Rhapsody of Succession

By Roy Baldwin

Creative Gateway

To My Friends

For encouraging and providing
the creative inspiration
and inspired creativity
to continue the Rhapsody series
into this fourth novel

Chapter One

The rain pounded the busy street. Strolling home, cosy under an umbrella and in her quiet inner world, she relished the melodic beat of her new Kate Bush album playing loudly through the earplugs of a trendy blue Walkman which Papa had bought her.

She was back in her early teens. The white elliptical arch entrance of the tall building scientist Professor Lauren Hind contemplated brought back deep and painful memories, long hidden. She could see her mother screaming hysterically and her father's face flushed red with panic as he carried her inside, blood pouring from her left thigh, throbbing in excruciating agony. The black Alsatian dog was more than plain vicious. He oozed unmitigated evil to be unleashed directly on the first unsuspecting victim, when his large yellow teeth and slobbery hot snout clasped her leg in a vice-like grip, tearing into her soft, white flesh. The hound had appeared from nowhere, bounding over a gate onto the pavement, barring her way and growling like an enraged spirit, water pouring off matted fur. He stopped, ears pricked up, staring menacingly into her eyes. Initially unsure, he suddenly sprang into action. Her father began beating the dog's head and body ferociously with his umbrella, loud yelps, screams and shouts intermingling in a blur of noise, until the beast finally released his grip and ran off down the road.

How much she missed her father. He would be ahead of everyone at this moment, delighted, comforting and optimistic with her predicament, seeing only happiness and goodness in her and the situation, whilst her mother would sense, without any words spoken, that all was not straightforward because all was never straightforward with Lauren from the minute she was born. Her mother judged mercilessly, but her father loved her unconditionally. How much she needed that sentiment right then. It was the twenty-centimetre rabies needle plunged straight into her stomach which had made her acutely nervous of hospitals from then on. Despite the fact that this building of memories had now morphed into the select Veronique Clinique, a small and expensive private hospital, the nascent phobias re-emerged, as intense as the direct light of the sun. She recalled recent events, of being roughly injected by Sergei inside Vaag's strange palatial yurt near Murmansk, when she had become delirious and nonsensical with plant poison. Her insides shook with an intense cold.

She could simply walk away. But her logical and capable mind began kicking in to drive out those demons, using arguments based on scientific rationality. She had to go through that door, whatever lay ahead.

The pretty reception nurse, in pristine white uniform and sheer black tights, greeted her warmly in a soft voice and directed her to a comfortable chair in front of a desk and laptop. That distinctive southern Mediterranean accent? Yes, definitely a Cote d'Azur lilt, which gave Lauren an unexpected frisson of comfort as did the radically changed environment all around. Everywhere was quiet and serene, no endless queues of distressed patients sat in rows of cold, hard seats like before and no medics in blue overalls rushing around with tense faces. In fact, she felt like she was entering her own purposeful Cassini

2

building, although her sharp eyes instantly took in the clinic's quaint retro furniture and dark blue colour scheme, and her mind began formulating more calming design alternatives. Odd, she thought, whenever stressed she would think in the same terms as her ex-husband always did.

"A muted pale green would look much better," Lauren remarked to the nurse as the laptop was switched on. The nurse smiled back unperturbed.

Lauren suddenly realised. This place was a chic French establishment in Brussels. Charlotte had been born in Nice but in her aunt's house, as Lauren had refused to go to the local hospital. She hadn't been in a hospital since, except once, for that awful eight-hour wait when her former husband had twisted his knee, imprisoned for aeons in an antiquated English accident and emergency in London, with no staff anywhere and the urine sodden chairs all ripped and full of holes. So much for the English free health system. She preferred to pay and by the look of the Veronique Clinique surroundings the bills would be big and fat.

As the receptionist called up her details, Lauren peered down the corridors. The place was ultra-modern and pristine clean. She noted, in the room opposite, an array of high-tech diagnostic equipment, glassware and rows of pumps with flashing electronic coloured lights and computer screens lit up. That gave her a deep scientific comfort, almost umbilical. Maybe she could have her babies in a laboratory this time.

She was directed to a small waiting room, and feeling a need to be private she sat apart from a couple of elderly patients. A voice in the distance called out whilst she pondered in a daze, trying to string her thoughts together into some coherent solution of exactly what it was she wanted from this place. Shit, she was sixteen once again … abort or deliver?

But nobody was abusive, lecturing, or shouting continually this time. Whatever came next would be her decision alone and she knew in her heart that whoever the father was, she was going to have them all. Job done. So why on earth was she here?

"Ah … bonjour. Mademoiselle Hind, oui?"

She realised the voice had been directed at her and returned from her reveries to see a tall, smiling man of similar age in front of her, dressed in a smart blue Dior suit and wearing an expensive white shirt and plain pastel matching tie. Some kind of tiny laser device hanging from his neck caught her attention, and she began instinctively working out the frequency of light and its potential significance from the unusual green spectrum being emitted.

"Mademoiselle Hind?"

"Excuser moi Docteur, pardon. J'étais occupé par autre chose, le laser. Parlez vous anglais? Je préfère parlez en anglais s'il vous plait. C'est possible?"

He looked momentarily flustered and took a quick peep at her notes, then peered back up through his bifocals. "But of course, Professor Hind. I am so sorry; I missed your correct title, remiss of me. I am Mr Jones, Edward Jones and Principal Gynaecologist at the clinic." He held out his hand as she rose from her seat. "Are you teaching at the local University?" he remarked softly.

She smiled. Behind those rimless Armani glasses, Edward Jones had that impish grin and mischievous look of her ex-husband and a comparable London accent. He was English down to his boots. She should have spotted it immediately from those handsome Anglo-Saxon cheekbones. She rather liked the prematurely greying hair too, but then a firm voice in her head rang out … no. She couldn't start fancying her potential gynaecologist, at least not at this stage. And she was missing

4

husband Philippe, still incognito somewhere in Siberia up the Lena River, wherever that was, undoubtedly having fun with Olga the gas engineer … fuck him … and she still needed to tell him. Perhaps the redoubtable Mr Jones would facilitate a suitable dialogue.

"Good morning Mr Jones," she replied. "I assume from your posh Chelsea accent that English is much more preferable for you as well."

He grinned back. "I'm impressed Professor Hind with your geographical accuracy. I'm actually from Surrey in England but spent many years in Chelsea, including taking my initial training. You're the first person to notice I had gone London native."

She laughed. "May I call you Edward and please call me Lauren, I hate unnecessary formality. And to answer your question, no, I'm not working at the University, although I once was an academic in Paris for some years. The title sticks forever and I like the cachet, as I am sure you do, being a plain old mister, Docteur?"

He looked at her intensely. This was no ordinary patient. For a start off he was used to professional deference at a first consultation. Professor Lauren Hind was decidedly nonchalant and unimpressed with his status, and quite stunning looking. Having triplets at forty-three also indicated a somewhat unusual woman, medical opportunity, and challenge. His friend Moyshe had recommended him, but Moyshe had, as usual, given the briefest of details except to say she was a scientist. He beckoned her to follow him into another room.

"Please come this way Lauren. I have my own personal private clinic and patient area at the end of the corridor, a little like a fashion concession in a department store, a complete microcosm in itself."

Ah, she thought, she could happily relate to the unexpected fashion analogy, which made her feel better still.

He continued. "It was a major reason I came here so I could pursue my own approaches unhindered and utilise the facilities which are first class. The Veronique Clinic is funded by Garoma, the nuclear giant in France. They initially wanted a facility to research radiation sicknesses, which one of my colleagues heads up. Then they diversified and hence my unit was born as it were."

She smiled. She had already assessed from his demeanour and mannerisms that he was intellectually rigorous and professionally capable, plus he had adorable laughing eyes … but that was par for the course if Moyshe recommended him.

"Yes," she responded gently. "I understand, and given their track record on safety I can see why Garoma wanted some credible backup. We do a lot better I can assure you."

Puzzled, he gazed at her again with that intense look she found growing on her. "I'm sorry Lauren, what did you say you do?"

"I didn't, but for your records I am the CEO of Cassini."

"Cassini? Seeking the moons of Saturn?"

She grinned. He knew some astronomy and had a sense of humour, not a bad combination for a medic. "We are a global power company providing nuclear services and forefront research, and in the future we will extend business to the rest of the solar system … including Saturn!"

He suddenly stopped before opening the door to his clinic, his eyes wide and mouth open. "Now I know where I've seen you. At my dentist's, residing on the front cover of Bloomberg. You're European Businesswoman of the Year. Oh my word, that is pretty incredible if you don't mind my saying so."

"Nice to know how wide my picture has become circulated," she replied with a laugh. "But it hasn't stopped me getting pregnant with triplets. You know the probability of that happening?"

"Depends on whether you had artificial insemination or conceived naturally."

"Definitely not the former, Edward."

"In that case, let's get inside. We have a lot of interesting discussion ahead."

"Yes, Edward, without a doubt," she said, immediately thinking for some odd reason of Mila and wishing she was there alongside her. Whenever there was trouble, her enigmatic Serbian friend, Mila, was usually to be found. Mila was very special as was their deep relationship. It was Mila who had guessed she may be pregnant in the first place and insisted on her doing a pharmacy test there and then in the Y&Y cafe, clumsily wetting herself in the toilet. But now Mila, with her Israeli Special Forces background, had become Cassini Director of Security and Intelligence. At least she could feel safe and secure at work.

But she still hadn't told Mila either about triplets. Nor had she told Charlotte her daughter, Svet her step-daughter or even Amélie, her best friend of twenty-one years, that she was pregnant. They all felt like daunting and individual challenges to commence that discussion, especially given their own suddenly acclaimed fecundities. She wasn't ready to face any of them. Only her Executive Assistants, Eva and Helena, sworn to secrecy knew and of course Annabella, who she would be eternally grateful to for simply listening like the sister she never had and only Annabella could be, practical and sensible with advice and care when she needed that support desperately. But she also needed more facts, and hopefully after this day she would have them, clear and unambiguous. Heaven knows, and then she could tell the most important person of all, her husband.

Chapter Two

With a pink modesty gown wrapped around her, she lay down carefully on the soft leather examination couch as Edward Jones reappeared in blue overalls, cap and mask but with the telltale gold Armani spectacles still perched on the end of his nose. His nurse, Adèle, had already briefed her on the range of examinations and what to expect and stood discretely to the side. Blood and urine samples had been expertly taken by Adèle and she was getting the results analysed immediately in his adjoining laboratory. Lauren was feeling decidedly impressed and comfortable with the Edward Jones clinic; no waiting for weeks on end for results. This was the kind of scientific efficiency and operation which gave her confidence, exactly as she would want to run it herself.

She must now, she reflected, be around two months. Already a small bump was becoming apparent, detracting from her usually impeccably slim figure. My God she thought again, how big will she become with triplets? With Charlotte she had not actually been that large and only showed publically at eight and a half months. Perhaps tight bellies ran in the family, as she remembered her mother who had been the same once saying to her father.

"I have all the initial results too from your local hospital examination ten days ago. They are excellent scans so I don't need to repeat them," he said confidently. He pulled up a contraption on wheels, like a shrunken dentist's chair but beautifully upholstered in purple, and clipped it securely to the side of the couch. "Can you slide across and put your legs onto these stirrups. Adèle is going to adjust this chair and then I'll take a proper look," pulling out a tray of gleaming stainless steel devices which looked to her more like a variety of workshop welding clamps and metal pliers. He picked up something resembling a fork with a handle and adjusting screw, similar to a piece of equipment she once used for cleaning radioactive pipes.

She felt distinct apprehension for the first time, as he switched on the laser device and she closed her eyes and thought of England as her ex-husband used to say. It was all over gently if slightly uncomfortably in moments, and thankfully he came up for air smiling. Back on the normal couch, she tried to relax as he drew up a stool.

"A bit early days Lauren but all looks excellent inside, definitely triplets. Were your previous births multiple by any chance?"

"You know I have had a child previously?"

"Of course. This is my job, like building bombs is yours," he replied with a grin.

She grimaced. "I can assure you that is the *last* thing I do. I had Charlotte at sixteen then nothing happened again, despite three previous husbands and a lot of trying at one stage, which is why I am so surprised now."

He frowned thoughtfully, glancing at her wedding ring as Adèle returned with the test results from the laboratory next door. "And your present husband? Is he looking forward to the forthcoming event?"

She hesitated. Adèle looked and then discretely left the room. She had been there before.

Lauren sighed then began slowly. "I may have a bit of a problem."

"Paternal origins? Or him being an arsehole."

She laughed at his directness and informality. "Both!"

"And how do *you* feel Lauren? Ecstatic or mortified?"

She gazed into his eyes. Edward Jones was a serious man, but that playful air gave her the confidence to stop dillydallying with her own inner feelings, be truthful and put her fears into his hands, something she would be averse to doing in all other areas of her life. "I've had ten long and hard days to think about my predicament, weighing up all the pros and cons as a good scientist should, which I'm sure you will appreciate."

He nodded.

"Actually, I feel completely overjoyed with the prospect. I have maturity, status, independence and money, a stability nobody can and will take away from me including my husband. I can give these children a loving home and a future, and enjoy the experience I missed when my daughter was taken away immediately at birth and adopted. She and I met each other for the first time last year and that has been so wonderful, and I'm a grandmother too. But so many lost years have passed by which can never be made up. I intend to be a woman who does have it all Edward ... I have the determination and the organisational skills, but I'm also feeling very frightened with the concept of the remaining pregnancy and giving birth to triplets at my age. So many things could go wrong with them and me and I want to minimise risks. Do you understand now?"

He patted her hand. "Totally. With me and my specialist team looking after you, then you will be in excellent hands here. Is it vitally important to know who the father is before birth?"

Lauren pondered again then decided. Sod it, Philippe can believe what he wants, but he will have to wait until they emerge. She had read up on prenatal paternity testing and was not prepared for the risks of invasive methods, and non-invasive techniques were unreliable causing even greater uncertainties. When the triplets come out she will know immediately. There was not exactly a wide variation of possibilities.

"No," she whispered.

"In that case," he replied, "we have one less risk to worry about. And more good news is that your blood and urine results all look fine too. You are a picture of health, even your blood pressure is normal and I expected that to be raised. I also asked for additional sampling of radioactive materials, given the nature of your work, but nothing to worry about; slightly higher levels of alpha particle emission but within safety boundaries."

"My fucking best friend Amélie," she growled, thinking of the thorium oxide powder covering Amélie's clothes after they found her lying in the Cassini lake.

"I'm sorry …?" he muttered.

"Apologies, Edward. An incident a while back, a long story, in fact Moyshe, who recommended you, was with me. One day I may even tell you." She smiled back …

<><>

They returned to his private office. She was pleased to get out of that awful gown; the design could definitely be more appealing. She would have to talk to him about that. What do men ever know about flattering women? Well, maybe some do.

He pushed his glasses up off the front of his nose and looked at her seriously again. She flushed, thinking that in the last fifteen minutes he had got to know every intimate part of her

12

body quicker than any other man alive, even Luis, but he was dead. Gosh, why was she thinking of that bastard again, but at least he couldn't be the father.

"So, would you like me to continue Lauren as your personal gynaecologist now?"

She laughed loudly. "You don't come cheap Edward but on this occasion you're hired!"

He grinned and blushed. Professor Lauren Hind would be a unique challenge, professionally and personally, but he was going to pull out every stop to make sure she delivers three healthy babies. He shuffled in his pocket for a prescription pad. "My speciality is genetic abnormalities. I would like you to start a special course of vitamin B12 with iron and other mineral supplements which I've tested for maximum effectiveness. Our pharmacy next to the entrance will prescribe immediately."

"Why?" she replied, intrigued.

"A precautionary deterrent against spinal cord deformities, more prevalent in older mums. Best if you start the course early in pregnancy. And a special request. Would you like to be a guinea pig for a new genetic profiling programme I am conducting here? The research is directly connected to my specialism and is now ready for final phase trials. The program is geared to highlight genetic abnormalities and produce a probability profile, enabling targeted treatments and aversion methods. All totally safe for the babies, like normal blood testing, only providing much more extensive results. Given your scientific background I would be happy to share the background theories involving mathematical genetics. The first phase has proved excellent for identifying Down's syndrome, without the risks of withdrawing amniotic fluid, something we may in due course need to consider. I thought you might like to participate."

She thought hard, her mind churning over all kinds of things, both innocent and mischievous at the same time, but with her being an older mum as he delicately hinted, she couldn't say no. She thought of Svet and Sergei and how he too would love to be involved in such work. "Yes, the proposition is irresistible to an old scientist like me."

"And, not so old, Lauren. Having babies in your forties is becoming de rigueur now for professional women, especially in the UK, who are increasingly leaving it late to conceive. Yes, riskier but now with modern technology and well trained midwives much safer than the old days."

"You mean like out in the jungle?"

"Definitely not a place for you to be giving birth to triplets. However you may, like many of my patients, demand a planned caesarean from the start."

"You mean they're too posh to push," she replied with a large smile.

He laughed, his eyes lighting up again behind those sharp lenses. "You've heard of that expression?"

"My ex-husband was a Chelsea guy and I picked up all kinds of bad habits from him including his quaint English aphorisms. I'm posh but I'll definitely be pushing!"

"Good. Obviously we'll agree all that later when your pregnancy has progressed further and we can see the full profile of the babies, just to be safe."

They shook hands and she started to proceed to the door having left a business card on his desk.

"Send your invoices and proposed appointment schedule to Cassini for the attention of Eva, my Executive Assistant, who will expedite everything immediately."

"Will the company approve of such payments, Professor Hind?"

"Listen Edward, I own the company, and this little incident occurred in company time, so I'm approving it here and now. Plus, I would like Cassini to sponsor some new gowns. I'll get the Luddite manager over here to advise you. As a good starter I can see Dior branded your suit. It will do wonders for all your posh clientele. Deal?"

His mouth dropped. He couldn't believe his ears but admired her chutzpah. "Yes … err … a deal," he muttered blushing with a large grin as she stepped cheerily through the door.

Chapter Three

Returning to the office in her new SUV, a flame-red BMW, Lauren felt a welcome wave of satisfaction flowing through her mind. She really had to phone Annabella to thank her for persisting with those pleas to find top level medical support, no matter what the cost. Annabella had been so unusually strident, even offering to pay herself, not that money was an issue for Lauren, but having a chat with Moyshe had definitely paid off. Mr Edward Jones would do very nicely for the moment. She thought again about Amélie and Charlotte, also pregnant, and would phone them each later. Now, she had the confidence to listen to their predicaments and discuss her own.

Her car phone, set far too loud, sounded. She turned down the volume and pulled in quickly into a supermarket car park.

"The Succubus representative is going to be late, probably about four pm now. Shall I rearrange your personnel meeting with Bella?"

A torrent of blank brain death began sweeping across her head. "Eva, who or what on earth is Succubus? Or am I finally going crazy?"

Eva giggled down the phone. "Sorry Lauren, I forgot to mention it yesterday. It's the code name for the Israeli fusion project which Mila has been negotiating on. You're meeting the research representative this afternoon ... err ... a succubus ... is a kind of female demon who does things with men when they're asleep."

Lauren roared laughing. "My goodness, you mean like a sexy vampire? Someone has an even greater talent for weird project names than me. I like the implication, we should recruit them onto our marketing team. Fine, I can catch Bella first thing tomorrow. I know it's important, she has a sensitive employment tribunal case coming up, which I want to avert."

"Is everything okay? Did your appointment go well?" Eva replied, worried about Lauren's condition but also intrigued to know how her consultation had gone.

"Absolutely fine Eva, all progressing nicely. And I now have a new gynaecologist, the delectable Mr Edward Jones who I think you would approve of. Mila definitely will. But he's anything but cheap."

They both laughed again.

"I'm so glad," Eva replied. "Have you told anyone else yet? Mila keeps plaguing me for meeting slots so you can go to Tel Aviv and I keep putting her off."

"After this morning, I intend to tell everyone by the end of the week Eva, so both your lips and Helena's lips must remain sealed tight for now. Oh, I'll be back for lunch."

"No problem. Great … see you later then," Eva replied, the lilt in her voice sounding distinctly uplifted.

Lauren was close to the Y&Y cafe and its salubrious interior drew her temptingly inside for a quick break and private reflection before returning to the hubbub at Cassini. The rest of the day was going to be very business intense. Sitting in a quiet corner, she ordered a refreshing herbal tea; the regular and copious cappuccinos had gone onto indefinite leave. She hadn't heard from Philippe for ten days now, but at least his absence had given her some space and time to think hard. She would wait for his call first. Obviously he was still finding it harder than either of them realised to settle down into a kind of normal marital bliss. His mindset seemed to be drifting towards being a part time husband, just like he had behaved with his former wife, Lyudmila. She wasn't sure how long she could tolerate that, especially not now. She needed him there alongside her more than ever, and she still loved him very much. But their relationship had been getting strained since returning from Murmansk and her normal resilience for emotional determination was weakening. The parameters had suddenly changed and something would have to give. Why the fuck can't he just phone? ... That damned Olga probably, whoever she was. She had to speak to Charlotte that evening, and find out if DG, Charlotte's Texan oil billionaire father-in-law and US Senator, but now her live-in partner, who was presently with Philippe on holiday in the depths of Siberia, was equally into vanishing mode.

She ordered a second herbal tea and began to write down some pointers for her Israeli meeting when her personal phone jarred in her bag. Just maybe it would be Philippe calling ... but it was step-daughter Svet, hopefully still enthusiastically pursuing her mathematical physics degree at Harvard.

"Hi Lauren, you answered quickly, it's great to hear your voice again. I'm really sorry taking so long to call but got hugely involved in a new group project ... actually in genetics would you believe? ... I find the mathematics absolutely fascinating. It's all Sergei's fault really." She giggled nervously but Lauren remained suspicious of her tone.

"Don't worry Svet, things have been busy here too, I understand, no problem at all. Spoken to your father yet?"

"No, actually. That's one reason I rang. Where is he? His phone goes on voicemail like permanently. Is everything okay?"

"Funnily enough he says that about you too," she replied light-heartedly. "He's still somewhere on the Lena River with DG and some old colleagues doing a hunting holiday, and seems to have gone out of contact, but he did warn me." She white-lied but didn't want Svet to get worried, but at least everyone, even his daughter, was getting the incommunicado treatment.

"Gosh Lauren, it's going to be getting really cold up there now this time of year."

Lauren grimaced, reflecting ruefully that there would be ample opportunities for him and the mysterious Olga to keep each other warm, and then immediately bit her lip for being so crass. More importantly she had Svet on the line and an opportunity to find out whether what Mila had disclosed in confidence had materialised.

"They're discovering their inner male again or something. You know how your father is, and he did need a break after Murmansk. I haven't heard from him for ten days except for one short text saying all is well. Actually Svet, let's forget your father for a minute. Mila and I had a chat. So what's the prognosis?"

Svet went quiet, then after a prolonged silence she began in a halting voice. "Actually I was so worried out of my mind. I had missed a period, panicked and phoned Mila. I know I should have phoned you first but my father would be so awful and I was unsure of everything …"

"It's not a problem Svet. I do understand, but I want you to know you will never have to worry about confiding in me on anything, and if you don't want your father to know, then he will never know, believe me. We both go back a long way now

19

on trust and respect and I will expect the same of you too. That's what being grown up is about. Agreed?"

"Absolutely Lauren, I'm so sorry. Thank you so much for that, it means a lot to me. But Mila was amazingly good and gave me all kinds of advice which I followed up …"

"So?"

"False alarm. A couple of nights ago I felt awful with dire stomach cramps and my period suddenly happened, but much heavier than usual. I reckon it was some sort of delayed reaction after all the trauma in Murmansk."

Lauren felt herself breathe a big sigh of relief and her tension inside evaporated as that heavy weight in her own stomach dissolved away. One problem less. She knew the real truth but was glad; often nature's way if all wasn't right. "Who knows Svet?"

"Only you. I haven't told Nadine or Sergei, not even Mila. I just wanted to talk to you. I'm so glad you're not angry with me."

"Of course not. Next time you have any personal problem you phone me immediately."

"Definitely. One thing though I did decide was that if I had been, you know, like pregnant, I was going to keep him Lauren. I thought about you and Charlotte, and I just couldn't have … But I know it would have been so disruptive for my life and ambitions. That guardian angel was around again keeping an eye hopefully for a better time in the future. Being with Sergei, there is so much more I want to do first. Anyway, I'm on the pill now just to make sure, but please don't tell my father."

"Of course not, I agree. But I am confident you would have coped and I would always support you one hundred and fifty percent no matter what anyone else thought, including

Philippe. Goodness, how mathematically illiterate I'm becoming!"

They both laughed and giggled on the phone, exactly as they used to. Lauren felt a huge wave of relief.

"You betcha, just one hundred percent will do fine," Svet joked back.

"Do you love him Svet?"

"Yes terribly and he loves me. I really want to spend my life with Sergei and I know our relationship is right for both of us, I just know it for sure, but I can't talk to my father, although not being pregnant makes it a lot easier. He will still go ballistic."

"Don't be so sure. He likes Sergei a lot and Sergei is joining Philippe and DG later this week for the last few days of their holiday."

"Really? He never told me."

"Don't worry, your father hasn't told me much either since he left. Men!"

"Yes, I agree. If necessary we can both live without them," Svet replied laughing.

There was another silence before Lauren decided. It was time to make an announcement. "Anyway, I have another secret to tell you. This time though, you are the first to know, and will be in strict confidence. Okay?" She heard Svet pouring out a drink.

"Just a coke but I've put a shot of vodka in for fortification because your secrets are always awesome and cool. You know, Nadine is still at College but she has a boyfriend would you believe, at long last, a real superbrain computing professor called Roland. And he's British but very handsome. He dotes on her and she lets him and you know Nadine, how detached and independent she is. It must be true love, she certainly likes older men."

"I'm pleased for her. She took so much pain and beatings in that hellhole of a cell in Murmansk. It would be really nice for Nadine to experience some normality again."

"But, you would never know Lauren, she is all healed up completely now and looks totally stunning. She is remarkable with those Chinese medicines and her inner discipline. Even Sergei is amazed at her recovery and she has got him looking more closely at her remedies of course. We all get on really well here, including with Roland. Oh, before I forget, I have changed my course too. I got so taken with genetics that I'm doing a couple of new biology modules. I want to combine physics and biology and eventually work in bioengineering. Sergei and I have discussed it extensively and he thinks it's a great idea and is totally supportive, predicting a massive future and opportunities in what is a new discipline. I could be right at the forefront in a few years and work with him directly. He's staying here in Boston for a while, planning an expansion of his medical research into the US, and wants to look at this area. I feel so happy. I hope you're not angry."

"Far from it Svet, go for it. There is nothing wrong with your heart and your science being in the same place. I know and I wished it had been like that for me … sorry … it is really of course with your father. And the moment Philippe calls I will square off Sergei and your new academic and career direction with him. I'm sure as long as you're happy, he will be fine. You really are growing up fast."

"Gosh I appreciate that, thank you. So, what's your big secret now I've put the vodka in? I'm all ears."

Lauren took a very deep breath. Short, sweet and simple, that was the only way. "I'm pregnant, I'm going to have triplets, Philippe doesn't know yet and … he may not be the father."

There was a deep void of silence as sweat began to pour from her brow. Why had she said the last part? She could hear Svet tipping the rest of the vodka bottle into the coke.

"That's like a sort of exploding supernova type secret," Svet replied in a monotone. "What you've just said is so mind boggling, I'm breathless here. I can't take it all in. I'll have to ring off. I'm sorry Lauren …"

The phone went dead. And Lauren walked immediately to her SUV and sobbed her heart out for a good half hour. That wasn't exactly a good start to revealing her plight to the world. She sent another text to Philippe to phone her urgently, the air with him had to be cleared quickly come what may.

<><>

Recomposed and back in the office, she was at least prepared for the Israeli meeting, all armed with reassuring and sensible scientific sureties, unlike the rest of her life. She was going to tell anyone now, who did or didn't want to listen, to get over it because her babies are all happening anyway. Eva, Helena and Annabella, presently sworn to secrecy, had been easy and comforting but others even Charlotte her own daughter may react like Svet. She hadn't told Mila either, still negotiating in Israel alongside her Cassini colleague Directors of Planning, Research and Marketing, Sonja, Juliette and Johann. She had been especially impressed with Juliette becoming comfortable and adept with the political complexities of the job, as she formidably led on new academic nuclear fusion research. Hence having a productive meeting with the Israeli Succubus, which still made her smile, was essential.

She was feeling sickly again especially and predictably in the morning. The smell of a cappuccino made her want to retch although at least she hadn't been actually vomiting. She remained comfortable with the entire global negotiations being conducted for reactor sales and the Cassini business position overall. Just as well as she simply wasn't feeling up to travel, although she had decided to make an effort to head down to the new Cyclops Centre in Cannes once she got the damned nausea under control. She grabbed the phone.

"Eva, can you do me a quick favour?"

"Hi, you're back, I didn't see you come in. Do you want a coffee… sorry I mean herbal tea?"

"A glass of cold mineral water would be lovely please. Can you call the Veronique Clinique for me and leave a message for Edward Jones that I would like some advice on morning sickness, which is becoming a bit irritating. I stupidly forgot to mention it when I was there."

"I'll get onto it right away. Actually, I had a feeling you may get sickly and I brought in some lemon and ginger herbal tea. My mother swore by it. Want to try?"

"Yes please Eva, thanks, and a chicken salad sandwich too if possible."

Eva laughed. "Mmm, your appetite isn't too bad yet is it? All coming up shortly. I just need to pop out for some things."

Three quarters of an hour later, and already feeling better after the ginger tea, she wolfed down her sandwich peering at the final spreadsheet figures for her meeting when a loud racket and laughing outside distracted her. The door opened and Eva walked in with an unexpected visitor.

"Adèle is here to see you. I found her at reception. We used to be old school friends and have managed a quick gossip on the way up."

Lauren smiled and got up to greet Adèle, impressed that Edward had responded so quickly, then she noticed Adèle pass an envelope to Eva, presumably his invoice already. She grinned.

"Hello Professor Hind, great to see you again and what a fabulous office you have here. Mr Jones insisted that I personally came immediately. I have some recommended diet and advice sheets, additional vitamin tablets and a little electrical device to use on your wrist which he has been working on successfully. We are keen to avoid anti-nausea medicines like Zofran, unless you get really bad. Is it convenient to run through them?"

"I'll leave you to it Lauren," Eva shouted through the door. "No other meetings now until four so you won't be disturbed."

"Thanks Eva, please Adèle sit down. Yes let's go through your recommendations. I'm impressed with the prompt care and attention, so I'll make sure Edward's invoice, you handed to Eva, is paid immediately," she responded with a laugh.

Adèle blushed and pulled out her folder … noticing the herbal tea bag in Lauren's saucer. "That's really good too, ginger is excellent."

"Never mind the tea," Lauren responded happily, pulling a special multimeter out of her desk drawer. "Now, let me take a close look at Edward's electrical device … mmm… that weak magnetic field I'm detecting already gives me some thoughts for improvement … Did you say he's patented this or thinking of it?"

Chapter Four

A few more days had passed uneventfully by. Business meetings had gone successfully. Apart from a few funny emails from Mila hinting at her mega-purchase of a luxury camel cashmere coat from an Arab trader outside Tel Aviv, all was amazingly quiet on the communications front, particularly from her husband. Lauren was feeling exhilaratingly upbeat having established that the combination of ginger tea and Edward's mini-magnetron on her wrist was doing wonders for her stomach first thing.

She was suddenly disturbed from a quiet early evening at home, reading her latest research papers, by a knock on the front door. Visitors were not expected. She looked through the peephole and saw Eva and Seb outside with some steaming cartons of takeaway food, and opened the door.

"Hi Lauren, on the off-chance we decided to try the new Chinese takeaway down the road and bought enough for you, if you fancy, all plain and mild!"

"Eva, how thoughtful and you too Seb, good to see you. I thought you were still away sorting out Juliette's security system at Cyclops? Come in both of you. To be honest I'm starving and was debating what to cook, so yes please."

"I see your appetite remains undaunted, are the remedies working okay?" Eva said nonchalantly, sitting down on the white mink couch.

Lauren stared momentarily at Eva then back at Seb looking his usual non-plussed and self-contained alpha male self. Eva suddenly went bright red.

"Oh gosh Lauren, I really do apologise. I sort of mentioned it to Seb but nobody else whatsoever, I promise, it just sort of slipped out."

Lauren grinned. "I suppose if I can't trust my own personal security then who can I trust? Pillow talk Eva?" she replied promptly, amused to see Seb's turn to blush under that somewhat wan smile. "Now we all have secrets to share. Anyway, I'm not going to be able to hide it all forever so don't worry."

Eva got up. "Actually, we also wanted to share something else with you," as she waved her left hand prominently in front of Lauren's gaze, the small ruby and diamond ring dazzling conspicuously in the halogen spotlights.

"Engaged?" Lauren retorted. "That is absolutely wonderful, I'm sure you will both be very happy together. Congratulations. That has made my night, really it has."

Eva beamed. "You sit down Lauren. I'll just go to the kitchen and warm up some plates for this food. Seb has brought a bottle of chilled Pinot, only eleven percent to celebrate. I'll go and find the opener," and grabbed the large brown bag from his hand.

"In the drawer next to the oven. Okay, but one small glass only for me, both of you." She sat down next to Seb. "I'm so pleased for you and Eva, Seb. I suspected a while back when her cooking offers became very regular. I assume you've settled into your apartment?"

"The pad is wonderful actually, and thank you Lauren for facilitating it all. Eva is fantastic, I wish I'd met her years ago. All my ongoing depression and getting over my brother's death has lifted for the first time. Oh, and I'm back early from Cannes because we completed the security job in record time. The environment is very secure in the temporary research building, and having vetted the new onsite security team thoroughly, Mila and I are completely happy with the set up. You can feel reassured, no problem."

"That's great to hear Seb, thank you. I've pretty well got over Murmansk but I'm certainly more alert to security issues than ever before, so I appreciate your work."

"And if I may say, it is fabulous news about you. I assume Philippe is over the moon too?"

Lauren grimaced and looked towards the kitchen, noting Eva totally absorbed with clattering plates and glasses. "I want to ask you in confidence. I'm sure you guessed everything in Murmansk was not as straightforward as sometimes it seemed when I was kidnapped. Vaag may possibly be the father, but I'm not sure. I don't know and don't want to know until they are all born and I still haven't told Philippe, who remains on holiday in Siberia … and I don't know how to."

"They?"

"Triplets, Seb. Eva missed that part?"

He laughed. "Yes! My word that is truly fabulous! Actually, I understand your problem entirely. Okay, a male perspective I have to say, but just be straight when you finally speak to him, no frills and no fuss, especially with Philippe. He's like me in that respect, just the facts as you know them, simple and short. If he genuinely loves you, which I believe Philippe does very much, then he may be initially unhappy, but he'll want to stand by you and support you completely. In any case, he may just as likely be the father so what has he got to lose? The same situation happened to me with my disabled brother when Imogen, my former wife, became pregnant. But loving her and her welfare were my priorities, which overcame my potentially violent reaction. Sadly, they both died at birth and nobody ever knew in the end, and now my brother's dead too. I'm sorry Lauren, that isn't going to happen to you, I know it."

She patted his hand gently. "Thanks Seb, no problem. I'm sorry to hear about Imogen. You've been hugely helpful, I can't tell you. Hey, perhaps now a new bright future with Eva is on its way for you too and maybe children at some stage?"

"Yes, definitely, I hope so."

They looked up and saw Eva staggering out with a tray of hot plates laden with steaming rice and vegetable dishes.

"Shall I put this food on the dining table Lauren? Seb can you lay those mats out please and bring the wine, glasses and cutlery in."

Seb wandered off into the kitchen. Lauren kissed Eva on the cheek. "Thanks Eva and I really am so happy for both of you."

<><>

Watching Seb and Eva saunter back to his apartment down the corridor, she finally was able to sit down, relieved that it wasn't too late but pleased with the evening's unscheduled treat. Her mobile rang. Perhaps it was Svet? She hoped so but she didn't recognise the number.

"Hi, it's me. Hope I haven't caught you at a bad time as I usually do. I just wanted to tell you that I'm not jealous."

It was Amélie, totally out of the blue, but what on earth was she on about? In fact where had she heard that phrase before recently …?"

"Sorry Amélie, as usual what are you talking about?"

"That you're on three and I'm only on two of course."

"Sorry?"

There was a moment's silence as Lauren pondered, puzzled, and then it hit her. Oh God … how could Amélie possibly …? "You know, don't you?"

"Of course I know brainbox. So does half the world probably now after the rumour and speculation in a comment yesterday circulating in Heat and other magazines. Is there nobody camped outside your apartment yet? Good job I have all the time in the world to read the gossip mags."

Lauren's heart sank. The story was moving on around the globe faster than she had any idea could be possible, but how? And where from? Thank goodness Philippe was still halfway up the Lena River. The last thing he would be perusing is celebrity magazines.

"Anyway," she replied. "What do you mean I'm only on two? Oh gosh, not twins surely … oh my goodness Amélie, that is wonderful … I'm sorry I've not been in touch, but this has all hit me like a sledgehammer."

"Listen idiot, you think I don't understand? Me too, and it should be me saying amazing to you, we both know the probability of having triplets … you are fantastic. Is Philippe over the moon, I assume?"

Lauren went quiet; that phrase too was suddenly cropping up with depressing regularity. "I haven't told him as he's ensconced in the depths of Eastern Siberia, out in the middle of nowhere with no communications on a hunting holiday with DG, and I don't want to …"

"Okay Lauren, let's stop there because I know exactly why you don't want to, and I have the same problem, so let's talk. You first. No holding back with your best friend. Issue and then solution, we're both good at that, especially as between us we may be bringing five brothers and sisters into the world."

Lauren laughed loudly. The usual Amélie as ever, bringing her brand of offbeat humour into this catastrophe. No, it isn't a catastrophe, they are all going to be beautiful and talented … "I'm worried because whilst I was out for the count in Vaag's abode recovering from the poisoning, I woke up completely naked and had been like that for at least an hour in Vaag's sole company. I don't know what he did; he claimed he had simply put me in a warm bath. Shit Amélie, it was Luis all over again."

"You have a bad habit of ending up naked and comatose with baddies, but so be it. I think my chances of Vaag being the father, given what he and I got up to in Grozny, are considerably higher. But I did fuck Rufus too. It was like a necessary marital catch-up after so long apart, inside the toilet on that flight to Stockholm. Wow I've never done mile-high before, pretty awesome. So what about you and Philippe? Did you get to shag him then? I assume, like me, conception time is around our Murmansk escapade together?"

"Honestly Amélie, do you have to be quite so glib and graphic, but yes. We managed it in that awful hotel in Kola before he left, it was quick mind you."

"Listen, we're both scientists, that is how we are, so get over it. We need the plain old simple facts, all the raw data, draw conclusions and then we get ahead of the curve … agreed?"

"Oh, Amélie, you're absolutely right, I've badly needed to hear that. I feel better already, so how is Rufus taking it?"

"He's remarkably cool and not perceptibly bothered on the basis that logically it's all now water under the bridge and he has me back. So I'm deciding to have a DNA done on placenta fluid next week and get it over with one way or the other. Whatever, I'm having them and we both are agreed, no abortions. You need to do the same, or are you thinking of aborting anyway?"

"I want them Amélie, more than anything in the world now so that is how it's going to be, unless there are medical reasons to consider otherwise."

"Hey me too, totally."

"And I've decided, especially in my condition, that I'm not taking the risk of testing until they are all born."

"Okay, we may deviate there. So you're just going to have to tell Philippe straight, and he can like it or lump it until they are born. No other conclusion really is there. Job done Lauren. Now, do you want to know what I'm doing with my life? You will be totally amazed."

"Oh Amélie, yes of course I want to know and I have already decided, what you've said is exactly what I'm going to do."

"Good, your best friend to the rescue, once more. Oh and before I forget, the Serbian Sleuth and your daughter both know too, about the triplets that is. They are both cool and happy just waiting for you to call them so don't worry about it."

Lauren sat back and drew breath, totally astonished. How was that possible? "What? Mila and Charlotte actually know already?"

"Well there is nothing that doesn't get past Mila's astute intelligence sniffing; of course she knows Lauren, she's known for the last week. As for Charlotte, hands up I confess. I told her inadvertently because I phoned her for advice, her being an expert on twins, and I assumed as one would that she knew … She's a fellow engineer Lauren and had it all logically and practically sussed in a microsecond, your own daughter remember?"

Lauren couldn't help laughing and giggling with relief down the phone; her tension was evaporating as quickly as liquid nitrogen on a hot stove. She was supposed to have been the one to offer sympathy and support to Amélie but somehow everything just got reversed. Annabella was right; it all finds its own level very quickly.

Amélie continued. "Good. Now that we're all finally back to normal, *you* are talking to Lady Westvale now."

"Pardon?"

"Sadly, whilst you, me and Rufus were roaming around the Arctic looking for Svet and her kidnappers, his father suddenly died — a fatal heart attack. Angus apparently had problems for years but told nobody in the family. Rufus, as the eldest of his two sisters and one younger brother, has inherited both the title and Westvale Hall. We tore up the divorce papers which had reached the final stage, phew, just in time. So, I am now Lady of the Manor and what a fabulous estate it is up here in Lancashire. Thousands of acres, all viable, because the return on the land and the range of other business activity, including weddings, covers the overheads and Rufus has inherited a shit load of money. I don't need to work ever again if I don't want to and neither does Rufus. So for the time being, fuck Rubidium and nuclear energy. Time for the good life, getting fat and bringing up babies. I might, though, put up a few wind turbines just for posterity."

Lauren couldn't believe her ears. Somehow Amélie, no matter what adversity, always seemed to land on her feet. She was really pleased for her best friend ... but also quite jealous, although if it came to it she could do the same thing. However in reality, certainly at that moment she still wanted her career, her company and the babies too.

"I'm pleased for you Amélie but here's a bet? A thousand pound Luddite dress that you come back to the scientific fold within twelve months? Not because you'll get bored but because you will simply be driven to it. You're a scientist to the core as you always said, exactly like me."

"Okay Lauren, you're on, I know exactly which Dior dress I fancy already, so you'd better reserve it in advance. Anyway, I want you up here soon and we can talk properly and have some fun. We need to chat and share. Mila will likely phone you I suspect. Of course Charlotte also has her own good news, which I assume you know from Mila. DG is definitely the father, she has no doubts, and she sounds very happy about it. I know you're not because I remember your face in the jeep when you realised they were in a close relationship, but my view is quite simple … she's happy and they are obviously in love. And DG is quite something Lauren, you know that, so let them get on with it and be happy for them. I've got to go, I'm getting tired. Let's catch up again soon."

"We agree for once Amélie about Charlotte and I'm whacked too. The quicker the nine months are up the better."

"Enjoy it Lauren, you will bloom decidedly, I can just see the photo ops in your Gucci maternity wear … bye."

"Bye Amélie and thanks so much, you really are a best friend."

<><>

The phone clicked off and she lay on the couch exhausted but at last feeling back in control of things. She really had to get a move on and tell Philippe. Half the world was gathering pace. She looked furtively out of the window. No paparazzi. Thank goodness she was in a gated community with security but she needed to get her presentational act together. Not exactly a royal birth looming, but there would inevitably be media interest given her press exposure over the last two years and possible concern from her business customers who needed to be reassured of continuing confidence in Cassini. She hadn't thought of those implications until then. She needed her marketing and press guru Johann on board quickly. She looked at her phone again. A text had come in whilst she was talking to Amélie.

Hi darling got your message sorry I've been out of contact - something wrong with the satellite phone. Igor has fixed it temporarily but battery almost flat. I'm fine but Olga has gone missing - hopefully not far. DG and I have to track her down quickly - wolves are out. Will reach a town on the river tomorrow and will phone. Hope you are well. Love you lots.

At last, she thought, contact. He is still part of this universe after all. Come on wolves, get running a bit faster ... no, not even I am that nasty ... or am I?

Chapter Five

Tomorrow never comes, so they say. Who, Lauren pondered, thought up that pithy trivia? She felt disappointed. No phone call again from Philippe so tomorrow felt yet again like another day. But to compensate, Mila was heading back to the office from Cannes and that brought a genuine smile and needed warmth back to her cheeks.

Lauren had successfully led an important morning meeting on the topic of nuclear energy strategies for Europe, addressing, amongst others, a couple of senior European Commissioners and selected advisers in their extravagant abode on the other side of Brussels. That massive curved building, she decided, was an obscene display of architectural ostentation and always made her uneasy, especially listening to the many young and articulate high flying civil servants openly discussing a myriad of strangulating policies to emasculate European Union nation sovereignties. The trendy concept of federalism, vehemently promoted by some of her own top-level European Commission contacts, was not one she favoured viewed from her global business perspective. But, having learned the hard way in the past, she chose her words carefully; there was enough at stake to remain outwardly and sensibly neutral for now.

No doubt this discussion forum had been prompted behind the political scenes by French President Jacques Chandrisé, her new friend and ally, who had done an amazing job promoting her Cyclops fusion centre partnership concept with JETR. A more distinctly informed coterie of scientific observers from all twenty-seven states had turned up. For the first time since her star conference turn in Beijing with Rosie, her interpreter and confidante in China, which already seemed so long ago, she felt truly back on presentation form. That was despite an early but brief heave in the pristine personal toilet of the Energy Commissioner, blaming a night of bad prawns rather than the retching smell of strong coffee mixed with cigar odour in his office.

Although she was pleased that this discomforting sickly inconvenience was abating significantly following the voodoo magic of electromagnetic bracelet energy, diet changes and vitamins from Edward Jones, she reflected briefly, with sadness, on the plight of Rosie. Rosie had saved her life twice, each time from terrorists both in Beijing and latterly Murmansk with that dazzling and totally unexpected display of Chinese martial arts and weaponry. Rosie was so incredibly special and gorgeous, why did she have to get shot? She really needed to find out how Rosie's spinal injury recovery, under Sergei's innovative medical treatments, was progressing, despite Rosie's vehement insistence to everyone, particularly Lauren, that she wanted absolutely no contact or visitors seeing her in a wheelchair. Rosie had obviously taken her serious gunshot injury very badly; perhaps Mila, her old friend, knew more. A discussion with Svet now seemed a very distant proposition since that disastrous attempt at coming out on the triplets. It would be nice to do something right with the Dubois entourage for a change.

A detailed conversation at the generous buffet table with a group of feisty female science representatives from the newly joined Bulgaria took her mind off family woes. Complimenting

Lauren on her prophetic and wide ranging nuclear plan for the next fifty years, the Bulgarians seemed especially clued up on recent Russian progress with fusion, some aspects of which she needed to check out with Philippe. A mild security commotion caught her eye at the top of the palatial room. Somebody uniformed was being led out in some distress. Then two very tall and smartly dressed blonde women, with a distinctly commanding presence, began marching through the crowd of bureaucrats, catching the swivelling gazes of an array of intrigued male and female delegates. She immediately recognised one of them. How could she not, viewing the sexy ankle-booted occupant of a vivid red knee-length Prada dress, a delectable bow tying up the neckline and temptingly fastened all down the front with large white pearl buttons. Her companion was equally stunning in Versace yellow.

"Lauren, you look fantastic and the Energy Commissioner tells me you're speech was so forward thinking and visionary that he will be raising it at the next EC Presidential summit. Oh, I'm sorry, can I introduce you to Dr Katrine Henrikson. Katrine is leader of the Danish Social Alliance Party, presently holding the balance of power in their coalition. We met last night in the Alamode Hotel next door."

"Last night?"

"Hello Lauren, I agree. Your speech was one of the most powerful I've heard for long-term advocacy of nuclear power in Europe. It was a wonderful proclamation of hope for a carbon-free energy future. In Denmark our Parliament banned the production of nuclear power twenty-three years ago, and as I'm sure you know we have put all our efforts into becoming world leaders in wind power. We export much of it, but I believe we must now revisit a wider energy agenda. Wind doesn't blow continuously, and this sudden mania for shale gas exploration in Europe worries me. Denmark still depends on nuclear generated power imports from Sweden, Norway and Germany and there are idiotic moves internally to even decommission our three national nuclear research laboratories, which is hugely short-sighted. I would like to use your speech as a political counterweight and overturn this unnecessary and costly diversion."

Lauren shook hands with Dr Henrikson, who displayed all the airs of a confident and clued up experienced politician. And she was highly attractive. They exchanged business cards immediately. "Good to meet you Katrine and I'm happy to help with your dilemma. I shall ask my Executive Assistant, Eva, to email a presentation copy with detailed notes over straight away. And if you need any further advice, please feel free to contact me directly."

"Thank you," Katrine replied. "So much appreciated. You would be very welcome to visit me if you get the time and see the research laboratories. They are, I understand, doing some interesting work which you may find useful."

"I shall definitely check my diary Katrine."

"Great. Sorry but I'm afraid I have to dash to the airport. We have a vote tonight on amending our equality laws and I need to be there. Mila, I hope we'll meet again soon, we've had such a useful discussion on energy security."

"I'm sure we will Katrine, have a good flight back to Copenhagen."

Lauren stared from one to the other as they shook hands, and felt a deep twinge of unease. She recognised that look … and hadn't seen it for a long time … confirmed as Mila glanced back at Katrine's pert bottom heading towards the exit, conspicuous in her tight dress. But Lauren had her own problems to contend with and she wasn't going to mull deep and hard about Mila right then.

Mila turned back and hugged Lauren, still bewildered to see her at the meeting.

"Mila, it's lovely to see you, but what are you doing here? I thought you were heading for the office later. How on earth did you get in? This was a very strict invite only and prepared weeks in advance."

"Katrine invited me last night; she said you were the star turn so how could I resist? You heard it from me first, but I predict she will become the first female Danish Prime Minister in due course. Anyway, more important, how is the mother-to-be faring? I know it's only been ten days since I last saw you but lots seem to be happening right now. You know I know don't you, hey how could I not know such amazing news, and I'm so pleased for you. I knew you were pregnant remember after that test in the Y&Y that I forced you to do … but triplets? That really is something … at least I hope you feel it's wonderful, but something about your demeanour tells me that not all is quite as you would like it. Correct?"

Lauren forced a smile. The usual perspicacious Mila and she still loved her deeply for it. "Grab two plates of that delicious looking salmon salad and let's go to the empty table by the window. Looks like the delegates are thinning out and I've already spoken to the most important people who left first, so we won't be disturbed. I want your opinion before we head back to the office."

Lauren grabbed some bottles of water and headed for the table, with Mila close behind clutching two plates of lunch. As they sat down Lauren remarked, "What exactly was all that commotion about when you walked in?"

Mila smiled, but was doing a poor job of innocently. "When I arrived there was a silly mix-up at the security desk who didn't have Katrine's faxed invitation from the hotel. Unfortunately the stroppy burly guy, supposedly head security, busted his shoulder accidentally when he grabbed at me and fell. They need to get fitter those guys, that'll hurt for a few weeks."

"Accidentally?"

"Well you know how it is," Mila replied with a mischievous grin. "The rest of them were too inept to notice."

"So how is Sonja? I got an email requesting a few days urgent leave whilst she was with Juliette at Cyclops, which of course I granted immediately. Something about an urgent family matter at home in Croatia?"

"Yeh, Sonja," Mila replied in a brusque and disinterested tone. "Her mother had a bad fall outside her apartment and broke her leg. Sonja is just going to get things sorted out, although her two brothers nearby could make more of an effort."

"Brothers? Sonja's never mentioned others in her family."

"No," Mila replied, hungrily tucking into the salmon and a large hunk of bread. "Everything became complicated when the family ties fell apart during the Bosnian war. But they did all reconcile eventually. Her elder brother is now a senior politician in Zagreb, active in Croatia joining the EU and much more interested spending time here in Brussels wheeling and dealing. Her younger brother is a local carpenter, busy with his small business, and their wives don't want to know. They are a waste of space for Sonja now her mother is getting old and frail. I offered to help out but Sonja wanted to go on her own. Hey, I thought this conversation was supposed to be about you not me."

"We can get to that ... out with it Mila, something has happened hasn't it over the last couple of weeks? I'm not totally mushy-brained yet although I suspect it's starting. And how come you arrived a day early?"

Mila coughed loudly. "Okay, yes, I'm uneasy. Something silly happened down in Cannes, only a week after we had moved into our new apartment. And you must see it soon Lauren, I'm really pleased, sea front, lovely view, mega luxury, but what else would you expect from me. Oh, forgot to mention ... after we all got back from Murmansk, Sergei needed some discrete and confidential advice on managing Vaag's massive wealth, not all as well hidden as it might have been.

"You've been handling Sergei's legacy?"

"Yes, in my other business I have serious networks for that type of work. It comes up often when we assist clients with security needs. Anja and Emmylou concentrate on wealth management from the New York office, I haven't done anything for a long time but this request was special, as you understand, so I personally sorted him out completely. He wanted to maximise his assets to begin his massive international medical research programme, but at the same time keep prying eyes well away. Brother Vaag had accumulated a lot of money Lauren, and not just a few million. We're talking billions of US dollars here and Sergei also wanted a secret trust fund set up for Vaag's myriad offspring. Let's just say the commission was generous, which I split with the team, but leaving enough for me to buy our luxury apartment outright with cash. Having been inspired with assisting Svet and Nadine on their Harvard luxury flat purchase, Sonja and I replicated the same approach — with a place twice as big and ten times as cool!"

"That's astonishing. You've both obviously been having fun whilst I've been fighting off the intrusive speculum of my new personal gynaecologist, Edward Jones, who I will add I will have to keep well away as he is far too dishy for your green eyes."

"Mmm … can't wait. Anyway, tell me all that in a minute. I can see from your expression that I'm not going to get away from here without telling you the full story, am I."

"No, Mila … you are most definitely not, and as your boss you are instructed to tell all," Lauren replied with a smile. "To be honest, I'm simply amazed with everything that Sonja has been doing for Cassini, and she is still able to find time for apartment hunting as well."

Mila suddenly looked serious. "That's part of the problem. I have to say the new job you gave Sonja is the best thing that has happened to her ever; for the first time in her life her true potential and ability is pouring forth. I'm equally amazed with her capabilities, and I honestly wouldn't want it any other way Lauren, the transformation is fantastic for her. But she has become so absorbed and determined with her work and her plans that our own life balance, and downtime with each other, have taken a bit of a knock … and I don't help, always being impatient and gadding about around the globe. But we've known each other long enough to manage all that."

"I'm hugely grateful too with what Sonja is achieving managing Cyclops — her work has definitely generated real progress. Both been tetchy I assume at home then? You should plan a holiday together and relax. So what happened?"

"You never met Rafael did you?"

"Rafael?"

"Sorry — better known as the lobster supplier in the old days."

"Oh … mmm … yes …"

43

"Don't worry. I know Sonja told you about him. Anyway, not so long back she bumped into Rafael, quite out of the blue, on the seafront in Cannes, he was there visiting and expanding his business network. I wasn't exactly overjoyed and it did upset her balance."

"I understand that," Lauren replied, sensing an uneasy tension in Mila's voice.

"You don't still think about that bastard Luis do you? Or both bastards come to think of it … or maybe the second one especially now?"

"Yes … I do … sometimes …"

"Shit Lauren, I thought so. We'll come to bastard two in a minute, because I know exactly what is the matter with you, and we need to deal with it."

"I think I have dealt with it … but go on …"

Mila drew breath and sighed. "The problem was Raphael began pestering over the next couple of days and then stalking her. He hadn't got over Sonja running off the way she did … unfortunately he ended up instead returning to Palermo in a wheelchair and won't be coming back any time soon."

"Oh gosh Mila. And Sonja hasn't been overjoyed with your remedial work I assume."

"That's an understatement, but yes, in a nutshell. She'll get over it but I can sense she's evaluating her feelings again … one way or the other … and being broody too has heightened her introspection. Sometimes Sonja is too seriously intellectual and focussed for her own good. Sorry, that's a silly thing to say especially to you, and I still love her for all she is … and I still love you, despite the expanding belly."

Lauren smiled. "Good, I'm glad to hear how much you love the most important people in your life. You both need to spend more time together and enjoy little things again. Perhaps Sonja will also reflect positively during her time in Croatia."

"Perhaps."

"I'll arrange a meeting as soon as she's back about rebalancing her work portfolio. There could be an opportunity actually. I'm thinking of promoting Helena from being more than Sonja's assistant and into her first management role as Sonja's deputy. Helena has equally shown outstanding capability and I want to encourage her onwards and upwards in the company. That way, Sonja's workload can be shared and we can appoint a new assistant for both of them. What do you think?"

"Brilliant, definitely worth doing, I agree about Helena. Anyway, let's get back to brass tacks … you! I can see from your pained expression that Philippe is retaining a frustrating penchant for continued wanderlust around the wild steppes of Siberia East, and is still unaware of the mega-news?"

"Yes … both he and DG remain in blissful ignorance … plus … I hope the wolves are still active."

"Sorry Lauren, I missed that particular last subtlety, but I think I have a sneaking suspicion; probably female?"

"Yes."

"I see the hormones, understandably, are on top note. But is there another reason why his convenient absence in the middle of nowhere is not too unwelcome? Because you have something tricky to tell him don't you? Okay, truth time, you know me Lauren, I'll get straight to the point. When you through survival necessity fucked Vaag back in Murmansk, I suspect you never quite realised the extent of the potential complications?"

Lauren grimaced. "You have a touching directness Mila which occasionally defies subtleties, but actually I'm glad you've said it because I'm expecting a call later today when Philippe reaches a town base and can recharge his satellite phone. The truth of the matter is when I was woken up naked by Sergei in a bath of hot water from that near-death poisoning experience, I genuinely don't know what happened in between, but I do know what Vaag was intending to do, and so was I by then if I hadn't gone all inconveniently ill and comatose on his shoulder as the action was about to start. That's all I remember … and sadly I wanted Vaag right then … God knows why or what was going on in my head, I was very confused. So, I don't know how to tell Philippe, Mila, that I'm pregnant and he may not be the father."

"I understand fully how you felt then, I wasn't stupid either and there were good reasons for your unease and imbalance as we both know, especially with the peculiar way Philippe had been behaving … we're both one of a kind Lauren and I understand you better than anyone. Are you having pre-DNA testing? You could get a sample done through Sergei?"

"No … I'd already decided against that, too risky given my circumstances, and Edward agrees. The identity of the father will have to wait until they finally emerge blinking into the sunlight. Then I think it should be fairly simple to know if Vaag was the father. But around that time of conception, Philippe could equally be the father."

"The Kola Hotel?"

Lauren smiled and dug Mila in the arm playfully. "Yes, how did you know, we were very quick and quiet?"

"Because when I took him back out into Murmansk he was rather red in the face considering it was minus eight outside," Mila replied laughing. "Look, when he calls be concise and to the point. Give it to him straight because he needs to know now, before anyone else puts two and two together."

"Amélie already has."

"I'm not surprised. She has a well-honed inbuilt radar for multiple shagging that would confound both the NSA and GCHQ combined."

"Pardon?"

"Never mind, but that proves my point. What's done is done. Sometimes a girl has to do what she has to do, you did, and he has to get over it, that's life. I believe he'll hot-foot it straight back to Brussels immediately and want to look after you no matter what, because Philippe loves you very much and will focus solely on the sensible and logical outcome … that he was the better man and so will be the natural father. Mind you Lauren, just how wayward were you? Because in theory each triplet could have a different father."

"Shit Mila, what have I gotten myself into?" Lauren replied, visibly alarmed at the prospects of that possibility.

"I'm sure when you ask the mysterious and delectable Edward Jones he will run off a range of infinitely miniscule probabilities that even you, with your mighty superwoman maths brain, will concede the impossibility in reality."

Lauren immediately cheered up, leant forward and hugged Mila hard. "Once again, I can't thank you enough for turning my head around. I'm so grateful. I love you."

"Good, just remember me well, boss, at bonus time. Now more interesting, Juliette came back with me too last night and will be in the office when we get back … she has some matters to discuss with you."

"What matters?"

"I'll leave that to her … but we all decided that given your impending contribution to increasing the world's population threefold then we want to take you out this evening for a small celebration. You can leave the serious drinking to us of course. We've booked a table at La Palisade … and no buts."

Lauren looked back blankly. "Sorry, who's we? Who exactly knows about my pregnancy Mila?"

"Well pretty well everyone except the press, certainly inside Cassini. And don't go blaming anyone. Rumours began in earnest when your sudden maternal blooming appearance caught the eyes of the more astute amongst your female management team, including reception. You can't keep a good gossip down, and your entire work colleagues think you're totally amazing and it's such fantastic news and are really pleased for you, so there's no need for any 'on high from the pulpit of the CEO' announcements. Johann has already prepared a suitable and very upbeat briefing for the press for your approval later, to go out today. And most important, our friendly Luddite manager wants to come in and discuss the possibility of your modelling their new range of Gucci maternity wear, at of course a massive discount!"

"Oh Mila," Lauren choked, tears falling down her cheek. "Gosh, thank you, I feel hugely better and I'm so genuinely happy about having the triplets. I really want them Mila and I'm going to give them everything."

"All that you were never able to give Charlotte? Yes I know … and Charlotte understands too. You two have been nervously circling one another for far too long. She needs you Lauren. Phone her later when she's having breakfast."

"I will … I'm going to be the woman who does have it all Mila. La Palisade is a lovely thought. What cabaret is on tonight?"

"Good … you deserve a little party spirit … now let's finish this lovely salmon and head back to the office, plenty to do. And before I forget, the 'we' tonight is me, Juliette, Bella, Giselle, Eva and Helena, all males are banned. I don't know who's on, but we have a good table at the front. Oh … and there may be a surprise guest."

Chapter Six

Walking into her office, she was confronted by a large map of the Cote D'Azur spread halfway across the table, with Juliette and Eva eagerly pointing at different locations from a list at the bottom.

"Hi Lauren, I'll just get you a lemon and ginger tea. Earl Grey Juliette?"

"Yes please Eva." Juliette turned around and gave Lauren a welcome gentle hug. "Gosh you look …"

"Blooming is the word you want. Don't worry; I'm aware everyone in the universe now knows too."

"Fabulous for you both … Philippe must be very excited as well."

"Actually, he's the one person unbelievably who still doesn't know, having been marooned with no communications on a holiday break in Siberia. However, I am expecting a phone call shortly to break the news."

"I'm sure he'll be ecstatic when he finds out, but triplets? Multiple births are fun. I've loved seeing the twins grow up, so similar but also so different."

"Twins?"

"Yes. I know I don't usually talk about my children but that's one of the reasons I wanted to see you and discuss some personal matters, if it's okay."

"I hope you're not going to tell me you're leaving us?" Lauren ventured with a measure of anxiety. "Not now of all times?"

"No, no, quite the opposite actually. The divorce was finalised last weekend, and I intend to move permanently down to Cannes with Isabella and Jonathan, who are sixteen and will shortly finish boarding school in Surrey. I intend to start them in an International School to study a broader Diploma programme, with subjects taught in both English and French. I was just showing Eva my shortlist of schools to choose from around Nice and Cannes, but I'm especially taken with the new Moulin School, specialising in science and technology and situated near one of the largest technology parks in Europe. Both twins are keen scientists."

"Like mother ... and father?"

"No, quite the opposite. Gregory is an international lawyer. For the last ten years none of us have seen much of him but we did benefit from the income and the large house in Clapham. Given his background, I am amazed he tried to contest an equal settlement of assets but he did and lost, with costs and an appropriate share coming my way including the recent proceeds from the sale of the house. He is relocating permanently to New York to move in with his long-term lover."

"Gosh Juliette, I had no idea. I'm sorry about all this ... Is she ... younger?" Lauren suddenly said before biting her lip, irritated with her own thoughtlessness.

"I'm not sorry at all. Gregory's gay and has chosen that path for a long time, so we never saw a lot of him as they grew up. I immersed myself in work and have other pursuits, and the children have become very independent. The money will enable me to buy a place that I choose this time, not a cast-off heirloom from his parents. They're very excited about the move and very much want to be with me in France. And Mila has offered to help me find somewhere suitably lush … her taste and eye for property detail is just amazing."

Lauren smiled warmly but was thinking wistfully. That all explains a lot. Juliette had always been cagy about her private life, and of course Mila had already identified the interesting nature of some of Juliette's 'alternative pursuits'. But a sixth sense unease swept across her mind with this sudden familial Mila philanthropy, especially given Juliette's secret disposition for chains, ropes and whips, and Mila's wobbly relationship with Sonja, also working alongside Juliette. But in the end they were all grown-ups and had to sort out their lives as they saw fit. She had enough concerns for herself. The important thing was that Juliette seemed as committed as ever to developing the Cyclops fusion centre by making a decision to relocate fully to the Cote d'Azur, which was excellent news. She would do whatever it took to ensure Juliette remained onboard because there was no comparable nuclear research director in the fusion field anywhere.

"Well Juliette, thanks for confiding, and I'm pleased your life is finally sorting itself out. I can understand how things have been difficult and you have my total support. We still retain the former policy of relocation expenses for Executives, so when you move from your Brussels flat please make sure you have a chat with Bella, every little helps. I actually did a science International Baccalaureate so I'm probably better placed than anyone to advise you and your children on that curriculum and on schools. Don't hesitate to ask."

"Goodness, thanks Lauren. I felt apprehensive about telling you somehow, I really appreciate it."

Lauren grinned. "No problem. Anyway, we have a good hour and a half yet before my next finance meeting with Herman, so down to business. How is that new modelling process for low temperature fusion going? I've been thinking a lot about the implication of changing the ratio of deuterium and tritium volumes and the role of lithium deuteride in the initiation process. My initial calculations imply that we may be able to improve the sustainability of fusion energy release, albeit at a higher but manageable temperature."

Juliette pondered for a moment. "Actually, I agree. Bhavika and I simulated your theoretical reactions on our mini-supercomputer at Pune, and we both concluded the same possibility, but the intensity of the initial laser simulation needs more serious thinking about. But we're confident of doing some small trials at Pune before replicating at Cyclops."

"At Pune University?"

Juliette suddenly cleared her throat. "I'm amazed Lauren that with … err … everything happening … that you can … well … do such intense abstract work," a vague stutter permeating her usual sharp clarity of erudition.

Lauren laughed out loud. "Don't be coy Juliette. What you really want to say is why hasn't my brain gone to mush like every other expectant mother at my age?"

"Well … I didn't mean to imply …"

"Don't worry, I keep reading over the hardest mathematics I can find to keep the brain exercised … anyway, those triplets share Philippe's genes so between us we should keep the intellect primed up … hopefully!" She immediately realised she had said what her subconscious mind already believed and felt happy.

Juliette relaxed. "I still remain impressed. Actually Lauren, Bhavika is with me. I asked her to fly in for the next week. She's only next door talking to Helena, but she's made some real political headway not only with our small research centre at the University, but especially with developing ideas for new approaches to our work alongside JETR. Can I ask her to join us?"

Lauren felt immediate pleasure. There was something almost irresistible about Juliette's deputy that always made her feel good inside. "Excellent, yes, that would be very useful and timely, I haven't seen her for some time." She shouted through the door. "Eva — can you ask Bhavika to come in please."

In a moment they were shaking hands warmly, as Lauren admired Bhavika's smart and figure hugging knee-length black pencil skirt with a teasing split at the bottom matched with an expensive crisp white blouse.

"Hello Lauren, it's good to see you again. Congratulations on the triplets, I really hope it all goes well for you."

"Thanks Bhavika, just as well you've popped in today as soon I may not be able to get over to India … I'll be too big for a normal plane seat!"

They all laughed warmly as Helena brought in some more refreshments and Bhavika's favourite Darjeeling tea.

"Helena, when I've finished with Dr van Woesik later can you pop in before we leave. There's something important I want to discuss."

"Fine Lauren, I'll see you later," Helena replied, feeling nervous with Lauren's serious tone and hoping that she hadn't messed up the formal Cyclops launch arrangements in two weeks time.

Bhavika continued, noticing that Lauren had admired her new outfit. "Actually, I took your advice and popped into Luddite first thing this morning and was immediately taken with their new work-wear fashion range ... this skirt is a Malene Birger."

"Really? Mmm ... must go and check them out ... ah well ... forgot ... I mean maternity work-wear!"

"Don't worry, less than nine months to go Lauren, a mathematically insignificant period of time and I'm sure your figure will be back in no time," Bhavika replied, grinning.

Juliette, sensing drift which she always hated, brought the discussion back to the task in hand and asked Bhavika to update Lauren on all the Pune University and nuclear India politics, plus new potential business relationships establishing, and the latest research work, now that the Cassini Indira Centre had taken on some promising physics postgraduates under of course Bhavika's watchful eye.

The following twenty minutes were spent with an intense question and answer discussion amongst the three, with Lauren scribbling a mass of reaction equations down on her portable whiteboard which Eva quickly rolled in. Finally Juliette summarised where the discussion should lead.

"Okay, going back to our conventional high temperature activity at Cyclops, we know from our testing work on JETR's equipment that their tokomaks are struggling with magnetic field strength restrictions on the plasma. Lauren, you remember that paper I produced last year which mathematically highlighted returning to the unfashionable stellerator design concept? Well, I've since picked up on interesting work coming out of the University of Wisconsin which validates my thesis that we should explore the use of a quasi-symmetric magnetic field, within a new stellerator type design ... and ditch the tokomak entirely. Bhavika?"

"Yes, I agree. So with my two postgraduates and Pune's super-computer facility, we have modelled up an optimised magnetic field geometry inside a conventional stellerator design which should dramatically improve plasma transport and hence fusion reactor performance. We've picked up that the Americans have a practical demonstration reactor showing this configuration works, but what I've done is to redesign the twisted field coils differently with a new quasi-symmetric shape. I think we should try and build our own demonstration reactor too."

Juliette cut in. "Lauren, we have the facilities at Cyclops and now the expertise, as I've recruited two new senior researchers from the US who have recently worked on stellerator design. In addition, we could incorporate and easily modify all the up to date diagnostic equipment we brought back from Ernesto's former Rome laboratory, so we can thoroughly measure the largest set possible of properties of the plasma and magnetic fields. Also, Ernesto is now focussing further at the Weitzman Institute on accurate measurement and this will form the basis of our initial Israel collaboration that I've been successfully negotiating with Mila. A separate paper for the next Board meeting is on its way for that."

"Budget parameters?" Lauren asked softly.

"I've worked out that the first EU grant we will receive through our partnership work with JETR will cover this proposal."

"Okay, approved, benefit of an autocratic Chairman. Go for it, both of you. This move, if successful, will significantly raise the profile of Cyclops which is excellent at such an early development stage." Lauren pulled her desk drawer open and pulled out a thick folder and handed it to Juliette. "I want both of you to read this carefully … stellerator designs were something I actually worked on when I was in academia in Paris, and I also caught that recent US research paper. I think you may find my latest musings, not for formal publication yet, rather helpful. I want you two to take everything forward and get the credit in due course. But I'm afraid I haven't had access to a supercomputer!

"No, just a super-brain Lauren," Bhavika replied. "You never cease to amaze me. How do you find time to actually run Cassini?"

"Organising my time to a microsecond and having a great team of Executives to do the heavy lifting, including you guys. But you've raised an interesting issue, which amongst my other predicament I am reflecting on as my heart still lies with the research as you can see. Mushy brain and business woman of the year or not, I don't want to lose that link with mathematics, where I get so much inner pleasure from, almost as good as sex, sorry Bhavika, I'm getting off the track."

Bhavika grinned. "I agree, as good as."

"Eva?" Lauren shouted again down the corridor. "Can you and Helena come in with that bottle of champagne the Israeli Ambassador left us? Small glass for me, but we should all have a little celebratory fusion toast … thanks both of you, excellent work."

Eva and Helena arrived with the drinks trolley and they all relaxed with some first rate Israeli bubbly, joined then by Mila from her hot desk next door as everyone began chatting loudly.

"Bhavika would like to join us tonight for your special girls night out Lauren, is that okay?" Mila shouted across to Lauren who was musing quietly to herself again at her equations on the whiteboard.

Lauren looked up and waved her hand warmly. "Absolutely yes, but Bhavika, I'm afraid I have to delegate you to drink for me as I will be sticking to soft drinks …"

"No problem … done. Mila has already said she will look after me if I get too inebriated and incapable."

"Yes, I'm sure Mila will," Lauren replied with a tinge of inner caution, watching Mila's enthusiastic conversation and wandering eyes having met Bhavika for the first time.

A bespectacled and serious looking male suddenly appeared at the door catching Lauren's gaze. Immediately she clapped everyone to attention. "Right everyone, celebration's over. I have some serious spread-sheeting to do with Herman; off you go. See you all tonight."

As they filed out to finish off the champagne in Eva's office, Herman wandered in and closed the door. "Sorry to be the party pooper Lauren. What's the celebration about?"

"New potential research business which we need to now reflect in these spreadsheets. Actually Herman, I'm glad you came in and I could get rid of them. I'm getting a bit tired, and gosh they're taking me out tonight too. Hope I can keep the eyelids propped up."

"What, more celebration?"

"Of course … well … my predicament, they want to cheer me up."

"Predicament? What predicament?" Herman immediately said a look of earnest concern on his face. "The finances couldn't be better considering how long the new Cassini business has been going."

Lauren looked at him and realised. "You don't know do you."

"Know what?"

"Gosh, you have been locked away in your office staring at screens the last week. The rumour has finally got out … I'm pregnant … with triplets!"

Herman's face went a decidedly paler hue. "Oh my word Lauren, I had no idea." He grimaced. "Err ... congratulations ... how is Philippe taking it?"

"He doesn't know yet, still away on holiday in the wilds of Siberia and out of contact," Lauren answered, trying to look cheerful but feeling tetchier than ever making constant excuses for him and that ridiculous situation.

"Mmm ... I'd better make a few long term adjustments to this financial spreadsheet," he replied.

Lauren raised an eyebrow ... he never said up or down.

Chapter Seven

Struggling to balance on her open toed six-inch heels, Mila carried a huge tray of drinks from the bar across the cabaret table to the front where the nuclear party were seated, her powerful biceps rippling sexily from her sleeveless dress. Juliette's' eyes were wide with admiration.

"How do you keep so fit, Mila? Those muscles indicate a different attention than just the gym to me?" Juliette chirped, loosening up far more than usual with the three vodka and tonics she had already consumed in succession trying to keep up with Bhavika, who appeared to have the alcoholic stamina of a water buffalo, Indian style.

Helena and Eva both looked up sharply. Juliette was always so proper and formal at least in the office, this was a new and unexpected side.

"Weights of course Juliette … and more," Mila replied giving Juliette a knowing look at which she blushed instantly. "Now Bhavika, I can see you're a woman of fashion taste like me, the way you've been eyeing my dress. Like it?"

"Yes, very much Mila. It suits you beautifully. Who's the designer?"

A voice from behind the pillar suddenly interrupted. "It has all the hallmarks of Karen Millen to me. She's becoming well known for that style of signature stretch and floral printed sleeveless shift dress, especially the contrast mesh panelling at the neckline."

They all turned, mouths open, as Lauren appeared, her blonde hair pinned up and elegantly wearing a beautiful blue stretch-silk organza gown, individually created for her by one of the MA students of the local Fashion College who's Governing Board she chaired. The design, cleverly and purposely hid her slight belly bulge.

Giselle was the first to speak. "Lauren, I'm just gonna say it out loud, you look absolutely the most stunning woman in this room tonight. Even inside those best boudoirs I know in New York City, I ain't seen a woman look so perfect. Don't you all agree ladies?"

Everyone nodded, taken aback.

"Thank you so much Giselle," Lauren replied, smirking inside.

The last time they had seen Lauren look so good was when she got married. Unknown to them, in Lauren's mind, that was exactly how she wanted to feel on this particular evening with Philippe definitely phoning later.

Mila continued, smiling warmly back to Lauren. "As usual your fashion analysis is as good as your nuclear; absolutely spot on. And I agree you look ravishing. I'll just go and get you a ginger beer."

"Thank you Mila, yes please." She smiled back at Mila with that particular look that each privately understood and which both of them wanted to feel right at that moment to assuage their individual concerns.

Everyone was becoming distracted with the food menu and discussing choices as Eva began organising the eating, waving at waiters and writing down preferences. The jazz cabaret was due on shortly when most people would be dining. But Juliette surreptitiously caught the nuance between Lauren and Mila, and thought, and then thought again. She looked up to Mila, who was turning to walk away, and waved a fifty euro note.

"Mila, can you get me a Moscow Mule and one for my drinking companion here please? Does anyone else want anything?"

"No, we've all decided to now stick to the house wine which is excellent … I've just asked the waiter to bring some red and white bottles to go with the meal," Eva replied with precision, noting that Juliette was sounding a little slurry.

"What's a Moscow Mule?" Helena whispered across the table.

"Vodka, ginger beer and lime, a concoction emanating way back from Manhattan and used to be served in a special copper mug. It was originally a wartime speciality and nothing to do with Russia," Giselle said promptly. "Are you sure Juliette you want to blow your brains out with one of those?"

"I'm up for it," Bhavika responded cheerfully. "No problem."

"On me Juliette," Mila replied with a laugh. "You're going to need that fifty euro note for the taxi to get you back home in one piece."

<><>

Finally, prompted by Lauren who had a recent craving for it, they all decided to have the house night special of fish and chicken paella and share two massive cast iron hot dishes of the yellow rice speciality, which were quickly brought out. Whilst waiters were dishing out their portions, the cabaret host leapt to the stage to announce the main billing.

"Ladies and gentlemen, please give a warm welcome for the Brussels answer to George Benson … Mr Jock McIntosh and his very own soul-jazz quartet."

62

As the applause resounded, three guys appeared all dressed in identical smart casual black shirts and jeans and took stools behind the synthesiser, drums and double bass respectively. Jock McIntosh then sauntered in, flashing a broad smile and picked up his Gibson semi-acoustic guitar off the stand. He stood in front of the mike, legs apart, adjusted the strap and his glasses, as the keyboard player and drummer began a slow blues intro. Then he launched together with the bass player into an accompanying set of complicated fast riffs, the room descending into reverential silence with the mellow sound, disturbed only by a slight background of clattering knives and forks.

Lauren, sitting between Mila and Eva, had been distracted at the start fiddling with her phone which had vibrated in her bag, realising that Charlotte had tried to call but the signal inside the room was decidedly poor. She would call Charlotte when she'd eaten. She looked up casually towards Jock McIntosh, appreciating the musical talent. She loved this type of jazz, when immediately she almost choked on her portion of rice.

She could not possibly be seeing who she was seeing … the idea was so surreal as not to be within the normal bounds of probabilities … but rewinding back her sixth sense she decided it was an acceptable outlier after all and smirked. She knew, as a former occasional performer, that he would struggle with the spotlights to make out the near-audience properly but equally she knew she couldn't be missed in her stunning blue dress … and waited for his gaze around the audience to settle on her table. When he looked her way, she noticed his face, just for a micro-second, perceptibly twitch and he dropped a note which her sharp musical ears caught and then he resumed, looking the other way. This was definitely going to be a fun evening, to be followed up at the first break.

Mila noticed a larger than normal grin across her face. "Out with it," she whispered in Lauren's ear. "You know that guy don't you. Former conquest then?"

"Well, he certainly knows me very intimately indeed."

Mila was uncharacteristically flummoxed. Perhaps also, Mila pondered to herself, it was not the best time for old flames to be turning up, especially as Lauren's hormones were obviously flying all over the place.

"Ok, Mila, you look pathetically beaten so I'll put you out of your misery," Lauren whispered back. "By night, you see the crooning sophisticated jazz guitarist, Jock McIntosh. By day, he is better known as Edward Jones, with a somewhat different and more sombre occupation."

"Jesus Christ Lauren … not your fucking gynaecologist?"

"The very same."

Eva, antennae always well tuned into Mila's asides, looked across. "That's Edward Jones, your gynaecologist? Adèle's boss, who sends me his bills? Crikey." She turned to Helena to tell her but immediately saw Helena in another world altogether, tapping her feet rhythmically to the beat, totally absorbed with the amazing Jock McIntosh, musician extraordinaire. Eva turned back to Mila and Lauren and they all raised their eyebrows and laughed.

"He can have that George Clooney effect on women I'm sure," Lauren remarked.

"But this is not like Helena … one little bit," Eva whispered concerned, with Mila grinning broadly.

Following a further set of soul-jazz classics, in which Jock McIntosh also sang in the definitive mode of George Benson, the first break came as the plates began to be cleared away for desserts, cheese and coffee. The wine on their table was duly replenished. Bhavika still looked as sprightly as when she came in, obviously hardened over many years by harsh Indian liqueur, but Juliette had become rather worse for wear, talking far too loudly, whilst Bella and Eva began hard to distract her from any conversation.

Lauren turned to Mila and whispered. "I suspect Juliette is reacting in some way to her divorce just finalised, but we have to stop her drinking any further. She simply can't take it."

"I know. I'll keep an eye on her. Her ex-husband was a barebacking addict, treated her and the kids like shit."

"What's barebacking?"

"Later Lauren, later."

"Anyway, whilst Jock the Jones is ensconced in a huddle by the bar, I'm just going to have a little fun. Watch me."

Lauren raised herself up from the seat and began a slow and casual stroll to the bar, all eyes turning. Jock McIntosh looked up furtively, fear creeping distinctly across his worried expression, but he had nowhere to run as he was on again in ten minutes.

"Jock McIntosh, how lovely to see you again, may I introduce you to someone at my table?"

His band members and friends looked around, and it was obvious they were wondering how on earth Mac could know someone so gorgeous and sophisticated.

"Yes, certainly Professor … a pleasure."

He whispered to his friends that the woman was a Brussels University academic he had met at a recent gig there, and they all nodded. Wiping his sweating brow, they began walking over.

She linked her arm into his and whispered. "Don't worry Edward, your secret is safe with me. I can see your fellow musicians have no idea of your daytime alter-ego. You really are a fabulous musician, I love it. And I do seriously want you to meet someone."

"Thanks Lauren. I really appreciate that. Need to keep my two lives firmly apart. Are those anti-nausea remedies I asked Adèle to give you working? We have an appointment next week too don't we."

"Yes, I feel so much better now. I have some technical ideas about improving your electromagnetic bracelet, Edward. On the house so to speak, but I want to be on a new patent. Look forward to being inspected next week."

"Don't say it like that Lauren," he said back, grinning, amazed at how gorgeous and mind blowing she looked.

At the table, Lauren looked hard at Mila and Eva then turned to everyone. "Jock and I are old friends from way back, and I just wanted him to meet a fellow jazz aficionado. Jock, can I introduce you to Helena Zharanowska, my new Deputy Director of Administration. Helena is a fine musician too, isn't that right Helena? Tenor Saxophone?"

They all turned mystified to Helena, who blushed profusely and wriggled in her seat. Eva mouthed 'really' to her friend, pleased and also unsurprised Helena had just been promoted by Lauren to Sonja's deputy, but even more amazed that Helena, who was always discrete about her private life, was a jazz fiend.

Edward Jones turned to Helena with an infectious grin and knelt on his haunches beside her. She was sat, demure, cross-legged and alluring in her mini-dress. "Do you really play tenor sax?" he asked, his eyes looking her all over.

"Yes, since a child. I was classically trained, then soul and jazz took over in my teens, but I never went professional. My big influence has been Charlie Parker and I love the Jimmy Smith band. You sound just like George Benson. Great voice."

"Thanks ... Wow ... hey do you know Lover Man? Want to gig with me as a guest? Me and the band would love to have a saxophone interspersed with the music, and jazz makes you live dangerously doesn't it? I've got a spare with me in a case behind the amp; it is a tenor. I've tried to learn for ages but I'm not really any good."

Helena looked up, her eyes flashing, and for a change thought here was a man who had a certain delectability and panache. There had been a real desert out there in her personal life right then. She was on a big high with Lauren's job offer in the afternoon, which she was looking forward to starting so much. She hadn't played on stage for ages … but why not? "Lead the way Mr McIntosh."

Helena got up, much to everyone's amazement except Lauren and Mila who understood completely, and walked onto the stage to inspect the saxophone. Everyone began returning to their seats. Lauren was very fond of Helena, especially after all that Helena had done during the recent 'Amélie in the lake' escapade.

"I'm just popping to the loo Mila," Lauren whispered and got up.

"Err, before you go there's a special guest tonight who is mmm … going with you," Mila replied waving to the end of the stage.

"Pardon?"

Suddenly, a tall and gorgeously dressed slim woman, with long curly black hair, in a tight fitting flimsy evening gown sauntered up towards the table. Lauren couldn't believe it, another 'just not possible' was happening. She had an immediate flashback to a rather special and pleasant evening once upon a time … in Palermo, Sicily.

"Annabella," Lauren cried stretching out her arms as they hugged warmly. "What on earth are you doing here?"

"I've come to look after you for a while. Don't worry everything is fine back at home with the children and Luigi. Angelina and the nannies have everything in control exactly as my sister likes it to be. I'll explain later. Come on, I need the loo badly too, I got delayed from the airport."

They strode off arm in arm as Juliette turned to Mila and uttered. "Gosh, two equal contenders now for the most beautiful women here tonight, don't you think?" a definite slur dripping from her voice, despite a major effort to control it.

Mila grimaced and tucked aggressively into her raspberry sorbet. She wasn't normally outdone but had to admit defeat for a change. She hadn't seen Annabella looking like that since they lived together in Rome, and it worried her.

Lauren and Annabella soon returned chattering incessantly, and then they both sat down quietly with Mila and Eva. The tables had been reset in smaller cabaret style. The last remnants of dessert, coffee cups and cheese were taken away, and more drinks were being provided with fresh orders taken.

Onstage at the back they could see Helena standing confidently with a large gleaming, golden saxophone, running quietly through a set of jazz scales with Jock McIntosh, releasing an impressive and pleasing arpeggio of sound. Then she slung the sax around her neck and strode purposefully, without any seeming anxiety, to a microphone stand next to the bass player. The show was about to begin again. Jock, aka Edward, strutted to the main mike and began.

"Hi everyone and welcome to the second half of our show. As you know, the best jazz is often the most improvised, and do we have a treat for you now. I am pleased to introduce our guest musician for the rest of the evening; she hasn't played with us before, but she has impeccable talent. Ladies and gentlemen, please give your usual warm welcome to Ms Helena Zharanowska."

The applause was deafening, especially from the Cassini table.

Lauren turned to the others. "Now, there on stage is a man who likes to take a bet on a good risk by intuition … which is why he is now my personal gynaecologist."

Annabella turned around startled. "Your gynaecologist? You must be joking Lauren."

"Nope, his real name is Edward Jones and he runs the top clinic in town. Jock McIntosh is his alter ego night-time passion, but a secret; neither his friends nor fellow musicians know. Funny, but as another alter ego musician, I have the same instinct too about Helena and her playing. She won't let him down. And doesn't she look lovely in that red mini-dress and cage boots."

"I agree wholeheartedly," Eva chipped in, fascinated by the sight of her friend onstage.

"Actually, Edward Jones took by far the biggest risk of his career becoming *your* gynaecologist," Mila added with a raucous laugh. "You're a wicked matchmaker Lauren. I assume from his demeanour and the way he's ogling Helena that he's single and between partners presently? She'll be blowing more than her saxophone later."

Eva coughed and Annabella playfully swiped Mila's arm. "Mila, honestly, you never change, sometimes you can be so over a top, isn't that so Lauren?"

Lauren smiled, saying nothing.

Eva turned to the others with a quizzical expression. "But do gynaecologists ogle? Surely they see so many women's private parts that ogling becomes a meaningless occupation?"

That set off Mila again. "Yes, Eva, believe me they ogle. Having that intimate knowledge of women confers a special understanding of what will and won't turn you on. Isn't that so Lauren?"

Lauren continued smiling and remained totally non-plussed, pleased with her first pairing off attempt on this occasion. Everyone was quiet as the first warm up of a standard long blues number progressed apace. The soulful and artistic improvised sound that Helena played with all her might was a joy to listen to. She certainly was talented, and Jock the Jones was decidedly hooked.

Eventually the finale arrived as Jock announced the number Lover Man and invited the audience to finish off the evening with a slow dance. Juliette, by then quiet and morose, was suddenly tapped on the shoulder by a giant of a man with a large shaven head and piercing dark eyes, and asked to dance as groups of couples got up. Juliette looked up, smiled and headed off to their amazement onto the dance floor, with Mila watching closely as Helena blew her way through the slow sexy number. Jock sang melodically, the swishing of the cymbals and the background melody of the organ and bass providing a sensual atmosphere for end of evening intimate connections and the whispering of sweet-nothings.

Juliette suddenly returned to the table looking for her handbag, distinctly unsteady on her feet. "He's asked me to go back to his hotel for a good fuck. I haven't had a good fuck with a man for years so I'm off."

Eva and Annabella looked horrified. Lauren pulled up a seat quickly as Mila stood up and helped Juliette to sit down. Bhavika and Giselle were at the other end of the bar area in friendly conversation with Indian friends of Bella, well out of it.

"No Juliette, that's a bad idea so you're not going anywhere, understand?" Mila said sternly, as the guy came over to the table, Juliette sitting with her head in her hands.

"Oi Blondie. She's coming back with me, so back off if you know what's good for you." He was English and unsavoury.

Mila smiled back calmly. "Listen sweetheart, I think you can see, she's not in a good state," she replied in a totally unexpected London cockney accent. "I'm bored with this dump, how about you and me go and have some real fun. Follow me and I'll get my coat."

He looked Mila up and down, smiled back and nodded with what was a much more attractive proposition, following her as she tripped sexily down the walkway towards the exit.

Lauren looked back at Annabella and Eva and whispered. "Oh my God, I don't have a good feeling about this. Shit."

"We all know Mila can take care of herself, which is more than can be said for Juliette here," Annabella replied casually, Juliette sobbing quietly on her shoulder. "What will be, will be as we Italians say."

Mila was back in five minutes, dusting her hands. "The head bouncer called a taxi. Sadly, Big Jack had to leave immediately to accident and emergency for urgent dental treatment, with a black eye and *very* bruised testicles when he slipped on the pavement. Shame, I was looking forward to that offer." She grinned.

"Bloody hell Mila," Lauren retorted but was truly thankful.

"Now," Mila continued. "Annabella you know the routine. We're used to this Eva from our former Sicilian hotelier days. We'll take Juliette back to her flat and tuck her in bed. She'll be fine tomorrow apart from a blinding headache and bad stomach."

Annabella grinned at Lauren as they all helped Juliette to her feet and began easing her towards the door and then the taxis. "I'm booked in the hotel opposite, where Bhavika is staying. I'll see you tomorrow okay," Annabella shouted back.

"Fantastic, I look forward to that. Bye both of you. Take care of her will you."

"What is the matter with Juliette? She looks dreadful, is she not well?"

Eva and Lauren turned to find Bhavika with her coat on, walking towards them. "Perhaps I should give them a hand. Sorry, I got caught up in a long conversation with Bella's Indian friends."

Lauren patted her arm gently. "Don't worry Bhavika, she's in good hands with Mila and Annabella ... I know from past experience. She'll be fine some time tomorrow. One Moscow Mule too many I fear. Juliette hasn't got the drinking stamina of an ox like you, unfortunately."

Bhavika blushed. "Lauren, I feel terrible, I never noticed and should have. I was a bit party wild at University, drank the males regularly under the table, the habit has sort of stuck."

Eva and Lauren laughed, both thinking that was quite obvious. "Anyway, Bhavika," Lauren replied, "I understand you're here until the end of the week and will also be seeing Sonja when she returns from leave. Can you pop in first thing tomorrow for an hour? I'd like to tie up some loose project ends that came to me whilst Helena was on stage playing, you know, from where we left our meeting. I've confirmed a revised budget now with Hermann for your exploratory work. We'll be fine without Juliette."

"Thank you so much Lauren, that's fantastic. See you then," Bhavika said, turning and departing to the exit. "I just wanted to say good night as well and thank you for inviting me this evening, it was a great night out."

"Bye Bhavika ... you have Mila and Eva to thank who organised everything ... bye," Lauren called back smiling and waving her off.

"Your diary is clear for the morning, a rare space for desk work Lauren. I'll text Annabella to come in at ten-thirty," Eva added. "Look there's Seb at the door. He promised to pick us up and take us back to our apartments, you don't need a taxi. Hope that's okay," as they both watched Helena disappearing out of the door, hand in hand with Jock McIntosh.

Lauren gave Eva a large hug. "Thanks. I don't know what I'd do without you, you're a real treasure. Actually it's been a really good evening, thoroughly enjoyable. But never forget. Wherever there's trouble Mila is usually not far behind!"

They giggled and walked briskly to the very dependable Seb quietly waiting patiently, and then the three headed home. She suddenly felt uneasy. Charlotte hadn't been phoned and Philippe hadn't called. Hey ho, tomorrow would be yet another day.

Chapter Eight

Clattering noisily with an irritating squeak, the electric roller shutters on her garage door slowly rumbled as she put her BMW away for the rest of the day. Following an excellent meeting with Bhavika, Lauren realised that a vital business file she needed on Johann's latest market assessment of nuclear opportunities in Africa was still lying on her breakfast table. She decided to return home and continue work from there for the afternoon.

Annabella had rung the office first thing to say once they had Juliette tucked in bed, she had decided to stay overnight and watch over her because Juliette had vomited badly in the taxi back and was still in severe distress, looking a very pale colour. She was then going out for some coffee and light breakfast for Juliette as the apartment was bare, and would leave Juliette to recover in the afternoon, by which time Juliette's mother would arrive from London, after Annabella had insisted that someone should stay with her for a few days. Lauren suggested that Annabella swap the hotel for her guest bedroom for the rest of her visit which Annabella enthusiastically agreed, hoping all along to be able to stay with Lauren over the next couple of weeks. She intended to organise appropriate planning and maternal things for her, promised when a distraught and confused Lauren had first confided about her triplet pregnancy. Annabella's recent experience of having two babies in quick succession was not going to waste.

But she also had another agenda in mind, and wanted desperately to talk it through with Lauren.

Mila, in the meantime, had headed straight back to Cannes to work on further security issues at the Cyclops Centre, and complete arrangements for her and Juliette, later in the week, to revisit Israel, assuming Juliette had recovered properly, although Mila was confident Juliette would be back to her usual self in two or three days.

Lauren mused over everything, realising that Sonja too would be back from leave in Croatia in the next few days and hoping that she and Mila could find some quality time to sort themselves and their future out. Deep down, knowing Sonja's strong personal capabilities to mend bridges and her long held depth of feeling for Mila, Lauren was confident they would quickly be fine, especially given the joint commitment made to living together in a new luxury apartment. She felt a warm all-over glow for a true and lasting friendship and admiration for Annabella's capabilities and caring nature. Given the turmoil presently she was looking forward to having Annabella around. She had to admit to an increased feeling of acute loneliness, especially after the upsetting conversation with Svet. Damn Philippe ... still silent ... not a murmur of a text, email or phone call.

She read steadily through Johann's latest Africa research, his proposed network of potential business contacts and overall positive recommendations, and made some notes to follow up discussion. Africa would be an interesting trip, one continent she had never visited. Suddenly her phone jarred into life, buzzing across the shiny table as she grabbed at it. For the first time the screen flashed up Philippe's mobile personal number. At long last, rapidly urging her brain into gear — he was back in some civilised area. But the call failed to connect, and returning generated a continual unobtainable number.

"Damn and shit," she cried out frustrated, with a seething anger, tapping endlessly at the screen to no avail. A loud banging on the door was about to make her totally flip, but she took a few deep breaths, realising that getting so upset and over the top wasn't such a good idea and logically would not solve any problem right then.

"Who the fuck is at the door, now of all times," she muttered.

Anybody coming into the building had to pass and be approved by the strict security concierge, but she wasn't expecting a visitor. She pulled open the door angrily and stared at the figure, and her face dropped with total disbelief ...

"What was it you said once, you look like you've lost a fifty dollar note and found a cent?" the smiling visitor said, on seeing the red, angry face.

Lauren, completely disorientated, dashed forward, arms outstretched and hugged her visitor hard.

"We'd better make the most of this Lauren, because in three months time neither of us will reach the other!" her visitor continued, reciprocating.

Lauren stepped back. "Gosh Charlotte, you're the last person I was expecting. What on earth are you doing here and where are the children?"

"So, are you going to invite me into your palatial apartment then?"

"Of course, come in, straight through into the sitting room on the right and take a seat. Nobody is here, only me." Lauren looked from left to right outside, all deserted, then closed the door and walked into the room. How did Charlotte find her and what was she doing here, all the way from Texas? And this must be the first time Charlotte had been into Brussels, let alone seen her apartment.

Charlotte was walking around the large room, admiring the paintings and the lovely contemporary furniture, staring thoughtfully at the luxurious white musk sofa. "I phoned Eva who kindly said you were working at home and gave me directions to your address, so I took a taxi immediately. Security was a laugh. When I told them I was your daughter, they looked blank, insisted on seeing my passport then declared that I must really be your sister, before letting me through. Seeing us together in six months will be a bit of a challenge for them, especially when they meet my new husband."

Lauren stared. "New husband? Actually, I think I need a ginger and lemon tea."

"Does that help morning sickness?"

"Most definitely, a special mix recommended by my gynaecologist. Do you want one too?"

"Mmm ... yes please."

Both smiled, as Lauren went off to boil the kettle. It was a strange way to heal the tension but somehow it worked. No more dancing nervously around each other afraid to talk.

Supping her hot drink, Charlotte nervously fingered a Luddite maternity wear catalogue on the coffee table, and began to speak. "One good thing is we both have the Hind genes of strong, logical and clear thinking, so thanks to Mila, I know you know and you know I know ... congratulations all round and problem solved! I came here because I was desperate to see you above anything else."

Lauren roared with mirth ... how alike Charlotte was ... daughter and sister combined and so lovely to just turn up.

"Okay, we've covered that one, err ... new husband next please," Lauren replied.

Charlotte patted her tummy. "Fortunately, this time only one is incubating inside; although it looks like multiple births as well as engineering runs in the family. There is only one absolute possibility who the father is, and I love him and he loves me, and when his divorce comes through we're getting married. Lyell has been very straightforward. He wants nothing and has already moved in with grandma and a Cherokee squaw on the reservation. DG is going to be more complicated, and Lorraine is fighting for a hefty settlement, but DG is confident his pre-nuptials with her will hold in court if necessary."

Lauren felt immediate apprehension. A sad aspect of her overactive brain was a capacity to accurately recall odd facts and figures, excellent when she and her former husband played pub quizzes in London, but in this case her daughter was a much more serious issue. "Charlotte, it isn't legal, certainly not in France. There was some sort of test case in the UK, and I wouldn't expect the US is any different, probably stricter especially in Texas."

"What isn't legal?"

"Marrying your father-in-law," Lauren replied softly, feeling her stomach churn purveying such news.

Charlotte became flushed. She was distinctly uncomfortable for a moment and then took a deep breath and a pause. "Sorry, I should have explained a while back, but it only came out when all these legal proceedings started and I had no idea. Lyell and I were legally married, but DG hasn't been my father-in-law."

Lauren stared puzzled. "I'm sorry Charlotte, I'm not usually so dense, but you'll have to explain."

"Because Lyell is not legally his son. Once DG and I reached a stage in our relationship when we knew ... well ... that this was it for both of us he came clean one night. I knew it was serious because he made me a meal ... spaghetti bolognaise, the only thing he can cook! Lyell was found as an abandoned baby on the reservation by DG's first wife, who was, as you know, Cherokee – there were complications, tribal and also her own family, all kinds of things and in the end DG, by then already wealthy and under pressure from his wife, 'bought' Lyell and they brought him up off the reservation as their son, but he was never formally adopted by either of them. And that is how it stands now. DG had already thought this issue through in the context of him and me potentially marrying and had quietly taken advice from his own top lawyers … so he isn't and never has been my legal father-in-law, plain and simple."

Lauren was completely taken aback, but then began to assemble and disassemble the facts, logically and clearly, and felt a huge sense of warm relief wash over her. Part of her conscious unease with Charlotte and DG's relationship was DG being her father-in-law; their age difference was not such a problem for her. "Did Lyell know all this and the twins?"

"Nobody knew only DG and the woman who Lyell calls his grandmother. When DG told Lyell the truth a month ago, his only reaction was he wasn't surprised but acknowledged and was grateful that DG always tried hard to bring him up well and as his own son. In some odd way they even seemed closer after that revelation. I suppose it explains why Lyell and DG were always divergent as adults and why Lyell never fitted into DG's grand plan for the family oil empire."

"Mmm … yes, I suppose it does. What about the twins?"

"This is not the time. One day, when they're older, DG and I will tell them, but not now, Lauren. Is there some reason why our family relationships are constantly riddled with complications, especially you and me?"

Lauren laughed. "Who knows, but it never gets boring does it. Well, I'm very pleased for you both. DG is an amazing and caring man … going back to Lorraine, will you do the same, I mean agree pre-nuptials?"

"No, because DG insists me and him are going to be forever and for the first time in his long life he knows he wants to wed the right woman for once. He's so looking forward to being a father again, and Lexi and Kat are overjoyed with having a new brother to look after."

Lauren smiled at how wonderful that sounded, but couldn't hide her inner grimace. Obviously Charlotte, in her usual organised way, had already prenatally sorted gender and paternity. "When you knocked, for the first time in twelve days I almost got a call from Philippe but the signal went … I'm still waiting … and he still doesn't know and …"

Charlotte interrupted, her eyes narrowed. "Philippe isn't back from that damned Lena River yet? But he was supposed to leave for the airport the same time as DG and also Sergei."

Lauren looked up and began to feel a sickly unease as Charlotte continued.

"Some woman in the party, a sister or friend of one of Philippe's associates with them went missing whilst Sergei was there over the last weekend. She apparently ran off into the night from their camp crying, so DG told me. He didn't know why, and the three of them took almost two days of tracking but they found her eventually, relatively unharmed but incredibly lucky, in an old bear den about five kilometres away, where she'd taken shelter and lived off berries and melted ice. DG reckoned she must have known survival techniques."

"So where's DG?"

"He's with me Lauren. He's gone into town to meet with some political colleagues who are here for a forthcoming US-EU summit on trade. We left the twins in Texas, in the safe hands of Delilah and Orlando. They have school of course, and they pass on their love and want to skype us all whilst I'm here. DG and Sergei left Yakutsk Airport three days ago. Philippe must have stayed on for some reason. Perhaps he's doing some business deals, you know what he's like. Yakutsk is apparently quite a large city, but it's freezing cold there now, the river was starting to ice over. And you say he still doesn't know? Well DG does now because I told him, but I know he won't have mentioned anything to Philippe, as I also told him to keep his mouth shut … politely of course … because we both realised immediately … there may be issues. Incidentally, he's hugely happy and so pleased for you."

"That's nice, thanks, I really appreciate that from both of you, but yes there is an issue Charlotte, which is precisely why I'm so cut up inside and putting on a brave face to the rest of the world, because I need to discuss everything with Philippe obviously, and this stupid Siberia situation and that damned woman, all make it worse of course."

"The woman? You know about her?"

"He sent me a text that the delectable gas engineer, Olga, had gone missing and they were going to find her … then their satellite phone packed in."

"You seem to think this woman Olga and Philippe are … err … close? DG said nothing, although these things pass him by. Sorry, I'm sure there is absolutely nothing."

"Yes, you're right, hormones, multiplied three-fold!"

They giggled, but Lauren just wanted to get this inane Philippe communications saga over and done with.

Charlotte poured another tea and became pensive. "I was the only one who heard Vaag when he broke into our hotel room in Kola that awful day. I realised, and so did Mila later, that kidnapping you had all kinds of motives for him … and I realise that you may have been in a position … where you had to say yes … in fact Lauren, between you and me … Shit I'm going to say it … I suspected you wanted to say yes, and I understand fully why if you did, I'm your daughter remember."

Lauren rubbed a tear from her eye and composed herself, drawing breath sharply. "I'm sorry Charlotte all that stuff went on. You're my daughter, I love you and you're right, I still don't know what was going on in my mind then, but equally I can't be sure anything actually happened because I went unconscious with the poisoning, then woke up naked in a bath of warm water. Conception was about that time, and either Philippe or maybe Vaag could have been responsible."

"So have a pre-DNA test then?"

"No, I'm not, I've firmly decided after weighing it up and there will be no risks taken. Gosh, triplets will be difficult enough at my age, and I want these babies so very much Charlotte because …"

"Because you have the chance and capability to give them what you weren't able to give me, and I so much understand that too Lauren … everything will be fine, trust me." She threw her arms around Lauren and hugged her. "He'll be back in no time, on the next plane from Siberia, and throw his arms around you. Olga the bear will be a distant memory. Anyway he has work to get on with … DG has offered him the chairmanship of Rubidium because Amélie of course, like the rest of us, is now indisposed."

"Rubidium? Does Mila know?"

"I have no idea, but I doubt it. Why?"

"No matter, I just wondered."

"No, the rest of the group pregnancies have been relayed from all angles of course by Mila, which is why I sound so knowledgeable. I also understand that Svet may have fallen under the spell of the Russian baby boom. Mila is hugely supportive and watchful of you Lauren."

Lauren smiled. Between Charlotte, Mila and of course Annabella, complete sense was finally emerging. She was very glad for all of them as best friends. "I know, and I'm grateful to Mila for so much ... Fortunately, Svet is in the clear, although listening to her description over the phone I'm convinced she's had an early miscarriage and not a heavy period, but that may likely be for the best. She has now taken steps to avoid a recurrence. But when I came to my situation, with Svet, and the possibility of the father not being Philippe, and I had to be honest with her Charlotte as I believe I should always be, after all she was there and the focus of everything we did in the Arctic to find and save her, but my whole revelation came as a big shock. She immediately hung up and we haven't spoken since. I feel terribly bad and upset now about the whole conversation."

"You did the right thing Lauren. Better to be honest and direct from the start ... Svet is only eighteen but she has a sharp scientific mind, and will be analytically mulling over the situation as you and I know too well. I'm confident she will be onside and supportive again. But I can see why you must talk to Philippe immediately ... Do you want me to ask DG if he knows any more about what Philippe is up to?"

"No, let's not complicate it further yet, I'll see if he gets through again. Where are you staying?"

"A place Eva recommended; the same hotel as Annabella is in, who I bumped into as I was going out ... I recognised her from when you got married. She isn't a woman to easily forget, so strikingly beautiful."

"No, true. Annabella is coming here later. Would you like to pick up DG and come to dinner too? That would be so lovely the four of us. Say seven? And we can skype the twins too."

"Heck, yes please. DG wants me to meet him and those goddam awful Republican politicians at the EU Headquarters now, some good business opportunity, as usual, so I'll just grab a taxi shortly and head on over there."

"I can take you, Charlotte …"

"No, no, I can see from those papers on the table you have some complicated research to get on with. I've got this app on my phone so I'll just …"

Lauren was staring at her own buzzing phone; the ringer was off when the screen lit up. "It's Philippe!"

"I'll just wait in the dining room for this taxi and if it comes I'll let myself out … go for it and good luck Lauren … see you later no worries," Charlotte whispered back.

<><>

"Hi darling, at long last we can speak. How are you? It has been a nightmare here but finally we found somewhere to charge my phones and get a normal mobile signal out. I want to head home fast."

"Philippe, it's lovely to hear your voice again." She suddenly heard the door clunk and saw Charlotte waving through the window and running towards the security gate. "Where are you?"

"Yakutsk, at the Arctic Fox Hotel. Only just got here. DG and Sergei have just headed off back to the US. I'm with Igor and Pyotr. They're waiting at reception for an airport taxi to get back to Moscow."

She was already feeling hot under the collar … she could sense he was lying through his back teeth by the tone of his voice, never mind that she knew DG had left days ago. "What about Olga? Did you find her?"

"Yes, a bit difficult and took a while, but she was fine."

"So has she gone too?"

There was a silence for a second. "Err … not quite … her flight has been delayed …"

She was rapidly tiring of this logistical gymnastics and went straight to the point. "Philippe, there's something important I must tell you … now … I'm …"

"Sorry darling, just hang on a second, Olga's waving at me from the boutique opposite."

Lauren could have thrown her phone against the wall, but took a deep breath and wiped her brow with a tissue. She couldn't believe she was having this conversation. She caught their discussion; his skills with a mute button were as bad as his emailing. 'Hey Olga, that short dress looks terrific, certainly goes well with the black boots, definitely buy both …' Giggling was evident in the background, more than one female voice, presumably the other friend, Nina.

Philippe continued. "Sorry darling, just got distracted for a moment, now what was it you were saying?"

"I'm fucking pregnant, and just for good measure, yes trouble does come in threes and I'm having triplets, oh and a bit of icing on the cake, I might organise a lottery quiz to guess who the father is. Prize … an all-in-ticket for the laugh a minute, fun and frivolity holiday guaranteed in the depths of Siberia, with Philippe's fucking trekking tours. Anything else you want me to get in before the phone cuts off and you return to the irresistible charms of your shitty gas engineer companions?"

There was a protracted silence. She began to pace the room, livid and red in the face, but took steady deep breaths, she was not going to upset herself, bad move, she had to calm down ... steady, analytical, logical and determined ... the scientific way. She needed that to see her through what seemed to be the most bizarre of situations, when half the world and his wife were aware of her predicament but not him, who didn't seem the slightest bit interested? What the fuck was the matter with the man she thought she loved and recently married in good faith? Was the Lauren Hind man-curse prevailing again this soon?

"Jesus Christ Lauren, sorry, you've every right to get mad at me, I wasn't paying proper attention, I'm really sorry ... what did you just say? You're pregnant and having triplets? Bloody hell. How long gone are you?"

"Two months. You don't sound exactly wildly ecstatic Philippe?"

"Sorry Lauren, it's just hit me like falling off a skyscraper, I just need to think. Gosh, yes, marvellous news, and ... err ... how are you feeling?"

"Well, you know Philippe ... triplets at forty-three, probably like passing gall stones, one quick heave, nine months and three clinks later and they're out in the bedpan ... I'm bloody scared, what do you think?"

He began to cough and put on a more cheery and comforting voice. "I'm sure we can both see this through and of course I will be supportive every step of the way, so anything you need, I'll get sorted immediately and ... err ... two months, so conception was around the time we were in Murmansk?"

"Yes, the Kola Hotel, if you recall. Probably the last time we did it, whilst saving your daughter who also has no inclination to fucking talk to me either. Sorry, I apologise that was unfair, Svet is fine, I take that back."

"She sounded a bit chilly when I spoke to her yesterday?"

"Yesterday?"

"Sorry … I mean last week … lost track of time a little here."

"I bet, especially out in the woods with the bears."

"That sounded a little cynical, Lauren."

For some strange and frustrating reason, perhaps, she thought, her legendary communication skills were also on the wane, she simply wasn't getting through. "Tell you what; let's forget the bears and wolves. Back to basics. When exactly are you coming home? That would be a useful start."

"You're not actually joking about who the father is are you. I remember that bastard Vaag, taunting mercilessly about you before kicking me to kingdom come. I'd put all that shit to the back of my mind, didn't want to know so I didn't ask. But now it's there again, clear as a bell."

"Maybe we should have talked it through, how you felt, before you set off."

"Not exactly easy talking was it Lauren with my jaw mangled and wired up."

"Look Philippe, let's talk sensibly and rationally now. It's possible something may have happened when I collapsed with the poisoning. I don't know because all I remember is waking up in a bath of warm water. Why are we having this conversation now? I'm pregnant, I want you here and as far as I'm concerned you're the father ninety-nine percent.

"But not a hundred percent is it Lauren. You were naked with him?"

"Well in a bath you tend to be as I recall, but I cannot remember how I got there … end of story. I'm sorry Philippe, that's it. Now when are you coming home?"

"He already had twenty-one children by God knows how many other women, so another three would be neither here nor there, would it."

"It's nice to be thought of by your own husband as another cog in the former Vaag concubine and child production machine, but I don't quite see it that way. I really am looking forward now to these babies. Yes, the last two weeks have been a huge shock to me and my system. But I want them Philippe and I'm going to make sure they have all the love, opportunities and care possible, with or …"

"With or without me you were going to say … Jesus Christ Lauren, you don't give a shit whether I'm the father or not do you …"

"Of course I do. This is terrible, why are we arguing? Just come home. I need you. I need my husband, is that unreasonable?"

"In that case you will have to go for pre-DNA testing immediately."

"Pardon?"

"You must do a paternity test before they are born. Olga has had that done. It was painless although in the end she had an abortion … but …"

Lauren screamed down the phone. "I don't give a fuck about that slag … nor do I want to hear about her … I think I detected a hint of a command tone from the all powerful Philippe … are you ordering me to do a paternity test?"

"Yes of course I am. What man in his right mind in this situation wouldn't?"

"Well, we can dispel that little fantasy of yours darling, because I have already decided … and I'm not. Seven months to go before they are born — then I think it will be pretty clear who the father is, don't you? I think you forgot. I don't take to being ordered about, especially by you."

"I can see you've become quite irrational and hysterical Lauren. It's a waste of time continuing. I'm cutting this call. I

88

have to think. I'm sorry but you'll need to give me time. This has all kinds of implications. Bye Lauren."

With that the phone went dead. She immediately redialled but he had switched the phone completely off and the voicemail immediately kicked in. "Fuck you, you bastard, I don't need you or your patronising crap." She threw her phone hard against the wall, smashing it into tiny pieces. She wanted to cry but was too angry and upset. Like father like daughter; why on earth did she get involved with the whole damned Dubois family? That little discussion went far worse than her worst nightmares could have foretold. She still loved him, she wanted him there, but no way would she be cowed by threats. They were her babies and her body, and only she would decide. The babies' interests and their health must come first ... surely he could understand that? Or is that sensitive male ego of his so bruised, twisted and battered in his mind that any semblance of compromise and coming to terms with the reality of where they both are, and then getting on with it sensibly together and finding joy and happiness with the future, were as realistic as nailing jelly to the ceiling?

An email pinged into her work smartphone, fortunately intact on the coffee table.

Hi I'm really sorry about our conversation and upsetting you. The news was just such a shock and I know I handled it badly ... I need to reflect ... I'm not very good with this sort of thing. I think it would be a good idea if perhaps we keep some distance for a little while. I really need to stay on in Russia anyway because I have decided to accept DG's offer to chair Rubidium and develop new energy business in fracking with Igor and Pyotr who are coming in. Igor will become CEO of a new Russian operation. Keep in touch by email and text, especially if you have any problems or are not well ... I just don't want to talk right now, I'm sorry. I love you. P xx

She retrieved a pan and brush from the kitchen and began aimlessly brushing up the remnants of her wrecked personal phone, tears streaming down her face. *How could that idiot love me and want to keep away? I can't comprehend any of it.* That mantra ran in a continuing loop relentlessly inside her head. She lay down on the couch, crying ... *this was not how their life together was meant to be* ... she was inconsolable, shivering violently, until her eyes closed with emotional exhaustion and sleep overcame her ...

<><>

The sharp light of mid afternoon peeping through the half drawn blinds of the large windows filled her sore red eyes as she looked up, disoriented, at a smiling figure sat next to her on the edge of the sofa, gently dabbing her forehead with a towel. She had a thin blanket over her.

"Oh ... Annabella ..." she mumbled incoherently. "How did you get in here?"

"I borrowed Mila's security keys before she left for Cannes. She has a spare set. Save you the trouble of getting new ones cut. How are you feeling Lauren? I can see something has upset you very badly. Do you wish to tell me? It might help."

Lauren struggled from out of her slumber and sat up, opening her handbag for a mirror. She looked in dismay at the reflection. "I look horrendous, I must get some makeup on and dab my eyes with something. I'm really glad you're here." She hugged Annabella hard, feeling the warmth of her body through the short thin dress, her figure amazingly lithe and firm, considering she recently had two children.

"First a tea, I see you indulge in ginger and lemon ... me too, I love that. I will put the kettle on Lauren."

"Good idea, I'll just freshen up," Lauren replied, heading for the bathroom. She emerged with a sprinkling of blusher and lipstick refresh, having dabbed her tired eyes with a solution. She smiled at Annabella who sat primly and patiently at the coffee table, running through the conversation with Philippe in her head and feeling tears welling up again, but fought this time to suppress her utter devastation. Her conscious mind had begun gearing up in the usual way to provide logical barriers and rational resolutions to this new crisis.

She retold the whole conversation, slowly and carefully, Annabella nodding and taking in every nuance and subtlety. A sudden flashback to the lovely time they first met in Palermo ran through Lauren's thoughts, as she strove hard to keep positive and prepare for explanations. Only with Annabella had she ever been so frank and open, and despite their last few years apart, it was exactly as if time had stood still and they were close, warm and intimate again, special and unique, a deep and indescribable feeling of sister comfort, different from Mila, something she had never shared with anyone, except now perhaps with Charlotte.

Annabella sat in silence after Lauren finished for a good minute, supping her mug of tea and nibbling a shortbread biscuit. "I believe you want me to be truthful with my opinion Lauren, as I always was. Do you want that still?"

"Yes."

"Leave him be now, let him stay in Russia, whether it's a day, a week or a year because only Philippe will be able to work through his interpretation of what has happened in his own way. Then he will return and either love and want you or equally not. You may never see him again Lauren because the impact of what happened with Vaag was hugely traumatic. The episode is deep and irrational inside his head, and he simply can't cope with you being pregnant with Vaag's babies. He sees the triplets, presently, as a curse, a deliberate multiplication of deep guilt … that he didn't try hard enough to keep Vaag away from you … and this is the penalty he has to suffer."

"Then I must do the DNA test immediately."

"No Lauren. The way his mind has set itself, even if Philippe is the father, he won't believe it. He has to work through this differently, and staying in Russia, immersing himself into a new business is already part of the journey to enable him to try and confront his demons over Vaag, once and for all. And that will take time."

"Gosh Annabella, you have a perspective nobody else has, not even Mila. Why?"

"Because I had a father who was exactly the same and I saw it … with my sister … long before you and I met."

"Luis? Oh fuck, I forgot."

"Luis and Philippe, as men, had a lot more in common than you thought. I always knew, but it wasn't something I wanted you to hear, but this situation has called for it. Angelina, once ten years ago became pregnant. Only Luis could have been the father but he wouldn't believe her, for silly, stupid reasons at the time in his head about the village priest … and she aborted it after six weeks because she could see no way then of coping with a child without him and losing him as a result, and it was one of the most devastating decisions she ever made. He never knew of course, it was as usual told to be a false alarm. I'm not going to let you do the same Lauren."

Lauren stared out of the window, her mind running in fast rivers of thought, rationalising, shaping and pitching the proposition, as if it were a difficult mathematical problem, the only way she could cope. She breathed in hard, returned to Annabella and gently held her hand.

"Thank you Annabella."

There was a moment's silence. No words needed to be spoken further, each understood the other.

Lauren continued. "My goodness, I almost forgot. I've actually asked Charlotte and DG to come to dinner this evening. What on earth can I cook? My social skills have taken a nosedive since becoming pregnant."

"And your cooking too, Lauren. There is hardly anything in your cupboards and fridge. You must get into a routine and eat properly and sensibly. So, I shall go out and buy some ingredients for one of my specialities and make it for you. You know who were the two best chefs in Palermo? Me and Sonja. And I taught her a recipe which is very traditional Sicilian; swordfish linguine with capers, mint, tomatoes and herbs. Very good for you … Will Charlotte like that do you think?"

"Sounds wonderful. Yes, I'm sure she will. She loves fish and DG will eat anything as long as there is plenty of it!"

"I passed a good fish shop near the tram stop."

"And there's a supermarket over the road, Annabella. I really appreciate it. Cooking has never been my strong point, sadly, but I've decided to improve once the triplets arrive."

"Good, that's more like it, you and Mila both. There are too many alpha-females around me!"

Lauren grinned. "I do recall those wonderful sardines in fresh tomato and mushroom sauce you amazingly rustled up on your island, after you had me tied up."

Annabella blushed, heading for the door. "Mmm … I'll hurry now to the shops and get everything. You prepare the table. I think a few weeks of being looked after will jolt you back to your old self. Deal?"

"Yes, deal. I'll go and look for my best tablecloth."

<><>

Hitting his head on Lauren's door frame, and apologising between expletives, DG was soon back to form, waxing lyrical, in his deep Texan drawl, about the Lena River holiday exploits to Lauren and Charlotte over a glass of white wine, and how they saw no bears or wolves but caught lots of fish. So he was well up for Annabella's cooking. Mention of Olga was decidedly absent, and knowing DG who was not renowned for his discretion, Lauren felt a twinge of relief. She was going to put that factor out of her head. DG, however, was renowned for his astute political skills, and following a verbal barrage from Charlotte before they departed, he was keeping his thoughts to himself.

"Lauren, it sure is great to see you again and you look … heck … so radiant, am I pleased to hear about those darn triplets. Guess my old friend Philippe must also know by now and …" A look from Charlotte forced a deviation to his flow of words. "… and must be making tracks like a cat on hot bricks back here, I guess?"

At that moment Annabella brought in a huge bowl of steaming pasta, mixed together with carefully prepared pieces of swordfish and herbs, the capers clearly visible in the tomato sauce. Charlotte, chattering away to Annabella, went to fetch the bread rolls and other bits and pieces.

"Doggone it Annabella, that sure smells delicious, you are some cook, I do believe."

"I have made a second tureen DG. I remember, Luigi said you demonstrated a big appetite down the nightclub you all went to afterwards …"

DG grimaced. "Don't mention that to Charlotte," he whispered. "She's darn forgot now I hope, got real riled next morning … I was a bit late because of Mila and Sonja … those girls sure can party."

Annabella and Lauren laughed, indicating that his secrets were safe with them. He turned again to Annabella.

"If you ever need a job over in Texas, I could sure fix you up as a head chef, no problem. Heck, just thought, last time we met was at Lauren's wedding. Only seems like yesterday." He turned to Lauren and patted her hand. "And now, between you and Charlotte we have four new additions to the family coming already, isn't that just something?"

Lauren giggled. He had no idea what Annabella was actually financially worth and she would of course keep that special secret to herself, as always. "Bring that wine to the table DG. No formalities here." She put on some quiet music in the background, Mozart concertos for piano and violin. She was just about to sit down when there was a knock on the door. "Take a seat everyone. It's only Eva; she's just dropping off some papers for me to sign urgently."

She closed the dining room door and stepped through the hall. "Coming Eva," she shouted and opened the front door.

Immediately, out of the side, a hand shot forward and grabbed her by the neck as another short and burly masked individual seized her arms and hissed in a strong Eastern European accent, close-up into her face, his breath stinking of tobacco. "Don't make one sound bitch. You will tell me now, and I will say this once. Luchenserkov. We know he's here. He live here. Which room is he? Tell me."

The first assailant pulled out a long and oddly curved blade. "Hurry, or I cut your belly now, tell me quickly, no scream and I relent — you don't want belly cut do you in condition? Speak."

She looked, terrified, into the dirty balaclava in front of her face at a pair of intense dark and cold eyes, a killer. She recognised that look immediately, it could have been Vaag reincarnated, except Vaag was much taller. Shit, what on earth was this all about and how did they get in? Why the hell wasn't Philippe with her?

The second man released his grip from around her mouth as she coughed. "Luchenserkov is somewhere in Russia, I live here with my husband. I don't know him. You're mistaken."

"Luchenserkov is your husband. We waste no more time, I cut belly first then we search."

"No …" She struggled hard and caught the door with a bang but they were strong as the first assailant with the knife tugged open her thin cardigan. Suddenly, he screamed out loud when a giant carton of steaming hot green curry completely covered his head and eyes from nowhere. Simultaneously, a fist shot from behind and caught him hard in the kidneys. He dropped like a stone. Before his companion could even release his grip from behind her, she heard a sharp crack to his skull and he also fell slowly to the ground. She stepped aside, her heart pounding, petrified that she would start contracting with the shock.

DG, alerted instinctively with his Special Forces background to the odd noises, had crept into the hall and taken out the man behind with one swift blow. Charlotte and Annabella, aprons still on, were stood behind him, mouths open and silent.

DG stepped forward to the figure outside advancing in. "Holy Moses, that there curry's strong. Hey Seb, great to meet you again, nice work, waste of good food though on these punks." They shook hands and Seb began pulling off the masks of the comatose assailants, unconscious on the ground.

Lauren looked outside to see Eva, standing there, speechless, rigid and white as a sheet, the folder of papers scattered over the corridor, and ran out to put her arms around her, amazed again at how detuned from reaction to something like this she had become. "Go on inside Eva. No problem now, everything is under control."

Eva came to and sheepishly picked up the papers. "I'm sorry Lauren, I was so startled. I know this is Seb's job but I've never seen him … well … in action as it were."

Lauren laughed. "And DG too … so at least you can feel safe with the man in your life now can't you," she replied, eyeing Eva's shiny ruby engagement ring, glistening iridescent on her finger.

"Yes, definitely. But who are these people Lauren?" Eva said walking in to greet Annabella and Charlotte with a hug each.

They all looked at Seb who was smiling, the identities of the men obviously known. DG cut in, picked up one in each arm with his enormous strength and dumped them inside the hallway and closed the door. "You know these clowns, Seb?"

"Yep, brothers, a couple of small time Latvian villains, drugs and petty thieving mostly and hired for occasional beatings. But they're not the brightest of the Brussels underworld and certainly no professional killers. They were asking for Luchenserkov, Lauren. Any ideas?"

Lauren shook her head, perplexed, as Eva and Charlotte came in with cloths and a bucket and wiped up the remains of the Madras curry off the dark wooden floor, putting the balaclavas into a plastic bag. Annabella had placed the tureen back on the stove to keep warm.

DG cut in again. "Luchenserkov? Say, that was Ivan, Philippe's best man Lauren wasn't it? Mmm … he never stayed long that day."

Eva glanced at Lauren and they both smiled. Whenever there was a weird mystery, Luchenserkov could be fleetingly associated … but supposedly being her husband? What on earth was going on? … Lauren's mind veered immediately to

Philippe. Surely to goodness, not all over again? What was he actually up to in Russia?

Seb was now on the phone. "Olaf, where are you? Great, can you get round to my place in the next ten minutes with Josef and Vlad? You'll never believe, we've got Hinni and Henni here and they've been rather naughty boys, but I want to know who sent them and why?"

He fished inside the groaning Henni's inside pocket and pulled out a wad of notes. "Five hundred now and then I'll top it up later when you report back. There's a red pickup of theirs round the side. Can you take it and them away and sort it for me. Keep them off the streets for a while will you. Cheers."

"Hinni and Henni?" Lauren mouthed back to Charlotte and Eva. They all giggled, feeling safe and assured with their macho guys now in control of things.

DG gave out his huge belly laugh. "Attaboy Seb, I like your style. Don't you like his style Eva?"

Eva grinned back with a forced smile, not knowing what to say, but she very much loved all of Seb's style.

Annabella came back in. "Just checked the food again. I have made plenty for six. You two are going to be hungry now your meal is down a drain. Lauren … is that okay with you?"

"Definitely, take your coats off. Seb, thank you so much, gosh that was timely you were around then."

"Actually Lauren, these two are relatively underworld softies. They were trying to scare you and obviously have been paid to do it," he replied, waving the rest of the notes. "But they wouldn't have harmed you in the end; they haven't got it in them despite the appearances. I can see what you're thinking. All part of my job … to know both sides of the coin and keep you and the team safe."

"I've heard Mila say that too, Seb."

He grinned knowingly. "Absolutely, Lauren. Say DG, can you help me get these two out the back by the bins? All seems quiet everywhere. Olaf will be outside now and pick them up. It's quite a dark street down that side, the lights aren't working. I noticed a breach in the security fence there as we walked in which first alerted me, but why the CCTV didn't pick them up or the alarm in the concierge go, I don't know. I'm not very happy with the security firm here ... I'll be moving, at the residents AGM next month, for a change Lauren, and in the meantime will be taking some of my own extra precautions, so you won't need to worry anymore."

"I'll back you up Seb ... and thanks once again." Lauren replied, totally grateful.

DG picked each one up again, ducked under the doorframe and he and Seb began dragging them along; they disappeared quickly through the back entrance. The miscreants meanwhile remained well out of it all, both semi-coherent. For Hinni and Henni it was sadly a touch of bad luck meeting up, on their first blackmailing assignment, with two ex-Special Forces operatives.

Everyone soon began to relax over dinner, and Eva, still jittery for the first half-hour, eventually calmed down after a few glasses of Lauren's excellent Pinot, and a special cuddle of course from Seb who assured her not to worry.

Annabella had everyone laughing over Luigi's not very expert attempts at his first nappy changing, and how her sister Angelina had shamed him into taking baby classes for men, a first in Palermo. She would be in Brussels for the following two weeks, and to nods of approval all round, confirmed she intended organising Lauren into a CEO mother-to-be routine. She described how husband Luigi had taken back the former Palermo hotel, where Lauren first met her, Mila and Sonja, from his younger brother who wasn't doing very well with it.

Now back with the old business, Luigi was happy again, especially when Annabella appointed two nannies for both her and Angelina, to look after their combined troupe of four young babies full-time. Everyone laughed at Annabella's unexpected dry humour and once again her English began to confidently improve as the evening progressed. Annabella discretely made no mention of Lauren's ex-husband, except to say that employing the nannies had enabled Angelina and her partner to pursue the development of their new design and fine art studio together.

DG, having consumed almost one tureen of the wonderful pasta sword-fish to himself, sat back contentedly, his huge bulk, resting relaxed in the chair. He pulled out a packet of three big cigars from his pocket.

"Say Seb, you fancy a smoke of one of these? They make your eyes water that's for sure."

Seb laughed. "I'll give it a miss DG; I gave up smoking many years ago, sorry."

Charlotte flashed across a sharp look. "DG, you are not back home in Dallas. Europeans don't smoke giant Havana's after dinner."

"Say Lauren I'm sorry, would have gone out in the yard anyway, but Charlotte's right. I'm gonna give up these darn things, too expensive anyway."

Everyone laughed again ... DG never usually had a spending problem, being an oil billionaire. He continued looking at Annabella. "You Europeans seem to have lots of fun bringing up your babies ... I'm beginning to like it over here. Heck Charlotte, I reckon the twins would love it too, don't you think?"

"Could be darling, could be," she replied with a smirk, as Lauren looked carefully from one to the other.

They were immediately distracted with Annabella returning from the kitchen with a strange looking dessert she had also made.

"My goodness, what is that? It looks absolutely delicious," Eva remarked, her mouth watering.

"A Sicilian speciality and is one of my favourites. Arabic in origin, the dish is called a cassata and is made with fresh ricotta cheese, sponge cake, marzipan and candied fruit. I couldn't get ricotta but did spot some Spanish requesan on the cheese counter, which is a good substitute, a whey cheese. I haven't used it before so I hope all is okay. Slice DG?"

"You betcha Annabella, your cooking is just simply awesome. Plenty of room left for one of those."

Everyone tucked in, marvelling at the exquisite and individual taste. Lauren was extra-pleased Annabella would be around for a few weeks. And she had become quite intrigued at Annabella's whispered mention of a recent call from Irena concerning a senior job with Aid Evocative as they uncorked the wine. But, most of all she felt supremely reassured. She knew Annabella loved Luigi, and being around her sister, Angelina, and especially their children, but she could see Annabella also needed other challenges in her life. And she had the financial means, family agreement and organisational skills to have it all, and was now determined to do so. Lauren pondered about Philippe. She loved him still, and wanted him around her, but she desperately also wanted her babies and she too needed the challenge of her company, her career and the research. Like Annabella, she had sufficient means and the management and organisational capability ... she would do the same. She was now crystal clear in her mind. Yes, she wanted Philippe alongside and supporting her, but it would be up to him to decide if he wants the same … and she would wait for now … but was unsure whether that meant forever.

The familiar Skype ring suddenly sounded up on her laptop as they were relaxing with coffees and teas.

"Lauren, I bet that's Lexi and Kat, they'll be home for lunch. Answer it quickly," Charlotte said beaming as Lauren ran to the screen and tapped her mouse.

The video link flickered into life. "Hi Grandma," Kat shouted all excited, with Lexi standing next to her, jumping up and down. "Look what I've drawn for you, using a new digital painting app on my iPad."

She held up a screen image towards the webcam and Lauren gazed at a remarkably life-like picture of her, in a fashion dress obviously taken from a photo and manipulated, sitting in a holding position with three babies, two dressed in blue outfits and one in pink, in her arms. It was amazingly good for a nine-year old with a vividly imaginative creative mind.

"My goodness Kat, that is really fantastic. How did you do that?"

"Lyell left some books on Photoshop before he left, so I've been learning on my laptop, then working the painting on my iPad. I'll email you the image, but it's quite large so I hope you get it okay."

Lauren could only wonder. They knew too, and seemed very happy with the idea even though they had once commented over the phone that any woman over forty was far too old to have babies, so Charlotte must have enlightened them somewhat.

"Why did you choose two boys and a girl?"

Lexi came on, her expression serious with that determination and scientific exactitude, which Lauren recognised in herself and Charlotte, a characteristic well inherited by Lexi. "Actually Grandma, we would really like three boys, which could be fun as we're so much older and bigger to boss them around, but in the end we decided that another girl would make a sensible gender balance."

"I'm afraid I can't make them to order Lexi. They may all come out the same, like three girls and be identical, the same as you two."

Charlotte giggled in the background. Her daughters were too much. Kat poked Lexi and shouted. "We're not identical Grandma, all Lexi does is look down microscopes at tadpoles … ughh … but I draw, Lexi's drawings are horrible."

"They're not horrible," Lexi replied in a shot.

"Okay you two, that's enough," Charlotte shouted from the table.

"Sorry Grandma," Kat replied. "Actually our guinea pig had three tiny babies last week and they're all different colours, she was very fat though. We can cuddle them now. Will you get very fat Grandma?"

Lauren laughed, then thought of three different babies from two different fathers and grimaced inside. "I might Kat but maybe not too fat."

"That's good. Can Lexi speak to Mom please? We'll have to go back to school in a minute. She's had an accident." Kat said with a gloating smile across her mouth.

Charlotte came immediately to the screen and saw Lexi standing with a great tear out of the knee of her jeans. "I fell off Orwell's cart at playtime, I'm sorry Mom, can I wear my new Levi jeans please, and I promise I won't do it again?"

"Yes, okay, but next time if you can't learn to look after your clothes then it comes straight out of your pocket money. Lexi, your scrapes cost me a fortune. It has to stop. Understood?"

Lexi looked glum. "Sorry Mom."

"Now go and get changed quickly and don't be late. Both of you say goodbye to Grandma."

"Bye Grandma." The screen went blank.

Lauren felt so much better again. There was much to be said for family contentment as she looked across to Annabella who returned her gaze with a wistful and clear acknowledgement. Annabella was right.

Seb returned from the kitchen holding his mobile phone. "Just had a call back from Olaf … didn't take long to prise the truth out of them. It appears that Hinni and Henni were contacted by someone from Amsterdam to do a job. They met her in a hotel there and …"

"Sorry Seb … did you say *her*?" Lauren said quietly.

"Yes, a blonde Russian woman. They were given an advance and a script, which you heard at the door, plus this address and instructions to find a certain Luchenserkov here, kick shit out of him and frighten you. They don't know who you are and are too dense to ask questions. They became very scared of hanging around when they realised from Olaf and friends how much they were out of their depth, and have departed Brussels, minus the pickup, both heading for London and family, and won't be back."

"A Russian blond, you say Seb?" DG asked. "Mmm … but why I wonder? And insisting Ivan Luchenserkov is Lauren's husband? Makes no damned sense, darn it."

Charlotte spoke up. "What does make sense is that someone wants Lauren indirectly frightened and scared, that there is some Russian connection and they know …"

"That I'm pregnant … they made a point of saying they would cut my belly open in my condition. My pregnancy is not officially global news yet, only a small number of people genuinely know and all of them are connected to Cassini, so it points to maybe someone having a grudge, maybe working in or connected to the company and they must know something about our Russian connections. I agree, it makes no immediate sense, and let's face it Seb, you and I know that I continue to be subject to occasional crank calls, threats and intimidation letters, the downside of having a face in the press and being in the nuclear sector. I've got used to it, and heaven knows, what I've faced the last few years is why I'm getting ever hardened to violence. I'm not going to let this worry me."

"Goddam it no, Lauren," DG said firmly. "I agree. Anyway seems like our punks have rode off into the wilderness. My gut feeling is it's a one off."

"I agree too DG," Seb added. "But I will increase security levels now and sort that fence tomorrow, and I'll discuss with Mila, to see if she has any angle figured out."

"No Seb … I trust you. Let's leave Mila out of it for now. She has enough to worry about with her other work. I accept DG's hypothesis, we'll let it rest."

Annabella and Eva had taken the dishes into the kitchen and were stacking up the dishwasher and tidying up. Charlotte came back into the conversation. "Actually DG, it's getting late and I can see Lauren is tired and so am I … in fact I'm shattered … jet lag probably."

"Never affects me," DG replied, "but I can see moms-to-be need their beauty sleep. Let's hit the trail back to the hotel."

Eva came out of the kitchen, hugged Lauren and they all departed quickly, leaving Lauren and Annabella to prepare for bed.

<><>

No more had been said or asked about Philippe, but Lauren felt certain that DG knew or suspected he may likely be staying on in Russia, and so did Charlotte. Discussion would be left for another day. It wasn't DG's fault, and she didn't want him to feel bad about asking Philippe to take on the chairmanship of Rubidium. In fact she was pleased that at least Philippe will be working alongside DG, rather than on some unknown project she had no connection with whatsoever.

As they drank a hot chocolate nightcap each, Annabella turned to Lauren and said quietly. "I understand exactly why you don't want Mila involved ... That is wise, let the Russian sleeping dogs lie for now. All should be fine in due course, believe me."

Lauren smiled, but she now had more to ponder than she realised earlier.

Chapter Nine

Jamming hard on the brakes, her BMW shuddered to an immediate halt with the merest slither of a computer controlled skid on the wet tarmac. She had spotted the last space in the municipal car park and swung in immediately, when a small stocky canine with a large burly head ran directly across her path, its elderly female owner in laboured pursuit, shouting and gesticulating.

Her heart was pounding. She exhaled a deep breath, not a good moment for her routine examination and blood pressure test with Edward Jones. A continued yelping around the front offside wheel arch made her stomach lurch again. Shit, she had hit the damned dog and it was injured. The owner, a tall woman in her mid seventies with smart, bobbed silver hair and dressed in a light-brown tweed suit, bent over and began dragging at the animal, which continued to yelp and bark. Lauren opened the door carefully and got out. Despite having the seat far back, sitting behind the wheel was becoming a noticeable girth discomfort.

She walked around the front of the car. The long lead had somehow caught on a brick and the end had then flown itself under the wheel arch and jammed under the tyre, pinning the dog from any further bounding off.

"My dear, I'm so sorry. Unfortunately, he slipped from my grasp when I dropped my purse and he's ever so lively still. He's only two months old, a pit bull terrier cross. I like dogs with character, don't you? Thank you for stopping in time. Quark, will you behave please."

Lauren watched perplexed for a moment. The woman yanked the lead free with a hefty tug, and pit-bull puppy, completely unharmed, was now firmly in her hand again.

She gazed hard at Lauren, with a keen and analytical concentrated stare. "I recognise you, my dear. You're Professor Lauren Hind aren't you, you run Cassini. I saw your picture in Forbes last week and very nice it was but I see they have photoshopped your profile. My goodness, how many months? Congratulations."

Lauren, relieved, held out her hand. "Quark is a rather unusual name for a dog if I may say?"

The woman laughed, "Yes bonkers isn't it, old habits die hard. My name is Leibstein, Naomi Leibstein."

"Dr Naomi Leibstein?" Lauren replied startled. Razor sharp recall had immediately located the appropriate neurone file. She was glad the fuzzy brain period had vanished along with the morning sickness. "Expert on Israeli nuclear developments, original pioneer — you wrote a book about the nuclear ambiguity which was neither denied nor affirmed. But they passed you over for a Nobel Peace Prize as punishment. Retired off due to ill health, I was sorry to hear that."

"You have a well informed memory, Professor Hind. Yes indeed, although it was some time back now. Actually, my health has never been better. Retirement? Well, do any of us ever retire in this business, my dear? But it does suit me to blend into anonymity in my comfortable apartment overlooking the park, where I can potter with Quark, alongside the faceless Commission bureaucrats jogging here. Hanging around Washington with Reagan became rather conducive to political brain death, but I remain active in the right quarters." She laughed and winked.

Admiring her expensive attire, Lauren had already concluded that Dr Leibstein had extensive private means or a significant pension. One other thing she also recalled. This woman, apart from being a renowned nuclear engineer, had been an outstanding but outspoken and highly admired science correspondent for the Washington Post, before suddenly disappearing off the map, fifteen years ago.

"Sorry Naomi, I don't want to appear rude but I have to get to my clinic over the road, my check-up is due. Four months actually and triplets; we've managed out that part of the public relations so far but intend to release it soon."

"Triplets? Gracious, you do have a lot on your hands, although I would never have known, you look in remarkable shape."

"Thank you."

"You have a good press person my dear. Edward Jones runs the clinic doesn't he? My granddaughter is under his care at present, I take care of the bills. A very able man, you are in excellent hands."

Lauren grabbed her bag from the passenger seat, pondered and then surreptitiously passed a business card into Naomi's hand and whispered, "Ring my mobile tonight, I need some advice."

"Of course, my dear. How nice to meet you. Good luck with Edward."

She watched as Naomi disappeared around the corner, dragging hard on Quark who was mischievously intent on going anywhere else but her way, then she hurried into the clinic, five minutes behind time. Lateness was something which she always hated with a vehemence.

Edward Jones hurried out and greeted her with a warm handshake and smile. "Lauren, great to see you. How are you feeling? You look much better now the morning sickness has gone. Let's run through some quick tests and today I'd like Adèle to do an ultrasound scan."

He led her to the examination room, observing the bump with a degree of concentration and thought. "Now, what are you? ... mmm ... sixteen weeks already?"

"Edward, I know I'm beginning to show but when I had Charlotte, it was only in the last month that anyone could even have suspected, which at the time was just as well ... I was following in the footsteps of my mother and grandmother who also had small bumps. But given there are three babies in there, logically shouldn't I be bigger? Is everything alright? I felt a kick yesterday for the first time."

"We'll run some more tests but I'm sure all is fine. Bump size is dependent on a number of factors. You're tall and have excellent posture, and very fit with all the gym and exercise you've rigorously pursued so you will have very strong tummy muscles. Given the gap between now and Charlotte, it's almost like a first pregnancy. I suspect you also have less amniotic fluid, which we can see on the ultrasound. All these factors may make you look like a pregnancy with one baby, I suspect they are combining. Unusual, but I have seen it before in multiple births."

Lauren grinned. "That means I can work longer."

Edward looked back, frowning. "Mmm ... we shall see, Lauren. Normally, I would expect, with triplets, potential bed-rest and no work whatsoever between twenty and thirty weeks, no travel and take it completely easy."

She grimaced.

He started with some routine tests and checked her blood pressure, the results coming back immediately. "All excellent, your overall health remains very good."

"I won't do bed rest ever, I absolutely hate lying in bed unless I really have to, even if I'm ill." Lauren replied vehemently. "But at the moment I feel fine, a little tired at night and I have delegated more work to my Executive team and going in to the office later and coming home earlier. I've reduced my travel, but want to keep options open to the very end please Mr Jones! Also I want no C-Sections; I am going to have a natural vaginal birth come what may."

Edward Jones remained non-committal. "Now I can see the determined, stubborn and won't be dictated to CEO and leader coming out, who has also been doing her research homework?"

"And, did you get that succinct description from Helena by any chance, Edward?" Lauren replied, laughing, sharp as a bullet. "She has a big smile on her face these days and her work output has doubled, so I approve of the description."

Edward blushed ... guilty as charged but wouldn't say. Then suddenly his face drew across a large grin as he blurted out quietly. "Actually Lauren, I haven't thanked you for introducing me to Helena. She is the most amazing woman I've ever met, and she plays with me now once a week at the club. I know you haven't been back since but the regular audience has doubled. Wow, can she blow a saxophone, and since she moved in she has reorganised my whole life and her cooking is so ..." Suddenly he realised he was talking to Helena's boss and Helena's boss was a patient. "Oops, sorry I shouldn't have said all that, I will get killed if she finds out ..."

"Moved in? So for a serial George Clooney bachelor, things *are* getting serious and probably about time in your case.

Excellent — don't worry your secret is safe with me, and I'm very pleased for both of you."

"Here's Adèle, the machine is ready. Let's get you hooked in. Normally, it would be too early yet to tell the sex of the babies though."

"That's fine Edward, as we agreed I'm happy to let nature simply take its course."

<><>

Despite being an experienced scientist and having seen no end of new and innovative discoveries, a profound sense of wonder enveloped her as Adèle carefully moved the sensor around her moistened belly, and they peered up at the screen. There they were, visible for the first time. She could see her babies, all three of them.

"Oh my goodness, just look at them, all cuddly and wrapped around each other, their little arms and legs everywhere. I never had an ultrascan previously, my mother strongly objected. She had strange views on some things and I was petrified at sixteen so I agreed. Aren't they beautiful? But how on earth, in those positions, do they line up to then come out in order?"

"That's why, Lauren, multiple births are not quite so straight forward, and why I want to keep all the options open, including a caesarean. I don't want you to continue beyond thirty-five weeks. But the way they're positioned, and their size, is encouraging for a potential natural birth. Agreed?"

"Yes, all options open of course, as a last resort."

"So far they look in good shape in there. Obviously, because there are three they will be tinier at birth than normal and weigh less than an average single baby, probably between three and four pounds. So by thirty five weeks, you will want all the strongest stomach muscles you can muster to keep holding them up. They are quite compact all curled together, fluid level is certainly not excessive."

"I can't tell their sex Edward, but with your experience are you going to hazard a guess?"

"Do you want me to?"

"Yes I do, now I've thought about it since looking at them, then I can have fun with permutations and combinations of names."

"Well, not absolutely definitive yet, but I'm fairly sure one of those is a girl. Did you say Charlotte has identical twins, your grandchildren?"

"Yes, identical female twins run through the family. My grandmother was also an identical twin … So give me the probabilities Edward, I'm a mathematician I can hack it," she said laughing.

"I'll leave the maths to you, Lauren. Most common is two plus one, but depends if they are fraternal or identical and how those eggs have been fertilised. Also common is two identical and one fraternal but they could all be fraternal too. If I was a betting man, given the run of identical twins, there may be a good chance they will be identical … three girls Lauren or if I'm wrong three boys!"

"Mmm … Philippe would like three boys I suspect, easier on the wallet when they all get married and less hassle when they're teenagers, especially if they like clothes as much as me."

"Has he not said yet?" Edward ventured quietly, his voice displaying surprise, and then he remembered the discussion about the father issue.

"No, Edward. Philippe is keeping things to himself and is very preoccupied with his new business venture in Russia." Lauren replied slowly and carefully.

"Mmm ... well, whilst Adèle goes down to the labs to get the results of the other tests, I'll just go into my office and type your notes up quickly." He moved the sensor for an optimum shot of the triplets and saved the image. "A copy of this should be printed off shortly for you as well. You can carry on lying there for a moment."

Thinking of Philippe, either happy father or badly done by ex-partner, made her uneasy. She had been doing her best to keep such thoughts out of her mind, through continuing her orderly focus on work and routines to take care of herself. These were definitely paying off, thanks to Annabella's lists and plans, steering her back to her normal organised self. Lying there on her own, her mind began to assemble all the things that had happened in the last two months.

The first two weeks with Annabella were truly wonderful. The experience of individualised caring, with which Annabella excelled, had provided the space, time and wherewithal to think and get her act together, a welcome jolt from the gnawing and growing paralysis with Philippe and his continued absentee attitude. She had been growing seriously depressed over him, but in the last four weeks an atmosphere of realpolitik had finally consumed each of them. The weaving and dancing embarrassingly around each other had metamorphosed into a steady and contented working arrangement of continuous email exchanges, and of work banter, interspersed with the occasional phone image, of the sort they did before they got married and he was off on his long treks. That was when she knew she was in love with him but wouldn't admit it. Now she could admit she was still in love with him but nobody would know it. Or, more to the point, nobody could understand it, although Annabella smiled and said no more ... she understood. It actually suited her now for him to be on a long sabbatical away. Philippe had faded out of view inside and outside of Cassini, because it had got around that he was now Chairman of Rubidium and was setting up a new business operation to develop the exploration of shale oil and gas deposits in Russia, otherwise known as fracking. Based just south of Moscow, he had a small office set up and had found a suitably austere three bedroomed apartment to live in with Igor and Pyotr, the three of them maniacally working their business networks for openings and political support. All wives, partners and children were subsumed into the dark recesses of outer space. Perhaps it's something about Russian men ... but at least they had a regular cleaner who also did washing and ironing for extra roubles per week. It appears Igor was a bit of a foodie and had trained as a chef in the Russian army as a young man, so he took care of the cooking ... photos of the smiling trio eating cabbage soup, borscht washed down with vodka, beef stroganoff and chicken Kiev, were emailed at regular intervals.

Stepdaughter Svet continued to be hard work, remaining aloof. She didn't want to talk about babies or her father who she had equally shut out of her life, and was pursuing her bio-engineering studies with a maniacal focus, determined to become senior science wrangler of her year, whilst continuing working alongside Sergei. Svet was becoming increasingly ambitious with amazing future plans. Lauren was impressed with her determination and pleased, because in the end, Svet was shaping up to follow in her own footsteps. Perhaps in due course they could get close again. Svet had to find her feet her own way after the trauma of the Murmansk kidnapping. Most importantly, Sergei remained loyal, protective, comforting and supportive towards her potential success.

DG had played a number of clever political lines. He was financially backing Philippe and letting him get on with the

Russian venture, but was well aware from Charlotte of the minefield of family issues about and remained silent, passing no opinions one way or the other or between. He had his own pressing issues within Washington and continued to spend much time in the US, and he was having particular difficulty getting his divorce from Lorraine finalised. She had cannily instructed a specialist lawyer to challenge the pre-nuptial arrangements, securing time to negotiate a better settlement. DG was veering that way; he had enough cash to be flexible. Over the previous twelve months his canny technology investments in US oil and gas stock had almost doubled ... and his net worth was now over four billion dollars, an incredible sum, so fifty million here or there was not going to cripple him if that's what Lorraine was demanding. But it was his relationship with Charlotte that pleased her especially. Because over a Skype call a couple of evenings ago, after a cheery discussion with Lexi and Kat about their birthdays soon on the 8th February and what they would like, and they both wanted new trendy watches, with bright colours and big dials, Charlotte finished up by saying that she was keen to move to Europe with the twins and be nearer to Lauren because they all missed her very much. Charlotte's engineering business in Texas was being well managed. With a new female CEO in post, Charlotte had decided, with DGs encouragement, to take a long and relaxing pre and post maternity leave this time. DG was also keen to spend some of his enormous cash on winding out of US politics, and having much more family time with Charlotte. He was not standing for re-election as Senator. He wanted to do something more philanthropic and had been discussing water purification and medical ideas with Sergei, whilst allowing his energy investments to continue to grow by encouraging and mentoring others doing the work, principally presently Philippe.

She suddenly looked up, startled out of her reverie, seeing the smiling faces of Edward and Adèle.

"The rest of the test results are fine Lauren, I'm pleased to see the blood pressure is down, so you must be taking your foot off some of the accelerator. Good … but no travel soon please … promise?"

She slid off the bed and shook his hand. "Of course. Thank you Edward for all your good work, hugely reassuring."

He handed her a large brown envelope. "Memento from today. I thought you would like a copy. Adèle will sort out your next appointment with Eva. See you soon."

She tripped out feeling quite elated from the clinic and walked steadily to her BMW. The weather had changed for the worse, skies darkening and a slight windy drizzle commenced as she searched frantically for her mini-umbrella, and realised she had stupidly left it in the SUV. But the SUV was only a few minutes away so she ploughed on, pulling her coat heavily around her.

She didn't intend to mention to Edward that she actually had two trips planned in the next ten days, and she was going come what may. First, she would visit Amélie, a long standing invitation with her best friend which she was hugely looking forward to, catching up and gossiping on the world, babies and energy. And she was hugely intrigued with Amélie's sudden Lady of the Manor role and how she was fitting into her new life. The second trip was vital business to Tel Aviv. Juliette and Sonja, with Mila's help, had finally secured a robust deal for Cassini, JETR and an Israeli Nuclear Research Centre to all begin cooperative fusion research. Not only was she needed to sign up the joint accord, but she had finally decided to work on the research side directly, with Juliette and Bhavika. This would necessitate some changes in both the structure of the company and key responsibilities ... and now was the time, after more practical reflection, to take that important decision ...

<><>

Putting the key firmly in her front door lock, she spotted one of Seb's security personnel discretely observing her and her apartment outside the security concierge. Seb was now Chairman of the Resident's Association, and the apartment owners were all hugely relieved and pleased when he proposed and recommended a change of security company. Many had already complained to the building owner about the laxness and unprofessionalism of the original crew, and been ignored ... but Seb wasn't the ignoring sort of guy and a new operation was already in place, as well as agreed expenditure on a range of up to date deterrent and surveillance equipment, including micro CCTV. New triple glazing and a refurbishment of the driveway to provide more parking was next ... Seb, with the unanimous support of everyone, was determined to raise the high standard of the apartments even further, and hence increase market values and saleability in a tricky housing slump, with Brussels facing a potential financial crisis. There had been no repeat of the Hinni and Henni episode exactly as Seb promised, but the mystery of the initiating Russian woman remained. And Lauren continued to keep Mila in the dark.

Once inside, she settled down to the evening with a light chicken casserole and rice, from a Russian recipe. She was making the effort to find the time to cook properly again. Finishing off a small glass of ginger beer, she pulled out the management paper she had finalised during the afternoon. She was going to split Cassini into two semi-autonomous divisions and retain overall control as Chairman of the new Cassini

Group. Cassini Operations would remain based in Head Office in Brussels and continue the successful sales, marketing and engineering services for their range of advanced nuclear reactors as well as overall financial and personnel management. Most of the research and demonstration had been relocated to the purpose built Cyclops Centre near Cannes. This and the Indira Research Centre at the University of Pune in India, plus her forward planning for the new Confucius Fusion Academy being built in Beijing in the grounds of the University of Peking, would all be rebranded Cassini Research. Juliette would lead the research and become overall CEO of the division. For the first time Lauren would take a new role, as an adviser for innovation and new projects. Now, she was in a position to follow her heart and her intellect, especially with her triplets on the way. Cavorting around the world, hard-selling her advanced Xenostra reactors to Heads of State and running the company day to day would be out. In, would be leading a serious forefront research endeavour and ideas generation to speed up a commercial fusion process … her true crock of gold at the end of the nuclear rainbow.

The paper was almost completed. She had to decide on who would take over the day to day running of the company. She felt sadness run through her body, remembering that in the early days she would be discussing such a major decision immediately with Philippe, always valuing his never held back wise and worldly input. Now, of course, his present distaste for everything nuclear as well as everything baby overshadowed her bothering to even try over the email. He wouldn't talk anyway. This was going to be her business decision alone … because Cassini was now her company.

She tipped the remaining ginger beer into her glass, sat back and then impromptu, grabbed her phone and dialled. A voice immediately answered with a quiet hello, but Lauren recognised the intonation immediately.

"Good evening Dr Leibstein, Lauren Hind here. Are you doing anything this evening?"

"Ah … Professor Hind. What a nice but not unexpected surprise. What did you have in mind?"

"Coffee and a chat in my apartment, I live about three kilometres from you. I can send a car."

"That would be lovely my dear. Will your driver be able to cope with Quark? I can't leave him but he does settle down at night. Would that be acceptable?"

Lauren smiled to herself … she expected that … although not a dog lover she would manage, and Quark did seem friendly towards her once they had formally met under the wheel arch of her BMW.

"Fine, may I call you Naomi?"

"Of course, I much prefer it; always hated my surname but my six grandchildren love it."

"You have grandchildren?"

"Yes, and five great grandchildren, all in Israel, but their parents sadly, I buried … died in a plane crash over Alexandria, terrorist plot you know, forty years ago. Parents should never bury their children Lauren. I was supposed to be on that plane but my only son and his wife swapped to do the meeting as I was unwell. A long time ago but it still feels like yesterday, however life must go on, and it did.

Lauren fell silent. Yes, no matter what, her life has to go on too and it will. "I'm so sorry Naomi. Car will be in half an hour."

"Thank you my dear, excellent, I will see you later."

Following a quick call to Giselle at the Cassini security desk, a car was immediately despatched. Lauren continued to reflect whilst she waited. She had taken another key decision that night. Philippe was right in one respect. It really was time to move … and she would head down to Nice and base herself there. The decision made logical and clear analytical sense. She would be close to Cassini Research, she loved Nice and the Cote D'Azur, and her heart was decidedly no longer in Brussels. The apartment, she would selectively let out to someone suitable because the market was plainly not good to sell. She needed to be nearer to Mila and become stabilising cement, as Mila's foundations had grown particularly wobbly in the last few months. But if she let her apartment she had to find someone she knew and trusted, she disliked the idea of just anybody coming into the place.

The bell rang and Lauren peered through her new spy hole in the thick security door Seb had put in, to see the now familiar looking and tweed-suited Naomi standing there, Quark panting hard next to her. As she opened the door, Quark bounded in with a loud yelp and headed immediately for the kitchen, sticking his great head straight into the kitchen waste bin for the leftovers of Lauren's chicken, wolfing it down and the tea bags in one gulp, tail wagging madly.

"Quark, come here you naughty boy, that's not how to behave as a guest in a new house." Naomi shouted, her face visibly alarmed at the thought of curtains being torn down and shredded, although he had never done that so far.

"Don't worry Naomi, I'm sure he'll be fine, do come in and take a seat, door on the right," Lauren replied softly, but feeling a distinct unease inside, desperately trying to hide her childhood dog fear. However, she had put down an anticipatory monster bowl of water in the kitchen and they both heard a loud slurping and murmurs of faint growling. Quark had certainly found his drink.

Naomi, looking nervously towards the kitchen, walked into the lounge. It was chilly outside and Lauren had lit her gas fire on low to provide some additional cosy background warmth, her thick velvet curtains already tightly drawn.

"What a lovely modern and spacious apartment Lauren. I do love your pre-Raphaelite prints and antique furniture, but what a super sofa ... the arctic mink covering indicates you have a penchant for chillier climes my dear?"

"A rather hazardous Russian adventure via Scandinavia last autumn. But the terrain was splendid."

"Yes, I agree, I loved Finland, lived there for some years when I was younger as a correspondent. All great fun. Ah ... the menace returns."

Lauren turned and Quark, now content, sidled up to her, tail wagging for a quick stroke, which she reluctantly did around his floppy ears, his short white coat, gleaming and shiny in the subdued light. He then gave a huge whimper and yawn, his powerful jaws and teeth displayed fully, and lay down on the rug at her feet in front of the fire and began to doze off, antics for one day, now concluded.

"He seems a powerful dog, Naomi, I know the breed. My ex-husband's English family used to keep them, Staffordshire bull terriers. Do you like this particular breed?"

Naomi smiled. "I know Lauren; a normal woman of my age would be expected to have a poodle or a corgi. Yes, they can be vicious and lethally aggressive if provoked, they are strong but they're also very family-oriented and loving if treated and trained properly. He's the third one I've had, probably the most boisterous, but he'll be fine in six months. Some have amazing track records of incredible human rescue from bad situations; they are very brave if their owners face danger. Proton died of old age, the other, Electron was shot. He took three bullets, but still pinned the assailant, who was a big man, down before arrest, but he sadly died from his injuries two days later."

"Shot?"

"I'm afraid, in my long life my dear, I've upset a few people. Nuclear politics and journalism are a toxic mix in some quarters. A few rather nasty agencies are still looking for me. But I don't want to alarm you Lauren. Now what would you like to talk about? "

"Coffee?"

"Yes please, black, no sugar."

"You'll have to excuse me, I tend to drink ginger beer now; sadly coffee disagrees. I hope it's temporary, being a former caffeine addict. I'll just get some drinks from the kitchen. I'm used to security issues too Naomi, and also done my fair share of nuclear upsetting. This place is very secure so don't worry."

"Yes, thank you, I noted the safety measures the moment I got to the gate."

Lauren returned with the drinks and biscuits and they resumed. Naomi had the appearance and the background of a woman who didn't waste too much time on social chit-chat, but preferred to get to the heart of the issue quickly … a characteristic Lauren shared fully. She always felt naturally comfortable with other female scientists.

"Essentially Naomi, I need an objective and independent adviser on certain matters working behind the scenes. Someone who is outside of my company structures, totally discrete and reports solely to me on an ongoing and informal basis, and doesn't mince her words. For that she will be paid well."

"And why do you think I might fit your needs my dear?"

"Because the subject matter is commercial nuclear fusion at the very forefront of development, the politics are potentially volatile and dangerous, and the location is Israel. And I'm heading for Tel Aviv next week."

"Well now that is a fascinating combination of challenges." She patted Lauren gently on the hand over the coffee table. "I think we may have a deal. I'm more flexible and mobile than you probably think. Fortunately, my widowed sister Ruth lives a couple of blocks away from me and she and Quark get on fine, so he can be looked after when necessary. In fact he and Toby are already bosom pals."

"Toby?"

"Her cat. Now, would you like your elderly aunt to accompany you? Perhaps you may be able to book an additional ticket." She fumbled in her handbag and pulled out a French passport, handing it to Lauren who peered inside … and her eyes expanded into saucers as she looked at the photograph of a dark-haired woman aged seventy-nine with the name of Leticia Hind clearly printed in alongside a Paris address. "Your father, my brother was a nice man, great tragedy he died from that accident so young. I do my homework, my dear."

"But the passport looks so genuine."

"To the controllers and their technology, it is. In my business Lauren, one needs fluid aliases and to know of course the right people to get certain jobs done. Not a problem."

Lauren stared at Naomi's face; the silver hair was so different.

"What you've been looking at today, is a wig. The real me is in that picture, although I dyed my hair earlier before the photo was taken. Gone off blonde to be honest, no offence my dear you look lovely. So what do you think?"

"I'll make sure Eva, my Executive Assistant, books Aunt Letty who hasn't been to Israel for years and is really looking forward to it, in for the trip. There may be one problem. My Director of Intelligence and Security, Mila, will be there. It is due to Mila and her network of Israeli contacts at the highest levels that this coming together of opportunities exists ... she is amazingly astute and very formidable."

Naomi laughed long and loud, needing a sip of cold water to stem her tickly cough. "My goodness Lauren, I should have guessed. The amazing Mila Krstic, of course it all makes sense."

Lauren looked up, startled with the ease of revelation. Mila was always ghostly to the outside world. "You know Mila? You know her real name?"

"Yes, everyone in the Israeli political landscape of any importance, present and past, knows Mila. She has a well-deserved Mossad reputation for thoroughness and ruthlessness. I actually knew her father a hardworking diplomat in my early days. He helped me develop my nuclear network. She actually works for you? Good heavens, that's a real coup."

"Yes, actually she saved my life last autumn; she was totally awesome given the challenges faced. But the moment Mila sees you then the adviser cover may be blown."

"And I don't need to know any of that incident either. I can see you're very fond of her and rightly so my dear. Mila is a stunning beauty. But I assume one of the reasons you want some independent advice is that although you trust Mila unreservedly, she carries some risks too, and what you are doing you want to feel risk free on all counts. Am I right?"

"Yes, nothing bad, but I need to make this important decision balancing nuclear research, Israeli politics and commerciality. The mix is too tricky to leave solely to Mila's judgement."

"Yes, I agree. The Israeli politics I would think Mila will have correct, but I must say, the world in general is very fluid over there right now as is the Middle East in its entirety. Allegiances are changing constantly. But the first and last issue in your list sits nicely within our domain my dear. Now, one advantage is that I may know Mila, but she won't know me. Officially, I faded off the radar a long time ago, a ghost put out to pasture forgotten many years back, certainly since she has been in the special operations field. I can see no reason why she should be suspicious of plain old Aunt Letty doing some sightseeing whilst you have meetings. I know Tel Aviv well of course."

"Thank you Naomi. I feel fine now. I'll pay you personally, a monthly retainer. What are your rates?"

Naomi laughed again. "The money isn't important my dear. At my age what am I really going to spend it on? I actually have a good income from books and investments and even a Belgian pension … got naturalised here many years back. I take assignments for the fun and to keep me active. A thousand Euros per month plus expenses will enable me to buy a few more frocks and plenty of grub for Quark; he's a big, expensive eater."

"Is that all? Are you sure?"

"Absolutely, we can review it after six months. You may not need me then."

"Okay Naomi, agreed. Oh gosh, I hope this place isn't bugged now since Seb reorganised all the security."

"No it isn't," Naomi replied, bringing out a small device from her bag. "This would have alerted me. State of the art Israeli electronics. From a technology perspective, I think you are going to have lots of fun."

"Yes, I think so too." Lauren said quietly, now relieved, peering down at Quark, snoring softly. "Another coffee? And you can tell me more about your grandchildren and great grandchildren. I only discovered my grandchildren last year, another rather long story."

"Long stories … describes both of us my dear, the burden I fear of being nuclear scientists. Now where shall I begin …?"

Chapter Ten

The whole evening had been spent scouring Google for airlines and suitable destinations to fly to with minimal travelling. She was simply dying to see Amélie, especially after receipt of her newly installed software, Zubefy, which Edward Jones's geek bass player in his jazz band had been developing. Zubefy was a Beta test version of an interesting concept of instant messaging over the internet as an alternative to texting. Helena had emailed a special copy of the development software, which she and Amélie could each download onto their Blackberry phones after having it tested for malware and spyware in the Cassini labs. Lauren was keen to support cutting edge innovation and the idea of buying small innovative technology start-ups, as a new part of her growth strategy, had been mulling across her thoughts recently. Something else to discuss with Amélie, who had been first off the mark with a sexy, zubefying image pose in her new, chic Candice Candide maternity ruche dress, in deep maroon with an asymmetrical front, and all for less than five hundred euros.

I assume you're jealous. Good. Can't wait to meet up and exchange protrusions.

Yes, very jealous, hate what Luddite have brought in. My fashion school is doing much better. Expect to bring their first creation when I come. Except Lady Westvale is inaccessible can't find a suitable airport!!!

Ah ... understand. There is a special daily flight from Brussels to Blackpool International. Full of Eurocrats and fucking energy gas gold diggers on reconnaissance. This area is rumoured ripe and huge for UK shale gas, over my dead body. Fuck them all.

Glad to see encroaching motherhood hasn't dimmed your vocal aversion to fracking. Environmental indigestion still?

Ask Eva to contact Dr Philip Broadbent in the Commission. He'll get you on a flight.

Comparing bumps was likely to become argumentative, as she could see Amélie's tummy had expanded to a larger diameter than hers ... and she had one more on board ... interesting how differently baby development took place. Suddenly her phone rang.

"I think we've amply demonstrated a proof of concept, don't you, and my fingers are tired tapping on these tiny Blackberry keys. Although I must say I prefer this to international texting, definitely quicker," Amélie shouted down the phone, elated that Lauren was coming.

Lauren moved onto the white mink sofa, wrapping a throw over her legs to get more comfortable, and immediately thought of Vaag ... Could their deceased tormentor presently be sharing more than a joint history of lustful desire, but some permanent living legacy, a generational succession? "How is Rufus ... err ... coping?"

"You mean our new lifestyle or not knowing whether the babies are his or Vaag's? The answer is amazingly well on both counts, as am I, and Rufus is content to wait until the little blighters emerge in five months, seeing as I remain adamant now about no DNA tests. Decided to follow in your footsteps, very wise, all made sense. At least there's only two to worry about."

Lauren smiled. "You and me both Amélie ... except Philippe and I ... well we're effectively kind of separated, although we maintain a semblance of homely communication through regular email. He can only cope with that. He's just moved from sharing a run-down apartment in Moscow with two associates to a new large apartment in Novosibirsk on his own, whilst they all develop the next great business venture. That's not all. Wait for it. DG is bankrolling him, he is now Chairman of Rubidium Inc and this venture will become a company division. And the business? Fracking in Russia."

There was a long silence at the other end. Lauren could hear some liquid fortifications being poured out, hoping it wasn't anything strongly alcoholic.

Amélie finally returned to the conversation. "Fucking shit, I don't talk to you for two months and World War Three breaks out and we're all living under Chinese rule. I know I've been idly playing at Lady Muck up here in my green wellies, but I had no idea whatsoever, although I'm not surprised Lauren."

Lauren lay back in reflection as more chinking of glasses sounded and an email pinged into her laptop ... that could wait ... although she had tried to sound flippant and unmoved with Amélie, the whole thing was drearily depressing with Philippe. Thank goodness she had the inner resolve and the financial means to cope.

"I can see you frowning, Lauren. I did hear you only have a penchant now for ginger beer from the delectably discrete Annabella, who is keeping in touch too. She's done wonders for you. The glugging you're hearing is only eleven percent very best cold Sauvignon, once a week. A girl needs some vices even now; in fact sex at three times a week has got miraculously better. My bulge turns Rufus on ... sorry totally tasteless and thoughtless. Given the drinking habits of either potential father,

130

then these children are already well fortified with the right genes for a tiny indulgence."

"You mean Mila hasn't spoken to you? ... I mean about Philippe?"

"Mila has become very quiet Lauren, not a word about anything but given the circumstances, that's not surprising is it? At least a few pigeon carriers have made the flight up to here."

"What circumstances?"

"Oh-oh, we're going to have one of our best friend conversations aren't we, I suppose I should have guessed. Don't worry, I'm sipping slowly. Whatever you do, don't get over-excited or shoot the messenger because she is doing an excellent job running your administration."

"What? Helena?"

"Yes ... ever since I did my lady of the lake routine in your grounds and Helena did a superb job with getting me back to compos mentis."

"Yes, I agree, Helena is super and becoming indispensable right now."

"Excellent, because she now has a professional external mentor who gives her regular spot-on expert advice?"

"Who?" Lauren responded feeling agitated that Cassini's secrets were being shared with all and sundry.

"Me of course ... who else, Lauren. We kept in regular touch after returning from Russia, and when you promoted her, Helena wanted some reassurance and independent nuclear sector career advice. She is keen, highly able and will go far and has no intention of getting pregnant like the rest of us, despite her proclivities with saxophones and gynaecologists. Yes, I know about that too, so I offered to be her personal mentor. I didn't think you'd mind but she wanted to keep it quiet. She felt embarrassed asking you. Another factor to consider is that your team and everyone around you, including Mila, believe you have enough on your plate without being burdened by other people's issues, so you're now on a 'needs to know' basis, whilst they all simply get on with their jobs. Subtle but sensible. Gosh, I'm now becoming your indispensable mentor and adviser too."

There was a further pause as Lauren began to inwardly digest the situation, which of course, now she thought about it, did make sense. And Eva was very cleverly managing her diary and presumably was also in on the plot, because there were definitely more personal things diarised and fewer meetings. And Cassini was doing better than ever so something worked. Less meddling by triplet factor resulting in higher productivity? … Lesson for post-five months too … and she was glad Amélie, as always her bluntest best friend, took an interest in Helena … But what was it she didn't know?

"Amélie, there are times when I'm so grateful for your friendship and sense. Thanks for looking out for Helena, keep mentoring please, that's fine, I'm totally happy with all you've said."

"Thank goodness for that," Amélie replied, relieved. "I wondered whether to uncork another bottle, sorry only joking. Okay back to Mila … and Sonja."

"Yes, I know they've been going through a rough patch but I feel confident they'll work through it, they're a strong couple."

"I'm afraid that reasonable and logical supposition may no longer hold water Lauren. I'm assuming you know nothing, and why should you, but Mila and Sonja have been separated for a month, and Sonja is living quietly in Helena's parent's large house, temporarily in Ghent. Of course most of that time, according to Helena, Sonja has been in Israel wheeling and dealing with Mila and Juliette, so hasn't needed to be home."

Lauren went quiet. Why had this momentous news passed her by? "Well yes, and the Israel work has gone very well, in fact so well that I'm thinking of making some major company changes, which I want to discuss with you and see what you think, you have more experience of this than me …"

"Fine … let's leave all that until you come. Is Friday still okay? Because whilst you've been whittling on, I've sent Eva a text to book your flight for Friday before your diary gets busy again. You can be back on Monday, so we'll have the whole weekend to ourselves. Oh … Eva has as usual just replied immediately with 'onto it no problem.' Done. Next? Oh yes, back to supercharged Mila. I know, I wouldn't dare say it to her face."

"Amélie, I had no idea about them. Sonja especially, and let's face it Mila too, are the consummate professionals and would continue to do their jobs well and together, and I haven't exactly been zipping about sensing the nuances in the air so would be the last person to know. I can't believe they've broken up though. What's finally happened?"

"No nuances Lauren. It appears that Mila has also rented her new apartment out to a very rich Bulgarian female entrepreneur, setting up a music business in Cannes … and is now living with Juliette, in her new villa with her two teenage children."

Lauren struggled to sit up, amazed and saddened but also very angry with Mila, not just for her usual addiction to action, flippety-flop and 'time for a change' treatment of Sonja who deserved better, much better. But of all people, to be shacking up with Juliette? She was hugely irritated and upset, but only she knew why.

"I simply can't understand what goes on in Mila's head sometimes, and Sonja is such a wonderful person, I really don't …"

"Yes, I know you're upset Lauren and I think I know why, but don't jump to the conclusion that this issue is all one-sided. It may also be that Sonja has some problems too, or may even be the problem."

"I know that tone of yours Amélie, and you know more, probably a lot more …"

"Let's save this topic for when we meet," Amélie replied carefully. "My advice, as your best friend and as a former CEO, is as long as they are doing the jobs they're all supposed to be doing, and doing them well, then the rest is not your business. They are all big enough and old enough to get on with their lives, the way they want."

"You're absolutely right and I respect that. I'm not angry at you but Sonja is one leg of the triangle which I do need to think some more about …"

"Yes, I understand. Anyway, make sure you pack your best maternal wear when you come because I am organising a little dinner party on Saturday with some special guests."

"What guests?"

"I'm not telling … On Friday I'll arrange for Giles, our Estate Manager, to pick you up at the airport in the Range Rover. You won't miss him, early thirties, tall, dark, bearded, single and handsome and shoots in a very straight line. You sound like you could do with some diversions."

"Don't you dare start trying to fix me up, Amélie," Lauren replied sharply. "You know what happened last time. Anyway, in my state I will remain very indisposed."

"Yes, I remember number three well too. You married him and then divorced him, so what's another notch to add to the bed post, Lauren?" Amélie replied with a mischievous giggle.

Lauren laughed back. Same old Amélie, perhaps it was time for some fun and relaxation … fuck Mila.

"Okay, see you then, and make sure you have a Candice Candide catalogue to hand too, I need a refresh."

"Hey, me too … will do … see you Friday, bye."

Lauren put down the phone. What she had just heard had not only reinforced her restructuring proposal but made her rethink about her apartment. She peered down at her laptop and opened the emails. The second one was from Eva.

Hi Lauren - hope you're having a relaxing evening. Just doing a quick check of late emails at the office which came in. Your flight is booked for Friday, I managed to get hold of Amélie's contact already. He phoned me back immediately, they think it's a bit of a coup you wanting to visit a potential UK fracking area so you're booked on, paid for by the EC! Also had a strange call from a woman by the name of Oriane Leroux, I would say from the voice in her late forties or so. She said it was a personal matter and wanted to speak to you urgently. I've texted her mobile number to your personal phone so you can call her at your convenience. Is there anything you would like me to do regarding her before tomorrow? Seb and I are going to a late night film later tonight … he's a real avant-garde French film buff would you believe! See you tomorrow. Eva

Lauren had no idea who Oriane Leroux was. She replied back immediately.

Many thanks Eva now go and have dinner and enjoy the film - that's an order!

She picked up her phone and immediately dialled the number which was answered after two rings.

135

A confident female voice with a soft and very pleasant tone responded in French. "Bonsoir, c'est Oriane Leroux. Comment puis-je vous aider?"

"Bonsoir aussi, ici c'est Lauren Hind. Est-il possible de parler?"

"Ah … Professor Hind, hello. Thank you so much for calling me, yes it is convenient to talk," Ms Leroux replied, switching immediately to a clipped and posh business English, not recognising or knowing Lauren was fluent in French. "May I continue in English, you will probably feel it is appropriate when I explain my reason for calling?"

"Yes, thank you that's fine, do continue." In the background Lauren could hear plates clattering and a general hubbub of people noise, realising that Oriane Leroux was probably out having a meal or in a bar, but that was her problem. Who was she and what did she want?

"I am calling you directly on behalf of your daughter Charlotte and her fiancé DG."

Lauren immediately felt a sharp pang of alarm, something must have happened to them but what? And why was this person calling?

Ms Leroux continued. "I'm sorry, please don't feel anxious. This is good news. They want to extend to you a personal invitation to their wedding in two weeks time tomorrow at the Mairie in Nice. I am their personal wedding planner; your daughter hired me two months ago but wanted to keep it as a surprise. It has been a difficult assignment, given that they are both divorced US nationals. I believe, from Charlotte, you already know the challenges, but all is in order and arranged. It will be a small affair, just the bride and groom, your grandchildren and your husband."

Lauren was totally stunned and incredulous. She suspected the possibility would likely arise, from Charlotte's last discussions, but not this way. "My husband?"

"Yes, I understand Philippe is working away presently and very busy in Russia but I managed to contact him. He phoned me, just before you in fact, and was very enthusiastic and confirmed he would be there. You will both be witnesses if that is acceptable."

"But of course, that's fantastic. I'm so pleased for them and it has been a wonderful surprise. Thank you so much for contacting me Oriane, please call me Lauren, I hate formality."

"A pleasure Lauren. Following the ceremony, a meal in one of Nice's best restaurants has been booked for you all and I have reserved a suitable suite for you and your husband at the five stars Bassanova Hotel, all within walking distance of the Town Hall. DG insisted that no expense be spared. Your daughter and her husband will need to return to America the next day with the children; however I am sure they will all be back soon."

"Back soon?"

"Ah ... I'm sure Charlotte will tell you more in person. I also asked your administrator, Eva, to check your diary for the date, which is a Friday of course and she said there would be no problem clearing the day, and you will have the full weekend then of course."

Lauren, her mind reeling with all kinds of issues, took another deep breath. "That is marvellous, and thank you so much for doing all this Oriane. Will I see you there?"

"My assistant Gabrielle and I will be in the background, just to make sure all is fine."

"I look forward to that. I can hear I may be disturbing your meal Oriane so I'll let you go. Au revoir."

"Not a difficulty Lauren, my husband and I are indeed having dinner, but that is fine and it's been a great pleasure talking to you. Au revoir."

<>< >

Lauren got up slowly. What an evening of revelations this one was turning out to be. Her plan had been to sit in quietly with a cosy research paper and do some mathematics, fat chance. Gosh, Philippe would actually be turning up in person? What on earth is he going to say when they meet for the first time since he went off on that damned Siberian holiday? Perhaps now he's truly coming round to the notion of renewed fatherhood. She smirked. Someone in her immediate family had been meddling, either Charlotte or DG and probably both to get Philippe and her together. It would be like going on a new date again. Maybe a short separation does have distinct advantages. She would have to ask Amélie's advice on well ... you never know ... maybe the Rufus effect might take hold after such a long time separated ... She ran through in swift succession; wardrobe, hair, wedding present, something for the twins. Gosh it was all so exciting. But first she dialled the last call of the day, as exhaustion was setting in.

"Charlotte, now what on earth have you been up to?"

Charlotte giggled back down the phone. "I just wanted to surprise you. I assume Oriane has been in touch by the tone of your voice. Can you come then?"

"Try and keep me away. But why Nice?"

"I'll tell you more when we see you, and there is a lot to do still and get the twins sorted. But Oriane has been amazing and even measured up my dress over Skype. I just need a final fitting ... looks gorgeous ... we'll be in Nice a couple of days before. DG has some business there he wanted to sort out at the same time. Sorry, but I'm going to have to go, I have an important management meeting in ten minutes. Just had a text which confirms Philippe will definitely be attending, so we've got our witnesses sorted. DG and I wanted a small family affair only, no fuss and no friends. And he's paying for everything including your flight, and don't argue."

"Okay, I won't grumble. That was a bit devilish inviting Philippe, knowing how we are?"

"Like mother like daughter, anyway it's about time!"

"Yes, thank you, I do appreciate it Charlotte and I'm so excited."

"Great, speak soon, Bye."

<><>

Lauren quickly drew the curtains and went straight to the shower ... time for bed. She was too tired to reflect on everything further, but would piece all the news together in the morning, with her laser-like focus. Maybe some real normality was finally returning at last.

Chapter Eleven

The sun was just rising. A sliver of light through the blinds cast a finger of yellow over her papers. Lauren had been concentrating undisturbed for the last two hours on the staffing figures, recent financial summaries and future projected income and expenditure. She had been at her office desk since five-thirty in the morning, determined to assimilate as much data as possible to finalise her most radical decision on Cassini Power since taking the company private with her majority shareholding.

She stared at the opposite wall, carefully modelling the scenarios in her head, having the mental capacity to hold and compare a series of events running simultaneously, a skill she had honed over many years of pursuing advanced mathematical research. She was pleased the method easily transferred into business processes. She reflected for a moment that it was a generally sad state of affairs, in Europe and the US that insufficient CEOs of private companies and public sector bodies had professional scientific backgrounds ... or were female. Far too little company decision making was undertaken using people sensitive and objective, data-driven logical processing, and too much on male machismo, egos and banal greed. She thought immediately of both DG and Philippe and roared with laughter. Maybe they were the exceptions that proved the rule.

Drawing back the blind slowly, a robin was sat outside on her windowsill, chirping and singing for all he was worth, a beautiful trill of notes flooding the room. He stopped momentarily and stared straight at her, unmoved and unnerved, probably remembering the occasional bread titbits she left out for both him and the finches, before resuming again at full throttle. That was a sign, she decided. The analysis was sufficient and conclusive, and corroborated her initial gut instincts. The decision was made. Cassini Operations and Cassini Research would be born today.

"Something has really cheered you up this morning?"

She turned to see Eva's smiling face at the door, also early, with two bowls of yoghurt, muesli and berries in her hand.

"I saw the light on and brought you some breakfast from the canteen, I figured you probably wouldn't be thinking of eating."

Lauren smiled; Seb was a lucky man to have her now. "Gosh I'm starving actually, I've been here some time, but I wanted to get something really important finalised before catching that midday flight to Amélie. Come and join me, I'll just make some tea; I want to tell you first. Then, as Company Secretary, you can get a meeting together of our Executive shareholders."

"Great. Oh … before I forget, your meeting with Bella at eight is cancelled. She's gone down with a flu virus and was vehement she would not be passing it on to you or anyone else."

Lauren pondered, but she had the staffing profile anyway so the detail could wait until Bella was back.

Eva continued but suddenly looked uncharacteristically glum. "Actually, instead, I've scheduled a meeting in at eight-thirty. She was insistent she wanted to talk to you urgently. Sonja has flown back from Israel."

Lauren looked up. She wasn't expecting Sonja back until after the meeting in Tel Aviv in a week's time. Eva's face gave away enough. "You look like you know more than you feel comfortable with, Eva. Am I correct?"

Eva nodded. "Some of us had guessed all was not as it should be between Sonja and Mila. Seb of course is very close to Mila and confirmed when I pressed him that things were not so good, but being the bastion of discretion and rightly so, said no more."

"I'm aware too Eva and I'm sad to be honest, but sometimes relationships become unexpectedly complicated — that's life I suppose, but Sonja as you know is doing a fantastic job here."

Eva nodded once more, before tucking into her muesli. "What do you want to tell me? I have a useful spare slot this morning so I can do some proper papers for when you come back."

"I won't mince words especially to you Eva, so I'll lay it all out straight. I believe we have sufficiently grown and reached the point for the next evolution of Cassini. So I'm splitting the company into two independent divisions. Juliette will become CEO of Cassini Research, with me as a roving adviser for innovation. I need to think about CEO of Cassini Operations, but both will come under me as overall Chairman. This move will simultaneously streamline and clarify our product lines and improve service and development for customers."

Eva stopped eating. "Actually I like the concept very much. So you'll be like a nuclear Bill Gates, all powerful but flexible … to suit your new lifestyle?"

Lauren roared with laughter. "Spot on Eva, I always love your succinctness but yes. My heart remains in research and innovation; time the reins of day to day marketing and operations are passed onwards."

"So who do you think should lead Cassini Operations then?" Eva asked coyly, twirling her bowl around nervously on the coffee table.

"I may bring in someone from outside. On the other hand I may go by gut instinct. Can you get an Exec meeting together for Wednesday to discuss? No, sorry, leave it until we all return from Israel … so the following week instead. And Eva, as usual lips sealed, including Seb. I don't want Mila getting wind of this until the papers are circulated."

"Understood Lauren, absolutely," Eva replied firmly, eyeing a white convertible BMW approaching outside, through the window. "I can See Sonja coming. Gosh it's almost eight-thirty, I'd better get going, there are a load of press releases Johann wants you to see and approve and I'll just assemble them first in some order with comments. Most of them are about the twenty percent increase of Xenostra sales to BRIC countries but one is about you and your blooming condition. Have you got time before you go?"

"Did you say blooming or ballooning?" Lauren said gaily.

"Probably both, I'll fetch Sonja. Do you want another tea?"

"Yes please."

<><>

Sonja, dressed in an irresistible Emporio Armani dark-blue trouser suit, looked her usual gorgeous and sophisticated self, her cropped blonde hair accentuating her sharp Slavic features. Her green eyes flashed straight to Lauren's gaze as she entered and gave Lauren a welcoming smile and generous hug. Eva behind began setting out some more drinks. Sonja had been locked in Israel for the last month, a very challenging assignment requiring all her diplomatic and networking skills. But Lauren could see the tell-tale signs of dark rings around

Sonja's eyes, despite the carefully applied makeup, as well as a look of tension over and above the work pressure.

Sonja sat down and Eva returned with a plate of toast and jam. "I'm sorry Lauren. I haven't eaten since last afternoon, is it okay if I eat some breakfast? I'm ravenous."

"Actually me too Sonja, despite having just consumed a large bowl of muesli ... well I suppose I'm eating for four now! Eva can you fetch a plate of toast for me as well please," she shouted through the glass door.

"You look marvellous Lauren and I can't believe you're having triplets. You should be the size of a house."

"Good genes and a strong stomach — probably the job gave me the latter."

They both laughed and relaxed as they always did. Lauren had a very soft spot for Sonja. A shared and accepted joint love of Mila had strengthened their bond. Sonja was like the younger sister she never had, along with Annabella. But especially pleasing had been the return on investment from her gut and impulsive appointment, on a whim with no track record, of Sonja as an Executive Director to revive and streamline the company management and operative business processes. She had done a brilliant job over the last twelve months. Sonja had called the business meeting, but Lauren strongly suspected that Sonja wanted to talk about something else. She did too, but Sonja was too reserved to be blatant, unlike the person they both wanted to focus on.

Lauren began. "I'm glad you dropped in, we've got as long as we need this morning, then I'm off to see Amélie in the UK at lunch time and share bump progress."

Sonja smiled. "That will be nice for both of you actually."

"Listen Sonja, Eva has already said you've left a thick folder on her desk of recommendations and comments on your Israel negotiations. I'm really grateful you took the lead. I've had both informal feedback and of course the invite next week to Tel Aviv, which I am going to whatever Edward Jones may say. Sorry, he's my gynaecologist. Apart from a few technical sticking points, we've finally got a partnership deal. You've done brilliantly. Well done. I can read all that now on the plane to Amélie."

"Really? The deal is now confirmed? I wasn't sure at one stage, the whole partnership concept became very fluid and unfocussed, but with Juliette's amazing research credibility and of course Mila doing her usual behind the scenes arm-twisting with certain politicians, I stuck at it to pull the jigsaw together. I can get very determined when I want to."

"I know, and I'm impressed. So ... err ... you're working fine with both Mila and Juliette?" Lauren suddenly said, wishing she could start again with that particular sentence.

Sonja laughed. "Okay, I think you want to talk about Mila don't you and so do I. I can tell you know Lauren, and I'm sure, as you and I always do whenever there's trouble, that you're blaming Mila. I want to tell you the truth and this will only pass between you and me. Our breakup is actually my fault, I'm one hundred percent to blame, Mila really tried hard, but my heart has gone Lauren, I don't know why. I think a combination of factors over time, not one big thing."

Lauren looked up startled for a second and surprised. This revelation wasn't at all expected, but she remained composed and gently encouraged Sonja to continue.

"I've been uneasy for some time, even back in the US. Mila and I want different things Lauren, I'm ambitious but I also have a deep desire for some normality and stability. We've lived on the edge for a long time, Mila is very comfortable with that, she's restless and inside still adventure seeking, but as I get older I think we're diverging. Doing this job has been a huge game changer for me, and I'm so grateful, I can't tell you. It has made me realise for the first time what I am capable of. "

"But I thought she was happy to consider adoption and even getting married, Sonja? She talked about all that before my wedding and you've bought an apartment together."

"No, Mila insisted on buying it solely, she's made a lot of money this year. I know, but nothing has moved forward. There's always something else diverting her attention that's more important. I don't just mean Cassini, because she has a big commitment to her own security empire in the US which is why she likes the flexibility, with you, as a consultant on the books. She works enormously hard but doesn't want to be tied down. That's why Juliette is well suited to Mila's needs right now and to each other."

"You know about Juliette?" Lauren said softly, eyes wide and amazed at Sonja's cool emotional rationality and composure.

"Of course, and I'm not angry, I like her very much. Anyway I can't be angry. There is something else besides all that."

Lauren began thinking over everything she knew about Sonja, and poured out another drink as Eva knocked with more tea and an urgent set of invoices for Lauren to sign for Herman. Eva looked casually from one to the other, sensing a distinct tension between them. She shuffled the papers together, hurrying back out. As Eva reached the door, she suddenly turned. "Oh Sonja, before I forget, Johann left a message that he's managed to book a table at Y&Y for both of you for lunch. He just wanted you to know."

Sonja smiled warmly, immediately cheered by that message. "Thank you Eva," as she turned back to Lauren who was watching her carefully. "Johann and I have agreed to work jointly on a long-term, proactive marketing and sales plan for

146

R&D outcomes emanating from Cyclops and the new Israeli Centre, assuming you sign up as planned next week. That way, we're ahead of the curve for maximising potential of our forefront research. Juliette has already written a paper for me. Johann and I will turn proven research into business channels."

"My goodness Sonja, that's excellent and fits in perfectly with my plans. I like your mind-reading capabilities! Go ahead, I fully support the work. You get on well with Johann then? Great. Now where were we?"

Sonja nodded and ever so slightly reddened. "Thank you Lauren. Things came to a head with my unexpected meet up with the lobster supplier, in Cannes."

"I assume *the* lobster supplier, the guy you told me you had had a long relationship with years back? Yes, I did hear about that from Mila. I understand she wasn't too pleased," Lauren replied carefully.

"That was an understatement Lauren. We just had a drink and a catch-up in a seafront bar. He was his old self and flirty but nothing serious, he's married with two children now and settled into a good family life. In fact he's married to Greta's sister, who incidentally is now running the old hotel fully with Luigi back in Palermo and doing a superb job apparently. The place has had a three million euro renovation, and trade has rocketed. You wouldn't recognise it, although where he found the money, heaven knows."

"Gosh," Lauren said, smiling, knowing of course who was secretly paying for it all and why.

"Mila went totally ballistic over the lobster supplier. That evening she shot out, confronted him, punched him in the face on the quay front, broke his nose and he slipped on the wet surface and then broke a leg. He won't be able to work for at least six weeks and a family to support. I was livid with Mila. I sent some cash to Greta to pass on to the family. But something about that whole incident clicked within me, I realised at long last what I was truly missing and where my feelings lay. I'm a rubbish lesbian Lauren, and probably always have been."

Lauren's eyes widened at the deep personal revelations that Sonja was pouring out, obviously needing someone desperately to talk to … she wished deep in her heart that she had been more attentive to Sonja, which normally in the past she would have picked up. Damn Philippe, but she wasn't going to damn the triplets. She could see Sonja needed to continue. But her own mind was rapidly formulating the solution she also wanted for her own business plans, an approach she hadn't discussed with anyone, including Amélie, but her gut instinct was coming into the fore again. Playing by convention had never been her strong suit, she liked radical.

Sonja had gone silent, her mind pulling together and trying to pick the best way to say her finale. In the end, she already knew intuitively that she and Lauren shared a strong bond and that being straight and unequivocal suited them both. She looked over directly and crossed her legs.

"Before I arrived today Lauren, I had an early appointment, specially agreed. I've been with Edward Jones; Helena kindly set it up for me."

Lauren took a light breath, not expecting that to be said in a million years, but her mind was already running fast across various scenarios, rationalising at lightning speed … like an experimental outlier was formulating, and an odd wave of relief permeated her from top to bottom. Perhaps fate was stepping in to take a hand?

"And?"

"I'm pregnant, five weeks, Lauren." Tears rolled down Sonja's cheek. "I'm so sorry …"

"Sorry? There's absolutely nothing to be sorry about, certainly not with me," Lauren replied softly, handing her a tissue. "No crying, that is fabulous. I know how much that news means to you, and it is no problem whatsoever in this company, so rest assured," Lauren replied, leaning over to pat her hand and suddenly for the first time that morning feeling a kick, or maybe two, and took a sharp intake of breath.

"Are you okay, are they kicking?" Sonja said a worried look now across her face.

"Yes, it's gone now. I think they were playing football, that's the problem when you have a team inside you. First match of the day actually."

"Gosh, that's wonderful and thank you so much for the support; I was worried sick coming here. I don't want to give up my job. I'll need some maternity leave near the end but I have everything organised, at least in my head, to do both, and will be back soon after Lauren. That's the plan." Sonja replied, feeling more cheerful.

"Excellent," Lauren responded warmly. She wasn't especially interested in who the father was, it would be up to Sonja to reveal if she wanted to. "I'm glad you confirmed all that, because I'm going to offer you a new job. Right now."

"Pardon?" Sonja sat bolt upright, totally disoriented by Lauren's throwaway addition to this difficult discussion.

"In a nutshell Sonja, I've been formulating the next phase of Cassini development for a while, including a restructure into two autonomous divisions, Cassini Research with its own CEO and Cassini Operations, the latter running from Head Office here and responsible for marketing, sales, services and overall running. I will become Group Chairman. I've just decided. I want you and Johann to become joint CEOs of Cassini Operations. You have excellent complimentary skills. Bella with personnel and Herman with finance and IT plus Helena on business processes will report to you. Johann will internally promote a marketing and sales deputy equivalent of Helena and with Jacques running engineering services, they will report to him. Perfect. You have ten seconds to decide, and will receive a raised salary and bonus scheme commensurate with status and responsibilities. You and Johann will be my direct reports, as Chairman, alongside the CEO of Cassini Research. Yes or no?"

"Oh my word Lauren, I don't know what to say ... no I do know ... yes please. Your offer is simply an amazing opportunity. Thank you so much and having the faith in me to do the job."

"Never questioned it, Sonja. I've been toying with the thought ever since I promoted Helena."

"But, there is one thing Lauren I should also tell you because ..." Sonja began slowly.

But Lauren had already been factoring more in as they were talking, her fast mind and attuned instincts completely happy with the consequences. "You don't have to tell me, I've already guessed. You looked like the cat that found the cream this morning when Eva came in with her message. Johann is the father isn't he? I have no problem with that or what I've proposed. If you think you can manage the combination of work and family, it will be like running a business together ... which is what Philippe and I are doing of course."

She bit her lip for the moment, because Philippe was not Johann, a quite different and more engaged and committed personality altogether.

"Yes ... oh ... gosh," Sonja countered, drawing breath before continuing slowly. "Johann and I have been seeing each other secretly outside of work for some time, it just sort of happened. We get on incredibly well. I love him Lauren and he seems quite besotted, heaven knows why."

"Believe me Sonja, I can see why. You're a real catch. I think you're both very well suited actually. Probably about time he settled down too, commitment doesn't seem to have been his thing up to now. What about being a father for the first time? Does he know?"

"No, I intend to surprise him over lunch. We've talked a lot about children and he's very keen. I haven't moved in with him but I use his tiny bachelor pad to stay in now when I've been in Brussels working, although most of my time of course over the last two months has been at Cyclops and in Israel. We need to both save up more and eventually buy something nice."

"Okay … I may be able to help in that direction. I intend to move permanently to Nice very soon and work closely on cutting edge fusion research at Cyclops, like a roving adviser, or as Eva put it, a kind of nuclear Bill Gates. Would you both like to move into my apartment? I don't intend to sell it. Nominal rent to cover the utilities and maintenance and security charges only. I'm not looking to make money out of it, the place is all paid for, but as you know the apartment is big, three bedrooms, comfortable and luxurious. You can both save up then at a sensible pace, and it does me a big favour too, letting it to someone I trust."

Sonja pondered and a large grin ran across her face. "I'll need to put it to Johann, but I think that's an amazing idea. I would love your apartment, the place is so beautiful."

"I'm taking the bed because I made it, and the mink sofa, that's about all. The rest of the furniture you can use. Deal then? What a great morning!" Then Lauren's face suddenly darkened, as she thought of the lobster supplier. "Perhaps there is one problem though …"

"Mila knows about me and Johann. You know how she is. She's known from the start, super-sleuth extraordinaire that she always maintains. We discussed everything and Juliette when we separated and she's calm and accepting. I actually wonder now whether Mila's anger with the lobster supplier wasn't really directed at me, but that she was trying to be protective of my developing relationship with Johann, having already come to terms with the fact that we were coming to an end. Mila may be temperamental but she is amazingly resolute and far-seeing."

Lauren leaned back, smiled and breathed a sigh of relief. Her head was spinning with all kinds of interesting changes ahead. "All the new structure and jobs are to be formalised at the special Executive meeting after I come back from Israel. I'm going to call in Johann now before I go and offer him the job too, but I'll mention nothing about babies. I suggest you head over to Y&Y and relax. You're both going to have a lot to celebrate over lunch! I reckon it must be the hafnium contaminant I once found in the leaking pipes, or as they say in English, something in the water. All this immaculate nuclear conception going on here, a rhapsody of succession all at once."

Sonja laughed. "Who else then Lauren? Are there more miscreants?"

"I have my suspicions, time will tell," Lauren replied with a large grin. They hugged and Sonja departed with a decided spring in her step.

<><>

"Eva ... can you buzz Johann right away. I know he's in his office this morning. Something important has come up I need to sort out before I go. Then I shall wheel my case down to the minibus. Giselle has promised to drive me straight to the airport."

"Sonja looked very pleased on her way out, in comparison with on her way in?" Eva chuntered, rattling tea cups onto a tray.

"No, Eva … you have absolutely no idea, okay?"

"Of course," Eva replied, heading out of the door with a grin from ear to ear.

Chapter Twelve

The sleek, grey-bodied LearJet cantered to a halt in the small airport. She peered down at her watch, noting they were around ten minutes early. The plane was comfortable and spacious inside for a small aircraft and the eight seats were all occupied, although as she perused the group of male passengers heading for the exit in front of her none of them looked like entrepreneurial oil and gas men, more bureaucratic meddlers seeking to enforce gold-plated regulations. She was sick of regulations, which were proving a difficult disincentive for investment in nuclear power in Europe. Amazingly, she was making some headway in Germany with the Xenostra reactor, but once again tricky coalition green politics and devolved regional banking were working against a smooth and rapid deal. But the Germans were impressed and surprised with the innovative quality of their engineering design.

Last person to emerge, she stood on the top of the steps and looked around at the flat expanse of coastline, the Blackpool conurbation and greenery leading away into the distance ... somewhere out there lay the Amélie homestead. Not quite Dallas, but she remained intrigued with aristocratic Britain and how the English landed gentry were adapting to the twenty-first century. The wind was getting up again and another squally wet storm from the Atlantic was predicted for later. She was just in time as she buttoned her jacket up, her Isabella Oliver white and blue patterned t-shirt maternity dress clinging tightly, bump well showing.

For once she was airport impressed, having sped through passport, baggage retrieval and clean toilets in record time. Refreshed and made up, she made her way to the exit spotting a small scrum of meet and greet people waving signs. A large white card with Professor Hind scrawled in untidy green ink caught her eye, held up high by a rather dishy broad shouldered and heavily bearded individual dressed in a smart brown Barbour jacket and matching check shirt. He looked like a modernised and upmarket version of D. H. Lawrence, apt as she was in the middle of re-reading Lady Chatterley's Lover again.

"Hi, I'm Professor Hind, Lauren Hind."

"Professor Hind, a pleasure to meet you," the mid-thirties dish answered, well spoken with none of the broad Lancashire accent she expected. "Giles Hardacre, Estate Manager. Lady Westvale has spoken extensively about you and your work. I hope to show you our new cluster of wind turbines I've erected which power our cheese making complex, Lady Westvale even designed the switching gear."

"Really? Nothing surprises me about Lady Westvale, Giles. Please, just call me Lauren. I ceased to be a real academic many years back, but the title continues to open doors," she replied jauntily, already feeling cheered arriving.

He took the handle of her case and pointed through the glass doors to a large black Range Rover SUV parked outside in the front. "Bit of a squall heading again this way, we'd better be off, it should pass quickly."

Shoving the big automatic into gear, they soon shot out of the airport drive and onwards along the coast road, past the famous Blackpool Tower entertainment area and out of the suburbs of Blackpool, a seaside town which looked like it had seen better days. They continued quietly through the much classier resort of Lytham St Annes, the clusters of individualistic bed and breakfast five storey Victorian houses dominating the seafront, until finally they hit the misty green countryside. In due course Giles turned off the main highway and she found herself travelling along the bottom of an undulating wide valley, the road following parallel to the line of a meandering river, the clear water frothing over smooth stones and pebbles. She liked it out here.

"This is J.R.Tolkien territory," Giles suddenly said, over the purr of the engine. "He was so taken when he arrived in the late 1940s with the unique Ribble Valley landscape of wide rippling rivers and deep wooded conifer groves, he became immediately inspired to write the Lord of the Rings. You'll find many names in the trilogy from here."

Lauren looked over at his windswept face concentrating on the road as they drove over a small humpbacked bridge onto a rougher minor lane. "Do you like literary description, Giles?"

"Oh yes, I'm an avid reader of English classics, Hardy, Austen, Wolf and especially of course D. H. Lawrence."

She giggled and stifled it quickly with a cough.

"Are you alright Lauren? Not far to go, we're just heading into the estate now," he shouted over, looking at her and her dress up and down with interest, when she realised her thighs were showing more bareness than planned with the bouncing about, and pulled the hem down sharply.

"So Lord and Lady Westvale have a sizeable estate?"

"Not as large as in the early nineteen hundreds. The then Earl of Westvale, the present Lord Westvale's grandfather, was forced to sell off a lot of land and tenured property during the slump in the 1930's. But it's still considerable, just over nine thousand acres, including tenants, and the family mansion remains intact. A splendid and restored Georgian building actually, built in the early nineteenth century on the site of the former castle which burned down after a feud in 1791. My family has worked and lived on the estate for generations, originally gamekeepers. But I did a Masters degree in farm management at the local University, which incidentally is very strong on nuclear engineering."

"University of Central Lancashire?"

"You know it? I'm impressed Professor Hind. Yes, in Preston the county headquarters."

"I did some guest lectures there once, up on the Sellafield reprocessing site a long time ago, although I have to say that area of the nuclear business is very much Lady Westvales's expertise."

"Really? My word, I had no idea."

"Anyway Giles, I get the impression that unlike much of the old English aristocracy, the Westvale's have been pretty successful since the 1930s at keeping financially solvent."

"Absolutely, all down to the energy and commitment of Rufus's sorry the present Earl of Westvales's father who was determined to make the land work commercially. So over the years, intensive and specialised agriculture, particularly rape seed, wheat and cattle rearing, combined with other entrepreneurial activity have been fully developed and, given the size of the holding, are very successful, especially the lines of organic produce, cheese, milk and meat, sold all over the country through one of the large supermarket chains. They also let the house for film companies, very lucrative. A number of major films and TV dramas have been filmed here over the last five years. That was all down to Rufus, who has enthusiastically taken up the mantle of his father with a host of new business ideas such as the wind farm. Lady Westvale has been equally amazing and keen, and considering her background has settled into things here remarkably quickly. The staff love her."

"Please, feel free Giles with me to just say Amélie and Rufus, I hate formality but I do understand conventions."

"Thanks Lauren, me too and actually so do Amélie and Rufus, but I needed to be sure at first …"

"Understood."

He noticeably relaxed as they continued, driving carefully on the narrow road to avoid a number of bad winter potholes due to poor council maintenance of the tarmac.

Lauren pondered for a few minutes then asked. "Are there any other family members involved with the estate?"

Giles went silent. "Rufus has a younger sister and brother. Cordelia lives there, she has her own suite at the rear of the house overlooking the lake, but doesn't get involved in the day to day running. She prefers to paint and things. His other sister emigrated as a teenager many years back to Australia and cut family ties, we don't know where she is."

"And Rufus's brother? Presumably he takes on some responsibilities?"

Giles remained quiet as he gathered his thoughts. "Actually, I shouldn't really say Lauren … but … well no. I'm afraid Simon is locked up in a secure institution ten miles away, diagnosed insane with paranoid delusions."

Lauren looked over. "I'm so sorry to hear that, I had no idea. Had he done anything, committed crimes?"

"Bad things, actually, very bad things. Two women in the local village committed suicide as a result. The whole situation was one of the family trying to pretend he was normal but Simon just got out of control. He stopped taking medication and spent hours on end watching unsavoury videos in his locked room, withdrawing completely before escaping one night into the village. This was while Rufus's father was alive of course. Don't mention I said anything Lauren. Simon isn't talked about anymore."

"In my line of work, total discretion is the norm Giles, so have no worries."

"Thank you Lauren," he replied, cheering up again as they turned the last corner and drove up a long sandy coloured gravel drive, neatly laid out between clipped, green lawns. They headed towards a vast country manor of stunning red brick and almost square, with the tell tale Georgian features she was so familiar with, having a detailed knowledge and love of furniture and architecture from that period.

The moment they drew up in front of a huge pillared porch entrance, a familiar figure emerged in a bright red dress and tripped down the steps to the car to greet Lauren with a warm embrace as she stepped gingerly from the high vehicle. The two sandstone lions guarding the entrance looked remarkably similar to those at Cassini.

"Welcome to the palatial pad. I hope you had a good flight and that Giles has looked after you well?"

"Great flight Amélie, Giles is exemplary," she responded, looking up to Giles flirtatiously, mischievously noting Amélie's sideward glance. "And you look totally radiant, I love the outfit. Gosh, you really are wearing Versace. How did you get it and to fit so well?"

Giles, blushing, called back from the Range Rover. "If you'll excuse me Lady Westvale and Professor Hind, I'll just leave your luggage at the side entrance, then I need to sort out a pumping problem in the milking shed."

"Thanks Giles see you later," Amélie replied before hurrying Lauren inside out of the driving wind, although the heavy clouds had now begun to lift and the sun was casting a gleaming umbrella of light over the huge house. Amélie linked Lauren's arm as she escorted her through the wide main hall corridor into a very high ceilinged and spacious drawing room, laid out with matching period antique furniture, undoubtedly family heirlooms. A log fire was burning slowly inside the beautifully decorated Adam fireplace, whilst Lauren surveyed the ornate Georgian coving and lush green, striped period wall paper. They sat down in heavy green velvet armchairs around a beautifully carved mahogany coffee table. Lauren was already very impressed and hugely jealous. Amélie had pulled herself up, amazingly, out of the former morass of nuclear intrigue, personal Armageddon and the destructive clutches of Vaag, into a lifestyle she looked to have been naturally born to. The fit was uncanny, and Amélie looked uncharacteristically relaxed and happy, a state of presence that Lauren had never seen since the days, way back, when they shared academic life at the Pierre and Marie Curie University in Paris.

"You look a little overwhelmed, I told you it was awesomely opulent," Amélie began.

"I am. Lady Westvale, even for you this lot takes some beating. I had no idea Rufus had such an aristocratic heritage. It's like the former CEO of Rubidium who decommissioned nuclear sites and this unbelievable Lady of the Manor are two different women. I can't get over it … and the lifestyle suits you so well Amélie. I'm really pleased for you and insanely jealous, especially of all the gorgeous English period furniture."

"Yes, I agree with you for a change, and at long last I think I've found something that is really me for the first time in a long time. But, don't get me wrong Lauren, aspects of the old business I have been missing, and I do keep up with latest developments. You never know, I may need to return to the

160

fold if Rufus misbehaves again. In fact I've been reading your latest paper on fusion. You made a mistake on the third page, I'll show you later along with the furniture, but it didn't alter your conclusions. A very bold way forward towards potential commercialisation. I assume Cyclops will be leading the charge?"

"Well, what can I say Amélie? You're pretty unique for a best friend, but yes and you remember the infamous meeting we had with President Jacques Chandrisé in the Elysee Gardens and he proposed a tie in with JETR? Not only has that finally happened but we are partnering up too with the Israelis. I'm off to Tel Aviv next week to sign the accord. I wanted to ask, what do you think now I've done the deed?" Lauren replied.

"Very visionary Lauren, well done … I assume the Serbian Siren has had a hand in the Israeli part? No, I wouldn't dare call her that," Amélie chuckled. "Actually, I really wanted to fuck him?"

"Yes, that was fairly obvious and sadly, decidedly mutual. Fortunately, First Lady Imke did a timely rescue of both of you before the guillotine prevailed. Anyway, you have your own Elysee now."

"Mmm … yes … thanks to Rufus … ahh refreshments."

A tall elderly man in a smart uniform and starched white shirt and bow tie knocked and entered. "Shall I bring some tea and cakes in madam?"

"Yes please William, ginger tea and some of that excellent homemade carrot cake of Yvonne's."

"Right away madam." He departed promptly out of the other door.

"Shit Amélie, you have a real English butler? In this day and age? Bloody hell," Lauren uttered, dumbfounded.

"Actually, butlers are really on the rise now, especially amongst the nouveau rich and Russian oligarchs hiding out in London. William is more of a historic relic, been in the family service for years and he looked after Rufus's father, and of course Rufus since he was a boy. If you think about it, a place this size needs some organising or it would run to rack and ruin in no time. You need staff ... cooking, cleaning, maintenance, gardening, security and they all need managing, which is William's job. I would call him the house factotum. The estate, which is also huge at least it is to me, has a factotum too of course, ably managed by Giles, who does a delectably brilliant job and is very business savvy. I could see you fancied him rotten; presumably he charmed you on the way with all kinds of historic gossip. I'm sure I could arrange a discrete night time call after hours?"

Lauren laughed. "Not in my state thank you. Yes, I got a background summary of the manor. I suppose you're right Amélie, it just seems weird, you at the epicentre, with of course Rufus. Where is Rufus actually?" she said, keeping her lips sealed about the family black sheep.

"Okay, in five months time then, you and me both! Anyway, I can sense from your noticeable and obvious lack of discourse on the subject that him-indoors remains very much outdoors in the wilds of Siberia, digging for fucking gas and denying the obvious fatherhood situation still."

"You could put it that way, Amélie, but I've taken your last comments to heart and thanks. I'm relaxed ... it's up to him now. We do keep in regular touch by email but he still can't talk to me over the phone. However, there may be a glimmer of light down the dark tunnel, because he has accepted an invite, with me, to wedding of the year in Nice in two weeks time."

"Wedding of the year?"

"Yes, Charlotte and DG are getting married, a quiet ceremony just with me, Philippe and the twins."

"That is fantastic, I really wish them well. I'd like to send them a present; can you let me know where and when?"

"Yes of course. Tea is coming."

They settled down over the tea and cakes, presented on authentic matching Staffordshire old china, to a further hour's worth of gossip and technical discussions of Lauren's fusion plans. Amélie agreed completely with Lauren's proposed reorganisation of Cassini, adding some refinement to the structure from her previous CEO experience in the US. Rufus would be back later as Amélie explained. He often spent Fridays in London down at the House of Lords and at his club, being one of the few selected hereditary peers left still able to sit and vote in the UK Parliament. Rufus was a cross-bencher, although Lauren guessed that his leanings were decidedly right wing Tory, not just from his background but the unerring commitment to free market enterprise and supporting small businesses with special committee chairing, which he was apparently thriving on. Amélie completed her Cassini recommendations before showing Lauren around some of the other ground floor rooms, the amazing upgraded kitchen and scullery and to meet some of the staff, the most important being Yvonne, Head Cook, who looked like she had just stepped out of a period TV drama, and who worked alongside her daughter Sophie. Amélie proceeded to take Lauren up to her room, as they each walked slowly up the wide marble staircase.

"My word Lauren, it whacks me out climbing these stairs, yet you seem a bundle of energy still. And seeing that we are bump comparing, how come your three equals half my two?

Not exactly mathematically fair is it," Amélie said with a grunt, catching her breath.

"All in the genes, darling. Plus strong, muscular innards, so Edward Jones tells me."

"And the gym I suspect. You were right I should have made more effort while the going was good. He's quite a dish isn't he, your gyno?"

"How do you know that?"

"I have my spies still in Cassini, but no telling even to my best friend, especially as she's the CEO."

They walked into Lauren's bedroom where William had deposited her luggage and she drew in a large intake of breath. The room was decorated almost identical to her master bedroom in the Chelsea pad that she and Amélie had been the last visitors to, same high ceilings and large windows. An unexpected but delightful surprise.

"Gosh, you have an amazing memory for design and colours. Oh my goodness that bed … now I recognise it, my old bed I made in the Cassini workshop … the four-poster you took away. Oh Amélie, how wonderful."

"I thought you would like it. This is now the prime guest room, and has, I think, one of the best views from the house. I had it done specially. There's an ensuite been added that I refurbished in the latest Italian sanitaryware at the end and the other door leads into a massive personal wardrobe."

Lauren gave Amélie a large hug. "Thank you so much, I'm really glad I came here, ten out of ten for sumptuous luxury."

"Good, and now you know where I am then you can come here regularly from now on, especially when the army of successors are delivered. We can dump them all on the nanny when I get her ensconced."

"You're having a live-in nanny?" Lauren asked, her mind running over the pros and cons.

"Of course. I have the space and the money. I want to spend lots of time with the children, and I want more babies after these. But I also do other work on the estate and I want time to myself to explore personal interests. Having a nanny will be practical and realistic. I know you haven't considered the idea, looking at your expression, and it goes against the grain obviously but you need to be realistic too Lauren, especially with triplets. Breastfeeding? I wouldn't fancy it for long with three. Be pragmatic Lauren, you *can* have it all. Build the help you will need into your planning when you move to Cannes. Believe me you won't regret it."

"Stupidly, I haven't really seriously thought through post-birth arrangements yet. There's been so much going on with Philippe and all that associated crap as well. But you're right; I will need to find a sensible work-life balance. And Annabella has been adamant about that too."

"Not like you … Lauren the long term, logical strategist? No, I understand, lots of emotional issues … but hey me too. It isn't stopping me being pragmatic, even if Vaag is the father."

Lauren pondered and pulled her mind deep into the issue with a maelstrom of instant analysis. Yes, Amélie and Annabella are absolutely correct.

Amélie continued. "Anyway, you look tired after the journey. I suggest you take a rest, sort yourself out, have a snooze then come down for seven, where we will have oodlings of ginger beer to start with. Rufus will be back just before then. I forgot to mention, we're having that dinner party at seven-thirty tonight instead, a slight change of plan because I have *two* special guests who will arrive later. And don't ask because I'm not telling you."

"Two?"

"Yes, isn't that fun? Right, I shall leave you to unpack. If you need anything just pull that cord over there, which rings a bell in the scullery and Sophie, who oversees the housekeeping, will sort you out in a jiffy."

Lauren looked at the red tasselled ceiling chord ... incredulous. "Really? ... This communication system is pre-transistor!"

"Of course, I'm an aristocrat — must play the part. See you later," Amélie cried with a snort and kissed Lauren on the cheek playfully. "Oh, before I go, just to warn there will be an additional family person for dinner, Cordelia, Rufus's fucking sister. She's twenty-eight and lives in a large suite at the other end of the house like God's gift, does fuck all but flaunts about, either spending all the hard-earned wealth or passing weeks on end like a hermit in her rooms. And she occasionally paints. Blinkered old Rufus is protective of his younger sister, so I can't do anything ... yet ... much as I would like to kick her rear out of the place for good."

Lauren looked back and smiled. Obviously the Cordelia, as described by Giles to a tee, would be quite incompatible with the intrepid Dr Helgudóttir, former global CEO and of hardworking Icelandic and Scottish stock. "Okay, no worries. I think I will have a snooze actually, I'm worn out."

<><>

Lauren, carefully unfolded and hung up her clothes in the dressing room and then selected her specially made sleeveless cocktail dress, which the MA fashion students in the College whose governing body she still chaired, had designed and made for her. The fabric was an expensive silk which Lauren had specifically chosen and paid for. The dress was adorned with a beautifully feminine abstract, floral design, in a sophisticated

166

palette of her favourite canary yellow, subtly accented with light and dark blue orchids and roses. Tied at the bust, she would wear the dress as a simple strapless gown, the chiffon body adding to the opulent and ethereal quality. She wanted to make a statement, as always especially to Amélie, and this dress provided the ideal opportunity, a perfect complement to the surroundings. Thank goodness Amélie had excellent electrical background heating installed, which not only had she designed but they were now generating from their own wind farm. It was the first modification to the house Amélie insisted upon with Rufus, the moment he had carried her over the doorway. One advantage for him ... being married to a nuclear engineer.

She gazed out through the high windows at the small lake to the rear, a fountain spurting away happily in the centre, and onwards over the extensive gardens and beyond, to a rural mix of undulating woods and cow filled meadows dotted with hay feeders and interspersed with cultivated land. Tractors were busy, preparing the ground for the coming year's crops, and in the distance she could see the handsome Giles, driving his own machine and waving his arms vigorously at some of the farmhands. She smiled, and felt that pang of Tolkien, but then decidedly veered swiftly back to D H Lawrence watching him, fishing out her Lady Chatterley's Lover paperback for the next steamy instalment when she went to bed later.

Stifling a yawn, she patted her old bed, a mild reminiscence of ex-husband sweeping past. He would have loved it here being the consummate fashion and interior designer; perhaps he wasn't so bad after all. Lucky Angelina. Wistfully, she lay down on the bed deciding to set her phone alarm to six, but instead exhaustion immediately overcame her ...

<><>

The quiet tap-tapping on the door made her sit up with a start as she looked blearily out of the blackness of the window. She had well and truly dozed off for hours.

"Come in?"

The door opened and a young woman in her early twenties wearing a smart dark skirt and frilly, white blouse was standing there smiling. "Sorry to disturb you Professor Hind, I'm Sophie. Lady Westvale asked me to see if you were okay or whether you wanted any help?"

"Gosh, thank you Sophie, please call me Lauren. What time is it?" Lauren replied sleepily. She gazed over to the large hands on the ticking grandfather clock in the corner. "Oh my goodness, it's almost seven o'clock! I must have slept solid for three hours. Damn, I didn't set my phone alarm. I'm going to be late for dinner." She struggled off the bed and pushed her hands through her hair.

Sophie spotted Lauren's clothes laid out in the dressing room. "Actually, dinner isn't until seven-forty five so you have plenty of time Lauren. Tell you what, I'll just go and tell Lady Westvale that you'll be down at exactly seven-thirty, I'm sure she'll understand. Then if you go into the shower and change and I'll come back up and dry your hair and do your makeup. I trained in hairdressing initially, no problem at all, we'll soon get you ready."

"Thank you Sophie, I'd really appreciate that … see you shortly," Lauren whispered, moving herself immediately into the shower.

Fifteen minutes later, Lauren was sat in front of the dressing table mirror, fiddling with a selection of bracelets, necklaces and rings, unsure of which combination as Sophie dried and brushed her hair damp-dry.

"That silk dress is absolutely gorgeous and fits you perfectly Lauren. I'd go with that sapphire necklace and gold bracelet which match those long lemon earrings, especially with the dress rings you have on. Would you like me to put your hair up?"

"Mmm … I agree totally," Lauren said, as the necklace was carefully put on. "Yes please, I don't have the patience and time normally to fiddle with my hair myself."

"No, I understand. Lady Westvale explained what you do. Your job sounds fabulous, you must see some fantastic places around the world," Sophie said, piling up and pinning Lauren's long blonde hair carefully, finishing off with a small pale yellow rose inserted from the vase of flowers lying on the table. "You look really beautiful Lauren; you do suit your hair up like that. Now, I'll just put these lashes on and dust some mascara around to finish."

Sophie, skilled and proficient, was soon finished. Lauren stood up and gazed at the whole effect in the full length mirror and felt more than satisfied, even her bump was only showing a little, the way the dress had been carefully cut and fitted.

"Stunning. I think you're ready for the ball now Professor Hind and it's almost seven-thirty. I'll just run down and alert Lady Westvale that you're now on your way."

Lauren finally sprayed on her best Chanel No 5 and made her way carefully, in her dark blue five-inch Louboutins, out of the room towards the top of the staircase and along the wide landing with old and grim looking ancestral paintings adorning the walls. She could hear a general hubbub and voices below.

"Ahh … here she comes, at long last." Amélie's voice rang out echoing over the wide, white marble. "Lauren, my special guests are here and quite excited to see you."

Lauren was perplexed, she peered down but could only see a couple of figures at the sides in the haze as she held onto the banister and decided to play Amélie's game, head held high, slow measured celebrity staircase walk. She had done this many times at heads of state events, but Amélie had never seen her pose this way and probably never realised. Time to make one of her well-practised grand entrances, but who on earth were these so called special guests?

As she descended, the mystery dinner guests suddenly sprang into view. She couldn't believe her eyes. Irena, large as life, was standing with her husband Peter, the former UK Prime Minister. She would never have guessed, and she hadn't seen Irena since the fateful escapade to Murmansk. How wonderful. Her mind flashed back to Annabella and the proposed job with the Aid Evocative charity which Irena chaired. What was Amélie up to? Peter's eyes were on stalks as she slowly descended to the bottom, nor had she forgotten. Being trapped and alone with him in the nuclear bunker in Chequers during the cyanogen crisis was a bit of an experience, fortunately not consummated to conclusion thanks to Rufus. But unusually for Peter, Irena was next to him. She had to remain aloof.

Irena held out her arms and gave Lauren a generous hug. "Surprise! We were up north for business and Amélie suggested dinner. I couldn't resist when she said you would be here. That dress is absolutely divine, I want one Lauren exactly the same. A little bird told me you're expecting triplets … excuse me but are you sure?"

"Irena, how marvellous to see you … yes, I'm very sure, I've even see the scan pictures but as I said to Amélie, I'm the lucky owner of strong muscly innards!"

They all laughed. Lauren turned to Peter who had put on a lot of weight since his forced departure from high office for the bright lights of international consultancy. Too many congressional dinners by the look of it, she pondered, over at the World Bank which he was now advising.

"You look totally ravishing Lauren, definitely the belle of the ball. Lovely to see you again," he said, kissing her on each cheek, French style.

She looked back at him and smiled. "Good to see you too Peter, I hope business is good?" deciding, as he looked at her with a leer she now felt uncomfortable with, that he had metamorphosed into a quite undesirable man, unlike the dashing and slim PM she nearly ... well that was definitely history.

She stared at Amélie, tall and equally stunning, her short and fringed spiky copper hair all twinkly with shiny bits sprayed in. She too wore a dark orange, sleeveless maxi dress, all nicely fitted, bulge just showing, with a daring neckline. In fact it was definitely a Dior, but a maternity Dior? Where did she get that dress? Thank goodness they weren't really competing, they both looked ravishing, to quote, and Amélie was smiling happily so must have felt the same. As best friends for so long they always, almost instinctively, knew what the other would wear.

Suddenly two more people stepped into the hallway. Rufus, dressed smartly in casual country wear and open-necked shirt strolled in, looking exactly the same, but slightly chubbier and certainly more relaxed. Amélie and aristocracy obviously suited him perfectly. Alongside him was a tall slim woman with long brown hair wearing a beautiful stunning white cocktail dress, finished with large pearls around her neck and all her fingers adorned with clusters of variegated coloured dress rings. The woman and Rufus were incredibly alike, the same long faces, dark brown eyes and high intelligent foreheads. Lauren immediately realised who this must be.

Rufus stepped forward and kissed her on the cheek. "Lauren, great to see you, you are as adorably blooming as Amélie here. We're sorry we've missed Philippe on this occasion but hopefully next time, yes?"

"Rufus, you look great and your house is so divine. I want one too."

"Cost you a bit though Lauren, bit more than a nuke," he retorted, quick as mustard, and they all laughed. "Now, can I introduce you to my sister Cordelia, who is a … err … an artist."

Lauren leaned forward, arm outstretched to shake hands, but Cordelia leapt towards her imparting a tight hug and a sloppy kiss on each cheek, like long lost buddies. She wore a delicate and expensive perfume which wafted across Lauren's nose. Lauren stood back. "Cordelia, how nice to meet you. An artist, that is interesting …"

"Yes, I know," Cordelia replied, her lips drawn tightly into a forced smile, her voice possessing a noticeably slow drawl, and with a very posh accent of the old fashioned intonation only heard amongst the English royal family or in old BBC clips. She was heavily made up, with dark black rings drawn around her eyes and a bright red lipstick. She could have been on the cover of a paranormal novel. Lauren couldn't help but be drawn to her piercing seductive stare, oddly hypnotic; Cordelia was very attractive with an hourglass figure. "You love paintings don't you Lauren, perhaps I can show you my studio later? I normally never show anyone my work, not even Rufus, but I would love to make you an exception. Would you like that?"

Lauren, mind in gear in an instant, noticed Amélie's expression and shuffle, but she already knew, well experienced these days in the signs and signals, not that Cordelia was exactly subtle. She was being chatted up, not by Peter as she might have expected, but by Cordelia, oh my God, stay calm.

"Perhaps over the weekend Cordelia. I know I shall be quite exhausted after dinner carrying this army around inside."

"Army?"

"Yes, triplets."

Cordelia thought for a moment … then smiled again, smacking her thin red lips and flashing her eyes. "Mmm … nice."

"Lauren?" Amélie intervened diplomatically. "You haven't quite met everyone for the dinner party." The others all looked at each other; this was obviously a surprise for them too, even Rufus. Typical of Amélie, on top form and enjoying herself hugely. "There is one more guest, lurking behind the curtain." Everyone turned as Amélie shouted out. "Time to reveal yourself special guest."

The curtain opened and a figure confidently walked out towards Lauren. This time her mouth dropped wide open and her heart beat instant palpitations, with a mixture of disbelief, incredulity and a huge wave of desire. This cannot be, she was dreaming, she had to pinch herself. Rufus also stared, with equal amazement. Irena, Peter and Cordelia stood back; they all could see the figure was someone special, to both Lauren and Amélie. But before she had a chance the figure held Lauren tightly with a long hug, tears running down both their cheeks with delight and amazement and whispered in Lauren's ear. "Don't ruin your makeup; you look adorable enough to eat. Yes it's really me, all fit and ready for duty again. And congratulations, internal army suits you."

Lauren stood back. "Rosie? How on earth? … It's not possible it can't be."

"No, all very possible Lauren thanks to amazing Sergei combined with very tough training and recuperation regime in Alaska. I walk again, spine fully healed. Sergei is fantastic man, but I think you and Svet know that already."

"Absolutely, but what are you doing here?"

"Amélie and I have kept in touch, and I want to thank her for personally supporting and funding US Special Forces recuperation programme which was especially tailored to my needs. Thank you Amélie."

Lauren was baffled, and also felt a wave of guilt wash over her because although both she and Amélie owed their lives to Rosie, only Amélie had made a special effort to get her fully well again ... Lauren felt frustrated with herself once more having too many stupid preoccupations, when the really important ones had slipped past without her knowing. But, as she always rationalised in situations like this, you can't go back in time, well not yet. They are where they are, so get on with the blessings in front of her.

"Amélie, you have done something truly wonderful for Rosie, thank you so much. Rufus knows the background, but just to say Irena, Peter and Cordelia, Amélie and I were in a very tight work spot last year. Nuclear can sometimes be a dangerous business. Rosie, with her own special skills got both of us out of trouble and saved our lives, at a serious cost to her, but now amazingly that is history and I can't tell you all how pleased I am to see Rosie today looking so amazing."

They all smiled and clapped.

"Right everyone, dining room to the right please, dinner is being served," Amélie shouted, as Yvonne and Sophie walked through with pots of steaming food, followed by Rufus and everyone else.

As they walked in, Lauren gazed at Rosie again, her slim figure tightly held inside her lovely red silk sleeveless evening dress, with the huge heels she loved to wear and her jet black hair, now quite long, swirling over her bare shoulders. She looked and sounded as wildly enticing as ever. Her shoulder and arm muscles were powerful.

Rosie sensed Lauren eyeing her toned body, as was Cordelia. "Look at muscles," she uttered, posing 'Popeye' style to both in the usual inimitable Rosie way. "Done more weights and press-ups than ever. Fitter even than before, don't you think Lauren?"

"Yes, Rosie, definitely, you are very fit," Lauren replied with a smirk, as Cordelia, walking the other side, laughed her head off.

They all sat down as directed by Amélie at a lovely old oak dining table, which Rufus declared had been in the family for five hundred years and at which King Charles the First had once sat and eaten and apparently so had Samuel Pepys, the famous diarist. He pointed up to a faded and cracked dark oil painting behind him, the once magnificent gold frame having badly deteriorated. "I intend having this picture restored soon."

They could all clearly see the same table, the King plainly visible and surrounded by another nine nobility supporters, although the room looked different as it must have been painted in the former castle which burned down. "This table and the painting were the only things saved in the great fire of the original ancestral home," he said, proudly. "You can still see scorch marks on the legs at this end."

Lauren was placed in the royal chair, with Rosie one side and Cordelia the other, whilst opposite, Amélie, Peter and Irena took their seats with Rufus at the head. A rich red tablecloth had been laid out with an array of immaculately arranged silver cutlery and an intricately patterned porcelain china dinner set. William came in with some assistants to formally serve, as the wine was uncorked and tasted.

Rufus explained whilst the food was meticulously dished out. "Sophie has dug out an old seventeenth century family recipe and modified it a little. Some ingredients and dishes no longer exist as we would recognise them now. Essentially, everything we eat today has been produced here on the estate, as it would have been during the time of King Charles. Our main meal is a type of venison stew which is what they ate in the picture."

"And Lauren, you and I are allowed one small glass of a special red wine we've brought up from the cellar," Amélie added playfully. "It's an Italian Barolo wine, made from the special Nebbioli grape. It has a wonderful aroma and has been carefully maturing down there for some years and should be just right now."

Rufus had the first taste. "Mmm … perfect. Enjoy everyone." They toasted, first the health of Lauren and then Amélie, their forthcoming broods, and finally Rosie.

Cordelia leaned forward and whispered across, making sure everyone heard. "What Lauren can't manage, I'm sure you and I can make a night of it, can't we Rosie?"

Rosie grinned. She had already made her mind up. She had a lot of downtime to make up for since being laid up with a fractured spine, and her press-ups were better than ever. Lauren looked briefly at one and then the other, and felt a weird combination of relief, anger and jealousy.

Amélie stared over and caught Lauren's subtle smile back … they both knew instinctively what the other was thinking … Rufus's fucking sister.

Chapter Thirteen

As the house staff began clearing up the leftover dishes from their 'eleven years of tyranny' dinner which Rufus, a Cambridge graduate historian, liked to call it, Amélie took Lauren, Irena and Rosie, with Cordelia trotting quietly behind, into the small but very comfortable drawing room where green tea was being served. Rufus meanwhile was keen to show Peter how the estate was sustainably farmed and how it had become self sufficient in energy, an issue the World Bank was especially interested in. Rufus was sensing a possibility of some potential demonstration funding.

"Let me show you the whole of the plans in my study, Peter," Rufus suggested. "And I have a good malt stowed away in there too," he added with a grin. "Just down the corridor." The two of them sidled out of the room and the women settled down in the luxurious armchairs and large sofa around the burning log fire, duly relaxed after the dinner.

Irena turned inquisitively to Rosie. "I don't know whether you know but the Aid Evocative project along the Mekong River on the Burma border has been going so well under Jie's overall direction. We have concentrated as you originally suggested on environmental issues and improving women's education and training, especially with the preponderance of mineral extraction and mining going on there."

"Yes, thank you Irena. Jie keep in regular touch whilst I recuperate in US. I advised from bed but she is very capable.

Ministry has been so pleased she has just been told to stay there for next six months and direct all operations."

"Really," Irena replied, surprised. "The trustees didn't know that."

"I'm sure Jie will tell you. She only got clearance for public knowledge two days ago. State press is already in area to produce good stories of course and show China in positive light with environmental activity."

"Wonderful." Irena turned to Lauren. "Annabella is looking to develop our work further in Africa on environmental improvement too, especially in areas beset with chronic pollution, health issues and poor waste management. Did she tell you? I'm so pleased she's now decided to become full time CEO from next month. Thanks for all the pep talk and advice you recently gave her, which really helped to make her mind up, especially now she has her domestic arrangements all in order. And of course the continuing Cassini funding support as chief sponsor of the charity is hugely beneficial. The intern, Joanna, you've kindly provided to work with Annabella as her assistant for the next twelve months has been settling in very well, especially in the new EMEA head office Annabella has established in Palermo, to compliment the new Asian office which Jie oversees in Shanghai. The trustees are very pleased, especially with the doubling of sponsorship this year thanks to the influencing effect of Cassini."

Lauren sat up. This was all news to her especially about Annabella, but she remained implacably unmoved except to say how pleased she was that Aid Evocative was doing so well, and that Cassini was benefitting internally and externally from having a strongly focussed environmental strategy. There certainly had been pep talks between them, but the other way around with Annabella pepping her up. She finally realised,

178

running back over their conversations when Annabella stayed over, the implication of Annabella's constant reference to not wanting to be tied down to just looking after the children and needing much more … my goodness … she will have her hands full as CEO. She was extremely pleased for Annabella, but even her day to day organisational skills would be challenged, although Annabella had the money to pursue her dream … and her mind was obviously set. Reminder to herself, she must make a quick phone call when she gets the chance this weekend to her second 'sister'. Africa was certainly going to be challenging and potentially dangerous, with vested interest, corruption and powerful warlords in the places she was likely to want to go with the charity, Aid Evocative.

Lauren looked at Amélie who was sitting quietly, absorbing everything as usual like a sponge, but also periodically watching Cordelia with concern. She didn't have long to wait.

"Irena?" Rosie said, having also become deep in thought. Lauren was mildly intrigued with what Rosie was thinking about. In fact did Mila even know Rosie was recovered? Nothing had been said. She seemed to have entered another fuzzy brain period where lots of things had been happening and she didn't have a clue about any of them … but perhaps she shouldn't whip herself too much. She had a major global and growing company to manage, triplets on the way, and a shit husband. She leaned back, miles away and smiled.

"Penny for your thoughts Lauren?" Cordelia whispered in her ear, running her fingers gently up the softness of Lauren's high cheekbones. Cordelia was now bored with listening about the real world. "What lovely features you have, quite Slavic, how do you keep your skin so soft and beautiful?"

"Regular use of creams, Cordelia, very French like me and being pregnant helps," Lauren replied in a clipped tone, and readjusted her seat position slightly, forcing herself to the very end of the sofa.

"I'm not allowed to be pregnant," Cordelia sighed, pouring out another green tea for her only.

"Sorry Rosie, what were you going to say to me and Lauren?" Irena intervened sensing something odd.

"I think you should both advise Annabella to take care in Africa, especially with vested Chinese interest. PRC is very sensitive to external meddling, as they see it, in Chinese affairs which affect security of mineral production."

Lauren nodded. She knew Rosie well enough to detect a clear red light warning message, and neither Annabella nor Irena, whilst being highly idealistic and committed professionals, were not sufficiently worldly wise to understand fully the implications of Rosie's statement ... another reason to talk to Annabella very soon.

Cordelia had now turned to Rosie and ran her fingers through Rosie's long and thick black hair. "You have marvellous hair and skin too Rosie. Tell me the secrets of Chinese women and their tricks for looking gorgeous like you. Is it all down to the green tea you drink?" She poured out her fourth cup and downed it in one go.

Rosie, being Rosie, unfazed and afraid of nobody or consequences, also liked to play games. "Cordelia, we Chinese women don't just drink green tea, we wash our hair in it all the time, lots of anti-oxidants repair damaged body tissue. Green tea also help to stay slim and young. And my big secret? I grind up pearls into powder, lots of amino acids and minerals for good complexion. Your pearls would be very tempting," Rosie added, fingering Cordelia's giant pearl necklace gently, lightly touching her neck and looking down at her ample breasts. "Finally, Chinese women all love lots of massage, get energy

180

flowing evenly through body, keeps illness and tired muscles at bay," as she gently squeezed Cordelia's thigh.

Cordelia began to appear quite flushed. "Goodness me, I love a good massage. I don't think I've had one for absolutely ages. Actually Rosie, I have a lovely set of Chinese prints I would love to show you, they have been in the family for three hundred years, as well as a trio of genuine Ming vases. Would you like to see them whilst Amélie and her friends talk more boring business? I can see you have an eye for art and nice things. I hate business, sorry everyone, I only know about painting."

"Yes, why not," Rosie replied, "I never miss a chance to look over nice things. Amélie would that be alright with you?"

"Of course Rosie, I'd forgotten about the Chinese art collection at the other end of the house. Please feel free. If we're not here when you get back, Cordelia can see you back to your room. I suspect we may have to retire earlier, I'm feeling very tired and I can see Lauren is too."

"Me too," Irena said quickly. "The jet lag again, I never get used to it ..."

Cordelia got up and held out her hand for Rosie and led her happily out of the room, chatting merrily, their stilettos clicking and clacking in unison along the wooden floor down the corridor.

Irena turned to Amélie. "As a clinical psychologist, I recognise certain aspects of Cordelia's behaviour are not quite ... normal?"

"Yes, she's fucking bonkers and an embarrassing pain in the ass in civilised company. Sorry Irena, please forgive the language, but sadly, Cordelia is one blind spot that Rufus doesn't see or want to see, and I simply don't know what to do with her."

Lauren laughed. "She's obviously cooped up too long all day on her own with only her wildest fantasies to keep her company!"

Irena and Amélie joined in, understanding exactly the nuances implied, but then Irena frowned and whispered quietly as they all moved their chairs closer together. "I believe there's more to the problem, Amélie. Am I right? What did Cordelia mean when she said she wasn't allowed to get pregnant?"

"Okay, too much brain power around this coffee table to fool anyone," Amélie replied with a sigh. "Gather round. Please keep this confidential, but she's driving me mad. Many aristocratic families have a long history of, let's say, close inter-breeding amongst a relatively small base of people and families. Cousins marrying, all that sort of thing … often the reason eccentrics reared their heads over time, but such families usually had the means and money to keep such issues quiet. Sadly, Cordelia is … how can I put it? … more extreme on that spectrum. Her mother, Cymbeline, was Rufus's aunt."

Lauren immediately spoke. "Hell, Amélie. You mean his father and his father's sister were …?"

"Yes, from childhood. Eventually the sister had to be put into an asylum and died there. Rufus and his elder brother Algernon, who incidentally also sadly died ten years ago in a farm accident here on the estate and was a big driver of the estate modernisation, were normal. Their mother, the last Lady Westvale died in childbirth, Rufus was only eight. His father buried his considerable grief in work and the estate right up to his own death a year ago when Rufus inherited the Earldom. His father never remarried, but had lots of Italian mistresses I understand; spent a lot of time in his later years in Tuscany."

"Hence all the Italian wine in the cellar?" Lauren added.

"Of course. Anyway, since a child, Cordelia was cosseted away and privately educated at home here, never mixed with kids her own age. The family were terrified she would be like her mother, a crazy nymphomaniac. Money of course was no object to maintain that status quo. She has a large trust allowance, her own suite, no responsibilities and her artistic whims were indulged. She became more withdrawn and socially peculiar and when she was sixteen her father had her privately sterilised."

"Oh my word, Amélie. But you've allowed Rosie to go off with her on her own?" Lauren sounded, her voice wavering with concern.

"Lauren, you and I know Rosie is very capable of looking after herself, and will be the last person to be intimidated by Cordelia's strangeness. And it's good for her to be with other adults for a change."

"I agree," Irena said softly. "To be honest, I'd strongly suspected Cordelia's problem the minute I saw her. Incest is one of the specialities of my private clinic and I did part of my doctorate in such cases, involving schizophrenia. Amélie, I believe I could help Cordelia, but she would need to spend some residential time down at my London clinic. I can't change the genetics, but our special therapy and counselling programme has worked well to slowly orientate cases like her to an acceptable semblance of social normality and independent living. Cordelia is highly intelligent and artistic; we have a good basis for working. Would you like me to speak quietly and confidentially to Rufus? I'm used to dealing with these family situations."

"Would you Irena?" Amélie replied, a distinct look of relief flooding across her face. "Your proposal sounds excellent, a lifeline not just for Cordelia but for me ... I'm really struggling to cope with her, and Rufus effectively washes his hands. I haven't the patience, even more so as the babies approach. She's the only wedge driving between me and him."

"Absolutely, call it a done deal, and because her situation would fit into our funded research programme with UCL, then the charge would be nominal. I'll speak to him before Peter and I go in the morning."

"Excellent. One final tea, then I'm afraid I have to retire," Amélie said, with nods all round. "Lauren, tomorrow you and I will do a tour of the wind farm with the delectable Giles, which I can see instantly by that twitch in your leg you're dying to do and you will be able to look at the special substation I designed."

They laughed, relaxed, and began to finish off the fresh pot of green tea. Lauren stared aimlessly at the thirty year old painting of the former Lord and Lady Westvale on the wall, not so convinced of Amélie's logic to send off Cordelia alone with Rosie. But she could only keep that concern to herself, although by the occasional look and comment from astute Amélie, she was increasingly convinced that Amélie knew about her own feelings and proclivities, especially about Rosie. The time was edging nearer for a heart to heart confessional with her best friend, although perhaps the best tactic was to keep Amélie guessing. In fact, the more she thought about it the more rational the logic was in doing the latter.

<><>

Lauren lay snuggled inside her old and very comforting four poster bed, the bedside light low, having devoured two more chapters of Lady Chatterley's Lover, her mind racing around with events of the day. The room was still warm, the thick solid walls offering excellent insulation, and she had put on only her short but comfortable blue chemise rather than her flannel pyjamas, not wanting to feel constrained. She needed to wind down having spent the previous half hour gazing through the long window which opened out onto the illuminated lake, the fountain still going quietly in the background. She couldn't get over the inconceivable return of Rosie, although guilt remained … Why oh why hadn't she made more effort? Of course one reason was that Mila had vehemently put her off, insisting Rosie didn't want to contact anyone whilst confined to a wheelchair. Was that actually true in the end?

A noise caught her attention, a quiet knocking. She looked up and realised someone was tapping at the door, and then the handle began to slowly turn. Shit … who was it? Why the fuck hadn't she locked the door, another stupid phase of forgetfulness. The thought of Peter outside made her shiver as she felt for something to grab, absolutely nothing, when a smiling face peered in through the opening. The long black hair made her heart calm down … thank goodness … but why was she creeping around? Rosie put her fingers to her lips and came in, closing the door quietly behind her, and walked over towards the bed stealthily.

"Don't want to wake anyone up Lauren," she whispered. "You like new Calvin Klein flannel pyjamas? It's so good again to wear nice clothes. I've really missed that."

"Yes, I bet. They're great; I love the deep red check. They really suit you," Lauren answered softly, admiring again Rosie's svelte slim figure and shapely thighs. "But what are you doing here?"

"Thought you would like some company … budge up, I'm sure there's enough room for a little one under that enormous duvet."

"But Rosie, this isn't …"

185

But it was too late as Rosie, in a trice, unbuttoned her top, threw it off and dropped her bottoms, Lauren gazing wide-eyed at Rosie's white naked body and pert breasts and remembering underwear never was Rosie's strong point. Next moment she dived under the covers with her arms wrapped cosily around Lauren.

"I knew from your eyes, that you haven't had a hug for a long time, I mean real hug in bed. No sex Lauren, I understand, I just want to hold you close. It's been so long and in my darkest hours, and there were many I can tell you, stuck in wheelchair with Sergei pushing me around from lab to lab. I thought only of you, and future immediately felt much better and I was determined I would one day lie in bed with you again."

Lauren turned to face her. Rosie looked so lovely, it was like the heady days they spent together in Shanghai and Beijing were only yesterday ... and she was desperate for a loving hug again ... and she still loved Rosie like she did before, special, forbidden, fleeting but very real and tangible. She put her arms around Rosie and held her tight, before then allowing Rosie to slowly lift off the chemise over her head. Their lips and breasts met. It was Lauren's first long kiss since Philippe cleared off three months before for the Lena River.

"I thought you said no sex, Rosie," Lauren whispered and giggled.

"Ah exception prove rule, good and useful English saying. Just a little sex then, but first I want to feel belly. Gracious you have army of kung-fu apprentices in there, I can feel them kicking with excitement."

"Yes, like their mother. Be careful Rosie won't you."

"Not got strap-on. For you only very gentle fingers for rub, like this," as Lauren groaned quietly, eyes closed with the

186

pleasure of Rosie's slow and delicate intimate touch, quickly giving her the fastest orgasm she had experienced for many aeons. Rosie gently put her hands over Lauren's mouth to stifle the scream.

"My goodness Lauren, that was very quick. Let me hold you close. You shake a lot."

"Mmm … Rosie … as good as in Shanghai … I needed that, I love you."

"Hey, I love you too …"

"Rosie, does Mila know you're … better?"

Rosie laughed. "No, not yet, I want to surprise her in due course. It's not necessary at this moment. I'm sorry to hear about Philippe … maybe in due course he will be back home, I'm very sure."

"You know about Philippe?"

"Yes, I'm still with Chinese intelligence, I never dropped my links. An electronic wire came through via one of my high level Russian contacts, the guy who led me to Murmansk initially and North Korea connection. It was about new energy exploration deals going on in Novosibirsk. I did some digging and amazing … up popped Philippe and some of his associates on computer. Another Russian contact thought he had left his wife … I drew logical conclusion, Lauren, immediately. He think Vaag father, yes?"

"Shit Rosie, you're as good as Mila at this intelligence stuff. Yes, not so much left as quietly uncoupled for a while, and he'll damn well have to sit it out until they're born. He can't take it at present."

"I'm not quite as good as Mila on sleuth … she is number one … but am close. I understand your problem … Philippe will come around. And Mila? She still with long term girlfriend? I believe she now based in South of France. Nice?"

Lauren felt immediately forlorn. "No. Mila is sort of …"

"I'm sorry. I know Mila very well remember for many years and she saved my life finishing off shit Vaag, I will always owe her. But Mila never do half measures. I assume she is on rampage again with sex?"

Lauren smiled then sighed. Rosie had an interestingly direct way with words, the bullshit carefully lost in translation.

"That sigh says enough Lauren, hey perhaps I am now in with chance with you," Rosie announced in a loud giggle.

"Maybe, Rosie," Lauren replied, holding her closer, when she noticed Rosie frown, then put her fingers to her lips.

They both heard it. A rustling near the window, behind the large velvet drapes. Mice? Suddenly the curtain opened wide and a man leapt inside through the opened window. Lauren sat bolt upright, transfixed at the sight before realising she and Rosie were lying naked together, and pulled up the duvet from half-way down the bed, wrapping it around both of them. The man was no older than his mid twenties, very handsome, fashionable stubble, with thick, swept-back dark hair and a toned physique. The problem was … he was also stark naked, a long knife in one hand and holding a massive erection in the other. Lauren was quite speechless, petrified and unbelieving of such a sight, her eyes drawn to the appendage, but Rosie was very calm, her eyes steadily perusing the problem target. She felt Rosie's muscles stiffen and a comforting hand rub her thigh reassuringly under the duvet.

"Hey big boy?" Rosie said calmly. "You look like you've come for some action. Tell me what you want to do; maybe we can accommodate that dick of yours."

Lauren looked alarmed at Rosie but saw her gaze, steely and unnerved, exactly like when Rosie stared out the terrorist about to kill her in Beijing, before instantly blowing his brains out.

Shit, she thought, another Mila moment. Why oh why does this follow me around … especially right now in Amélie's bed.

The man smiled. Then Lauren realised. That look, those eyes, the stare and the long face … they had just left the female version an hour before. Oh my God, he must have escaped. Cordelia's brother, Simon, the crazy rapist or worse by the sound and look of him. Rosie must also have guessed, the likeness was such a close match … but Rosie didn't know about Simon.

"Actually ladies," the man said in a slow and very proper English accent exactly like Cordelia. He began dragging in a riding whip from the bay window. "I'm just in the mood for a threesome, not had one for a while. Blondie, drop that duvet and pull it down please, or I'll cut that expanding belly of yours open from end to end. I want to see the full package first. Do it," he hissed.

Lauren went white and let go of the duvet edge as Rosie pulled it down off them. Lauren shivered, her complete nakedness on show.

"Like what you see then? Does your sister know you're here gorgeous?" Lauren looked. Rosie had guessed too.

"You know she does Chinese whore. You've fucked her all night, and I'm going to do exactly the same to you in return. Then I'll decide whether to cut both your bellies open, I like to do that, and my sister likes me to do it too, but," he yawned, "it all depends how good a fuck you are Blondie."

"In that case, I think you should warm up on me first, I'm a Chinese whore who loves whips big boy and I've got lots of room for you."

Rosie swung her legs out of the bed and slowly stood up as he gazed over her body, his erection hard and horizontal.

"I rather like that idea, Chinese. Come to me slowly. And you Blondie, not a move or this knife heads straight between the eyes. You watch first. Then it's your turn."

Lauren gazed, petrified of what all this would be doing to her babies, as Rosie moved sexily towards him, her hips swaying, looking like an expert practising from a Chinese sex manual. She reached him as he lowered his arms still holding the knife, and held him close, gazing into his eyes. He was mesmerised, but that was always the irresistible Eastern allure of Rosie, for men or women. She reached around his bare back as he tried to guide himself into her, gripping the tops of each arm. Lauren suddenly heard two sharp cracks immediate and fast like a blur. He screamed out, piercing and agonised. The knife clattered down onto the wooden floor. His legs buckled with the pain and he fell clumsily to his knees, his face contorted in agony.

"Sorry big boy, no more wanking for a while I'm afraid," Rosie muttered and hit him hard in the side of the face. "Fucking crazy amateur." He fell prostrate onto the floor unconscious.

"Lauren, quickly, someone will be knocking shortly. He'll wake up in next few minutes, I give measured blow and no damage to beautiful face, only dislocated joints in each shoulder. Painful and slow recovery though, like double sports injury. Shame really, big boy would have been good fuck. Pass me that whip whilst I tie his hands and ankles. Throw me my pyjamas and spare pink dressing gown hanging up. Put your chemise and dressing gown on, switch on kettle and get cups like you make two coffees, and then we wait."

In a moment they had their nightwear and dressing gowns on. Rosie cut pieces off the leather whip tails and bound his hands and feet, then dragged him towards the wall, pushing his back against it. He was coming round, groggy and moaning pitifully. She wrapped a large towel around him so he looked almost respectable. Lauren's heart was still pounding as she sipped a glass of water … my God, what if Rosie hadn't been there? It appears, she mused, that Cordelia had likely been colluding with her brother to facilitate his escape, probably bribing someone at the asylum. They were both as deranged as each other, but he was doubly dangerous.

Within the next few minutes, on cue, there was a loud knocking at the door. She heard the stentorian voice of Rufus and the door knob rattling. "Lauren, are you alright? We heard banging noises, open the door Lauren please or William and I will break it open."

Rosie nodded to the door, putting boiling water into the tea cups. Lauren tentatively opened it wide to see Rufus and William standing there with alarmed expressions and Amélie with Sophie behind. Irena and Peter were blearily opening their bedroom door and peering out to see what the commotion was about.

Rufus immediately stepped in, noting that Lauren looked shaken but seemed unharmed, then spotted Rosie, kneeling next to the man, holding the knife.

"Very sorry Rufus. Lauren and I were just having night cap and chat when he entered from window waving knife and willy at us, looking like dirty old Chinese man, but without mackintosh." She pointed to the open window as they all gazed incredulous. "Ladder, I think. I'm afraid I had to deal with him immediately, security training as you know instinctive especially with knives, but he will soon recover Rufus, not badly hurt although he will be in pain now. Is he relative?"

Rufus looked woefully at Amélie. "Fuck, Amélie. How the hell did he escape, and get in here? Jesus Christ. It's Simon.

He's supposed to be locked up in a secure institution; God knows how he got out."

"Ahh, Simon?" Rosie replied. "I assume he is brother of Cordelia?"

"Yes, but he is not very well, not well at all. Lauren, I'm so sorry you had to witness all this. Are you sure you're alright?" Rufus continued, staring disconsolately down at his young half-brother, bound and groaning on the floor."

Amélie went up to Lauren and hugged her hard. "Oh Lauren ... how could that bastard Simon do this ..."

"Hey no harm done all of you, I'm fine. I've got pretty battle hardened over the last few years," Lauren replied, smiling and feeling a huge relief. "And I can feel the football team kicking; I think they enjoyed the match too." They all laughed, tension dissipating and smiles all round, except for Simon.

Rufus turned to William and Peter. "Can you both help me get Simon downstairs and into the study? I'll call Bowderdales. I expect they're looking for him already."

"Rufus?" Lauren said, looking at Amélie. "Something Simon said about Cordelia; I think she knows and somehow helped him, possibly using an insider."

"Bloody hell. Amélie, what are we going to do with both of them?" He stood there with his head in his hands, completely flummoxed. Simon was now standing, grimacing in a lot of pain, silent and sullen. William and Peter took him gently by the arms and began to lead him downstairs carefully. Suddenly he turned and muttered back. "Damned Chinese woman Rufus, she's evil. She's fucked everyone in the house even Cordelia. She and Blondie were in bed together, I just wanted to join in the fun ... Chinese bitch."

Amélie, stone-faced, watched Lauren carefully, who used every effort in her body to appear dismissive. Rosie was her normal unreadable and inscrutable self. Rufus turned to Lauren, Rosie and Amélie, as Simon was led down the stairs. "Now you can see the problem, constant delusional sexual rantings and uncontrollable voyeurism, which is exactly why he needs to stay locked up."

Irena suddenly walked in. She had gone quietly down to talk to Cordelia and corroborated Lauren's suspicions. "Rufus, I've given Cordelia a sedative. She was in tears; the reality of what she'd facilitated had finally hit her. It's complicated of course, especially with Simon. I'll walk with you to the study. I have a solution if you want me to try, but I will need them both down in London. I have secure accommodation for Simon, in fact very secure."

"Irena, yes please," Amélie said, with Lauren nodding. "Rufus, what do you think?"

Rufus smiled at Irena and held Amélie's hand. He knew how trying this issue was becoming for her and their relationship. Bold moves were needed. "I agree, excellent suggestion, we've tried everything else. Money is no object Irena. I know from Lauren how successful your treatment methods have been proving. We'll agree arrangements before you go at lunchtime. Now, I'll just go and wait for the men in white coats as it were. I can see Simon will need some hospital treatment, but thank you Rosie. Your prompt action saved Lauren and the rest of us from potentially a lot worse. Everyone back to bed please, rumpus is over, an order from the Earl of the house!"

They all laughed. "I think we can finally have nightcap, Lauren. Amélie you want to join us?" Rosie said. "Then I head to bed too. Enough excitement, I think, for one day."

Amélie tired out, nodded and smiled back. She had suspected but now knew for sure, but it didn't matter and never had. In fact, if she'd thought harder she'd known for a very long time.

Lauren knew she knew, but had no idea for how long or why. She felt quite relieved. They all chatted for a further twenty minutes.

As Amélie eventually followed Rosie out of the door, she turned slowly back to Lauren, vigorously fluffing out her pillows. A good night's sleep was desperately needed.

"I was right wasn't I?" she said with an Amélie smirk.

Lauren looked up and smiled. "Of course you were," not knowing or caring at all what Amélie was referring to.

Chapter Fourteen

Sitting quietly on a smooth rock, the unexpected sight of different coloured graffiti of every shape and size imaginable stretching the entire length of the sea wall sickened and surprised her. Jaffa was such a lovely old town, an ancient port city steeped with history and culture. Why had the Israelis allowed such desecration and not made any attempt to clean up the mess?

Mid morning and the water was quite calm. The waves lapped gently against the multitude of rocks and pebbles revealing a small sandy area carved out along the small strip of beach. They had walked down from the hotel briefly so that Lauren could clarify final thoughts, in the fresh sea air, about the lunch time partner sign up ceremony at a government building in the centre of Tel Aviv. A car was coming to pick her up at noon.

"You need to study the history of this place," Naomi Leibstein now transformed into Aunt Letty, said softly. "Especially, all that has happened since the early 1950s with the mix of inhabitants. Then you will understand. I can see that such vandalism disturbs you, but it is part of a safety valve to keep local tensions from flaring. The demographics of Jaffa are a population of around fifty thousand people, two thirds of whom are Jewish and a third Arab."

They had sauntered to the beach through a beautiful series of well-kept gardens interspersed with old Arab buildings, passing by a small Islamic museum. She saw a mosque, the minaret prominent amongst the buildings behind and began to reflect. There were many complications to the politics of working with Israel, especially given the sensitivities of the entire nuclear agenda from bombs to power across the Middle East and Iran. Did she need this collaboration for Cassini?

Letty cut in. "My advice is you must ensure there is an easy and transparent get-out clause before you sign off. If future cooperation was not to your liking for any reason then you will be able to cut and run."

Lauren nodded, fiddling in her bag for the draft summary and her iPad to which Sonja had emailed a pdf of the final full agreement. She would never allow Cassini to be held hostage or be forced to act as a pawn between competing European, Israeli, American and Arab interests. They looked through both files. Quickly, Lauren found the relevant chapter heading and supporting paragraphs. Sonja had annotated the final draft with extensive notes stating that she had indeed inserted a break clause after Lauren's comments of concern. The drafting was legally perfect. Cassini could cancel the partnership anytime without notice, reason or penalty. Sonja's attention to detail was exemplary; Lauren remembering her concern was triggered by a throwaway remark from Mila in the Y&Y before she left. She turned to Naomi. "Good. It's done. I'm satisfied in principle with the rest too."

"I agree Lauren. The opportunity to accelerate your own research given the technical trials using new magnetic materials being tested at Weizmann is significant, so worth attempting. Out of the three organisations, only Cassini has the practical wherewithal though to commercialise. They think they have, but JETR is well behind comparatively. On the plane, I digested three research papers from JETR and Weizmann; the Cyclops work is definitely, in my opinion, ahead. You have an excellent research head there."

"Yes, that's Dr Juliette Curwen, my first senior appointment and worth her weight in gold neutrons. Gosh Letty," Lauren exclaimed pointing to the road. "I can see her and Mila up there, walking along the seawall. They should be with us shortly."

Letty tapped her arm gently. "Something you should know quickly. Mila, as she has a bad habit of doing, has overreached a little and linked herself into a high octane network of extreme right wing politicians. They may be using her Lauren. I think, once you sign up, it may be wise to reflect on Mila's role here in Israel."

"How do you know all this?" Lauren asked, mystified and surprised that Letty should be able to track Mila of all people.

"Trust me. I have a very sophisticated network of informants, contacts and high level officials here. Mila has not been around for some time. Allegiances change. I spend half of each year in Israel and keep on top of the political hue. I have another disguise for that. In fact this is my disguise! Okay Lauren, I know how sharp Mila is but I think I can fool her."

"You look amazing Letty."

"Introduce me innocuously and then I'll slope off back to the hotel and go for a walk into town. I have a few visits to make. If there is anything else I dig up important you'll get a text."

"Okay, done … I'm used to this. Will you be alright for the rest of the day?"

Letty giggled mischievously. "I shall end up having a long lunch with Ephraim, an old flame from University days. He's getting a bit of an ancient crock now, but still has that twinkle in his eye … like me! I'll see you for dinner later."

<> <>

Juliette and Mila were now about thirty metres away and in animated discussion as Lauren waved. Mila waved back madly. Lauren could see Mila had a spring back in her step, curious about the body language. Thank goodness they weren't holding hands, but their proximity and the way they were looking at each other said enough. Lauren felt a wave of deep unease and irritation welling up again ... and it wasn't only jealousy. She had already formulated something in her head, an action to relay when she got the first opportunity.

Mila came bounding forward looking even trimmer, dressed in a smart, knee-length green Prada business skirt and jacket over a beautiful white blouse, her blonde hair cropped short and spiky again. Juliette brand and style matched Mila equally but in black and pale crème. They were professionally stunning in appearances. Each gave Lauren a generous hug, and then Mila stood back admiring and complimenting her newly tailored, smart maternity dress and jacket made by the fashion school again. They were now using Lauren as a maternity model for the best student designers, which she was very happy with supporting having guest-lectured a couple of classes on entrepreneurship.

"Mila and Juliette, can I introduce you to my Aunt Letty who flew with me for a short break here whilst we work. She's been staying a few days back home ... we've been having a lovely family catch-up. Letty is seeing some old friends here."

Letty shook hands with Mila and Juliette in turn, then having made a few banal comments about the weather picked her walking stick up off the rock and said her goodbyes, walking slowly back towards the town in another direction from the hotel.

Lauren was trying to stay comfortable and normal, and observed Mila instinctively doing her usual careful and concise intelligence assessment on Letty, her brain obviously whirring around at speed with an array of notions. Letty was cleverly disguised but she looked Jewish, certainly she would to Mila, but then the Hind family had a Jewish line running through her father's side anyway and Mila knew that.

Mila laughed and joked about their stay so far in Israel, relaying antics which she and Juliette had been getting up to in the hotel, all harmless fun, but they were obviously having a good time together. Juliette had transformed back to her sharp and uncompromising self since the unfortunate drunken escapade in the nightclub. Mila appeared unperturbed about Letty and Lauren breathed a sigh of relief. They walked to a quiet cafe a little further down the sea front and ordered tea and some snacks, sitting privately in the far corner around a large table.

"You've each done a fantastic job along with Sonja to get Cassini to this stage. I just want to thank you both warmly, to be reflected of course in end of year bonuses and a raise in your Luddite allowances ... I'm saving mine until a return to body normal!"

They all relaxed and chatted aimlessly, whilst the drinks and some mid-morning local Arab delicacies were brought.

"Now," Lauren continued. "Having read through the complete draft and summaries, I'm happy with what we're signing up to, and I've had a confirmatory chat with the legal people and Sonja too earlier. I just wanted this briefing to give us all a final chance to air any issues or concerns which may still be on your minds."

Mila ran through some of the political challenges, which she felt confident to handle, and confirmed that Weizmann was seconding Ernesto, with his new fusion team, as their lead partner collaborators. Pleasingly, this was exactly what Lauren wanted. Although, Mila added, it came with a few minor internal deals and promises which she didn't feel it necessary to elaborate on.

Lauren's mind ran back to Letty's warning, but she said nothing.

Juliette had concerns about ensuring that certain lines of research within Cyclops needed to lie outside of any sharing agreements with either JETR or Weizmann. But Lauren was already ahead with full reassurances, especially as the work referred to was the development area she would be leading on herself and be subject to the highest security protocols between her and Juliette from now on.

Satisfied that all was concluded, Lauren took the opportunity to outline her Cassini restructure. Juliette was ecstatic with the offer to become CEO of Cassini Research and especially with the raise in salary. Lauren then confirmed that Sonja and Johann would become joint CEOs of Cassini Operations.

Mila looked thoughtful and distant before finally saying. "So where do I fit into your plans Lauren? Operations or Research?"

"Neither," Lauren replied. "You, Seb and your security operatives remain outside of mainstream, an ethereal floater, ghostly and apparition-like as you always prefer, but reporting directly to me only. I thought you'd like that?"

"Of course she does, Lauren," Juliette chipped in patting Mila's hand. "Perpetuating the air of mystery and surprise is exactly you Mila, isn't it?"

Mila laughed her usual belly chortle. "Of course, that's fine Lauren."

But Lauren sensed Mila's response was a little forced and that something deep inside her was amiss, probably around Sonja. "Okay, so let's head back to the hotel. By the time we arrive the car should be waiting, and then I hope we can meet the dignitaries and enjoy lunch. Oh gosh," she groaned, rubbing her tummy. "The mention of lunch and I get a triple kicking, I think they're definitely taking after me."

Mila smiled. "That's for sure ... and Philippe as well of course," she said squeezing Lauren's hand gently. "Oh, and before I forget, there is likely to be a special guest at this reception. The Israeli Prime Minister was insistent on being there. He is keen to meet you personally Lauren, so that's all fixed up ... same table, next to you."

"My word Mila, you have been politically busy. I wish you'd warned me, I would have chosen a different ..."

"No need, you look stunning Lauren. But be careful with the jokes, he's not a very humorous man. Cost me a bit setting that up but no worries. It will help you a lot."

Juliette paid the bill and they set off back through the garden, chatting and enjoying the unseasonal warmth and the sun. The temperature was edging towards twenty degrees.

As they passed a large chemist's shop, Juliette suddenly grabbed Mila's arm. "Those sunglasses, there in the window with the large black frames. I just fancy them, mine are horrible. I'm just going to try them on, won't be a minute."

Mila and Lauren stood outside under the shade of the awning, as Mila passed her a bottle of water from her bag to drink. "Nice try Lauren, and I have no problem you feeling you needed to do it."

"Sorry?" Lauren stopped drinking and looked directly into Mila's eyes. She was smirking from ear to ear.

"Aunt Letty, aka Naomi Leibstein. Shit Lauren, sometimes you underestimate me terribly. Don't worry I won't tell a soul. So why is she here? She's good, highly respected, with a huge amount of knowledge on Israel and your sector. I have to say, her disguise was first rate too, but you know me ... disguises are my super-speciality remember."

Lauren certainly remembered. How could she ever have forgotten that fateful night with Luis followed by Mila's covert party video of her naked when they first met in Palermo? She was thrown, as always, by some unexpected Mila effect.

"Damn it Mila, I wasn't trying to undermine you. I just wanted some totally objective assessment of this deal on all fronts, there's a lot at stake. What the fuck do I know about Israel?"

"I know, I understand that totally and what the fuck do I know about nuclear?"

They laughed and the frosty mistrust dissipated. Mila continued. "And has Letty provided you with what you were looking for?"

"I don't honestly know what I was looking for, but she's been hugely helpful especially on the nuclear aspects."

"Good. But remember Lauren. In this business everyone has an angle, nobody does anything for nothing. I'm not talking about money and that includes Aunt Letty."

"Okay Mila, knuckles rapped firmly again. Now what's really irking you? I could tell in that cafe you were edgy, especially when I brought up Sonja's promotion. Listen, I'm not taking any sides. She's brilliant, and it will be good for the company and me ... and Sonja."

"I agree wholeheartedly, I'm really pleased for her. I think it's a super decision and prescient."

"Prescient?"

"You don't know do you, but then nobody does, except me of course. Sonja and Johann were married secretly last week. I wish them well though."

"Shit Mila."

"Look, I'm happy with Juliette for the moment; we get on well, it fills a gap, as ever. So give it to me straight Lauren, what is it you actually want to tell me?"

Lauren looked firmly into Mila's eyes. "I think you should take a bit of a sabbatical … six months … all the security is fine under Seb presently … give you a chance to sort out your own intelligence business as well."

"Okay."

"Okay? Is that all?"

"Yes, fine. But I want you to know, I still love you as much as ever. I'll be watching your back Lauren, whether you want me to or not and if you run into any danger, I'll be there immediately. Don't try and stop me … that's what I mean by okay."

Lauren was biting her lip; her insides were in turmoil … how could she do this? … The one person in the world who understood her totally, but that was why. They both knew that space between them, for a whole host of reasons, illogical, emotional, even nonsensical, had to happen.

Juliette came bounding out of the chemist's shop with her expensive pair of shades firmly on view. "So what do think? Hey, you two. You look like you've lost a five hundred euro note and found a shekel. We've got a mega signing shortly and hopefully a nice matching lunch, no time for the grumpies."

Mila laughed again. "We're fine Juliette, just chewing over a bit of nostalgia. Let's go guys, best heels forward, chests out and bellies in. Oops sorry Lauren … only joking. When I had my two kids I was the size of a house, and they were one at a time, I don't know how you do it. I thought I was fit!"

Lauren forced a smile, she had to cheer up. She'd made and taken her decision, life moves on as does business. "Yes, better get a move on. Big step forward for all of us."

Lauren looked across at Mila, enough had now been said.

"You've had children Mila? Gosh, where are they?" Juliette asked wide-eyed, looking quite shocked.

"Tell you another time Juliette," Mila replied, sanguine but calm. "But yes, been there and had the tee-shirt a very long era ago. Hey, there's the car waiting outside. Mmm ... a stretch limo ... now that is Israeli reception in style Lauren as befits your well deserved global reputation."

"I agree," Juliette added, linking one of Lauren's arms as Mila linked the other, both giggling. "You're flagging a bit; you need a helping hand from your trusty Executives."

"Thanks guys," Lauren cried, forcing herself back into CEO mode. "Hope there's a hairbrush and a mirror in that car."

"I'm sure he can wait five minutes while we do a quick freshen up," Mila replied.

"You betcha, girls."

<><>

They arrived just in time to be greeted by an entourage of bureaucrats and scientists from Israel, JETR and a few of Juliette's top researchers and engineers from Cyclops, all eager to become part of a new nuclear fusion community and lead the global race to commercial energy success. The Israeli Prime Minister bounded down the steps to greet Lauren, like a head of state. The whole atmosphere was low key in one sense but surreal in another. The only thing missing was a red carpet ... but this was Israel, and Letty had briefed and warned her extensively on what to expect, and especially on what to say.

Lauren glanced as the Prime Minister nodded briefly to Mila, and they exchanged a brief smile, then taking the lead, he guided Lauren into the building. A phalanx of heavy-helmeted and armed security stood very visible around the outside and on roof tops.

The rest of the ceremony, speeches and signing went quickly and smoothly to plan. Lauren and Juliette were led to a specially prepared area for photographs with the Prime Minister and other senior officials and scientists within the new partnership. She suddenly recognised her own press manager amongst the small coterie of journalists, and then unexpectedly spotted ... gosh ... it was Johann, standing in the corner smiling. What on earth was he doing here? There was obviously a greater desire than she had been led to believe by the Israelis for some managed publicity ... undoubtedly to serve some forthcoming political issue, remembering there was a US summit shortly on Palestine. She strained her mind back to some of the concerns which Letty had raised. She had to think laterally about how developments may be used, both in her favour but possibly against, depending on her global expansion interests. This deal had a lot of complications ... working with the People's Republic of China amazingly was relatively straightforward in comparison, but that linkage in itself could be a complication.

Holding a soft drink in the interlude before dinner, she began to amble across to Johann when Mila, who had been oddly absent during the main proceedings, suddenly sprang from nowhere next to him and whispered something in his ear. Then she turned to Lauren, waved and disappeared down a corridor.

"Johann, so lovely to see you ... but why are you here? I didn't think it was necessary, but actually now the way things have turned out, it's probably just as well."

"No, I understand Lauren, but once Sonja had briefed me fully on what was happening here, I decided to come and bring Zake … we need our own precise cover story for Cassini, not just a biased up Israeli version."

"Yes I agree, I didn't think fully, lesson learned."

"Actually we have to thank Mila. She managed to ensure, literally in twenty four hours, that Zake and I got the correct passes and authorisation."

"Yes … Mila has … lot's of connections here of some importance I realise. What did she say to you as I was walking over?"

"Oh, she was just wishing me and Sonja all the best … and no hard feelings, she isn't going to tear my head from my shoulders … thank goodness. Actually I have something I need to tell you about."

"I know too … congratulations to both of you … I'm sure you'll both be wonderfully happy, especially with the baby coming. Sorry Johann, I know about that as well, and it's great news. Hey, I have to say that don't I," she added patting her tummy.

"Thanks Lauren. Sonja and I really appreciate the support and everything you've done for us … we'll make sure Cassini heads for even greater heights."

"I hope so," Lauren replied with a grin, thinking of future dividends. "Now, I insist that you join our table for dinner with Juliette and Mila.

But Mila had gone and didn't return … either to the event or to Cassini.

Chapter Fifteen

T he weekend couldn't have come fast enough. This
would be one of the most significant times in her life
when she would witness her own daughter marrying.
Fresh and white woolly clouds scudded slowly across the blue
sky, a good omen. At least in Brussels it was going to be a
pleasant day and she expected the same when she got to Nice.

She had heard nothing from Philippe since learning he
would be attending the wedding. She knew he was busy and
absorbed with setting up the new Russian fracking arm of
Rubidium, but was dismayed that her own emails and texts had
been ignored again. Perhaps it had been a mistake to say she
was looking forward to seeing him. In principle she still did, but
she was beginning to tire of the perpetual tension and peculiar
avoidance of a grown-up discussion on their future together.
Walking on egg shells was becoming tediously irksome. Amélie
had been blunt and forthright in her assessment and advice.
She knew Philippe well and understood better than most the
good times and bad times of any relationship. But Amélie, who
shared her frustration, had seriously suggested that if Philippe
wasn't willing to discuss the situation in the same way that
Rufus had done, even agreeing to support Amélie
unconditionally, then maybe it was time to up-sticks and find
love elsewhere.

"You're a highly attractive and desirable woman with so
much to offer the right man," Amélie had insisted. "Don't

remain tied to a loser, if Philippe turns out to be a loser, because none of your predicament is your fault. Everything you did was to protect or help him and his daughter in those terrible hours in Murmansk."

Lauren reluctantly conceded that Amélie had a reasonable perspective, but the point of inflexion would still remain birth time ... and until then she had enough to worry about, not just with her own condition but especially the changing business of Cassini. She was so relieved to be financially independent. Which was why she was pleased to enjoy a great weekend with the family and forget her personal problems. It wasn't every day she would soon acquire a son-in-law twenty years older than herself. She giggled outright thinking of the irrepressible DG. Lauren had come to terms with the Charlotte and DG age difference factor a long time back and DG, despite his quirks, was a good, trustworthy and supportive man, and truly very, very wealthy ... She admired his new plans to wind down from the oil business and political front line in Washington and devote time to both his new family and wider global philanthropy.

She stared disconsolately at her suitcase. What else should she take? She was at least pleased with her 'mother of the bride' outfit she had picked up the day before, and carefully packed the dress in. And especially, she was enthralled with Yves Leguerre, the new young manager of Luddite, who had advised her of a range of specialist occasion dress creations by Aubrey Johnson, a new British fashion designer she had never heard of ... well not until she returned for a special fitting. Aubrey Johnson had flown in straight from London Fashion Week to measure up and approve the final tailoring of a beautifully soft and feminine knee-length floral print dress, with matching silk jacket and floppy hat in air force blue. Yves had arranged this opportunity specially, not just because of his immediate awareness of Lauren as a special client, but because Luddite could provide a unique dress to serve jointly as an occasion and maternity outfit. This area of retail design was Aubrey's specialism and as a former fellow design student with Yves, she was keen to develop the concept further. Astutely aware of the promotional value, Lauren had brought along Johann to manage the public relations. In the subsequent half an hour after happily trying on her new outfit, a deal had been done for Lauren to model Aubrey's new range at Luddite, in conjunction with a future big photoshoot and new editorial articles on Lauren and nuclear creativity, to be trailed in Paris Match, Vogue and Forbes.

A loud banging on the front door disturbed her reverie. She peered through the keyhole and flung it open with delight. Standing outside were Sonja, Helena and Eva, holding small presents all carefully wrapped.

"What are you three doing here? … Especially at the weekend, you should all be out clothes shopping!"

Eva immediately replied, smiling. "We've already been Lauren. There's a new exclusive gift shop opened next to Y&Y, so we've each bought a small wedding present for Charlotte and DG. Don't worry they're all light, I'm sure we can squeeze them into your weekend case. We weren't sure what to buy them, but they'll make nice additions around their new house … I'm assuming they're getting a new house?"

"That's so kind of you all, I know Charlotte will appreciate it, especially as the wedding is literally a very limited family affair with no fuss or friends," Lauren said cheerfully. "I had the same problem … What do you buy a man who has the money to purchase half of Belgium?" She held up a small gold framed oil painting. "I commissioned this from Gabriel Rousseau, a well known artist in Paris who has a style comparable to Van Goch. He painted it from a nice family photo of Charlotte, DG and the twins I took when Philippe and I were in Dallas. What do you think?"

"It looks beautiful. Charlotte can hang it up in a special place, what a great idea," Sonja said. "Now we all reckoned you would be struggling to pack, so we've come to help, and take a peep at your new dress that Johann keeps telling me about endlessly."

"Yes, and we have plenty of time," Helena added, "because Edward, Seb and Johann have gone to the football match in town, some boring world cup qualifier between Belgium and Brazil, and they intend celebrating in the pub afterwards."

"Err, you mean commiserating, I think Helena," Eva said with a laugh.

"Whatever, just an excuse for a boy's day out … so where's this exclusive dress then Lauren?" Helena replied. They peered into her suitcase and groaned with jealousy and admiration at the dress, jacket and accessories all carefully packed."

"Can't see the matching underwear?" Sonja commented, as they all giggled.

"Listen all of you, the size I'm getting, the smalls have to be well hidden these days, not displayed for all to laugh at! But I'm glad you like the dress … oh … and these are the shoes." She pulled up a pair of blue, patent leather, Jimmy Choo four-inch stiletto pumps, with a matching, dainty clutch bag. They all drew breath.

"Gosh, you will look lovely," Sonja continued. "I always thought only Mila wore Jimmy Choos and that you were a Christian Louboutin kind of girl?"

Lauren felt wistful at the mention of Mila. She hadn't heard from her since the departure into thin air from the Israel event.

"True, Sonja ... but these were irresistible and Mila always has excellent taste ... only ... actually I haven't heard from her, have you?" Lauren replied disconsolately.

Eva grabbed Helena and they headed for the kitchen to make some drinks.

"Yes, don't worry," Sonja replied. "She's fine and making good use of her sabbatical, doing what she loves best. She's in the Louisiana swamps with her new swat team head, Debbie, and training up some new recruits, all female of course, as a rapid global response unit when needed. Anja, Bernie and Emmylou are concentrating from the New York office on the growing lucrative computer hacking and data stealing market."

"So, she's keeping in touch with you?"

"Yes of course and with Juliette. I think Mila feels it's best if you and she maintain some space at the moment, but she sends her love. Don't worry Lauren, it's actually Mila who needs the space, from you, me, Juliette and the normal world ... that's how she gets ever since the Bosnian war, which permanently destroyed something inside of her. Occasionally she has to submerge herself in that closed macho world of special operatives, spies and subterfuge. It recharges her, she'll be fine, believe me ... and so will you."

"Thanks Sonja, I needed to hear that, I was feeling very miserable about what I said to Mila."

"Believe me Lauren, your instinct was spot-on, it was absolutely the right thing to do."

Eva and Helena returned with pots of steaming tea and coffee and some small cakes they had bought on the way. "Time for a break, then we finish the packing for you and get you to the airport on time Lauren," Eva said as they all nodded and recommended gossiping about the new blond hunk of a security guard who Seb had just recruited onto the main Cassini gate ...

<><>

An air of anxiety hung over the proceedings. No sign of Philippe. Lauren was sat in an anteroom in the beautiful neo-gothic Mairie of Nice, with Kat and Lexi chatting aimlessly about school, friends and then excitedly about moving to their new house in Nice which they had nice photographs of but had forgotten them, and Mom had borrowed Kat's iPad to take some last minute pictures of her wedding dress, so they couldn't show her either but insisted Mom would look very beautiful. The house was news to Lauren, obviously another surprise which Charlotte had been keeping.

"It's a huge big house on a hill and looks out over the sea Grandma," Kat explained. "Mom and DG call it a villa."

"Actually, looking at the outside of the villa and the rooms inside, I would say it was very like our ranch in Dallas, so we'll feel at home very quickly. At least that was what Orlando said," Lexi added, not wanting Kat to dominate all the conversation as she often tried to do.

"You'll miss Orlando and Marcie won't you, all that wonderful cooking?"

"Oh no Grandma," Lexi continued. "Orlando and Marcie are coming too. There's a small house for staff in the grounds, like at home."

"Really?" Lauren said, thinking about the usual snail-like speed of gaining non-EU French residency status for DG and Charlotte, plus Kat and Lexi, as well now as Marcie and Orlando, all US citizens. Then she realised. DG and Charlotte would be treated as preferential economic entrepreneurs, not only by bringing huge sums of money into the country but they would be setting up new businesses. Undoubtedly, DG had the best financial and tax advisers and also political contacts to effectively work the normally sclerotic and bureaucratic French system.

"It's all become quite complicated," Kat then said, with a serious expression. "Marcie's daughter is getting married to Howie, who is a plumber, and Delilah is also staying on because our house is going to be lived in by Hank, Mom's factory manager, who has six children, and the eldest is the same age as me and Lexi and they will look after the new family, instead of us."

"Gosh, everything back home has been happening very quickly."

"Yes," Lexi said solemnly, "And last week Mom took us to see Aunt Juliette, who we met at your wedding Grandma, and we met her children who are twins and much older than us, but we visited their International School in Nice, and we really loved it so we will be able to start next week, in the Juniors, and we can learn French too which will be so cool, but all the other lessons are in English thank goodness, especially science. There are other American children there too, our age, so we'll be able to make new friends really quickly. And they have much better classrooms than our old school in Dallas and so many computers, and even iPads in lessons Grandma. Isn't that great?"

"Really great, Lexi. I'm so pleased you're both so happy," Lauren replied, quietly flabbergasted at the speed of transition which her daughter had been masterminding … but then Charlotte was a chip off the old block, once her mind was set to get priorities sorted. She smiled, before feeling tense again, wondering where on earth Philippe had got to and what they were going to do if he didn't turn up. She dialled his mobile number … unobtainable as usual, frustration gathering pace in her head.

213

The end door suddenly opened. A very pretty woman in a light grey suit and pinned up black hair came through and walked confidently towards them. "Bonjour Lauren, we spoke on the phone. I am Oriane Leroux, organiser of today's wedding for your daughter. I see Kat and Lexi have been keeping you busy."

Lauren stood up and shook hands. "How nice to finally meet you Oriane, you have done a wonderful job here; the ambience, flowers and everything are lovely. But I'm worried that my husband isn't coming, and about the witness requirement."

"No problem, I have spoken to Charlotte and DG and they are happy if I act as the second witness with you. Now ..." Oriane said, looking at her watch. "Shall we all walk next door? The bride is finally ready and we must go very shortly. Girls, can you take a posy each from the table please."

Suddenly the door burst open again with a loud bang as everyone turned around, startled. In walked Philippe, red in the face and panting but at least dressed very smartly, as he always knew how, in a dark and expensive blue designer suit, which perfectly complimented Lauren's dress. How did he know? He rushed forward to Lauren and hugged her hard, all to her amazement, before she could blink or get a word in.

"Darling, I'm so sorry I'm late. The plane from Moscow was delayed with a snowstorm. Have I missed it all?"

She stepped back and looked at him, the first time for three months. He had put on weight, too much Russian stodgy food, and his head was no longer shaved. His hair had grown and was trimmed in a short and neat military style. But it was the dark beard, trimmed but very ample, which threw her. She had seen him with sexy stubble but never a full beard, although it suited him in a pleasing nineteenth century kind of way. He looked like an archetypal outdoors Russian oil man that she expected they would all look like.

"No," she replied, catching her breath. "Literally, the ceremony is about to start, just in time as usual. You look … mmm … well …"

He looked at her face carefully and then down to her bump, which, whilst prominent, was well styled into the dress. His mouth opened and his expression turned incredulous, as if he was confronting a raging tiger with a chocolate rifle, then instantly he reverted to standard Philippe mode. He composed himself and looked into her eyes. "You look so beautiful, I've missed you."

They kissed for a second, as Kat and Lexi whispered 'ahh …' in unison, and her heart fluttered stupidly like when they had gone on their first date in Palermo, and she began to immediately believe they were back together at last.

Oriane intervened with a cough. "I think we'd better go, the bride and groom will be getting anxious."

"Of course," Philippe said, pulling Lauren's arm into his and taking charge. "Come on girls, time to see Mom getting married!"

They walked inside and Lauren gasped seeing Charlotte looking so beautiful in her special Jan Lea maternity wedding dress. Charlotte's baby bump was the same size as Amélie's, but in the light-crème princess ball gown, her whole profile looked perfect and wonderful. Charlotte's hair had grown longer, and she had darkened the normally mousy blonde to a light brown, her hair flowing freely around her left shoulder with a matching flower pinned in. The organza wedding dress had a strapless neckline, complimented perfectly with elegantly beaded embroidery, and was finished off with a corset lace-up back and billowing skirt of cascading, silky, organza ruffles. Oriane gazed from bride to mother and back again, her mouth wide open seeing the huge similarity in looks and expression, and how gorgeous mother and daughter both were.

Lauren hugged Charlotte gently, careful not to disturb her dress, whispering into her ear how lovely she looked.

"So did you at your wedding," Charlotte whispered back with a grin. "I didn't have much time to get my dress made, but do you like it?"

"Beautiful, it really suits you, what a fabulous design."

DG, standing to his full six foot seven inches, was dressed very smartly in a dark grey suit, and began shaking Philippe's hand enthusiastically. Both immediately set up conversation, guffawing and joking over some issue or other, undoubtedly to do with the business, as usual. He then walked over and hugged Lauren. "Darn it Lauren, you look tremendous. I would never guess you had three little ones in there?"

"Strong muscles, DG. We nuclear people know how to conserve our energy and keep taut."

DG roared, his loud, booming voice echoing around the room, making an ancient vase nearby on a plinth shake precariously, as mayoral aides coming in stared back alarmed.

"Glad to see your humour is as sharp as ever, hey you'll be my mom-in-law in a minute. Best looking one I've ever had."

"You betcha, DG, and the last I hope," she replied, happy to be in his company again, a bear of a man who instantly made a woman feel safe and secure … then she thoughtfully pondered at Philippe, chatting to Charlotte and the twins who were becoming very excited.

Finally organised, they all followed Oriane who led them slowly down to the old historic room, where the marriage ceremony was swiftly and efficiently conducted, in style, by the Mayor of Nice. Rings and kisses were exchanged, documents duly signed and witnessed, and they were led out to the beautiful grounds for an array of family photographs in different poses and combinations, which Oriane had skilfully arranged and prepared. Finally, they returned inside to a small reception room for nibbles and a glass of expensive champagne which DG uncorked with gusto.

Whilst they all began chatting, Lauren watched Philippe again … she couldn't work out exactly what, but something wasn't quite as it should be. He was distracted. Certainly, he'd said nothing about how he had been getting on, or even asked how she was doing. He was almost avoiding her by engaging immediately in conversation with everyone else, even Oriane and her partner. Lauren thought perhaps that was to be expected, given the period of time they hadn't seen each other and the circumstances. They needed to return gradually to normality. Anyway, when they eventually headed to the hotel which DG had booked, he would have the opportunity to wind down and they could talk properly.

She was about to go and talk to Charlotte about the new villa when DG came over.

"Well Lauren, that whole episode went fine, mind you I've had plenty of practice at this I suppose."

"Me too DG," Lauren responded and they both smirked, knowingly.

"What I came over to tell you and Philippe, is there's a slight change of plan. Thanks to Oriane working closely with my advisers to cut through this French bureaucracy crap, you ain't going to that hotel anymore, because around now all our furniture will be moved in and sorted in our new house in Villefrance-sur-mer, just east of Nice. Lovely sea port, darn I think I said that name right … and Orlando and Marcie will be there cooking the best set of wedding breakfast rib-eyes you've ever tasted in your life. Heck, we've got fifteen bedrooms so you're staying with us. Charlotte and I have decided that's what we want to do for our honeymoon."

"Oh DG, that's fantastic," Lauren replied, throwing her arms around his neck and giving him a kiss. "Kat and Lexi told me you've bought a fantastic property which sounds just like the Half Moon Corral."

"Sure is splendid, not of course got the land around it for ranching, but I'm through with that … Charlotte's house back in Dallas we'll keep, but I sold my own place and got a good price on it, so thought I would just splash out for Charlotte and the twins. Heck, you can't take it with you can you?"

"You certainly can't."

"Yeh, new home cost me a few dollars, well I knocked the price down and finally got it for a bargain thirty-five million Euros. But the plot is around twenty thousand square metres, main villa about fifteen hundred and with a caretaker's lodge and adjoining guest house where you will both stay. Plus, there's a much better swimming pool. But the view? Doggone it, heck you can see all around the bay, and the sea, trees around everywhere up on the hill. Never lived in a place right on the coast like that in the US. I'm looking forward to it. And I've bought a little yacht too. Gotta fit in well with the locals, Charlotte says … so she's being refitted and will be ready for sailing after Easter."

DG suddenly pulled a thick wad of fifty Euro notes out of his pocket. "Hey, I'm just gonna pay the Mayor his wedding fee … guy wants cash so I'm giving him a bonus too for conducting us a real great ceremony. I just love all this French pomp and occasion … all got to me first at your wedding in Paris … have to admit I had me a great time that day too, Lauren."

218

Lauren smiled. She was intrigued with DG's formulating grand plan, the relocating to Europe in style to be immediately in pole place alongside the elite super-rich, oligarchs, celebrities and billionaire residents along that expensive strip between Nice and Monaco. She began to think about her own needs. Obviously she didn't have the resources or require the grandeur of such a huge residence, but perhaps she should look for somewhere east of Nice too rather than towards Cannes, and be near to Charlotte and the twins. Forthcoming Cassini dividends, according to Finance Director Herman, would be good in the summer especially for her as major shareholder. Cash and profits were flowing in from the mega deals with Beijing and the building of five advanced Xenostra 2 reactors in China. She had also bought out Philippe's Cassini shares. He needed to raise more money for himself and his new fracking venture, one of the few communications they had sensibly agreed on over the last twelve weeks. She could probably now afford a couple of million Euros for a new place ... and she adored the sea, and the weather in Nice was so much better than in Brussels. The area reminded her of Palermo. She thought fondly again of Annabella ... and then of course Mila. She grabbed a tissue. Too many raw emotions were rising all in one day.

A small voice chimed up behind her. "Don't cry Grandma, we're not in the tiniest bit sad, in fact Lexi and I are so happy now that Mom has got properly married, and DG is such fun. Lyell got married too last month ... to Charlene, on the reservation. She paints totem poles and sells them and wears freaky Indian clothes."

"Really? No. I'm very happy too Kat. Grown ups sometimes cry for lots of reasons."

Lexi walked up and interrupted. "Grandma, Oriane is talking to Mom about someone at the desk downstairs, who is looking urgently for Philippe."

Lauren raised her gaze across the room, spotting Philippe and DG in animated and humorous conversation with the Mayor and some of his male staff. Over by the door, Oriane was waving her arms and gesticulating, an unhappy look across her face, matched by Charlotte, who immediately went outside. Lauren began to walk across to follow when Oriane frantically beckoned her to the window. Suddenly the door at the end opened and a lone woman strode in and stood around quietly, clinically surveying and assessing the environment. She was tall, at least as tall as Lauren, mid to late thirties, long legged and powerfully built, dressed in tight blue designer jeans, long black boots and a fur jacket. Her face was rugged and hard but eerily attractive, long with high cheekbones and a concentrated stare which bore into any recipient of her intense gaze. But most compelling was her hair, a long red mane of thick ringlets, like Svet's locks on steroids. Immediately everyone else in the room turned around and gasped.

Lauren watched as DG's smiling expression turned to an immediate grimace and he mouthed something sharp and succinct to Philippe, the only part of which she could make out was fuck. It was Philippe who fascinated her most. His reaction was such that she wished she had her phone camera ready, just to capture that split second moment, from one second laughing and joking to the next, a paradoxical mix of sheer terror and joy in his eyes and his body. He obviously didn't know what to do, standing there transfixed, unlike the usually masterful Philippe where women were concerned.

Lauren's brain ran into overdrive. The woman slowly turned and stared hard and coldly at her. But Lauren's brain needed no more prompts, the logical conclusion of the unexpected guest had been reached in a microsecond … the she-wolf had arrived and no introductions would be needed.

A growl from DG prompted Philippe to finally move. He strode across, confidence renewed, to greet the woman with a polite handshake … she obviously expected something warmer. She exchanged words with him and then both of them walked across to Lauren, still standing and staring impassively at the two from the end window. Oriane beckoned to the twins and took them out of the next door … to show them the new toy museum at the end of the building. Charlotte walked over to her mother.

"Lauren," Philippe began. "Can I introduce you to Olga, I think I may have mentioned her, Igor's sister, she came on the Siberian trip. Olga has had to fly here specially, there seems to be an urgent business problem requiring …"

Both women ignored him, watching each other. Olga jumped in and held out her hand for Lauren to shake, which she didn't. "Hello Lauren, I am pleased to meet you, Philippe has told me much … you are nuclear researcher yes?" Olga spoke in English with a strong Russian accent, her green eyes flashing some sort of calculation as she glanced down unemotionally at Lauren's obvious state of pregnancy, then back up again, before staring coldly at Charlotte.

"Global company CEO and Chairman actually Olga … gas engineer aren't you? Oh of course, Philippe did mention your name. You got lost in the woods and the wolves came looking for you didn't they?" She sensed Philippe shuffling, the tell sign of his acute discomfort … excellent … now what the fuck was this slut doing here?

"I was never lost, I talk to wolves and I don't need men to look for me, ever," Olga replied with a defiant tone which quite amused Lauren, deciding that in another life, Olga may have been her sort of woman, reminding her of Mila in many ways. But the crazy mane of red hair, a blatant Philippe weakness for his daughter and former wife all rolled into one ... shit.

Olga continued. "I apologise for crashing the gates, but I come immediately from Novosibirsk, I need to warn Philippe about major catastrophe."

"Novosibirsk?" Lauren asked with feigned innocence.

Philippe cut in, sensing a confrontation looming between the two women which would get out of hand. "I'm sorry darling, forget to mention in the last email, Olga has joined the business team too ... well ... she is ... err ..."

"Chief Engineer. I lead fracking explorations team; already we drill hard in area with two small rigs, test results so far excellent. Philippe, we have no time for social chat ... you come back with me now, office ransacked." She pulled on his arm.

DG had finally walked over and decided to intervene, ignoring Philippe. "Whoa there Olga. I don't know why you're here but this is a social gathering, like for my wedding day, not a fucking Russian drilling site, and Philippe is my guest for the weekend."

"Don't worry DG," Lauren said sternly. "I suggest, Philippe, you take your Chief Engineer into the anteroom outside please and have a private discussion about your problems in Russia. Olga is obviously very concerned about your welfare, making such a long and special journey to get here; you need to talk to her ... *now*."

"Yes, of course darling, I agree. Follow me Olga. I hope your journey has been really necessary."

Olga glowered as they walked off together. She immediately began laying into him in harsh sounding and shrill Russian.

Once they were out of the room, Charlotte turned straight to DG. "Why on earth is that awful woman marching in here and disrupting everyone's day? Do you know?"

"Yes. Olga came on the hunting trip with her friend Nina and they did the cooking … must admit they rustled up a mean steak out in those forests. She's Igor's sister who is in partnership with Philippe running this new fracking venture out in the USSR, which I'm supposed to be sponsoring … I knew she was a gas engineer with an excellent track record, spends most of her time outdoors … but actually her being part of the team and now heading up a new drill pilot already … darn, that's news to me. I think little ol' Philippe has some more explaining to do. Lauren, sorry all this is going on … but you'll be pleased to know that them-there rib eyes are cooking nice and slow over at the new house … and I'm sure as heck looking forward to moving on and out of here soon."

"Thanks DG, as always you're a star. I do approve of my brand new son in law …" Lauren said, with a playful dig from her daughter, both grateful that some family normality remained. Fuck Philippe, at it again even on this special day.

But Charlotte looked hard at DG; no mention had been made to her about another woman on the Siberia trip … their honeymoon pillow talk already had an agenda booked, and it wasn't going to be sex … although, she pondered, it would be the first night married in their new house … okay perhaps she will be relenting this time.

She tapped Lauren on the arm and whispered. "The Russian Amazonian is coming back, with Philippe following hard at her ample rear."

Olga and Philippe, who was red in the face with a worried and aging expression which Lauren had last seen in their wild Sicilian helicopter flight fiasco, quickly rejoined them. DG motioned to Charlotte. "Philippe, you and I have some talking to do later. Charlotte and I and the twins will be out by the desk Lauren. Oriane has just phoned the limo to take us all over to the house. See you and Philippe down there."

She nodded, as they walked off.

"I'm so sorry darling," Philippe began. I'll have to return immediately with Olga back to Novosibirsk. There seems to be a serious problem, exactly what is going on I have no idea."

"But we have good idea, don't we dorogoy? Please fetch my coat and yours … it is with desk, flight to Moscow in one hour, I have booked private jet."

Philippe, appearing extremely uncomfortable, glanced tentatively at Lauren, who refused to look back at him, still staring at Olga, brazen, assured and commanding … and formidable … she suddenly felt sorry for him, he looked quite pathetic. He walked quickly out for the coats.

Olga continued. "Well Lauren, it has been nice meeting you, I'm so sorry to disrupt your plans with circumstance, but Philippe and I really have to get back to Russia. You are expectant shortly I see … you know Philippe … he always say to me that he hates children … and I hate them too. Obviously he cannot be the father. Good luck."

At that Olga marched to the door as Philippe walked back in, and grabbed her matching mink fur coat and put it straight on, leaving Lauren standing alone, speechless and red with rage. But she knew this was the moment to really stay rational and calm, she must not get upset with the bitch.

The moment she saw him stare momentarily at Olga, with that old tom-cat look he once reserved for her, she knew for certain … he was fucking her senseless and Olga had every air about her of being insatiable. He put on his own coat and walked over as Olga tripped down the stairs.

224

"It's not what you think Lauren, but I honestly do need to leave, I don't know what's going on over there but it doesn't sound good. I'm sorry for ruining our first weekend together." He tried to kiss her on the cheek.

"Fuck off Philippe and don't bother coming back, ever."

He stepped away clearly upset and confused at Lauren's reaction. "Hey, I'll email you immediately when I'm back ... and we can rearrange another weekend together if you like as soon as ..."

But she turned and walked briskly away, towards the door Olga had come in from. Out in the other hallway, she gazed outside. The sun was shining, the surroundings were busy and ... she didn't want to cry. Her instincts had been right and had primed her subconscious. She already knew in her heart that she and Philippe were never going to spend a night together again at DGs, she just knew it. And already she was rational and clear in her mind ... she would carry on with her own life, business and ... let events take their course. She had triplets on the way to worry about and soon loads of hard earned money coming in, and decided that she would definitely trigger that move down to Nice as soon as possible. She heard footsteps clattering up the stairs and saw Charlotte, struggling with her dress, coming towards her with a big smile. They quickly hugged for a good half minute. Lauren felt genuine warmth and real affection ripple through her from head to foot. She felt happy once more.

"Thanks Charlotte ... for just simply being here. I couldn't have a more beautiful and loving daughter. Thank you so much."

"Same goes for you too Lauren, best mom in the world. The twins and DG are waiting in the limousine. I can see Philippe has already left with that bitch … I'm sorry my scheming came to nought."

"Not your fault, sometimes these things are meant to be. I'm resolute about all this Charlotte … I have enough to concern myself with … and it will be up to him in the future. We'll just see how everything pans out, nothing hasty … yet! One thing though. How would you feel if I moved to a reasonable distance from your house? I've decided … I want to be near my family and I love this area of France."

Charlotte beamed and hugged her again. "That would be fantastic. Kat and Lexi would love it … and DG. Your family want to be near you too. You and I can start looking whenever you're ready."

"This weekend will suit me … nothing like getting on with implementation is there?"

"Absolutely agree … anyway, time for a nice meal, and I am dying to show you around the new pad … I'll miss the ranching but the rest of the place makes up for it."

"Great, let's go Charlotte … DG and the twins will be fretting down there."

Chapter Sixteen

Making their way in the old Bentley, up through the short winding drive, Lauren looked across at the expansive area of immaculate gardens beside her and then behind at the vast view of the coastline and the pretty port of Villefranche-sur-Mer, dotted with a myriad of boats and yachts. They had climbed about a hundred metres up on the side of a hill into which various individual large houses had been built. They passed a couple of smaller villas, not far down the road for sale, which Charlotte promised they would go and look at the next day. She could smell the sea air the moment they jumped out of the car, a slight coastal breeze blowing. Lots of shrubs and flowers were already beginning to bloom. The temperature had been nudging twenty degrees the whole week, so spring was arriving even earlier and faster. Everywhere, she noticed lovely trees of all kinds and sizes including small palms. A massive swimming pool was quietly bubbling away to their right.

Orlando was outside, just like in Dallas, trimming away at the hedges. He wandered across with a broad grin on his face, as DG waved and walked straight into the villa to check how things were, the twins skipping after him. Charlotte stayed back with Lauren.

"Well now, if it isn't Ms Lauren again, and how elegant you look if I may say. It's so lovely to see you once more. I hope you had a good journey up here. Marcie is just finishing off dinner, those steaks have been marinating all day, so they should be finger-licking delicious."

"Orlando, it's amazing to see you here too ... are you enjoying the new environment?"

"Gotta say, Ms Lauren, this place is fantastic and the fresh produce, vegetables and meat and fish you can get from that there port is just so wonderful. We've only been here a week, but already if feels like home. We miss Selena of course, but she's coming to visit next month ... and like you and Ms Charlotte, well, she's also in the family way. Congratulations."

"Thank you Orlando."

"DG tells me that Philippe has just been called away to Russia urgently on business, sorry to hear that Ms Lauren, but I'm sure you'll enjoy your stay here. We've got you all sorted out in the guest house, other side back of the building and the best view of the sea in the whole place. I'll just take your luggage right over there."

He took her cases and wheeled them off inside, as the chauffeur parked the Bentley in the enormous three car garage at the other end. Charlotte took Lauren's arm and insisted on a quick walk around the grounds first to relax.

"DG loved that English car so much that he's gone and bought it, and Jerome has been taken on as chauffeur and security. He used to be with the French Foreign Legion, would you believe? Special Forces trained. He's Oriane's brother. And DG has asked Oriane to become his very own personal assistant. We have been impressed so much with her handling of everything French and bureaucratic, of which there is plenty in this country. She was hesitant because of her own wedding business, so we've bought that too and she can keep overseeing it as well with some new staff, but on triple her present salary."

"DG has always appeared to be a real wheeler and dealer but seeing him in action first hand? … Now I can really see how he's done so well in business and politics," Lauren remarked.

"Yes, and I shall continue to chair my engineering company in Dallas, but just be directly hands off for a while. I have an excellent management team in place … I fancy being a more relaxed new mum for the time being and we can afford to do it, but it keeps my own independent income coming in too."

"And that is so important Charlotte, I agree."

They both smiled; a mutual understanding for why.

The front of the house had a similar Mediterranean appearance to the Dallas Half Moon Corral ranch, but less Spanish looking, with five large archways fronting the lawn. Over the arches was a balustrade balcony with another level behind again, leading into the top floor of the house. There were many shuttered windows front and back, and at the side of the building, rising to an extra storey, was a round tower culminating with some sort of observatory including a telescope. Between the main house and the guest house was a huge adjoining and beautifully tiled long balcony, full of tables, chairs and loungers, all strategically placed for choosing sun or shade. At the far end of the rear garden stood a small, two-bedroomed detached villa, where Orlando and Marcie lived.

"This place is quite amazing," Lauren said, taking in the whole extent of the massive plot, carefully cut and laid out into the hillside.

"The twins love it already, probably because their bedrooms are twice as big as in Dallas! Also, further down on the main road there's a regular bus service into town, and a daily school bus which the twins can use to go to school on their own, once we are all settled into a routine. It's very safe around here generally, and the residents of this side of the hill all pay towards a private security service, who discretely watch property and children. We've already chipped in our bit. I like it for Kat and Lexi to become more self reliant, as I had to be as a child."

"That sounds good all round, I agree."

"Now, before we go inside and I can see you're just dying to look around, me too since our furniture was flown in this morning from the US, I have to confess. DG and I have a little surprise for you. He insisted and I agreed."

Lauren turned around, mystified. "But what is it? I've got to say, this place is a big enough surprise."

"I'm not telling but let's go in now."

They walked straight through the entrance hall into a huge oak floored sitting room, painted a subtle shade of pale cream with a white ceiling, at least twenty metres square and the centrepiece of the whole house. Glass fronted doors led off to other rooms, presumably Lauren assumed, to a dining room, study or other reception rooms. A large coffee table on a red Persian carpet was surrounded by alternate white and pale brown armchairs and matching sofas, with deep velvet piles and fringed sides, lit by old antique table lamps. Other furniture was dotted about, including cabinets, a sideboard and various paintings, as well as the floor standing lamps Lauren recognised from Dallas. Also brought from America was the massive home cinema screen, and of course, pride of place at the end, DG's gun cabinet on the wall plus the seven foot stuffed black grizzly he shot in the Rockies.

"I didn't need or want to bring too much, just some of our personal stuff. Everything else is new; I chose it all locally and the same with the bedrooms. We started pretty well afresh." Charlotte said, Lauren wide-eyed with a pleasant jealousy at how lovely Charlotte's home already looked. "Now time for your surprise, close your eyes."

Lauren couldn't for the life of her imagine what they had cooked up, but she did as she was told, as DG crept inside and opened the door to the dining room … to allow a group of people to tip-toe in.

"Okay, you can open your eyes now."

As she did, a loud roar of 'surprise!' rang across the room. She stared incredulous. How on earth was all this happening? DG was just too much. In front of her stood Eva with Seb, Helena with Edward Jones, Sonja with Johann, Annabella with Luigi and there at the end grinning mischievously was … no … not possible … Amélie and Rufus. She stood speechless; her mouth wide open.

Amélie rushed forward and gave her a giant hug. "This is on behalf of all of us. DG said he wanted a little party to celebrate, so we've all come to provide one!"

"Oh my goodness, everyone is here, this is so fabulous and thank you all for coming. I'm so happy."

"Good," DG replied beaming. "Charlotte and I told everyone Philippe had to urgently get back to Russia and he apologises. I kinda wanted to get the whole Murmansk team together but …"

Sonja immediately continued. "Amélie and I tried to get Mila and Rosie too, but as usual both were on secret location somewhere and completely unobtainable. But we did manage a little bonus. Turn around Lauren."

Lauren turned and standing behind her … impossible … but there they were … Svet and Sergei, with the twins jumping up and down excitedly alongside them.

"Svet?" Lauren cried. "Sergei? I just don't believe it."

Svet, looking her usual resplendent self, red hair flowing, ran forward and gave Lauren a huge hug, whispering in her ear. "I'm so sorry for behaving badly, I was frightened. You look so lovely Lauren. My father is a pig; I never want to speak to him again. Oh, and Nadine sends her love … she's on vacation in Iceland with her computer professor boyfriend and is sorry she can't make it."

"Nothing to forgive, I understand and I love you Svet as ever. I'm just so pleased to see both of you. Let's talk about your father later, don't let him upset you … he'll come round, I promise."

"Okay," she whispered then drew back and smiled as Sergei came forward and gave Lauren a gentle hug.

"Thank you for saving Rosie. I've seen her recovered and you are the most amazing doctor Sergei, it's truly wonderful what you've done for her," she whispered.

"Most of the success was down to Rosie and her incredible determination and fortitude," he replied. "But I am pleased the new stem cell treatment worked. Fortunately, there was enough spinal cord left to regenerate it fully. I've already had a chat with Edward Jones here, your gynaecologist. He's very keen to collaborate in this area … me too."

Lauren stood back and smiled warmly. Perhaps this really was a new beginning, seeing all the people around her she loved and admired. This was true family … at long last …

A loud hand-bell ringing out at the opened double doors took everyone's attention. Marcie marched in declaring that dinner was being served and not to let her specially cooked steaks go cold. They all trouped into the adjoining dining room and sat in matching pairs, with DG insisting that Lauren take the head of the table.

Chapter Seventeen

Giant helpings of Marcie's trademark pumpkin pie, alongside lashings of copious rich-red Burgundy wine, which DG insisted on pouring out in gallons, finished the enjoyable wedding breakfast, Texas style. Whilst Marcie and Orlando with some helpers began to clear up, DG as usual insisted on all the men trouping after him outside for a mandatory cigar. Although this time, noting that two doctors were amongst the guests, he agreed to allow objections in return for a toast all round from his large bottle of Russian vodka, hidden behind the gun cabinet and out of sight of Charlotte. On the way to the balcony the guys all followed DG down a long winding spiral staircase first to inspect the new wine cellar from which the afternoon's excellent Burgundy had been selected ... hundreds of bottles having been left behind by the previous Ukrainian oligarch owners, who had hurriedly departed for Dubai.

Charlotte and the rest of the female guests slumped into the sitting room armchairs, chatting amongst themselves, whilst Marcie brought in a large pot of coffee plus tea for Lauren and Amélie and a plate of small chocolates.

"Grandma? Why is that called a wedding breakfast when the time is the middle of the afternoon?" Lexi suddenly piped up, sitting and pondering with Kat, next to Lauren.

"It's an old English tradition," Lauren replied. "Hundreds of years ago, when two people got married in church, they used to have a long break from eating for religious reasons called fasting. Hence the word break-fast, get it?"

"Mmm … that still doesn't seem very logical to me … because you're not English, Grandma, and neither is Mom and DG?"

"Ah, but I spent a lot of time living in England when I was young," Lauren said gently, smiling at Lexi frowning the same way with a problem as she did as a child.

Kat immediately rose out of her sofa slump. "Was that when you were married before, Grandma? Before Philippe?" she said, with a mischievous grin.

"Yes, it was," Lauren replied gently.

"So where is your previous husband now?" Kat asked, keen to pursue her interesting line of enquiry. Lauren pondered at this style of Kat probing; she was becoming far too grown up, noting Annabella opposite, also with a mischievous grin.

Charlotte behind had picked up the conversation and rose immediately out of her seat. "Okay you two, no more pestering Grandma, she's very tired after a long day. Orlando has now cleaned up the swimming pool and got all the pumps working again. It's still quite warm out, so why don't you both go to your rooms and play and then in half an hour you can have a swim when your food has gone down."

"Yippee, yes please Mom. Come on Lexi. Want me to beat you again on my new Nintendo car game that DG bought me?" Kat shouted, suitably distracted.

"I've worked out a mathematical system, so prepare to be a loser," Lexi replied as they ran out together and up the stairs.

Lauren looked relieved. Annabella came and sat next to her.

"Children get abominably inquisitive, just when you don't want it," Annabella remarked. "And Kat is a creative, they love to break the rules and be awkward. Look at me …!"

"Yes, and especially your sister Angelina," Lauren replied, both amused at the joke.

Charlotte finally came back after checking Marcie and Orlando were coping with the new kitchen arrangements, and suggested that they all went for a stroll around the grounds to walk off the lunch, a proposal everyone wholeheartedly agreed. Outside they looked up amused towards the balcony to hear copious bellowing and laughter, with great plumes of smoke rising in bursts like an American Indian war signal, DG and Luigi trying to out-puff each other followed closely by Rufus and Sergei. At a discrete distance on the next table, Seb, Johann and Edward remained smoke free, but with large tumblers of vodka in front of them.

Kat and Lexi in their swimming gear were already splashing merrily in the pool, Orlando keeping a discrete eye on them. Eva, Helena and Sonja had gone to look at the formal garden of shrubs and the orangery at the far end, whilst Lauren strolled the other way with Svet. Charlotte and Annabella were some distance behind, chatting avidly. Amélie had run inside to fetch her digital camera off Rufus.

Svet finally began to open out now they were alone. "You are definitely blossoming beautifully Lauren, and I love that dress. Where did you get it? Considering you're having triplets I'm surprised that you're not ... well ..."

"Like an elephant you mean?" Lauren replied, amused. "Everyone says the same thing, but according to Edward, whilst unusual, some women have very strong stomach muscles and are predisposed even with multiple births to only showing a little ... I was the same with Charlotte, smaller of course. Nobody guessed then I was even pregnant until eight months or so. We've done all the tests and everything seems fine inside, and whilst not definitive yet, indications are they may all be girls."

"Gosh, that is so …"

"Yes, cool … in fact ultra cool, positively absolute zero … I'm so pleased you and I are speaking again Svet. I understood totally how you felt over the phone but I was, I admit, very upset and miserable about it ever since. I should have been more sensitive."

"I really am sorry, and it will never happen again. You were right to tell me as you did. I just needed some time to rationalise. Something you perhaps need to know. Obviously I talked it through with Sergei, who also understood. He was annoyed with me reacting like that. What he did tell me was that six months before Vaag met you, and after his twenty-first child, he had a vasectomy done in a private clinic, but later Sergei was asked to arrange a reversal. I think it was when he had decided that he was going after you and to destroy my father and began planning that terrible set of events. After tests, Sergei wasn't convinced the procedure fully worked and that Vaag was, like not producing live sperm, or not enough, but he never told his brother, out of fear. What Sergei reckons is that the chances of Vaag being the father of your triplets really are miniscule, and that my father is genuinely their father too."

"My goodness, that makes me feel much better Svet, but truly, I'm still waiting until they're born. And Edward recommends the same."

"Sergei agrees too, don't take the risk. I went to visit my father last month for a long weekend. He paid, I wasn't keen, still really nervous about what happened first in Kiev and then Murmansk, but he insisted and Nadine agreed also to come. She was pretty relaxed about it and my father paid for her too."

236

"I had no idea. He never mentioned it. You actually went to Moscow?"

"No, Novosibirsk?"

"But I thought Philippe has only just relocated there, to get the business started?"

"No, he lied, Lauren. He's been there almost the whole time wheeling and dealing with some fucking oligarchs, sorry for swearing, who control a large oil and gas field nearby. I know from Sergei that my father has become Chairman of Rubidium and that DG has been backing the start-up finance to explore this fracking technology in Russia, but I don't think DG really knows what's been fully going on?"

"So what has been going on?"

"I'm worried. You would have thought he would learn lessons from the last few Russian ventures. I understand my father is a serial entrepreneur, hey, I did a module last semester in setting up your own business ..."

"Yes," Lauren said and grinned. "It shows!"

"But he has responsibilities now. He should be here with you. I told him all that, but he just grimaced ... something awful happened to him in the Arctic ... like he's trying to reinvent himself to cope and then the triplets on top. He refused to discuss any of it and went mad at me ... then that awful fucking whore Olga turned up."

"Turned up?"

"Yes, he put Nadine and me up in a luxury hotel down the road from his so called poky apartment, but actually it was quite luxurious and spacious, with two large bedrooms. Olga, according to Sergei, has been working with him since moving to Novosibirsk. She likes the outdoors and gas exploration and just looking at her, it's obvious she has a ravenous sexual appetite, for men and according to Sergei for women too."

"How does Sergei know all this?"

"Because he was out there with them of course, and DG, the last week of the holiday on the Lena River … Sergei is a very perceptive man … DG was oblivious and only concerned about the hunting and food, but Sergei took in the nuances … he only discussed it with me after you and I fell out."

"But Philippe told me that Olga had got lost and they had to search for her for two days, in danger of bears and wolves."

"That was a lie too, Lauren, I fear. It was a put-on ruse to get my father and her on their own, away from the others. They all split up, keeping in touch by satellite phones, DG leading the other party and my father 'found' her apparently so she and him were together for a day before they all reunited."

"But Olga must have been in a bad state?"

"You must be joking Lauren, Olga could tear a bear's head off in one go. She is super-strong, action woman type, and was brought up to survive in the wilds of Siberia. No, it was an excuse to finally do it; she had been frustrated up to then."

"Do what?"

"Can I speak frankly please … always we have shared confidences and never had secrets …"

"That will always be the case Svet, I love you, and you know that."

"I'm certain she seduced him at that point … which then continued and she quickly ends up in Novosibirsk as right hand person. Igor does all the administration. My father and that woman do the real power and deals together. He had been careful, tidying up when Nadine and I arrived at his apartment, but Nadine saw her things hidden in the other bedroom, when I distracted him, and there were other indicators, her toothbrush, makeup spotted, even a tampon box in the wardrobe."

"You mean Olga is living with him? Fucking hell, Svet. I can't believe it. Actually, a quick question. What does 'dorogoy' mean in Russian?"

"It means darling, why?"

"Then yes, I do believe it."

Svet realised what must have been said … deliberately by the scheming whore. "I'm so sorry Lauren. The moment I saw her with that hair, like my mother's and then the way she gazed at him all the time, I knew. Sergei was right. She's obsessive and dangerous. When my father and I were alone, I went mad and he got upset and defensive, denied it all, but I know my father when he lies better than anyone … and he knew I had caught him out. Nadine and I cut short our trip and we flew back early. I was so incensed and upset with him; I wouldn't let him take me to the airport. He's showered me with phone messages, emails and texts since but I ignore him. You deserve better than this behaviour Lauren, whatever the hell has gotten into him? I just wish he had never gone back to Russia then we would all be together like before."

They walked on quietly, out of the estate and down a path that took them along the hill with immense coastal views. Charlotte, now with Amélie and Annabella, was still behind but they were absorbed in their own conversations.

"Listen Svet, I've done more crying over your father and his behaviour over the triplets than enough … I've become so hardened and immune I can't feel anything left to cry about any more to be honest, no matter what he does. I'm hugely sad and disappointed with Philippe … and after meeting that fucking bitch Olga, not surprised. Sorry, my turn to apologise. As I said earlier, I'm doing nothing hasty, nearly four months to go yet, and the triplets and Cassini are my priorities. Then at that point, when they're born, Philippe can decide. I still love your father, Svet, but the way he is presently, I can't do anything. I simply haven't the energy. He'll have to come round, but I still have some faith in him that he may."

"I do hope so," Svet replied, linking her arm tightly as they walked on. "Gosh, I don't know about you being tired, I'm exhausted. Shall we sit on one of those seats over there and wait for Charlotte, Amélie and Annabella to catch up? What a view!"

"Mmm … wonderful … so I've also made a big decision. I'm going to move down here and be near to Charlotte permanently. I've also restructured Cassini so that I can concentrate on forefront nuclear research at our Cyclops fusion centre near Cannes."

Svet kissed her cheek. "That's fabulous. I think you've made an excellent decision, wow … mega-cool."

"When are you going back to Boston with Sergei? There's some villas for sale further on down that road. Want to come and have a look with me and Charlotte tomorrow?"

"Yes please. Sergei and I can't leave here until Monday morning. He wants to go back via London for a few more days. He has a medical meeting there and I intend to visit some school friends who have left Russia and also living in London."

"Great, tell you what, don't bother looking for expensive hotels. I still have my apartment in Chelsea. You can stay there if you want; everything inside is all set up as I left it last. I'll just call the agency that looks after it on Monday and they'll arrange to meet you and give you a key, plus a box of food."

"That would be fun … I'm sure Sergei would like that too … he can afford expensive hotels but to be honest Lauren … we both get really sick of them … there is no way he would ever become like Vaag, Sergei is so anti-materialistic."

"Deal then … all sorted."

240

They continued chatting and catching up about Svet's progress in her studies, her course now having changed to bioengineering. Sergei's latest research work was being extended to Alzheimer's, a final frontier Sergei regarded as the greatest potential future catastrophe as populations rapidly age worldwide. After the amazing success with Rosie he was exploring and funding the use of stem cells further, with a small group of like minded medical researchers, the reason they were going to London to consider setting up a new brain research centre.

"Svet, my gynaecologist Edward Jones is a brilliant man and has a high level London medical network ... he may be useful to Sergei."

"On to it, I chatted to Helena quickly. Sergei and Edward are already talking, I'm sure there are a number of areas of stem cell collaboration they are keen to explore."

Suddenly a quiet voice whispered over their heads. "So you two, what are you plotting then? I can see those furrowed expressions."

Amélie had crept up behind them with Charlotte and Annabella at her heels. They joined Lauren and Svet on the other bench, as Charlotte tried to point out which yacht amongst a large cluster of boats moored at the port in the distance was DG's he had just bought.

"It looks absolutely huge, Charlotte," Amélie exclaimed, as Annabella finally spotted it with her sharp eyesight. "I can actually see it now; the other boats are like little dots."

"He's a big guy, needs a big toy," Charlotte said and they laughed heartily.

"When are you all going back?" Lauren asked.

"Rufus and I have to catch a flight early morning," Amélie replied. "I'm afraid we have the annual village spring fete to open, such is the lot of an aristocrat's wife. Why?"

"Me too," Annabella added. "Angelina and … err …your ex … are putting on a major art exhibition at the hotel. Luigi and I have to be there, although Greta has got it all sorted."

"No problem, I'm going house hunting tomorrow … so it will be just Charlotte, Svet and me because I know the others also have to get back too. They have a business to run, mine!"

"Definitely boss. So, you're house hunting?" Amélie exclaimed with a laugh. "Excellent and about time too. Brussels is so passé, even for me; this is definitely the place for rich aristocrats, celebs and global CEOs. Reckon I should join you some time too, although Rufus is such a staid-in-the-mud Englishman he really loves the food and weather!"

"All decided then … I reckon it's time to head back and see how the smokers are getting on," Lauren said.

They got up and walked towards the villa, taking in the warm early spring sunshine and the first sighting of a green lizard sliding over the rocks …

<><>

Lauren wasn't aware that Charlotte had other issues running through her head. She had a big dilemma brewing; in fact she had two major dilemmas troubling her and talked about both quietly to Amélie and Annabella whilst they walked over.

The second dilemma, Charlotte, Amélie and Annabella agreed had now been resolved, much better than they expected. They realised, with the body language giveaway, that Svet had unburdened some truth-telling with Lauren up on the coastal path, which was just as well; they too all knew about Olga and Philippe two weeks before. Between them they agreed to keep quiet, concerned to ensure the knowledge that Philippe was into an affair remained well away from Lauren for the time being and hoped the wedding would bring Lauren and Philippe back together. Olga turning up in Nice upset their calculations.

In fact Rosie, having been alerted by Amélie that her gut instinct said something was seriously amiss over in Russia with Philippe, had quickly found out more through her own Russian agent contacts in China. Olga had some form, and was on the mild alerts of Chinese intelligence, although anything further would need closer digging out. Certainly Olga, the raving Russian sexpot with flaming red hair, had been graphically explained in Rosie's inimical way, the rest had been easy to surmise. Rosie, after telling Amélie, had contacted Mila ... aware already of Rosie's full recovery, and Mila had contacted Charlotte, who also had been guessing. In the end it was unanimous ... to keep it all from Lauren ... allowing DG, when appropriate, to be told the detail and then speak to Philippe quietly and try and resolve an end to the affair.

But of course Olga had spooked the grand reconciliation plan ... maybe she even guessed she had to get out in front quickly, which was one of the reasons for her turning up. Whatever, the parameters had changed. Lauren had probably worked it all out anyway at that disgusting juncture, and Svet undoubtedly had now confirmed it. Certainly the notable tension between Svet and Lauren had evaporated.

The remarkable thing was how sanguine and unperturbed Lauren was appearing to her daughter and best friends ... she seemed like Hilary resolving her Bill transgressions quietly ... by getting on with it, head held aloft ... high achieving women with a similar steely resolve to sort out what they wanted in their own way. On that basis, Charlotte and friends were all less anxious ... even Mila felt calmer down in the mangroves at least for the moment.

However, Charlotte's first dilemma was of a somewhat different order … and one which Amélie was going to have to think hard about over the weekend. Charlotte would ring early the following week. This dilemma could be explosive … for a whole set of new reasons, some tangible, others quite unpredictable.

Chapter Eighteen

Amélie could hear the landline ringing incessantly in the distance but nobody was seemingly around to answer it. "What use is having a butler if he doesn't deal with the trivia," she shouted exasperated, as she marched from the other side of the house, realising how unreasonable she was because she had, of course, given all the staff the day off in lieu of the weekend village fete. Where on earth Rufus was she had no idea. He was never where he should be.

The determined ringer was not giving up; she recognised the trait and worked out who it was. Amélie was, by then, almost out of breath. "Hi Charlotte," she gasped. "Sorry, had to run the length of this vast place, no servants anywhere. I'll just grab a chair. Phew … that's much better."

"You've got servants?"

"You betcha, hey I'm Lady Westvale, it goes with the English aristocrat territory, so have to act the part. Downton Abbey, which I bet DG loves, has nothing on us. Actually they are all fabulous people and totally indispensible, same as your Orlando and Marcie, especially in my condition. Pretty soon, running like this will be out of bounds!"

"Yes, me too, I'm glad you got back alright. It was all a bit of a rush in the morning with everyone shifting at once."

"Having six bathrooms did help, no congestion whatsoever with all of us morning-miserable women hogging the space … I must get Rufus to convert a few more rooms here … the

English aren't so big on bathrooms. Anyway, how did the house hunting go?"

"Pretty good. A mile or so down the main road we looked at a lovely villa. Similar views to us, six bedrooms and a manageable garden with a massive pool, which of course the twins approved of immediately. It also had a small and self contained granny annexe as the English owners called it ... which was quaint ... but perfect for a potential live-in nanny. The owners were desperate to return to the UK for family reasons."

"Did she like it?"

"Loved it and so did Svet. It was beautiful and newly furnished and certainly gave her an idea of what she would like. They offered to include much of the furniture as they couldn't take it back to the UK, which was enticing. The less hassle she has moving the better. But she's decided to employ Oriane to quickly locate and shortlist a range of other properties and search out suitable contenders for her taste and needs. Then Lauren will fly down for a day, look and decide, with me."

"Excellent. So, did you manage to speak to Mila?"

"Yes, amazingly I tracked her on her personal mobile. She answered immediately on some satellite device ... I could hear frogs croaking. She said she was going to wrestle with an alligator shortly to show the trainees and I needed to hurry, I didn't know whether she was joking or not."

"Mila doesn't joke about those sort of things, believe me she wrestles with alligators daily ..."

"Honestly Amélie, you're as bad as Mila. Anyway, when I asked her opinion she wasn't at all helpful, in fact became distinctly antagonistic and unfriendly. She thought, in no uncertain terms, that it was a bad idea and would destabilise

Lauren further and that I should abandon the notion totally. I thanked her politely and left her to the crocs."

"Mmm … I suspect there are lots of reasons for her reaction, but I don't agree."

"What reasons?"

"Tell you another time, but my perspective is quite the opposite. You should go for it. I did, despite family opposition. I was fourteen. And when I found him, living like a hermit on the Isle of Skye after enduring a long, rough boat crossing from Iceland, running away from home with a backpack in the summer holidays after a huge steaming row with my mother, it was quite surreal. He didn't know what to do at first. He'd never even seen me since I was two, so I just stayed and hung around, helping him with his pottery kiln. We got to know each other gently and gradually, and I realised he was actually quite an amazing man, self sufficient, artistic and living alone, at one with nature and his huge library of books. There were two sides to the arguments. And every summer holiday from then on I spent time solely with him and never regretted any of it. Sadly, he died last year in a care home … but I was with him."

"Heck, Amélie that sure is some story. So you really do think I should track down my father? I want to desperately and have done so for such a long time. I can't get rid of a burning curiosity and a need for closure. But how? I don't have any notion where to start. And talking to Lauren right now simply isn't sensible, at least on that I do agree with Mila."

"Tell you what, I have an idea. My ex, Michael, is a senior detective in the London Metropolitan police force. With a little bit of persuasion from me, I'm sure with his extensive contacts and network he could track down the whereabouts of your father. And Michael would be quite objective and independent, no agenda to follow."

"You mean like Mila don't you."

"I never said that Charlotte. Mila is undoubtedly an amazing sleuth, but having an objective search done takes any stray emotions out of the equation, and there are plenty between Lauren and Mila. I'll explain the request to Michael and pass him your email so you can liaise directly. I assume you have some facts and data of what happened when you were born and when you became adopted, for him to work from?"

"Yes, lots of information from my adopted parents. What do you mean plenty of emotions between Lauren and Mila?"

Amélie paused to think carefully, feeling her face reddening at the other end of the line. She had stupidly passed an unnecessary remark, forgetting that Charlotte has the same razor sharp scientific synthesising skills as both her and Lauren. Shit. "I'm … not sure how best to say …"

"So I'll say it. I think Amélie, what you're trying to tell me is that my mother is bisexual. Don't worry or feel embarrassed, I know. I've known ever since we were all together in Russia. Mila and Rosie are so extrovert and obvious, and publically proud of their orientations and out there flaunting, everybody can see that. But Sonja and Lauren are far more subtle, careful and sensitive. But it became quickly obvious to me that my mother has very special and private feelings for both Mila and Rosie, and those feelings are reciprocal. It doesn't matter to me at all, some of my good friends in the US are the same, but this isn't something I would discuss with DG, unless he raised it and it became an issue … although I have to say, outside of his usual machismo blustering, even DG is a lot more sensitive than he appears. And especially so concerning Lauren."

"Yes, Rufus is the same, which is nice. To be honest Charlotte I only put two and two together recently and I've been close friends with Lauren for over twenty years … like you it makes no difference whatsoever … but I'm impressed with your tuned-in antennae, normally it's me who doesn't miss a trick."

Charlotte laughed loudly. "Probably because I'm too much like my own mother at times! Do you think Philippe knows?"

"Yes definitely, you and Lauren are almost indistinguishable at times!" Amélie replied, chortling down the phone. "As for Philippe, I would surmise that Lauren has approached that particular challenge on a 'needs to know' basis, and has decided Philippe doesn't need to know … you probably noticed that Mila especially is always very careful in front of him and doesn't flaunt with women. Also Russia is not exactly a cultural bastion of LGBT rights either."

"Yes, you're right. I'm sure Philippe's underlying problem remains the issue of whether he's the triplet's father, but that doesn't excuse his behaviour with Olga. Anyway, Olga is bisexual, that was blatantly obvious to me and everyone around, she even flirted with Lauren as they talked, which probably disoriented her even more. Will Michael need paying?"

"No, he can't work for money, more than his well paid job is worth and he has three kids and my sister to support. It will purely be a small favour for me; he'll just do some digging on the side pro bono. He owes me a few anyway, like not telling my sister, who he ran off with and married, that he had a brief affair last year with a police intern … see, I don't miss all the tricks."

"Great, thanks, okay a deal, I really appreciate this chat. Must go, I still have a lot to sort out here and I start my pre-natal classes tomorrow … DG has promised to come too, that will be a first."

"I haven't thought of that, at least you know what to expect. I must book myself in Charlotte, a good idea. Can't see Rufus agreeing, although the babies are his first too …"

"I think you're wrong, Rufus is a big softy … he'll love to be there with you and participate."

"Mmm … maybe you're right… will be in touch."

<><>

The next few days were very busy for Charlotte and she was especially grateful for the twins demonstrating to DG, who was immensely impressed, how to fold a nappy properly, although how they knew she couldn't fathom … until they admitted they had watched it done on YouTube. Michael had sent her a private email introducing himself with a long list of points he would need information on, so he could then run the data through his computer system. She began to assemble the information from her box of private things which had just arrived from Dallas. The rest of her US furniture had also begun arriving, so chaos continued throughout the week as the twins assembled their own beds back together, and she began trying to mix and match her personal things with the new furniture. Fortunately, DG was a man of little emotion and sentiment about old things and clutter. As far as he was concerned he would just buy anything new immediately … except of course for the old seven foot black grizzly which took pride of place on the cargo plane and now stood in the sitting room … she was hoping that monstrosity would have gotten lost down in Lyell's Cherokee reservation, but sadly, not this time.

Especially exciting was that Oriane had begun some discrete searches in the neighbourhood of any property not on the market, but which could potentially be for sale … and was given a tip off about a lovely villa just on the edge of the port.

The property was set back only half a kilometre from the seafront, but a quick walking distance into the old port town itself, with all the health amenities, restaurants, shops and a Carrefour supermarket nearby. It was further away from La Ponderosa, as DG wanted to call their new house, than the villa they had already seen, but still only a walkable three kilometres, albeit uphill slowly. The specification looked very enticing. Oriane had already been to speak to the owners, a Dutch elderly couple wanting to retire back to Holland. The property was old but extensively renovated, with a living area of five hundred square metres, six bedrooms and beautifully decorated inside, with lots of unique features and superb views of both the countryside and the sea. But the plot was very intriguing, not only extensive at five hectares, but had stables, a massive swimming pool and a separate two bedroomed caretaker's house … ideal again for a live-in nanny. She knew her mother loved horses and had one as a young teenager, or the stables could be turned into a workshop for Lauren's furniture making hobby, or both. Oriane had taken a number of inviting pictures which she had printed out. Definitely, this was a villa Lauren needed to see …

The wind was blowing, as ever, cold and hard across the large water reservoir near the dam of the Novosibirsk hydropower plant. Wrapped up in thick protective clothing and standing out of the chill behind a large concrete block, Philippe contemplated the mighty river Ob, wending its way northwards, and peered over the vast plains towards the Ural Mountains. He had a lot on his mind and had to make some important decisions. The weather was changing fast in this continental climate, where the harsh extremes of winter dissolve away rapidly into a milder spring as April progressed.

Much of the dirty, slushy ice and snow was melting, and in a week or two's time would be gone.

He was fairly certain who had been behind the break-in and ransacking of the offices two months before ... it had to be either Rinde or Kharkov, some sort of pathetic warning. But there was no way he was going to pay their demand for additional 'consultancy' fees, over and above the normal expected backhander. He now had the technology and the wherewithal to make the shale extraction happen, and they knew their own reserves were diminishing ... the low hanging oil fruit had been extracted long back and their ageing drilling equipment and out of date knowhow, exactly as DG had originally predicted, were reaching their technical limits. They had five more years before yields pumped out of the ground in these fields would be next to nothing. They could all be rich with fracking, the geology in the area was perfect ... but why did these idiots have to be so excessively greedy, to the point where sensible business could no longer be worthwhile? Oligarchs and perestroika had simply not gone to the grand plan expected by Gorbachev in the late eighties that was for sure.

And he had to decide what to do with Lauren ... she wasn't returning his calls or answering his emails. The one discussion when he had managed to catch her late at night recently hadn't gone well. She hung up again, and DG especially had certainly stirred up a hornet's nest calling Olga directly and telling her she was an unwelcome whore and to clear off. That couldn't happen. Olga was indispensable now to the exploration plan ... at least he had finally smoothed things out with DG, who seemed to have plenty to occupy him fortunately with his new yacht and getting life together down in Nice ... good for him.

But Olga was so angry, threatening to cut DG's dick off and hang it on the wall if she ever saw him again.

He was feeling more disposed to the triplets, especially after seeing Lauren in Nice and he was pretty sure he still loved her, but that bastard Vaag and what he'd done to her and to him was too hard to cope with in his head … and Olga tore his emotions apart too, she had become addictively irresistible … and Svet? Their relationship was now so bad, also refusing to talk to him? What a fucking mess he'd got into. Only one sensible thing left to do … what he always did when cornered … fight hard, in this case for the new business and see gradually how the rest goes. He'd invested too much cash and hard labour into this project. There was no way those fucking oligarchs were getting their way … and he still had influence at the right levels … at least he expected he still did, although the new President was less known to him personally, a very hard war veteran character with a murky security background … but then who didn't have that background in power in Russia?

"A rouble for your thoughts my sweet darling."

Philippe turned around quickly, his body tensed on high alert and then he immediately relaxed with a sigh. "Olga, you startled me creeping up like that, and why have you got a handgun strapped to your belt? All that nonsense when we first met about needing me to show you how to shoot. I reckon you're a better shot than me."

Olga sidled up and wrapped her arms around him, holding him close, her breath steamy in the cold, standing slightly taller in her fur boots and tight black jeans, her jacket and hood tightly buttoned down with her thick mane of red hair flowing out freely over her shoulders.

"I take no chances now. I shoot balls off oligarchs. Come to tell you that I have completed final field survey using oil and gas software you stole from DG's fracking manager. Big progress, test result all stack up good. Now we can start the first full drilling, only fifty kilometres from here. Have you got DG's twenty million dollar loan? … Need lots of money to order equipment from China."

"Hey, I thought you didn't want anything more to do with DG after what he said to you?" Philippe murmured, stroking her hair.

"DG very useful to us with money and expertise so no, I am big pragmatist, but still I cut dick off when I see him," she said looking very serious. "Ah, also came to tell you, Rinde no longer a problem … found floating in the Ob last night in two halves. Chainsaw. Isn't that good?"

"Jesus Christ Olga, I was only talking to him two days ago. I was confident we now had a deal and could end this stupid feuding and get going. That's a major setback and a worry that someone is becoming extremely serious about wanting to stop us."

"No worry, Kharkov immediately bought up Rinde's gas fields so now we deal with only him … and I speak earlier and he no longer a problem either and agree to take ten percent of the profits not forty."

"Why?"

"I remind him of some indiscretion he indulged in at Novosibirsk State University many years ago with English spy. New Russian President is not very happy about sodomy, or foreign spies. Kharkov agree immediately, deal done, we start on his land once I get leasing agreement tomorrow, which you and my brother can sign up to."

"How do you know all this? Have you spoken to Igor about it?"

"No, but my brother always does as I tell him. I didn't spend all my youth running around Siberian woods shooting bear. Anyway, my lapochka, enough work you are cold. We go back to apartment, I tidy up, we drink vodka and I cook you the best pelmeni you have ever tasted. Wild boar, I shot early this morning, hanging up in garage. Yes? Then we have sex."

Philippe felt all kinds of instinctive tensions and alarm running through his mind … and thoughts of Lauren filtered into his consciousness as well. "Food sounds good … then maybe an early night I think …"

"No, Philippe, we have sex … otherwise at your age dick shrivel up and drop off, not good … and …" Olga began gently caressing his face and kissing his neck "Aren't I best sex machine you ever know?"

Philippe felt himself going hot and hard again … he couldn't keep his hands off her as they kissed passionately before Olga grabbed his hand and led him back to the apartment at a fast pace.

<><>

Lauren was counting the days off … two months to go. She had been tiring more easily in the day and needed regular afternoon snoozes in the office between meetings, although nobody minded. She was quite indulged by Eva, Giselle and Bella to ensure she didn't overwork as the transitional arrangements began to work their way throughout Cassini, and for the Brussels base to concentrate on operations and services.

Sonja and Johann were sharing an office as joint CEOs and already leading the regular Executive meetings which Lauren discretely kept away from, after having quiet discussions first with the two of them. But it was clear that Sonja too was now showing distinct signs of her own pregnancy and Johann's bachelor pad was way too small for her. However, Lauren had maintained momentum with Juliette on establishing the research priorities for Cyclops and the new Israeli fusion partnership and the big day was looming … her move down to Villefranche-sur-Mer, and then she could hand over her apartment to Sonja and Johann at last.

The previous weekend, she had flown down to stay with DG and Charlotte and to pursue an in-depth assessment of Oriane's final shortlist of properties to consider. A number had come and gone very quickly. Oriane had liaised in detail with every property up for serious consideration, and the list eventually came down to six. Oriane had then taken her wedding business photographer with her to make a short video which was sent on for Lauren to watch on her iPad, with additional commentary by Kat and Lexi who Oriane allowed to help with the editing. The very first villa she viewed with Svet still sailed through the sieve until the end … then she viewed in detail the old villa with the large plot, stables and beautiful design down in the port bay. That was it … she had exactly the same feeling as she did with her existing apartment. Love at first sight, and already began to decide what horses to buy and to show Kat and Lexi how to ride, once the triplets were born of course. Once down in Nice, she looked inside and around the plot, and was prepared to make a cash offer there and then but her dream villa was expensive, the owners demanding four million euros and not a centime less. But after further negotiation and a promise of a speedy sale, they agreed at three and a half million, especially when Lauren offered the services of her Cassini lawyers to complete the sale free of charge. The purchase would take up all of her dividend just paid for the year, and much of her savings, but she was very pleased and immediately phoned Svet, Annabella and Amélie to tell them of the good news, who were all as excited, and would visit as soon as they could.

Philippe, sadly, had become an increasingly distant memory. He didn't figure in the decision making whatsoever, especially as she, as well as Svet, had refused to talk to him since the Olga fiasco in Nice. She was prepared for a long game where he was concerned, with no indications, as yet, that Olga the Siberian Serpent had gone from his life.

And it was a very quick sale, no major problems and some minor repairs undertaken simultaneously. Oriane assisted with the French purchase process ... the exciting part was that she would be moving in the following weekend, and with Eva and Helena's help had already packed up and put out to storage all the personal belongings she would take.

As with Charlotte's purchase, the departing Dutch owners were leaving much of the new furniture and fittings, totally unsuitable to take to colder climes in Holland, and Oriane had already identified a range of upmarket furniture stores in Nice and Cannes where she could choose the rest. She had decided to dip into her special savings bank for furniture, the money her father had specifically left her in a trust fund, only accessible after her mother died. He would have liked her to spend it that way ...

On the way down to Edward's clinic, she had a number of wistful and nostalgic moments thinking of her Belgian chemical engineer father and how sorry she was that he never saw the triplets or even experienced the family pleasures of Charlotte, his first grandchild ... which made her even more determined to now make the most of her new family setting in Nice, with Charlotte, the twins and lots of babies, all manageable around her planned research work with Juliette. She pondered sadly about Mila, still deliberately keeping out of contact and spending most of her time in the US with her new security team. Juliette had rarely seen Mila either, but was so

257

preoccupied with her own family and her new responsibilities in Cannes, that she too hadn't had time to get overly miserable about it all.

Lauren realised she was missing Mila terribly and the feeling wasn't going to go away but was getting worse … and she resolved … time to break the deadlock.

The BMW gently pulled into the car park. Helena had kindly driven her to the clinic. Edward had continued to be wonderful and maintained a regular watchful eye on her condition, so far so good. She hadn't raised it and he hadn't said it … so bed-rest was still off the agenda. She was showing significantly now, but still no more than a normal pregnancy to everyone's amazement. But once she had moved into her new luxury Villefranche-sur-Mer villa, she had a sensible programme mapped out of lots of rest and working from home, so Edward should be pleased.

"Lauren, before you go in, there's something I want to tell you. I'm coming in with you. I have an appointment with Edwards's colleague, Claudette … who will be looking after me."

Lauren, struggling to undo her seat belt, finally yanked it open and off, smiling affectionately. "Oh Helena, that's wonderful, I'm so pleased for you. Well you couldn't have a better guy as the potential father."

"No, I know and I'm so happy actually. I think you've started a bit of a Cassini trend."

Lauren looked over, intrigued. "How?"

Helena went quite red realising that she may have unwittingly spoken out of turn, which was not like her, but it would be out anyway soon. "Err … perhaps when you get back in the office … you might want to ask Eva how she is …"

"Oh my word Helena, I don't believe it, that is amazing … there is definitely something in the water at Cassini!"

"Actually Lauren, Bella is getting a bit grumpy … that soon nobody will be left to work in Cassini, only her and Hermann … and there are rumours that his girlfriend in IT is also pregnant. I didn't dare mention that."

Lauren roared laughing. "I think Hermann had better budget for a nuclear crèche, it's about time anyway. I'll have a chat with Bella and Yvonne, we'd better do some staff planning and a few temporary promotions to ensure maternity cover is effectively managed … anyway she's still got Giselle … mind you I wouldn't put it past Giselle to surprise us either!"

Helena relaxed and smiled. "We'd better go, or we'll both be late."

Chapter Nineteen

The rhythmic clanking of metal cups against the bars grew louder as she walked along the gangway towards the heavily fortified visitor area at the end. A thick wodge of green spittle shot out of one cell, missing her, but landing over the uniform of one of the guards.

"Why don't you fuck off, you ugly piece of bear shit," she cried out lashing her fist towards another grinning imbecile, face pressed against the next set of bars, who was simulating masturbation.

A burly guard, with the dimensions of DG and shoulders of an ox, pulled her away. "Ignore those freaks; they've only been here two weeks, all waiting on remand. Once they're inside the main cells they'll soon settle down, especially when the other ten in the cell beat the crap out of them." He roared with glee, a huge bunch of keys jangling from his thick leather belt.

"And Professor Dubois, why is he still on remand too? He is innocent man, should not be in shit place like this piss-hole," Olga demanded, now feeling frustrated that Philippe had been locked up for three weeks in the notorious Vasilov Prison and nothing seemed to be happening.

"Careful, Miss, with that tongue of yours. Professor or not, we don't care in here. He's treated just like the next load of dregs. All of this lot are on the take in some way or other, usually drugs or vodka. I understand your husband is different, money laundering?"

"Trumped up lies. Professor Dubois is patriotic Russian, doing good for all the country and is innocent man."

The guard laughed. "That's what they all say. He's behind the booth at the end of the far row. Speak through the phone … you have fifteen minutes."

She marched quickly to the booth and sat down on the hard wooden bench, staring at the dishevelled sight of Philippe behind the dirty glass. He was shivering. It was cold in the building but his prison clothes were thin. He managed to raise a smile; Olga was the first visitor he had been allowed.

"God almighty Philippe, how have you ended up in here? You look bad. One minute you were in the office, the next gone no sign of you anywhere. I expected to see you floating in Ob. Thank goodness, after Igor pestered police and paid a few roubles, we found out you had been taken here by armed authorities. You are not allowed lawyer, what should we do? I have told nobody … particularly DG."

"I had no choice Olga … they burst in with Kalashnikovs saying I was wanted for state violations, illegal business and money laundering. I'm sure this is the work of Sergiu Kharkov. He warned me not to meddle in local politics … I had been putting pressure on him, through my normally reliable contacts, to relent to a five-percent fee and a cash sum of a million roubles once gas begins to be exported."

"Can I bring food and warmer clothes babushka?"

"Probably, I'd appreciate that. I'm alright, sharing a cell with eight others and a couple of slop buckets. Three of them are stark raving out of their heads and scream crazily all night so I get little sleep. Fortunately, I can at least look after myself. The most aggressive had his arm broken and the others realised I am army trained and have left me alone. The food is shit, gruel and mouldy bread. I look worse than I am, don't worry."

"If I get in there, I kill them all in one go."

Philippe smiled again, in turmoil reliving Murmansk once more. He had also been thinking about Lauren having plenty of time, but Lauren wasn't there and Olga's devotion, loyalty and affection couldn't be doubted. That was all he had.

"Something has gone wrong Olga, allegiances have now changed. All of the oligarchs, including Kharkov apparently, have decided they don't want fracking to be explored in Russia … too much investment needed and there are still ample normal reserves, they just want to move from field to field as each one empties. They're not interested in investing in Russian energy for the long term future, only immediate quick returns from easy and cheap extraction, where environmental concerns are ignored and backhanders flow extensively to retain political support. And an influential group, led by Kharkov, together with the state gas company have lobbied the President … claiming I am working Russian soil for US interests and am a dissident who wants to see the present government fall. Hence the trumped up charges, this of course has happened before."

"You mean like Khordokovsky? … You not exactly Russian billionaire and are politically uninvolved so not make sense."

"No, but DG financing this venture, is on both counts and a US senator. Somebody tipped off Kharkov about the secret backing by Rubidium, I don't know who. They're taking no chances. I've overreached and fallen on the wrong side of the political divide through my stupid arrogance. A quick trial is set tomorrow … I appear before a judge. I wish I had stuck to prospecting in the EU like Poland or even the Ukraine but not here. I've been naive, Olga."

"No naive or arrogant, Philippe and you wouldn't have met me … I think I know who betray you … they will suffer believe me. I love you and will not let you down, unlike all others.

What shall I do? ... DG has phoned number of times and I make excuses. He is asking for you for update."

"Wait until tomorrow, and then you must tell DG whatever the outcome. Hopefully, I may be let off with a warning. I'm optimistic, after all this government owes me some favours for what I did for the previous President. But I may have to leave the country quickly ... I'll need cash for border guard bribes. Shit, the fucking bell is going already. You'll have to go."

"I prepare, my angel. And if you leave, I leave too ... we are inseparable. Bye, my darling, I love you." She blew him a kiss through the glass as two guards grabbed his arms and led him away.

He felt so much trepidation and wished he had never gone to Siberia but had stayed with Lauren in Brussels. His complicated life had suddenly become a giant nasty puzzle, sliding down endless snakes into a deep pit of despair. But he had to stay resolute and muster all his inner strength to climb back up the ladder ... although how he could deal with Lauren and Olga if he got out quickly, he had no idea. The thought sent a chill through his body ... his stupid old weakness for ravenous Russian beauties, which even Vaag had mentioned, had now gone too far. But he would take one step at a time. He had to get out in one piece. He felt confident after his private discussion with the prison governor the day before, offering him a few well received promises again. Maybe he would be back home in Novosibirsk in the next twenty four hours ...

<><>

They were finally getting into a better routine, but early morning chaos prevailed that day in Charlotte's kitchen as PE outfits, drinks and books were being urgently assembled. Charlotte had left early for her new clinic in Cannes for a prenatal check-up with Oriane and left DG in charge of getting the twins to school.

"Lord above Kat, where on earth have you left your plimsolls? Go in your room and look under the bed please," Marcie bellowed in her broad Texan twang, as Lexi then dropped her orange juice all over the floor.

"Sorry Marcie," DG said. "I'll get that lot wiped up, and then I'll sure as hell have to drop them off at school now as they've already missed the bus."

"Say, DG, I am mighty glad that Ms Charlotte ain't around or she would blow a fuse, take my word."

"Sure as hell you're right Marcie, me too. Ah …Orlando has just brought the Bentley to the front door. I'm going to take a drive myself and see how the yacht refurbishment is going, crack the whip if those varmints are behind. We want to have our first cruise out at Easter. Hey Marcie, I want you and Orlando to come as well on the maiden voyage. You both deserve a break for all the hard work you've done since we've been here."

"Well … thank you DG. Me and Orlando sure do appreciate that."

Suddenly DG felt his mobile vibrate in his jacket and grabbed it out quickly. It was Philippe, at long last, where on earth was he? "Hey, little old Philippe, you got some good numbers to report back to me today?"

"I not Philippe, sorry DG, this is Olga."

DG's instincts were that this was unfortunately going to be a long call. Lexi and Kat were finally ready and waiting patiently to go.

"Say Orlando, can you drop the twins off at school please, some urgent business just come up on this here phone. Sorry girls, but I promise to pick you up end of day instead as a treat."

"Yes sir, DG, not a problem," Orlando replied, picking up schoolbags. "Kiss DG goodbye Kat and Lexi then let's fly or you'll be late for math."

<><>

"Just hang on Olga," DG replied quietly and walked briskly to his study and closed the door. "Now, I thought I'd told you to fuck off out of my business, so why are you on this phone?"

"I always will be with my Philippe, DG, but today we make no swearing please. Something very bad happened and I need to tell you."

"Okay Olga, go ahead, I'm listening," he replied sharply.

"Three weeks ago, Philippe was taken by armed authorities and brought to Vasilov Prison where criminal charges have been filed. Trial was this morning. He is now on his way to Labour Camp at Krasnokamensk, near Chinese border, a long way away other side of Siberia. He has just been sentenced an hour ago to fifteen years."

DG, totally dumbfounded, could hear Olga weeping quietly. "Olga, listen to me, this is terrible. What on earth has he done? That place is notorious for political prisoners. The Krasnokamensk prison is one massive uranium mine and processing plant where prisoners are made to do hard work in appalling conditions, once in there you sure as heck don't come out alive."

"I know place well. Philippe do nothing, charges all trumped up. Bad politics and vested interest by key oligarchs and state gas corporations in normal extracted oil and gas. They don't want fracking in Russia."

"So what has Philippe been charged with?"

"Fraud, money laundering, illegal business activity and now murder. Oligarch recently found in local river. All lies. This phone is safe, you can talk freely. Philippe made sure it not traceable."

"And where is Igor? Can't he do something? He has excellent connections, which is how we got as far as we did."

"Igor? He is gone already, to safe place out of Russia for now. Investment money safe in Swiss bank. He has no stomach for fights, my brother always been a weak man."

"Fuck, this is bad, way too bad for normal actions. How far up the chain has this fiasco been ordered, do you know?"

"Very top, after oligarchs do serious lobby."

"Okay, now listen carefully Olga. I have influential political contacts; the US-Russia bilateral network is not all bad, far from it, behind the scenes. I'll work on that and try and get him home. It may need some oiling of wheels but that can be arranged."

"Home is here DG, in Novosibirsk with me."

"Now listen Olga, and listen well. Home is not Russia but in Nice with his wife, Lauren. Do you understand me?"

"Nice? She moved there? Philippe not know. We love each other so he stays with me. She has betrayed him, I know for sure and she will suffer for that betrayal."

"What stupid nonsense are you talking about Olga? Lauren loves him. What do you mean she has betrayed him?"

"She has told Russian authorities about you and the US backing Philippe and our business venture to undermine him, because he doesn't want her or stupid babies. I know for sure. Lauren will pay at some time in her life."

DG felt an immediate alarm running through his body as he listened to her, Olga sounded as crazy as they all said she was. What the fuck had Philippe seen in her? He used his political instincts and decided to softball back, despite his desire to bawl and threaten her in his best language off the line. Olga would be likely needed, unpalatable though it was. "That is total nonsense and I'm sure if Philippe heard you say that, he would tell you in no uncertain words. Lauren is loyal, honest and loving, there is no way she would even think of doing such a thing. I know you're upset and I do sympathise with that, but you and I and Lauren need to work together to get Philippe out of this rat-hole he's found himself down in. You understand me Olga?"

There was a long silence … he waited patiently.

"I understand. What do you want me to do?"

"I want lists of names, backgrounds, as much information as you can get quickly on those oligarchs, their companies and anyone else in the food chain who has got a vested interest in seeing Philippe locked up. I will put my chief analysts onto digging up some counter-dirt and prepare the way to influence the President for a re-think. Philippe had a lot of influence with the former Russian President. You have secure email?"

"Specially encrypted … Philippe already do all that. I get you data, not a problem. But new Russian President has his own network of acolytes, criminals and oligarchs, playing one against the other. This is part of problem, but most are corrupt, some borderline and could be bought, especially with exit from Russia to London."

"Heck, I'll get to work today Olga, you get me the data pronto. Phone me in a week from a secure phone again."

"I see what I can do. I am sorry for all this, in fact fracking business potential really amazing. I plotted all results on advanced exploration software, planned full next phase to get first gas out and we started full drilling already. Suspended for now, and rest of equipment sent back safely to China for storage. Have spent five million US dollars, but will make sure site is secured. I too have contacts."

"Okay Olga, we can stand that loss for now. Yes, pity all this has happened, in other ways you and I would get on darn well, I see you have a high business drive and serious determination."

"Which is also why Philippe love me ... but you will hear no more from me of Lauren."

"Good, will be in touch."

<><>

DG waited till noon, sat back down at his desk, thought for a minute and then picked up the phone for the US Vice President, a former congressional friend. But what he didn't know back in Novosibirsk was that Olga was not going to forget Lauren at all. She had already been formulating plans ... and wanted revenge, painful and permanent revenge.

Chapter Twenty

The twins had finally gone to bed after playing their latest computer game, as a treat for finishing their math and science homework early. They had both been put in the top stream at their new International School and Kat had started piano lessons whilst Lexi chose violin for their music classes, activities they had not had the chance to do in Dallas. But both were confident that Grandma would be able to help them progress on either instrument, having mutually agreed that Mom and DG were both pretty useless.

Charlotte had been pleasantly amazed at DG's willingness and capability to help the twins with their new French lessons, not realising that he was fairly competent with the written language, albeit rusty for conversation. DG eventually explained that he had learned French when stationed in Vietnam as a Lieutenant Colonel, as many of the former Indochina colonialists still used legal documents in that language. She had also learned French at school and was rapidly picking up her facility again. They both were resolved to mix with locals and use the language when out and about.

Relaxed by the fireplace, a few logs burning to keep the early evening spring chill at bay, DG sat alone, ponderously weighing up some of the suggestions from his chief business analyst and political colleagues to overturn Philippe's jail term. He had been talking on the cross-Atlantic phone all week. True to promise, Olga had sent a surprising amount of information over, some of which was quite damaging and had definite political leverage in the right quarters. But of course financial lubrication along the chain would be needed … it wasn't the amount of money that bothered him, but who to target. Get it wrong and the whole plan could backfire and Philippe would end up with his sentence being doubled. But a bigger problem was looming, and he had to resolve it that evening starting with Charlotte.

"You look tired darling, you've been preoccupied all week," Charlotte remarked, swirling around her half glass of Sauvignon, following the lovely lobster meal that Marcie had cooked from a local recipe in town. "Want to tell me what's on your mind? Is it business or politics?"

"Actually, a bit of both Charlotte. I need your help to translate some documents in Russian, would you be able to do that?"

"You betcha, you know how good my Russian is, and it certainly came in useful in Murmansk. Anyway, how come you've got stuff in Russian? I thought Philippe and Igor always translated everything first for you. I'm glad that awful woman Olga has been sent packing … hopefully, Philippe will be making a visit here very soon, especially with Lauren moving into her new villa tomorrow. She's so excited and the twins and I are …"

DG interrupted. "Darn, I'm afraid things aren't quite so simple." He leaned forward and topped up both their glasses of wine.

"Dutch courage?"

"I've got to come clean with you and then talk to Lauren and I need your help."

"Okay, spit it out darling. Looking at your expression, something has gone badly wrong hasn't it."

"That's an understatement. Sit back … here goes … straight as it comes."

DG then went through the entire situation, Olga, the armed site entry and abduction of Philippe, the sentencing to fifteen years and finally the high level progress he had made behind the scenes to try and influence the crisis and get Philippe home to Nice.

Charlotte listened quietly, saying nothing, as she took in every piece of information, nuance and position analytically and precisely, her brain, background and training kicking in to full effect. This was akin to the moment when one of her oil rigs went on fire. She needed a disaster management and cool headed mindset, which she was as good at if not better than DG who usually fired at everything that moved headlong, guns blazing from the hip … although in this case she was amazed at how calm and calculated he had been on the specifics of the challenge, presumably, she thought, because of Olga slap bang stuck in the middle of everything.

"Have to say, that old varmint Dan Ackroyd has done an excellent job on my behalf with the Russian Prime Minister, who, it turns out, has a very high regard for Lauren apparently. He is keen to explore nuclear business with Cassini, to expand their reactors … worries about long term reliance on their own oil and gas and environmental concerns, there is some real bad shit lying around in major lakes in Siberia."

"What? The Vice President has got involved?"

"Absolutely, he owes me one, like his position for a starter. The Russian PM has promised to discuss Philippe's predicament with the Russian President, although the two men don't see eye to eye on everything, but there may just be at least a compromise somewhere. I've promised a Cassini deal which will be especially advantageous."

"This situation is appalling DG, what you've been doing is amazing and I'm really proud of you, but you can't promise Russian deals from Cassini … you have no influence on Lauren's company and know even less about the nuclear business."

"I know, but a little foreign hard currency subsidy coming through a different channel will help won't it?" he replied with a wink. "We should know more in the next ten days. But I can't keep this from Lauren any longer. She'll be assuming that Philippe, not answering any emails or calls, is doing a continuation of his bad behaviour, and she's built that wall of hellfire steel around her to protect herself from being hurt and bide her time … Doggone it I admire that in her, I see where you get all that from Charlotte."

She laughed. "Okay, but Lauren must be told straight away. I suggest tomorrow, when she's in her new house. I looked in yesterday and most of her furniture and personal stuff is already there, and Oriane has done a brilliant job, from sketches Lauren made, of getting it looking beautiful. So when she arrives in the morning, she will be almost good to go, no chaos. We've all been invited round tomorrow night for a housewarming meal. Oriane has booked someone to come in and prepare the food. I suggest just the two of us go over, but the twins visit Sunday instead and play in the pool. They'll be disappointed but I'll find some excuse. I know my mother. The moment we say we wanted to come without the twins, she will know we have something important to discuss. It won't be a problem."

"Not much of a housewarming is it?"

"She'll be much more concerned about Philippe and what to do. Believe me DG, I think the same way. She may be very upset, we'll have to cope with that and comfort her, but I

272

believe that wall of steel, like her iron tummy, will hold up … Lauren isn't a global CEO of a major company for nothing … and we have plenty of time for real fun, all of us, once we get Philippe home. Like a lifetime full I hope. I'll do the translation in the morning."

"Doggone, Charlotte, you should have been my Chief of Staff when I was the whip in Congress. Let's finish this wine and have an early night, time for our own celebrating."

<><>

As Lauren approached in the taxi straight from the airport, the first thing she noticed was the new array of shrubs and flowers around the doorway, making the drive and parking area look so much nicer. The lawns had been cut and there was a real air of tidiness and order around … she was surprised, anticipating living in a disorderly manner for at least a few weeks.

Oriane opened the door to greet Lauren as she struggled a little out of the rear door, and ran over to pay the taxi driver a fifty euro note. "Lauren, I hope you had a good flight down. Here, let me take your case."

"How lovely to see you Oriane," Lauren replied, shaking her hand warmly. "I must say it feels strange coming here for good, despite the fact I have done this moving thing so many times in the past. But this house feels special somehow. I don't know why, but the moment I saw it, I fell instantly in love. The way the garden has been tidied up, those flower re-plantings and the beautiful lawns … all look wonderful."

"Let me show you inside, I hope you like it. We've been busy working the furniture to how you wanted everything."

Lauren sauntered through the front door, noting it had been revarnished and then gasped with complete surprise. The place was lovely before, now it was just stunning. Not only had Oriane completed the paint redecoration but had matched the selected furniture left with her own shipped down. Nothing looked out of place, even the new curtains were up. Everywhere looked home from home, she wouldn't have to move a thing, her white mink sofa and oak coffee table were there exactly as she wanted. She walked through to the kitchen, admiring the additional tiling and the entire refit with new worktop appliances. And finally she walked into her bedroom, complete with re-assembled workshop bed and her trademark white silk sheets, and plump pillows divinely ready for instant sleeping in.

"As you know, the owners had left the place in good condition, but we decided to give an extra bit of a makeover so you would feel instantly it had your stamp on it, Lauren."

"You and your team have done a brilliant job. I don't care what it costs; just bill me as soon as possible. Never have I wanted to pay for something so happily. Thank you Oriane."

"Actually the work and my time are already paid for … DG insisted vehemently and you mustn't argue, as he'll get it back on tax relief. Now before I go, as requested, I have managed to locate a rather special potential housekeeper, who can start immediately. Her CV and references are in this folder. I am happy with all background and security checks. Her name is Marie LeClerk and she has dual English and French nationality. If you would like to meet her now, I have asked her to wait in the dining room or I can arrange a more convenient time."

"Now will be fine thank you Oriane, please ask Marie to come in. Gosh that was fast. Now I understand why DG asked you to be his Executive Assistant, I should have been quicker off the mark!" They both laughed.

Oriane departed and quickly returned with a tall and pretty slim woman, similar age to Charlotte, in a tight black pencil skirt, smart blouse and short brown hair. Lauren immediately recognised an Yves St Laurent stylish outfit and a stout pair of matching Louboutins, always a good start. The woman walked briskly over to shake hands. "Good morning Professor Hind, it's a pleasure to meet with you at last."

"At last?"

"Yes, my great-aunt, who I believe you know, has told me glowing things about your work, you have a fascinating job.

"Your great-aunt?"

"Yes Letty, my Great-Aunt Letty."

Lauren smiled. "Then please take a seat Marie."

Oriane returned with a coffee, a tea and a plate of biscuits, and then headed for the door. "I'll leave you both to it. Lauren, if you need anything over the weekend, please give me a ring on the mobile and I'll sort it out immediately, and I'll check by next week to see if everything is okay."

"Thanks Oriane, see you soon," Lauren replied, leafing through Marie's CV with interest. "Now Marie, I see you've been a governess to members of the UK Royal family, you've served in the UK Royal Air Force in Afghanistan and you're now a writer, and you have a degree in Egyptology. References are impeccable. That's an interesting career for a twenty-nine year old, so tell me more …"

"I write action thrillers based in war zones, and have three published so far. My father was also a writer, Pierre LeClerk, you may have heard of him?"

"My word, *the* Pierre LeClerk? The man who spied on Moscow for fifteen years undetected during the cold war?"

Marie smiled. "Yes, I also occasionally assist Great-Aunt Letty with her work. She thought you may want a housekeeper and I fancied living down here, I was becoming bored with the London scene. And I love babies, children and cooking."

Lauren rather liked the look of this young woman. And Naomi had obviously been watching her back too which was kind and thoughtful. Her instincts were good. "I think you and I should get on fine, Marie. You're hired. Now I know there is a caretaker's house at the back but I haven't had time to see that yet."

"Oriane showed me around earlier, it's perfect. Oh, and they delivered your red BMW X5 whilst I was here, so I've put it in the double garage for you."

"Do you have a car Marie?"

"Yes, a rather ancient Porsche Carrera, I'm afraid. I understand that you wanted someone to prepare a meal for your daughter and family this evening, a sort of house warming party?"

"Yes, I cheekily asked Oriane if she could hire someone, I'm too exhausted and don't know the shops yet."

"If you want to then I'm onto it. How would you like my special seafood paella, done French style with a nice original recipe, followed by crème brûlée dessert and of course cheese and biscuits? And Oriane has left some baguettes and salad for you in the fridge for lunch and a selection of wines to keep you going. I've put them in the wine cellar."

"A perfect suggestion, yes please. Heavens, I didn't know there was a wine cellar either ... I shall unpack my case and just have a quiet mooch around the new pad everywhere, then I'll probably have a snooze ..."

"Whilst I get on with the meal tonight ... thanks for hiring me Professor Hind, I'm looking forward to working for you ..."

"Me too Marie ... Leave your Porsche in the garage with my BMW, so much safer."

Pleased that most of her clothes were already packed away in the dressing room, Lauren gazed happily at the wonderful view of the sea from her large bedroom window balcony, and then she lay down on her familiar bed, staring up at the ceiling.

Perhaps, she pondered, life really was on the up again. Pity though she hadn't heard from Philippe for three weeks, he was obviously busy, but she had a good feeling he would soon be coming home. She fished out a dress for the evening and sent a text to Svet and Amélie.

Moved in, wonderful, please come soon.

Immediate response:

You betcha - Svet, Nadine and Sergei

Amélie was probably opening another fete or something. Travel exhaustion was overcoming her, as her regular afternoon snooze time accelerated … her eyes closed for sweet dreams.

They were sitting casually at the table, finishing off the local brie whilst DG topped up his glass of red Burgundy. Marie returned from the kitchen and began to clear away the plates.

"Heck Lauren, your new housekeeper is a darn good cook. Marie, where did you learn to make such a delicious meal?"

"Thank you DG," Marie replied quietly, picking up the dessert dishes. "Cooking is a genuine hobby, I actually did a Cordon Bleu training programme in London and have presented on television on a few shows."

Lauren looked up. "Really? DG's housekeeper, Marcie, is also an amazing chef. She told me she has a lot of French family recipes from Louisiana, going way back to slavery times. You might enjoy having a chat with her?"

"Excellent idea, pop over any time Marie, Marcie will love to chat, especially about cooking. She ran her own restaurant one time in Dallas," Charlotte added.

"I'd love to do that, thank you Charlotte."

Lauren cut in. "Marie, once those plates are in the dishwasher, you're done for today. Thank you so much for making my family housewarming dinner a big success. I think you'd better sort out your cottage at the back and unpack. See you in the morning, and then we can chat about my routine and things to do here."

"Thanks Lauren, I'm already unpacked, but I've got writing to continue. Evening is the best time for me."

"You're an author, Marie? What is it you write?" DG asked curious.

"Army based thrillers. I'm working on my fourth novel, Drone Death is the title. I was stationed in both Iraq and Afghanistan."

"Well, I'll be blowed. Send me a couple of your books Marie, I'd love to read them, might learn something about modern warfare and these darned drones doing the rounds," DG replied.

"Sure thing. When I see Marcie I'll bring some round," Marie said, pleased with the interest from a former senior officer.

"Now ladies," DG continued. "I'm just heading for the yard for a quick smoke of one of my Havana's. No use asking you two to join me, I know, so I won't even try. In fact after tonight, I'm gonna make some effort to give these puffers up and start to get fitter again. May even get to a gym."

"Good," Charlotte cried, patting his belly. "About time. See you shortly."

Charlotte and Lauren, now alone, continued casually chatting about babies and where to start buying clothes and baby paraphernalia in the port town. But Charlotte was becoming increasingly anxious. Once DG was back they just had to tell Lauren. "How long ago have you had any communication from Philippe?" she asked casually.

Lauren pushed her cheese plate away and became thoughtful. "Not for the last three weeks, no response from emails, or texts and he must have changed his phone which is now a dead number. I assume he's very busy out on site in the middle of some Siberian nowhere." She looked at Charlotte who was struggling to hide a grimace, and her face had become flushed. "Okay Charlotte, do you want to tell me? I can see something isn't right, I felt you were a little tense all evening."

Charlotte shuffled in her chair and coughed, as DG walked back in and immediately clocked the facial expressions. "DG, I think we should discuss ... err ... the problem now with Lauren."

"What problem, Charlotte? Does it concern Philippe?" Lauren interjected.

"Okay, darn it Lauren," DG replied. "Here goes, but I want you to listen to everything first and what's been done, then questions? Deal?"

"Yes of course, deal. Don't worry, you know me now and how I like to process information, exactly like Charlotte, so give it to me straight and sequential. I'm absolutely fine with that."

<><>

DG slowly and carefully ran through the events in Novosibirsk as relayed by Olga, careful not to overplay her involvement. Lauren listened, concentrating in her familiar way, impassively, as when faced with a serious technical or mathematical problem. That was how she always coped and it had fared her well. However, once DG got to the point of Philippe being sentenced to fifteen years in prison, he stopped when first one then a small series of tears, dripped down her cheeks.

"I'll get onto what I've been doing next Lauren, but you talk. Charlotte and I are so doggone sorry to be the bearer of such bad news, especially today. Here, take this tissue, sorry it smells of tobacco."

Lauren blew her nose, laughed at DG's apology and wiped the tears away, trying hard to compose herself quickly. She was massively upset and numb inside. She'd already rationalised through the Olga affair, after all she hadn't exactly been a paragon of virtue either, but remained optimistic that she and Philippe would get back together soon; she had no concept that such a catastrophic thing could happen. Why was Philippe such a damned idiot? This was even worse than Murmansk. At a stroke, Philippe was gone from her life for good, and she hadn't or couldn't do anything about it. She knew all about Krasnokamensk, the largest uranium site in Russia. Anyone sent there never came back alive. If the radioactivity didn't kill the prisoners, the hard labour and harsh conditions would. Shit, shit, shit.

"I can still get on a plane to Moscow," she said resolute. "Is there anything I can do? Can Mila help? Actually I'm glad you told me today because this is the start of a new life for me, so we may as well commence with sorting out Philippe at the same time."

"Lauren, this is way beyond Mila's pay grade and almost beyond mine. But let me tell you now what I have been doing … we have a plan, of sorts."

"You mean this goes up as far as the Russian President?"

"Yes. Philippe, unknown to me and I could kick myself for not being more closely involved, has gotten himself into far too deep water somewhere along the line."

"One of Philippe's great strengths, DG, is his perception for new business and his networks … but his big weakness is arrogance and not listening, and he sadly has a particular blind spot for his own country. I'm fine both of you; you've defined the problem and it's now time to work through potential solutions. How can we get him home?"

"I've got the US Vice President back-channelling," DG began. "He has a direct personal line to the Russian Prime Minister. Now we have one key asset there Lauren. The PM, Ivan Breshneryev, has a very high regard for you and your nuclear achievements. Information internally, which had been passed up the food chain, was either deliberately omitted or it wasn't known, I mean the connection between you and Philippe. I suspect Olga, in the middle, also threw off the scent."

"You mean that whore was passing herself off as his wife too?"

"I suspect that has probably been the case," DG replied slowly with a heavy heart. But Lauren was unmoved and unsurprised. Olga was already well factored into the toxic mix.

"The Russian President is a recent appointment; do we know how Philippe fits into the new political regime?" Lauren then asked.

"Again, my suspicions are … not very well. Either Philippe underestimated his personal appeal to the new President and the strength of the reactionary oil and gas oligarchs he was trying to outwit, or had no idea of the level of corruption and favours being exchanged. The new President, interestingly, doesn't have a KGB background but was Special Forces, same as Philippe. That may be an issue, perhaps they were rivals one time. I'm expecting a call from my Chief of Staff in the US first thing Monday. We should know more then. In the meantime Lauren, we need to hold tight. And all this must be kept solely between us three, no publicity and no press, nobody must know a darn thing."

"Lauren, tomorrow I promised the twins they could come over and play in the pool. Then perhaps we could all walk into the port, lunch on me … and just relax," Charlotte added, anxious to divert Lauren from any move towards airports.

"That sounds lovely, I look forward to it. I'm not going to jump on the next plane to Moscow. In my condition, I'm next to useless anyway and to be honest, Murmansk hasn't exactly fired up any great desire to return to the old USSR, DG."

DG roared in a great bellow. "Excellent, now time we headed home Charlotte, I'm whacked."

Lauren was quickly in bed pondering hard, immensely grateful and relieved DG had instigated tangible political action. She needed to get information on Ivan Breshneryev and the latest Russian nuclear policies, and then perhaps some business or economic leverage could be figured out. But she was equally determined not to let this new and irritatingly habitual Philippe setback ruin her life. She was massively upset and she would do all she could to get him out, but she had responsibilities and challenges too, and felt so physically tired … she was fast asleep in half a minute.

DG and Charlotte were lying in bed. "Actually Charlotte, there's something else bothering me, that damned woman Olga."

"What about her?"

"It was something she said. She had it in her head that Lauren had deliberately betrayed Philippe and orchestrated his prison term, and she made veiled threats. I quickly dissuaded her of that nonsense, but it's been lurking in my darned mind ever since. I need Mila's number … do you have it? Her special number? I need more information on that woman, something isn't ringing right. She's not just obsessive; I think she could be dangerous."

"Bloody hell DG, you mean Lauren is in danger? Here in Villefranche-sur-Mer? And only now you mention it?"

"I'm sorry Charlotte, hard to tell, but actually I already oversaw one aspect of security. When I talked to Oriane, she chose Marie with particular care. Her stint in Iraq wasn't a normal behind the scenes female support. Because of her outstanding abilities and fitness, the UK command moved her and half a dozen other women from special reconnaissance to direct combat in the SAS, as a highly secret six month trial, see how women could fare. The Brits are further ahead than our own high command, still stuck in a darned time warp with regard to women on the front line. She did well in the field."

"You mean Marie is like some sort of Brit GI Jane?"

DG laughed. "Yeh, I suppose you sure could say that. Marie already has a cache of weapons in her living quarter ... I've also quietly briefed her. I was going to tell you, don't glare like that honey, but the situation has sort of moved on faster than I thought."

"Wouldn't it be a good idea to tell Lauren? What about Seb?" Charlotte responded frostily.

"Seb is excellent but he's not a lot of use to Lauren down here when he's stationed in Brussels. Seems like Marie is almost there with Lauren, she'll complete the full communications tomorrow. I don't anticipate any problem. And she will make a great housekeeper and nanny. Marie isn't like Mila who will live and die the cause for the rest of her life. She volunteered out of the services, worked for the Brit Royal Family looking after a range of children ... and is a writer ... wants a different life, but she sure as hell will look out for Lauren, I'm well satisfied."

"Sorry, I yelled," Charlotte replied, cuddling into his huge body under the duvet. "I'm glad you've got my mother covered, you're quite the son-in-law aren't you."

"She's my prettiest mother in law by far, I sure as hell have gotta look after her or she'll be after my blood," DG answered, smirking, as Charlotte dug his ribs playfully.

"Anyway," Charlotte continued. "Olga has form. Lauren mentioned the scene at our wedding to Amélie, who mentioned it to Rosie, who did some digging and it appears that Olga is known to her network in the Chinese security services. See, you don't know all the intelligence around here, big boy."

"Darn, you're right, outsmarted again by women. That is very interesting. It means Olga is more than I thought, and now when you look and listen to her that all makes clear sense. She's obviously got a special operations combat background so I'm right to be worried. If Rosie knows, Mila will know. We don't need to contact her. You got Rosie's number?"

Charlotte nodded.

"I'll call her in the morning. Rosie's recovery is darn remarkable; she's a real Chinese warrior. If I break a leg again, I'll be on the first flight to Sergei, believe me honey-bunch."

"Hey big boy, all that wine you've drunk can't be good for you at your age either."

"Nothing wrong with my best parts, all in good working order, but in your condition I think I'll have to sit it out in the wings for a little while longer, although that pert white butt of yours might benefit from a bit of a rub instead?"

"Mmm ... guess that'll have to do for now ... well go on, I'm waiting," she purred.

But Charlotte had even more intelligence which she wasn't going to share with anyone ... yet. During the afternoon she'd finally received an email back from Michael ... the result was positive and intriguingly fascinating, much more than she could have ever dreamed about.

Chapter Twenty-One

Charlotte was relaxing in the bath, gazing incredulously at the email on her iPad, reading the summary over and over again. Michael had been remarkably quick, and although he had offered the extra services of a private detective he knew in Avignon that wasn't needed, and the agency didn't sound exactly salubrious anyway. Amélie had already warned her that Michael wasn't too choosy with his friends, another reason they divorced.

Confidential:
Your father's name is Henri-Gaston Landry and his address is The Gendarmes, Paris Parade, Marseille. This is a large detached mansion. The enclosed Google picture shows you the extent of the property behind the iron railings. The area is one of the most upmarket in Marseille, neighbours and surroundings highly affluent, as is Monsieur Landry.

He is 56 years old, French national, a widower and has been a successful artist all his life and specialises in painting bespoke urban landscape commissions, usually for large design and architectural companies worldwide. There are no records of any convictions or felonies and his tax affairs are in order.

He has five sons, the eldest is twenty six and the youngest is nineteen. They are all marine engineers and single, only the youngest one still lives with his father when ashore. The others are scattered around the globe, three live in Singapore and one in Hong Kong. His wife was a banker, she died five years ago of breast cancer.

Not only is Henri-Gaston Landry rich but he garners regular attention in the local press these days as a bit of a playboy, has had flings with various well known celebrities and is notorious for extravagant elite parties and gambling, but yet is supposedly shy and private. Little is known about his past and he doesn't do interviews. The attached picture, grainy I'm afraid, is the best I could locate.

I hope that is sufficient Charlotte, Good luck! M

She studied the picture again of a tall, slim and handsome man, with thick greying hair, helping a leggy female in a tight short skirt out of a limousine, who she immediately recognised as Claudette Gauguin, an actress half his age. Charlotte uncannily took after her mother in so many ways, good looks, character, intellect, but she definitely had her father's nose and a similar smile. She was hugely intrigued. Marseille wasn't that far. She decided mid-week, the day DG was flying to Washington for three days, she would drive over to The Gendarmes quietly and just look where he lives.

DG was sat in the garden on a wooden bench, the sun nicely warming up to be another fine day. He dialled a special security number on his mobile which was immediately answered. "Hey Dan, what you got me? I hope something a little more positive than when we started."

"DG, I'm glad you called, just got fifteen minutes then I gotta go … meeting with the President's Chief of Staff, I can't stand the bitch."

"No, me neither, so spit it out."

"Interesting discussion with Prime Minister Ivan, this incident was news to him; he'd been kept out of the loop, and got quite incensed. Sounds like Moscow have even worse insider politics than the White House. A rich oil and gas man, Kharkov, an oligarch, had gone straight to President Ilyushin, old mates from the army. You know how it goes from there."

"Yes, just as I thought. Now about Kharkov, I know that son of a bitch, a hard drinking bastard and even richer than me. So what's happened?"

"Ivan has followed up through his own meeting with Ilyushin. Kharkov had never mentioned the marital link between Lauren Hind of Cassini and Philippe Dubois and Ilyushin wasn't pleased either, but for some reason he wasn't prepared to waive a full deal. It appears that for now, judicial irregularities have been invoked and the sentence has been commuted … from fifteen to three years. Philippe will remain at Krasnokamensk but is not being taken off hard labour for three months, and only then will be allocated to farm duties. He'll be notified next week. It was said by Ilyushin that Dubois still had to pay a price, but wouldn't specify why, one can only speculate."

"What will it take to get them-there three years right down to zero Dan? What's the real price on the table?"

"Amazingly, not money directly. Ilyushin is annoyed with the Chinese being the first to get their hands on a great deal with Cassini for a number of those advanced Xenostra reactors being built around Beijing. Russia hasn't got the technical expertise to replicate them but has formulated a fifteen year plan to expand nuclear power, so it can export more oil and gas to Europe for longer … until of course the shale oil flows like honey from US soil, which it will within ten years, then they'll be in deep shit. I reckon a Cassini deal with Russia, even more favourable than the Chinese, may swing some positive leverage. I'll leave that one with you DG, let me know and I'll alert Ivan who has promised to negotiate directly on behalf of the Russian government, but only with Lauren Hind herself."

"Fuck me Dan; she's nearly seven months pregnant with triplets. There is no way she's getting to Moscow!"

"I'll leave you to figure a way, although even then there are no guarantees."

"Thanks Mr Vice President, you've done terrific for an old friend. Good luck with the pension bill; it's time something was done there. I'll be in Washington end of the week and I'll call in and have a beer."

DG immediately walked briskly to the fridge and cracked open a cold Belgian lager. He had one more call to make. Now where had Charlotte got to, they had to go and tell Lauren …

<><>

DG, swigging from the beer bottle, checked his watch. She shouldn't be asleep quite yet; the phone rang numerous times then was answered by a panting voice. "Yes?"

"Hey Rosie, it's your old friend DG, how you doing? You're a miracle I hear. Congratulations, I'm so pleased to learn you're up and about and very fit already."

"DG, how wonderful to hear your voice. I always been fit, you know that, especially for you," she giggled back. "Just pulling some weights, muscles getting nice and strong, I even fight Mila now."

DG roared down the phone. "You sure ain't lost your sense of humour, girl."

"Now DG, I know you, and DG not make social calls without deal. I assume you want to know about bitch Olga? All okay, Charlotte tipped me off, I already done useful work."

"Darn, that wife of mine is always one step ahead. So what you got me Rosie, anything useful?"

"You betcha, did I say that with good Texan twang? Yes, I get much more from Chinese intelligence. Olga Zavrazhny; she is daughter of Vlad Zavrazhny, ring any bells DG?"

"Zavrazhny? … Shit Rosie; he was a top commander in Spetsnaz, killed in Chechnya some years back. A grizzly operator who never took no prisoners. You say Olga is his daughter?"

"Yes, brought up in wilds of Siberia, elder son Igor is academic wimp … became diplomat and is now working with Philippe, which of course you know. Vlad brought up Olga like real son he always wanted, taught her all Spetsnaz skills including Systema martial art as child … outdoors gas engineering suit her well. She can look after herself like me and Mila, and frightened of nobody. So potentially very dangerous woman, especially if she blame Lauren for Philippe being locked up."

"I think we've got some movement there Rosie, can't say any more yet, politically sensitive, but Philippe may find life a little easier next week."

"Understand, that's good. I know Krasnokamensk, just over Chinese border. We have agents inside of course, keep an eye on Russian uranium. I get Philippe a phone then make contact and find out how he is and report back to you. If good you tell Lauren, if bad we keep to ourselves."

"That's a humdinger thing Rosie, many thanks. I sure do appreciate that."

"One day, you thank me properly DG, okay?"

"Mmm … maybe Rosie, just maybe."

She laughed loudly, mimicking him. "One final thing then I return to weights. Russian President, Leonid Ilyushin? He once was lover of Olga for long time. She eventually kick him out … and then she went off with Philippe. He and Olga know each other before, many years back when Philippe separated from first wife … so Ilyushin not very disposed to Philippe anyway and job will be harder to get him pardoned. I have alerted Mila, as you would expect. She already doing work too, no need to contact, she knows you have security for Lauren all in hand."

"Thanks Rosie, I assumed you would. Shit, all that stuff with Olga and Ilyushin all makes some sense now. Well, we're gonna try and shoot the hog anyhow."

<><>

Her first full day at the newly commissioned Cyclops Fusion Centre, and Lauren decided that a management by walking about exercise with Juliette around the new research building was a good way of introduction to the staff, and see the extent of the large site. Everyone had now transferred from the temporary building opposite, from which an impressive amount of work had already emanated. This was the first time she had seen the completed physical manifestation from a continuous stream of plans, modifications and tears from Herman when he saw the costs. That was until she had assured her Finance Director that a substantial European Union subsidy was definitely being made available, so they should let Juliette go for bust, even if she was fickle about her laboratory and workshop space requirements. Monsieur Le President, Jacques Chandrisé, had been as good as his word, honouring his pledge to get the best Euro-agreement done, although she still wasn't convinced that Amélie hadn't sneaked back into the Elysee and satiated their obvious joint admiration for the other. She laughed, reminiscing about that day, a prelude to arranging her marriage there … then felt a wave of immediate sadness thinking of Philippe. Damn it she couldn't even visit him … the labour camp was off limits to all outsiders.

She had effectively allowed Juliette a significant amount of latitude to get on with the completion of the purpose built facility, not only because she had complete confidence in Juliette's business capabilities, but coping with babies, Philippe, restructures and Israel, she couldn't stomach any more detail, happy to be a backstop, directing problems towards solutions. And there had been remarkably few.

The white-fronted and ultra-modern design of the main building positively hit her senses as they drove up. Marie was now taking her into work and would pick her up later; she didn't feel comfortable any longer squeezing in behind the wheel. First impressions were the five storey building was so much more technologically and architecturally upbeat than the old Brussels headquarters, with lots of modern smoked glass frontage, plentiful researcher offices and a lovely large reception. Surprisingly, the replication of the front lake, albeit smaller but with fountains and bronze lions that she did love so much in Brussels, worked well. She realised that Juliette had added homely design touches, astutely aware that at some stage Lauren would be unable to resist the draw of the research buzz being created. And Juliette was correct of course, she couldn't.

Sitting at her desk, she gazed around her new, well-lit office facing over the lake, more spacious than at HQ and with large windows letting in copious natural light which she adored. Juliette had furnished her working area very comfortably especially the inclusion of luscious, orange buffalo hide armchairs and a matching sofa around the teak coffee table. Next door was a small, adjoining office for a personal assistant … presently empty. Lauren was missing Eva badly and the welcoming aroma of morning coffee. With the expected knock on the door, Juliette walked in, dressed in an immaculate white Dior business suit … living with Mila was obviously rubbing off

… but a few paces behind her was someone else, an equally smart looking woman, early thirties, in a dark blue Versace trouser suit, with long black hair and beautiful brown eyes. But the facial features and the concentrated gaze? She was eerily familiar.

In front of the visitor, Juliette adopted her usual formal approach with a warm handshake … hugs later. "Lauren, welcome to the new Cyclops building and your new office, mine is one door down. Can I introduce you to Nirmayi, who I've appointed as your new Executive Assistant?"

Lauren shook hands with Nirmayi who smiled back warmly. "Good morning Professor Hind, it's a real honour meeting with you, I've been an admirer of your leadership in the nuclear sector for a long time."

"Well, thank you Nirmayi."

Lauren pointed to the armchairs and they settled down into the firm and comfortable fabric. "I'm impressed with the decor in here Juliette, how did you guess my taste so well?"

"Eva spilled the beans I'm afraid, but I can see you like it."

"Absolutely, the whole environment here from walking into reception right to the office feels so fresh and new, there's only so much you can do with a dog of a building like Cassini HQ. But the purpose build has exceeded my expectations. The final outcome really does look like the architectural drawings for once. Now Nirmayi, tell me about your background and experience," Lauren said, weighing up Nirmayi, who unusually she hadn't directly appointed for such an intimate position to grow into the job together, like Eva. Already, though, she liked Nirmayi's confident poise and dress sense, which unlike Eva, she definitely wouldn't have to train up.

But it was the accent which she hadn't expected. Very sophisticated, and a perfect posh English. Fairly quickly, Lauren learned that Nirmayi, also fluent in French, had gained a top first degree at the London School of Economics, an MBA at HEC in Paris a top European Business School she was familiar with, and had worked as a senior project manager for the waste management Director at one of the largest UK nuclear sites. Intellectually bright and business capable, Lauren could immediately envisage a different role for Nirmayi from Eva … a bridge, or a translator for her personal research and her wandering Bill Gates style ambassador activity with the rest of the business, particularly operations and services.

"Excellent Nirmayi, I'd like you to start immediately. Your office is next door; take your time to look around. The rest of the morning I shall be inspecting the site with Juliette, then at noon I'd like you to come with me for lunch and we can have a more detailed chat about your role … listening to your experience and qualifications, I propose to tweak your job, but it will become more demanding than maybe you thought."

"Thank you Professor Hind, I relish business challenges that will be fine. I'll go and set up my computer and sort out all the data, communications and security protocols."

"So from now on just call me Lauren, I hate formalities as Juliette knows. May I ask? Does Nirmayi have a meaning? I know many Indian names do."

"Yes, it means 'without blemish'. Actually Lauren everyone usually calls me Nimi too."

"Very apt Nimi and I shall do the same. I'll call in to your office later then we can go down to the restaurant, chat and start diaries."

<><>

"Gosh Juliette," Lauren said giving her an informal hug now they were alone. "You've tracked down a unique individual there, with all of Eva's capabilities plus the nuclear business project management experience. Now why does she look so familiar?"

"She should do. Nimi is Bhavika's younger sister, although they grew up along quite different paths, but are now, as seasoned professionals, very close."

Lauren smiled. "Of course, the family resemblance, I am stupid, that is an interesting turn up. Well, if she's like Bhavika, then Nimi and I should get along very well."

"To be honest Lauren, Nimi is much nicer, far less strident and very subtly sophisticated. She grew up with her uncle, a cancer consultant, in London. Quite why, I don't know. But Bhavika suggested her, and of course I love and admire Bhavika too, well I have to she's my indispensable street-fighting Deputy!"

They laughed and Juliette carried on. "The final design and additional facilities of this building, once that huge EU grant was confirmed, gave me the opportunity to think more laterally around the wider research spin-offs from the nuclear fusion focus. I went to visit the Paul Scherrer Institute in Switzerland, which of course has a long and prestigious reputation for applied and pure research into nuclear physics as well as other linked areas. So having been inspired by their multi-disciplined approach, I thought we could replicate the layout and vision, on a smaller scale of course. We are approaching a hundred staff in here now, which will double after signing up the Israeli-JETR partnership, to make us up to ninety percent capacity already. So when we walk around, you will see state of the art research workshops and laboratories already functioning in solid state physics, lasers, robotics, nanotechnology, new materials, and electromagnetic development. I've also appointed a Head of Partnerships … who is signing up memoranda of cooperation with the Universities of Pune, Peking and Pierre and Marie

Curie in Paris, your alma mater. What we need to do is ensure that other spin-offs and intellectual property from the fusion research can also be captured and either licensed or developed into additional commercial opportunities and income streams, as I did when I was at UCL in London."

"That's fabulous Juliette, well done, exactly the philosophy I envisaged for the new Cassini, managed vertical and horizontal diversification. And that is exactly what I want Nimi to do. Be the interpretive link to me to ensure that I can drive pure research towards applied innovation …and then more money for all of us. I don't need an Eva style Executive Assistant to ensure I run the business daily, because I now have you, Johann and Sonja to do all that heavy lifting," Lauren replied triumphantly, feeling good about getting her vision together in the first hour of sitting in her office.

"Then Nimi should be perfect," Juliette replied contentedly. "I got your first appointment right." Suddenly Juliette went very quiet and thoughtful. "Before we head off on the tour, there's something I want to tell you before anyone else, or you find out on the qt."

"The qt?"

"Sorry Lauren, London slang, I mean quietly or off the record." She took a deep breath. "Mila and I are finished, well, what I mean is we're no longer living together. Actually what I do mean is she's moved out by joint and very amicable and professional agreement. It would never have worked out, we're so unlike each other and … to be honest, eventually, I want a relationship which has permanence and a new family start and Mila is in transit. And I've realised, I want a man back in my life. We both needed and benefitted from a temporary fling and you probably understand why, given where we were both coming from … but it's run its course, well and truly. I don't know how long her sabbatical will be, but all she seems to want to do at the moment is bite heads off alligators in swamps."

Lauren roared laughing, realising she was subconsciously beginning to copy the DG belly laugh, well she had the belly presently. "I'm sorry Juliette, yes that is so Mila, I'm sorry it hasn't worked out …"

"No you're not Lauren and neither am I … these things always work out for the best though," Juliette replied, joining in the amusement, both understanding the essential Mila.

Lauren felt a huge wave of relief run through her body … she was actually very, very pleased to hear that news. She felt a kick from one of the three footballers, also excited, reminding her to get back to work. "Let's go then. Oh yes, I've now decided to name the facility the Cyclops Fusion Institute and your job title is CEO Cassini Research Division and Institute Director, the academic gravitas seems more appropriate. But first stop … you must show me the cafe. I could do with a reviving tea and a large piece of carrot cake."

"Me too actually … good idea," Juliette said. "Then straight to robotics; you have to meet Buster the nuclear dog, who can run fearlessly into a fusion zone and retrieve stuff where mere mortals only quake."

Lauren's first week had gone well. She and Nimi carefully worked through and agreed a brand new Executive Assistant job description, and they both managed to master the new high tech coffee machine which had now been installed in Nimi's office. Nimi's first job was to liaise with Johann and Helena and arrange an inauguration ceremony with lots of good publicity with selected customers and university partners. Swinging her legs out of the passenger door, she had barely touched the ground when Charlotte's old Dodge pickup she had shipped over to France, came racing into the driveway. Smiling faces were greeting her for a change ... and the twins were with DG splashing in the pool.

"How did they get here?" Lauren asked, curious.

"School bus dropped them off nearby. I said I was coming later, when you got in."

"Marie and I have had a good woman to woman talk yesterday," Lauren said, smiling mischievously. "I understand her background more thoroughly. She says the weapons are discretely hidden. DG has been scheming again hasn't he, but I do appreciate it, and she's now liaising with Seb as well. Pretty amazing, I reckon, having a housekeeper and future nanny who writes novels and totes a gun like Mila. So that saves you one confession for the day."

DG, who had walked over with a towel around him, looked relieved. "Sure am glad about that, thanks Lauren. You're real battle hardened these days since Murmansk but better to be safe for all kinds of reasons."

"Name me some more then DG," she replied promptly.

"Well, Rosie got some intelligence on Olga ... we all know she's a bit crazy, but she might also harbour a grudge and start getting nasty ..."

"You mean with me? Because Philippe is now imprisoned for fifteen years? I don't think so DG. My female assessment is Olga the Fearless will be promptly off around Russia looking for the next best opportunity and person to latch onto now that Philippe is incarcerated forever; she's obviously that sort of woman. I'm not going to let someone like her bother me ... I've got enough to occupy my brain."

"I agree," Charlotte added. "That's the last we'll be hearing of Olga."

"Anyway," DG began again. "Reason we both came is we've got some good news, just been confirmed officially."

"What news?"

"Philippe has had his sentence commuted from fifteen to just three years, following a little behind the scenes intervention and some irregularities discovered."

Lauren's face lit up. She couldn't believe it and threw her arms around DG, kissing him wildly on each cheek.

"Hey steady on, mom-in-law," he spluttered, taken aback by the big show of affectionate thanks.

Lauren continued. "Now, how much has it cost you, because I will transfer funds from my reserve account tomorrow, believe me."

"Doggone it, Lauren. No need for that. But it hasn't cost anything yet, apart from clarifying a few political realities. But there is one request ... a special deal or two for Russia on the Xenostra reactors, better than the Chinese got. Looks like you have a big fan in the shape of the Russian PM, Ivan Breshneryev. Now such a deal may push a little more in Philippe's favour, as well as add to your profits."

"I have one problem," Lauren responded. "The reason we never pursued Russian interest, and I'm aware of their need to build more nuclear capacity, has actually been down to Philippe, who steadfastly asked me never to do business directly with his own country. He never really clarified why, and I never pushed him. He will be very unhappy but that's too bad. I'll get Johann and his top sales team onto it tomorrow to start the ball rolling."

"I think I probably know why," DG replied. "Philippe is essentially an honest man, hates corruption and crooked dealing. You're gonna need me on this ... because part of the agreement will be some money will have to go to a company based in Liechtenstein, and I can do that."

"Liechtenstein?"

"Somebody's personal holdings high up the food chain. Don't ask. You can't and nor should you get involved in that, not with Cassini and your ethical stance worldwide, which has gained a lot of admirers I can tell you. Trust me on this Lauren; this will be part of my atonement too. If it wasn't for me going all bull-at-a-gate on fracking in Russia, then little old Philippe wouldn't be slammed up in the jailhouse."

"And I support him on that too Lauren," Charlotte added.

"One other conundrum," DG continued. "Breshneryev insists on meeting you in person to close any deal. I've told them you ain't flying anywhere right now so he said he'll come to you, but not company premises … he wants to meet you … here in Nice. Up for it? … I can fix that I think. No need to arrange security, there'll be a contingent of heavies with him. Ivan is one of the good guys over there, and a great opportunity to get my first special guest on the new yacht. Refitters are ahead of schedule, 'Nodding Donkey' should be putting out to sea in two weeks. Doggone it, better raid the piggy bank quick, still gotta pay for it."

Lauren thought hard then warmed to the proposal … she would definitely meet the Russian Prime Minister … and on DG's yacht that would be very cool, as Svet would say. Philippe would be extremely unhappy with the whole concept, but if it helped to get more time off his sentence then he would just have to lump it, because the meeting was going to happen, with his blessing or without it, not that he was in a position anyway to object. "I'm for it DG, but first I need to get Johann's team over to Moscow and start the preliminaries. Once they look positive then the invitation can be made … gosh, the name of your yacht just kills me."

"Me too," Charlotte said, joining in the laughter as the twins looked over to see what all the fun was about.

"Excellent. Now, just so happens that as I've got my swimming shorts on, if you don't mind Lauren, I'm gonna jump right back in that pool with them-there kids and Marie and have a good time."

"Enjoy," Lauren shouted after him as he bounded towards the pool, hollering to the twins, before diving in with a massive splash. She turned to Charlotte, who was facing towards the sun, eyes closed and relaxing. "And what about you? What are you up to during the day now you've got the family into a routine?"

"Oh, you know, just pottering about and liaising on the engineering business with my CEO, making sure noses are on the grindstone, that sort of thing." Charlotte laughed weakly, aware of a redness creeping over her cheeks, because she had one big secret to tell someone … Her visit to see the abode of Henri-Gaston Landry, except more happened than she anticipated …

Chapter Twenty-Two

The exchange of pleasantries was brief. Amélie was impatient. She wanted to hear the full story, curious about Lauren's teenage love-life which had never been spoken about over the last twenty-one years they had been friends. "So fire away Charlotte, what happened when you got to his address?"

"It was a longer drive than I thought, just over two and half hours and I was tired when I arrived in Marseille. But I have to thank Michael for perfect directions and the house photo was very useful. After a refresh and a coffee in a cafe down the road, I parked in the street and just gazed at the house, with no plan at all in my head. The residence is a massive detached villa with extensive grounds, and tall, black painted railings around the perimeter, so you could see the place fully. A couple of expensive Mercedes cars were parked outside. Everywhere was very quiet, no sign of life in the house."

"So having arrived there like a stalker staring in, surely you had to do something? You couldn't leave without doing more than stare? … I certainly wouldn't have done," Amélie cried, continuing with her impatience, especially when her normal mindset was always to confidently march in, confront and demand whatever she wanted.

But Charlotte didn't know what she wanted, especially once she'd got there.

There was a long pause. "So?"

"Okay here goes. I'm desperate to tell someone. The whole experience was really quite surreal."

<><>

Having stared at the outside of the building for nigh on twenty minutes, Charlotte, never normally a woman lacking in confidence, finally did decide. She had been weighing up the pros and cons, one issue following the next logically and sequentially, carefully trying to balance potential action and reaction and the long term consequences. But somehow the cons were significantly outweighing the pros, frustrating her even more. To hell with the consequences. She brushed her hair, applied some more lipstick, put her smart jacket on over her dress, and got out as elegantly as she could muster from the car and began to walk to the front. Opening the gate, she strode confidently up the drive and stood in front of the bright blue door ... then pressed the bell, twice.

After about half a minute, the door slowly opened wide and a woman stood there, early fifties, smartly dressed in a green uniform, presumably a housekeeper of some sort. "Bonjour, Madame. Puis-je vous aider?"

"Parlez-vous anglais s'il vous plait?" Charlotte replied, already feeling this was a bad idea, especially as her conversational French was still rudimentary.

"Oui ... how may I be of assistance?" the woman replied, staring down at Charlotte's very obvious bulge under her dress.

"Monsieur Landry ... is he at home?"

"I am sorry Madame, which one do you enquire for? The young Charles or his father Henri-Gaston?"

"Henri-Gaston."

"Is Monsieur Landry expecting you? Do you have an appointment?"

"No, but when he knows I am here, he will want to see me," Charlotte replied, her stomach churning six to the dozen, because that was already taking a big liberty. This could become a huge disaster. She wondered whether it would be best to just turn and walk away, while the going was clear.

The housekeeper looked down again at Charlotte's bump, pondered carefully then decided perhaps she should find the master of the house after all.

"Please wait here one moment, I will just go and find out. Your name please?"

"Charlotte?"

She continued standing there for at least a minute. Fortunately, the midday sun and growing warmth was shielded by the shadow of a large, nearby cherry tree, just into pink blossom with an adorable scent. She was desperate for a drink of water and a pee. She heard raised male and female voices jabbering in French, a serious debate ensuing inside, when a tall, slim male with flashing, blue eyes and a sexy grin, around twenty years old, dressed in trendy jeans and a black leather jacket, walked straight out of the door.

"Don't worry Charlotte," he said, still grinning and heading for the gate. "My father is on his way."

She turned and stared back, the smile and the expression … the same … that must be Charles, his youngest son … and her half brother. Her heart began to pound as she heard footsteps clattering down a wooden staircase and Henri-Gaston Landry appeared at the door.

She gazed at him all over in an instance. Like his son he was tall and slim. He looked a lot younger than fifty-six, clean shaven with a thick head of grey brushed-back hair. His skin was smooth but also lined from the sun; he had an alluring tan. He was wearing old jeans and a green, scruffy thin jumper and waving a small paint brush in his hand. But instantly she recognised the handsome look, the nose and the chin. Henri-Gaston Landry was a man with significant presence. She tried to imagine him when he was Lauren's lover, she sixteen, gorgeous, precociously bright and innocent, and he twenty-eight and probably married, and immediately felt that magnetic attraction her mother probably fell for too at the time.

He smiled warmly and like his housekeeper gazed at her bump and pondered before speaking in English, with a deep voice like DG but with a lovely lilt of an accent. "I'm sorry Madame. I believe you are English and I understand you insist on seeing me, but I'm afraid I don't know you. In fact I don't know anybody called Charlotte. I think you must have the wrong address."

Charlotte stared up directly into his eyes. There was no mistaking him. This was her father. She wasn't leaving.

"Actually Monsieur Landry, I'm American. No, it's true we haven't actually met before. I'm Charlotte … your daughter … and you're soon to become a grandfather," she replied boldly, no longer feeling hesitant. Then she added. "And would it be possible to use your loo please? I'm desperate."

She wished, every time she had back-tracked that initial exchange with him, that she had taken a picture; the quaint image of his expression, which turned from pleasant apathy and mild irritation being disturbed by some idiot woman, to one of sudden, deep contemplation, staring at her features. Features which were noticeably and unmistakably his. His past ran chillingly through his body, back in time as he began estimating Charlotte's age. Then it clicked … the colour drained from his face, his jaw sagged, as he looked at Charlotte properly and saw a ghost, a ghost who was then sixteen years old, who vanished abruptly from his life, snatched away and disappeared, but now suddenly reincarnated outside his front door. But of course, Charlotte and Lauren were so alike.

"Jeanette, Jeanette, where are you? Come here quickly," he shouted back into the hallway, and the housekeeper suddenly appeared breathless from the rear of the building. "Can you take Charlotte to the downstairs cloakroom and then bring her to my study please, together with a large pot of tea and some of those delicious cakes you baked." His smile returned and his face had regained colour, becoming quite flushed. He directed Charlotte inside the house, looked around outside furtively and shut the door quickly.

Charlotte, at last feeling hugely relieved, stepped inside the large study as the housekeeper shut the door behind her. Henri-Gaston, now dressed in a casual cheque shirt and smart Diesel jeans, stood up promptly from his chair and walked slowly towards her. He took her quietly in his arms and held her tight, cheek to cheek as she had her four inch heels on despite the struggle, she feeling the smoothness of his skin and a faint whiff of aftershave, he sensing the alluring odour of Chanel No5 and realising the woman he was holding had style, sophistication and wealth. An emotional force field was zapping from one to the other, enveloping them in a cosy net of hope, desire and incredulity.

"I always suspected that she was pregnant. I knew in my heart but they never would tell me … we were wrenched apart by that awful woman, her mother, and her father suddenly cut me off. Mon Dieu, Charlotte, you are so like Lauren. I can't believe it. What on earth happened to her? … Did she marry in the end?"

He poured tea out in china cups and handed her a plate of small cakes … which she grabbed as she had missed lunch.

Charlotte realised that having entered her father's house and now having met him without any proper plan, meant she had no idea where to start ... there were so many jumping off and on points and also many gaps which she still couldn't fill about Lauren's past life. She began by explaining that immediately after Lauren gave birth, she was adopted by an American couple and brought up in the US but that her adopted parents had been tragically killed in a plane accident when she was eighteen. She had to simplify her own life ... that she set up an oil and gas engineering business in Texas, had twins from a former relationship and was now recently married to a US Senator. Her father was fascinated, but kept returning the discussion to Lauren. She quickly realised that he wanted to know as much about Lauren as about his lost daughter, and that was extremely tricky. His mouth dropped with disbelief when she described Lauren's ascent to become Chairman and CEO of a global nuclear energy company. He had no idea, had never heard of her or Cassini and obviously his arts and culture networks and social patterns were a million miles away from any familiarity with scientists.

Lauren was only sixteen, their affair and his love for her had been intense and she had always been at the back of his mind, but his life had moved on so quickly in the fast lane of art, money and celebrity, then in the end a large and happy family materialised until his wife died prematurely. He simply assumed Lauren had faded away into a life of simple normality ... The notion that she was an international business superstar in the science, nuclear and energy world and a Forbes businesswoman of the year was too much for him to comprehend.

She found it hard to believe that although he had five grown-up sons, they were all single, playing the field with no serious relationships which had produced children, so Kat and Lexi were his first and only grandchildren. A tear ran down his cheeks when she showed him recent photographs … he wanted to meet them soon. And that was the point where she sensed major difficulties … because his fascination with Lauren was so strong he wanted to meet her too.

He talked extensively of his family, the four boys stationed in Asia as marine engineers and Charles, still living with him, the youngest one, who had just decided to switch University courses … into design and not follow in the engineering footsteps of his brothers.

Time had marched on. Charlotte did say Lauren had moved to Nice to be near her new company research institute, not far from where she and her husband, DG, also now lived, but used the excuse that she still had a lot to learn about her mother, and that they had only found each other twelve months before. He nodded. Jeanette suddenly reappeared, reminding Henri-Gaston that he had an important evening reception to attend.

He apologised, but she could feel herself breathing a sigh of relief. She wanted more and she wanted her father to meet the twins and DG but she needed to think … how could she approach Lauren on the whole issue of Henri-Gaston?

They got up and exchanged cards.

"Do you mind if I call you Henri?"

"Actually Charlotte, I would be very proud and happy if you wanted to call me papa, like the boys … I feel no shame or trepidation being your father at all."

She suddenly came to the realisation, in an instant, that in fact she too was happy to do the same. She hugged him "Thank you Henri, I'm sure I will in due course. I know we want to meet again soon, but will you be patient, give me time to adjust to this momentous change, talk to my immediate family … and talk to Lauren? Please don't contact her first ... can you promise me that?"

"Yes, of course. No need to rush, but I am dying to meet my grandchildren, that is all so incredible, I can't take it in."

"Of course, and I'm sure Kat and Lexi will be excited too and want to meet you. They know I was adopted, but no more than that."

"In all the discussion, you still haven't told me?" he said coyly.

"Told you what?"

"Whether Lauren actually married and has children?"

Lauren breathed deeply. "Yes, Lauren is married ... to Philippe," she replied quietly. "He is Russian and presently ... err ... based in Russia on business. No, she hasn't got any other children." The rest and the present were far too complicated for any explanation further.

His face flagged on hearing she was married, but then his smile up perked again and his eyes sparkled when she said Philippe was based in Russia. A potential incendiary scenario could be quickly generated if she wasn't careful ... she needed advice ... and she could only really talk to Amélie or perhaps Mila if she could locate her.

As they walked to the door to say goodbye, it opened and Charles walked back in. "Ah ... Charlotte, you're still here with my father I see. Papa, don't forget we have to be at the town hall by six and make that speech, all bibbed and tuckered," he said laughing, eyeing Charlotte up and down with a look of intrigue and latent lust.

"Yes I know, Charles," he replied irritated. "Now, can I introduce you properly to Charlotte ... meet your new sister and as you can see, soon you'll become an uncle."

The second occasion when she wished she had that camera.

"Pardon?"

"Charlotte is just leaving, but we'll have plenty of time to get to know each other better, bye, take care on the way back. We'll speak soon."

They hugged and she pecked a speechless Charles on the cheek. "Bye brother," and flounced down the path, floating in a vacuum from the rest of the world into her car and away back up the motorway ...

<> <> <>

Amélie listened hard and carefully before any pronouncement, but Charlotte really needed some sort of impartial steer ... and Amélie had been there before too, although her circumstances were quite different. "Okay, here's my take," she said slowly. "By all means meet your father again, get to know him better, and plan to introduce him to your family. But my advice is do not tell Lauren, not yet. She has so much to think about right now, perhaps this is a complication in her life too much ... I think at some stage you will have to explain more in a simple fashion to Henri-Gaston and then see how it goes. Take it all slowly. And don't tell Mila either, at least not yet."

Charlotte pondered over the phone, weighing up the pros and cons. Amélie made sense. Now the pros greatly exceeded the cons, but her own instinct too was to try and leave her mother out of the mix for now ... after all this was her real father, she was his daughter and Kat and Lexi his grandchildren ... and to start there. When a suitable time came she would discuss openly with Lauren, and she fervently hoped Henri-Gaston would respect all that for now and not try and contact Lauren directly himself. She had to take that chance ...

Chapter Twenty-Three

The line was crystal clear but an echoing satellite delay was hindering their discussion, so Lauren kept it brief and succinct. "Johann, I'm glad you personally took charge of this Russian assignment, I assume you have your top team of negotiators with you?"

"Absolutely Lauren and having the title of Cassini CEO has definitely opened more early doors for me. Today we finally see the senior aide to the Prime Minister, plus the Minister for Energy and a representative of one of the state oil and gas companies, which seems a little odd but we'll see. I suspect we're going to look immediately at comparative costs per megawatt of Russian gas versus Cassini nuclear. We've done well for only three days — the basis of a deal is potentially coming along. But do you really want us to go below two billion US dollars for a trial reactor?"

"Yes, but negotiate hard, keep that in your back pocket if necessary. I will clarify the finances with Hermann; this business deal has complications but we will remain profitable per unit."

"Okay, the line is awful, I'll report back tomorrow with a summary of progress for you and Sonja."

"Thanks, Johann. Is Sonja alright? I see she has electronically diarised working from home quite a lot, including today?"

"She's getting tired from a full day at the office. She can take rest breaks from home more easily as she is pestered less, although she works the whole day through still."

"Tell her to ease up from me and do like the Chairman, a nice snooze in the afternoon … I approve it wholeheartedly. I'll speak to her anyway tomorrow"

Johann laughed. "I will, thanks Lauren, speak soon."

She sat back in her old office chair, taking stock, as Eva walked in with a large pot of Assam tea, now becoming a firm favourite, before immediately departing with Helena down to Edward's clinic for their respective check-ups. A few days before, Lauren had taken an impromptu fast train to Brussels with Nimi, to show her around the Cassini HQ and introduce her to everyone. She had decided that a comfortable and relaxing train journey, supported by taxis and the best five star hotel in town, especially as she was accompanied, would be perfectly fine. She desperately needed a break and planned to head back to Nice after lunch, relaxed and looking forward to gazing at the French countryside in a first class seat.

There was a knock on the door and Nimi strolled back in having seen around the engineering services workshops. They discussed Nimi's new project management modelling software, populated with a variety of potential commercial routes to market of some of the existing research spin-offs … top of the list was Buster, the robot dog.

"I know he made you laugh on your first day, with that silly programmed bark but I've been through the research thinking in detail with Dheerandra Singh, the new robotics section head. Not only can Buster go inside highly dangerous radioactive areas and do repairs, but Dheerandra has built and programmed a smaller prototype puppy, Razz, using a revolutionary leg joint, designed at the University of Pune.

311

Bhavika tipped me off. Razz can run over a variety of rough terrains on those four legs, with forty kilogram packs on his back at fifty kilometres per hour."

"Good heavens, but what's that got to do with nuclear energy?"

"I would rather suggest Lauren, who would be especially interested in that sort of capability?"

Lauren shook her head. She was now thirty-three weeks, feeling apprehensive and her concentration was not as tip-top as she would normally like, to fire back. Fortunately, despite Edward's continuing incredulity, she hadn't increased much in external size for the last month and a half, like she was reaching some limit, although scans of the triplets and tests showed all remained well. He had called her not only a phenomenon in business but one in multiple births too. She was still working, but only half days as she did tire easily, but felt good and Marie was doing an amazing housekeeping and driving job. She was just eternally glad bed rest had not been ordered, although she was technically supposed to be confined to barracks on the Cote d'Azur. She hadn't told Edward she had popped up to Brussels, he would only grimace, and Helena and Eva were on strict orders to say nothing. He now insisted on knowing her weekly itinerary and a bed had been booked ready in a very good Nice maternity clinic which he had personally vetted with Adèle. The moment she had anything like a contraction, she had to phone him immediately. He even carried a special Lauren alert device.

"The military."

Lauren sat up slowly. That word jolted her wavering concentration right back. All of Cassini's products and services were sold to governments and were non-military, when she had an immediate leap of thinking to the whole concept of military, energy and combat … there was a channel here to market which everyone had ignored.

"Nimi … I like your thinking. I want an estimate from Juliette what Dr Singh's moonlighting budget would be to complete Razz as a commercial demonstrator, then I want you to do some confidential blue-sky thinking … around future military needs, involving nuclear and technology, but all support functions and non-lethal, definitely no bombs, that is one line we will never cross."

"Onto it Lauren, I'll start after lunch. Main competitor is probably Google would you believe? Oh, while you were out, I had a call patched through from Cyclops, someone called Irena? She wouldn't leave a message but said she would try later. To be honest, she sounded distressed. Would you like me to follow it up for you?"

Lauren stared out of the window, feeling both concern and puzzlement. All she was aware of was that Irena and Annabella, now Aid Evocative CEO at last, had gone together to the Democratic Republic of the Congo to set up a new Central African base for the charity. That move had made Lauren uncomfortable, knowing the appalling legacy of the old US built and failed nuclear reactor there in the capital which had been left to dangerously rot in a sorry state.

"No thanks Nimi, I'll follow up myself … Irena is Chairman of our key sponsored charity, Aid Evocative. Strictly speaking outside of our research remit, but key as a front to our ethical stance and corporate social responsibility as a nuclear company … bear in mind the issue of ethics and not only profit when thinking about the military … I know that's a tough call but you wanted some challenges!"

Nimi smiled and shut the door quietly on her way out to have a chat with Bella about the pension scheme, noting to

313

research Aid Evocative thoroughly anyway. Lauren poured out a large mug of black tea and ran through everything on her desk. Talk of military had made her immediately think of Mila and Philippe. The clandestine meeting with the Russian Prime Minister on DG's splendid and unbelievably huge yacht couldn't be arranged yet for six weeks, by which time she might have somewhat expanded her family … but DG confirmed some goodwill payment in advance had headed to Liechtenstein already. Philippe had to continue with hard labour at the camp and was breaking rocks for a new road to the latest uranium mineshaft. She had to get him out before he ended up in there. But she was pleased that he was still in good mental and physical shape, now receiving better food and was already much fitter and had sent his love … thanks to Rosie and her ability to contact him secretly. The sentence reduction to three years had decidedly boosted his morale. Olga had vanished into nowhere thank goodness, and Mila may as well have done as communication with her was zero … for which Lauren still badly blamed herself.

It was Charlotte she was now concerned about … who was definitely hiding something. Lauren knew her daughter almost instinctively these days, they saw each other constantly. Only Amélie seemed uncharacteristically normal which made a change. Happy, and loving her English Establishment life even more, now that both the errant Simon and Cordelia were both securely institutionalised in London and being treated by Irena. At which point she dialled Irena's mobile number, which was answered after a couple of rings.

"Hi Irena, Nimi, my new assistant said you tried to get hold of me earlier. Great job you're doing with the treatments so I hear from Amélie, so is everything with Aid Evocative going

…" Lauren stopped when a great sob sounded loudly over the phone. "Irena? What on earth is the matter?"

Irena continued sobbing until finally there was a pause as she tried to pull herself coherently together. "Lauren, I'm sorry, I'm inside a specialist clinic in Nairobi. I'm recovering from a bad shoulder wound and in so much pain you would never believe. Peter is here, he's just gone to get a drink. I was shot escaping. It's awful Lauren, I couldn't believe the place could be so lawless … and Annabella … oh my God …" She began to sob again.

Lauren shot up in her chair, got up and began pacing the room. "Start again Irena, slowly, what's happened? Where is Annabella? All I know is you were both heading off to the Congo."

"We arrived last month in Kinshasa and began to set up the Centre. An Israeli charity, No Zahoot, was also there and we joined forces having similar objectives, their focus being using technology to assist the poor and uneducated. But they had already learned a lot about local communities and politics from experience over the last year. We quickly got our health clinic running. Annabella is amazingly organised and caring Lauren."

"I know. So what happened then Irena? Keep going, I'm listening."

Irena cleared her throat. "An unknown militia appeared two days ago inside the building, twenty men in army fatigues, a couple of armoured pickups and all heavily armed with Kalashnikovs; a real dirty ragtag bunch, just as you see in media news clips. Annabella was out in town getting supplies. They bundled about ten local women, the nurses and two doctors into the truck and then shot dead one of our German doctors who tried to run, and a couple of the local security staff. Cold and merciless, shot in the back and no remorse, it was horrific

315

Lauren. I tried to reason with the leader who spoke English … they wanted medics. They had raided the old nuclear reactor site, which is a joke apparently, virtually unguarded and no proper security and somehow found a cache of radioactive material … for ransom to the highest terrorist bidder. I assume dirty bombs. But some of them are now sick with what sounds like acute radioactive exposure and poisoning, including their juju witchdoctor. The women were additional hostages to bargain with, probably with the intention of raping them first. The moment Annabella returned, without hesitation she raced off to the platinum mine where they were held temporarily to rescue the women. I jumped in our truck with her; I just couldn't reason and stop her. When we arrived, the leader immediately spoke to her first, ignoring me, and then grabbed her too, and let the other women go who all ran off screaming into the jungle. They decided they had secured a much more lucrative prize. I jumped in the truck, and they shot at me as I raced off, I got hit in the shoulder. I can't tell you the pain, what it felt like, but I kept on going with adrenaline to the army HQ, and collapsed inside. Nobody wanted to know, most of the commanding colonel's soldiers were out of town fighting some insurgency near the Rwandan border. The next thing I knew I was in Nairobi being treated … the Israeli CEO had got me flown out there drugged and comatose. Oh God Lauren, Annabella's been kidnapped by those thugs, God knows what they're doing to her. As the leader dragged her off by the hair, the last thing I heard was Annabella shouting your name, over and over again. I don't know what to do. For some reason, whoever these people are, or whatever they're doing, Annabella is just a sacrificial lamb along the way. All I get is obfuscation and claptrap from our own Foreign Office and Peter has no political clout whatsoever anymore."

Lauren's brain went into overdrive. She had to make that call, which she never ever thought would be necessary again. And fuck everything, Annabella was special, uniquely special to her, and in her last moments of freedom, her own name was the last thing on Annabella's lips.

"Irena, concentrate now on getting better. Leave this with me. I have contacts in this business. Believe me I am going to get Annabella out."

"But you can't do anything in your condition. Gosh you must be due now?"

"I've got plenty of phones Irena and a loud voice. I'll let you know, I do have some influence still."

"I'm so grateful, Lauren. I've got to lie down; I need a shot of morphine again. I'm so sorry, really, really sorry ..." She began to sob again.

"You get well, Irena. Bye."

<><>

Lauren sat down calmly and immediately decided. She checked her smartphone. The DRC was once the Belgian Congo with ties remaining so presumably there were likely to be flights direct from Brussels to Kinshasa. She didn't care that it was wildly impetuous, crazy, nonsensical, illogical and downright dangerous. Annabella was too important to her. She couldn't let her down, why did she shout her name? She couldn't rescue Philippe from Russia, but she sure as hell wasn't going to ignore Annabella. She booked herself on a United Airlines flight out, leaving in three hours time; thank goodness she had her passport.

After telling a puzzled Nimi to clear her diary for the next three days, Lauren walked casually out of the familiar old gate and jumped into a taxi. First stop was the Democratic Republic of the Congo Embassy, where she persuaded the Ambassador to sign off a temporary seven day travel visa for academic liaison. They waived the yellow fever certificate on condition that she stayed in the main commercial part of Kinshasa. Her international name, a gamble, fortunately carried some sway. On arrival at the airport, she immediately bought a small case and some additional clothes and toiletries; she could buy more when she landed and would purchase Congolese Francs at the Kinshasa Airport. Fortunately, everyone spoke French in the DRC. She had her iPad and did a quick survey of everything relevant to the trip. She went to a currency exchange and bought a couple of thousand US dollars and stuffed the cash into her bag, before booking herself online into the five star Magnum Hotel, one of the few places to accept credit cards. Finally, at check-in, she declared convincingly she was only twenty-seven weeks pregnant, which was accepted and allowed without a medical certificate from Edward Jones. She even had a complimentary upgrade to business first class and joined the five other people, having plenty of room to stretch out and snooze with a full empty bay of seats to herself.

In fifteen minutes she would be airborne on a flight taking eight and a half hours. She was now exhausted but also calmly elated and pleased she had taken the decision to go, despite all the risks. Life was one great risk anyway ... especially married to Philippe, and this couldn't be any worse. Finally she sent a quick text to Charlotte, before settling down, phone switched off, for a long snooze and dinner later.

Gone out of town on a trip and will be away for a few days. Please tell Marie and Nimi - nobody must worry. Will explain tomorrow. Love to the twins and DG. Lauren

<><>

Back in Nice, Charlotte immediately contacted DG and then phoned Nimi, before going round to Lauren's villa to see Marie.

Everyone was totally mystified, but DG took steps to alleviate concern, suggesting they leave things until at least the morning and see what Lauren says. At that point they would take any action if there was no response ... emphasising that Lauren was free to make her own decisions any way she sees fit, and whilst heavily pregnant, wasn't in quarantine ... whatever the reason she was acting out of character, it must be a good one.

Alarmed though Charlotte was, Marie and Nimi, now also back in Nice, agreed with DG, and they would all touch base first thing in the morning, once something clearer was known. However, Charlotte already had suspicions and serious misgivings, because she was still keeping her own secret. And once they had returned home, had dinner and DG was outside having a quick cigar, she quietly dialled Henri-Gaston who she had seen three times since, back at his house. She assumed, in a moment of despair, that Lauren had found out and they were meeting ... but he knew absolutely nothing, and was as mystified as Charlotte, insisting that he was maintaining his agreement of strict anonymity and no contact with Lauren. Charlotte was finally getting to know and trust her father ... a complex man with quite a florid past, but she liked him more and more, and their relationship was getting stronger and mutually accepting. Charles was turning out to be good fun, very relaxed with his new sister and openly informative when they were on their own, about their father's colourful lifestyle. Unusually, Henri-Gaston was celebrity girlfriend free, because his latest muse had decided to date Charles instead, but then she was only twenty-three. Brothers Daniel, Michel, Bobby and Jacques remained mysteries in Asia for the time being, although photos of them all revealed a similar likeness to her too. Daniel, the eldest, was a year younger than her, with eighteen months separating the others, which she found illuminating, especially when Charles confided that her father had always been desperate for a daughter.

<><>

Morning arrived in Kinshasa. Lauren bought more clothes in one of the hotel lobby shops, suitable for the humid and hot climate, which remained the same equatorial constant temperature around thirty degrees centigrade. She ordered breakfast, and was surprised by the sophistication of the hotel and the immediate surroundings, looking across from the dining room at the wide and busy main road outside and the new University building opposite, one of seven others apparently. Some tourists were about, but the main guest client groups were besuited business people, including a significant number of Chinese males, she assumed after land grab deals for the underexploited commodity resources in the country. Did that include uranium? She began flicking through her iPad again, taking in some key information to quickly understand her environment, all totally alien as she had never visited Africa before. Standing earlier on the balcony and looking across the city, the view seemed surprisingly modern and green with lots of new buildings, office blocks, cranes, definitely an air of a distinctive modern city … not what she expected. There was real business to be had here, and why should the Chinese grab everything? When she returned, she would set Nimi and Sonja onto assessing business potential for Cassini, there was obviously an educated and technologically savvy workforce somewhere. Her preconceptions of the Democratic Republic of Congo had been shaped up in childhood from her father, who had worked as a young graduate chemical engineer in the former Belgian Congo. She reflected on what he used to tell her as a little girl. Since independence in 1960, much had moved on. But this vast country, three times bigger than France, had

320

been riven by civil wars, factions and unstable corrupt government and now militias everywhere, constantly fighting government forces and each other, presumably to control large swathes of resource rich areas.

And it was such a militia that was holding Annabella … the question was what would it take to free her and quickly? She had the address of the new Aid Evocative clinic and that was all. She would have to try and find it and get there, but quickly noted from scanning online articles that Kinshasa, like many urban cities in third world countries, had massive rich-poor contradictions, and although her immediate surroundings were modern and western, lots of the rest of the massive city were shanty towns and slums. Characteristically, that was where Annabella had set up her new base. A wave of unease and trepidation ran through her head, but she had to be strong and plough onwards.

The time had arrived to clear the air, and she had to assuage concerns back home about where she was and why. Finishing the last large croissant and jam, she dialled the number which she hoped she would never dial again. It was answered in two rings.

"Hi … I'm glad you rang Lauren because I really miss you. I'm done in Louisiana, but I wish your call wasn't on this phone. You're in trouble aren't you? Where are you? Explain everything slowly and carefully."

"I'm in Kinshasa, Mila, but I'm not in any danger."

From the momentary silence, even Mila was stunned.

"Mmm … my calculations indicate you're due in about two weeks. Didn't get on the wrong plane by mistake did we? In fact how did you even get on a plane at your stage? Who else knows you're there and most importantly why?"

"I fooled everyone, because I'm just not that big. Nobody but you knows I'm here. Annabella has been taken hostage from her new Aid Evocative health clinic and rape centre by a local militia, who have stolen nuclear material from the defunct old reactor which the Americans had built in the 1950s. They wanted medical assistance for radiation sickness, but decided that Annabella was worth good money to bargain with. Irena escaped but was badly shot ... she's safe and in Nairobi being treated. I have to get Annabella out Mila. I don't care what it costs."

"I wish I had your stomach muscles. Just hang on a second ... okay ... I can get there by tomorrow. I need to have a passport and visa made immediately. I'll contact DG and Charlotte with reassurances so nobody else sets off and does something silly. Charlotte can reassure colleagues in Cassini."

"I've moved from Brussels, Mila. I've bought a villa near Nice and am now based at the Cyclops Fusion Institute."

"I know that and a fabulous move. I'm so pleased for you. As I am technically still a Cassini Director, I do read the Executive minutes which Eva kindly emails me. Where are you staying?"

"The Magnum Hotel."

"Okay, no problem ... mmm ... best place in town, that's good. Now you stay in the hotel, don't do anything risky or go anywhere ... and during the next fifteen hours I'll do some digging and then be there. Agreed?"

"I've missed you Mila, it was a stupid idea sending you off like that."

"It wasn't ... I badly needed the space to think hard about my life, it was a very good decision taking a sabbatical, believe me. Priority now, we have to get Annabella freed from where she's held. I assume any ransom demand will be communicated through Aid Evocative?"

"Yes, the base is shared with an Israeli Charity. They are involved together … the CEO is Manny Wertheimer."

"Wertheimer?"

"Does he mean anything to you?"

"Possibly. If anything changes Lauren, ring me or if you hear about the demands. See you soon."

The phone rang off dead.

Lauren sent a text to Charlotte, Marie and then Nimi.

I'm fine. I'm in Kinshasa and will be with Mila who will contact you shortly and explain. Nobody must worry or do anything. Sorry for the clandestine messages and sudden disappearing, but there's a problem which I personally need to resolve and I didn't want anyone dissuading me. Please don't phone.

As a fresh pot of tea was brought she made a call to Irena, still in a hospital bed, but making progress and now expecting to be out in the next few days.

"Irena, go straight back to London and rest, I'm so glad you're feeling better. I'm in Kinshasa, Mila is coming and we will do the negotiating … I need the number of Manny Wertheimer, the Israeli CEO who is the contact point for ransom discussions. Mila and I are going to take care of it and get Annabella home."

"Kinshasa? My God Lauren, how on earth in your condition have you got there? I should be there with you, but I feel so weak."

"Long story, but now unimportant. I'm fine, but tricky negotiating is something I'm much better at than you and you know Mila, she is very experienced with these situations and conditions. We'll get Annabella out, I promise. We should be back in a few days."

"I'll text you the number immediately we finish. We have a substantial reserve in the charity now, had some recent large donations and government help … we could access up to a million US dollars if necessary."

"Leave that all with me Irena, we'll see what we can do. Get well quickly, and then you must come and stay at my new home in Nice for a break, I've not long moved in."

"Okay and thank you so much for what you're doing for Annabella. I can't express my gratitude enough."

"Annabella is very special to me too Irena. Speak soon"

Irena's text immediately pinged into her phone. She was glad she chose a decent hotel with satellite communications. Lauren began to walk back to her room; she needed to talk urgently to Manny Wertheimer in private. And she was going quickly to the hairdresser … she suddenly decided she needed a change.

Chapter Twenty-Four

Having had a four month spell deep in the hot swamps and mangroves of Louisiana, the temperature and humidity around Kinshasa felt quite pleasant in comparison ... acclimatisation was not going to be a problem. But Mila felt distinctly concerned about Lauren's precariously imminent birthing, plus not being acclimatised to a debilitating place like Central Africa. And yellow fever, which she had managed to get a quick booster, was a serious danger in this part of the world. At least Lauren had promised to stay in the hotel.

Mila strode confidently up to the reception desk in her white linen Prada trouser suit, having faxed her details in advance. The manager was there to greet her in English.

"Dr Heinemann ... welcome to the Magnum Hotel, I hope you had a pleasant journey from the US on Congo Airlines. I'm sure you will find our business suite perfect for your meetings with Chinese bankers. We host a lot of events relating to China here. If you need interpreters or translators we can provide. Your room details and security key card are here and you are on the same corridor as Professor Hind."

"Thank you Mr Beko. May I ask ... I am expecting to meet Professor Hind straight away? Do you know where I may find her? Is she in her room?"

"Ah … I'm afraid not. Professor Hind apologises and will be back later. She had to go out to a meeting. She has left you some information."

Beko fished under the desk and handed her a large brown envelope. Mila remained externally unperturbed, but inside was fuming. Where the fuck had Lauren cleared off too when she was told how dangerous the place was?

Beko continued. "Before I forget, you do have another visitor though. She is relaxing in the bar and says she is Head of Security for the Denang Cobalt Mining Company."

A warm glow immediately spread through Mila's body. It couldn't possibly be, but she hoped it was. As she walked quietly into the busy and dimly lit bar area, with juju music playing loudly, African businessmen swivelled in their seats to leer at her imposing and sensual appearance, swinging her hips provocatively, her short blonde hair and stunning looks an unmistakable attraction. There was only one person sat on a high bar stool, legs dangling, with a large cocktail in front of her, who unmistakably would fit Beko's business description. She walked up to her quietly from behind.

"I see North Korean army fashion has been and gone and that cool African militia is in vogue now … and I'll have what you're drinking please, with a slice of mango on top."

The visitor spun around with a huge grin … and they hugged warmly for the first time in a long time.

"Rosie, you look absolutely fabulous, but where on earth did you get that gear? Only thing missing is the AK47," gazing all over at the pressed green and brown camouflage, tight short sleeved shirt and baggy trousers with smart leather army boots, finished off with a matching peaked cap.

"You like? Hate North Korean look now, but you know what Mila, female militia here, they are very cool women and know

326

how to dress practical and stylish. I copy, but African women have bigger boobs than me, have to work on that with more sex, but you like muscles? I think Sergei's treatment not only heal spine, but also provide big strength ... I lift one third more in weights than before and am fitter than ever."

"In every way, Rosie," Mila cried, laughing out loud. "But why are *you* here? Chinese interests I assume? Let's talk over in that corner."

They sat down at a table in a small annexe to the bar away from the noise and the crowds. Mila opened the envelope which Lauren had left her.

"Been here three days," Rosie began. "Had call from Beijing Ministry, they very concerned about reports of recent looting of fuel rods from old Triga reactor at University, all edgy over terrorists and dirty bombs especially in Africa. Asked me to investigate. I phone Nadine to find where you are, see if you know anything ... she put me onto Debbie, your new special ops leader with very sexy sultry voice who confirm you on way to Congo. So I assume Israeli interest?"

"Well it wasn't, but now I think it will be. I can see you don't know the rest of the story either ... things have got complex here, Rosie, and potentially very dangerous. I believe Manny Wertheimer is pulling the strings on this heist, you remember him?"

"Wertheimer? Ah yes, I remember, we go back long time to Israel, Russian Jewish émigré. You and I tracked him for weeks, once Zionist fanatic, but suspected of internal treason for leaking nuclear secrets. Fled back to Russia and ended up killed in big security shoot out in Turkmenistan."

"Except, he isn't dead. He's fronting a clandestine Israeli health charity, here in Kinshasa. I made a call to some of my Jerusalem contacts ... they knew he was alive, but thought he was in Iraq. They're pretty sure Wertheimer is linked to a group of well funded Palestinian militants and Al Qaeda."

"Shit Mila, that not good for Chinese either … we take him out."

"Except there's another odd but unconnected twist, you and I cannot ignore. Wertheimer linked up to another charity, to share and jointly run a new heath centre down in the slums. The militia who stole the rods, went there for radiation sickness help, and ended up taking the link charity CEO hostage for a big ransom."

"That's not good, but what's it got to do with you or us?"

"The charity is Aid Evocative, run by Irena who you know, with her new CEO Annabella, the hostage."

"Annabella? I know of her, she very close to Lauren, I am sure they had affair once."

"Annabella is also very close to me, Rosie."

"Ahh … now I begin to understand complexity."

"Not quite … because Lauren has got involved to try and negotiate Annabella's freedom. Lauren is here, in Kinshasa at this hotel, and I should have been meeting her now."

Rosie stared back hard. "Here? Lauren here? But she due very soon. You joke!"

"Yes, no joke."

Rosie let out a long string of Chinese expletives.

"You rarely swear in Mandarin, but I agree the whole situation is very bad."

"You miss final piece of story Mila, and why I swear more. When Wertheimer was roaming around Chechnya, whose brigade was that traitor running dog leading?"

Mila took a swig of her long iced cocktail and chewed at the mango, thinking hard. "Zavrazhny, Vlad Zavrazhny … oh fuck, this is becoming extraordinarily bad." Mila swore in Yiddish. "I would lay odds that Olga is here or on her way here, which is why that crazy bitch disappeared into nowhere, plotting and planning."

"She is formidable Mila, Spetsnaz training in martial art; she may also not be alone. There is bigger plot here I think. Annabella is sadly dispensable cog enroute … now a much bigger prize in town … who is not only worth much money but has invaluable technical knowledge and can be tortured to give up secrets … by Olga."

Mila tore open the envelope fully, read the note and handed it to Rosie.

Hi … hope you arrived safely. Sorry I've been bad, never much good at doing what I'm told, as you know, but needed to act quickly following a phone call with Manny last night. Went first thing to visit the Health Centre and met Manny, who was very friendly and concerned and offered to act as a conduit for negotiations to free Annabella. He introduced me to his negotiator, Chidi Bena Lala, a local tribal elder, but well educated in the US in astrophysics and speaks excellent English rather than French. He drove up on a motorbike with a tame pet female gorilla, Vega, on the pillion seat, the name made me laugh of course being an astronomer nerd. Chidi had brought her up from a baby abandoned in the forest. We then went to his house to meet his wife, Manny and I followed, then he left Chidi and I to discuss further. It appears the militia want half a million US dollars to free Annabella, who Chidi has seen and she is being treated well, with food and a proper bed, which made me feel so much better. I have authorisation from Irena and the Aid Evocative Board to negotiate around that sum of cash. They want to pay and release Annabella quickly and get her home. Returned to the hotel with Chidi's security to get changed and have gone back to his house, where we will sew up a quick deal later with their leader, a man called Mwata, don't know his full name. I trust Chidi who has the obvious respect of his local community and is kind and generous. But as a fellow physics academic, he knows all the deadly dangers of spent fission rods and has informed the government who will be taking armed action to retrieve the stolen material. Chidi has his own armed guards everywhere around his house and I feel very safe. I expect to be back early evening, with Annabella's release secured ... but need your advice on how to transfer the cash which is already wired to a Kinshasa bank and ready.

Mila looked hard at Rosie and immediately began carefully thinking through the next steps. "It's time to reignite our old partnership. Your assessment Rosie? I'm just making a phone call first. Damn it, this phone is out of charge, I'll just get a spare from my bag in reception." She returned ten minutes later to see Rosie also on the phone and making plans.

Rosie finished her call then began her assessment. "I once say to Lauren, you have incredible brain like giant planet but can be terribly naive about people, particularly bad people. But this is very clever deception. Chidi, I am sure, is good man and being used by Wertheimer so he can get hands on Lauren. We need to get to Chidi's house quickly, neutralise danger to Lauren, rescue her and Annabella and at the same time deal with Wertheimer. We also need more guns, given scale of plot."

"Agree. I've just spoken to the Israeli Prime Minister about the gravity of the situation we have unearthed, and he will speak to the DRC President, authorising access to immediate cash for hostage release if necessary. Both Presidents will want to try and avoid depleting the charity finances. We must now deal with Wertheimer, once and for all. You're right Rosie, we need help. Fortunately my gut instinct, as it always is with Lauren, was triggered before coming. She and Kinshasa don't

330

mix. My senior operative Debbie and my new special ops team I have just trained up, Alyssa, Diamond, Destiny, Michayla and Chloe are all on their way here. We have a private jet now. Iris, my commercial pilot, will be landing at the main airport in an hour with weapons. They are very formidable, all like Nadine.

"Those names, they all black and sexy too like Nadine?"

"You'll have time to think about sex later," Mila replied with a laugh. "But yes, all young African-American graduates, looking for adventure before settling down into business. Can you get more of those uniforms? We need to blend in."

"I too on phone to Beijing. Am authorised to take all necessary steps to defuse danger, so as well as conducting agreed assessment, will find materials then send special Chinese nuclear team to retrieve and securitise. This guy Mwata, he is known to my new militia friends who will provide uniforms. Bad, greedy and hard and has loyal team of followers, but most will run away at real trouble. They look tough in back of pickup truck behind machine gun, but weaken at knees when fight starts and heads depart from bodies. We take them all out. Your team will meet Jetta, Evette, Vandra and Zody. They hardened and special forces trained female militia, P30 commanders, know area and jungle like back of hand. I take Jetta and Evette, find Wertheimer first and eliminate him at clinic. We have nice plan, use wiles. Like all men he will have weakness for beautiful black temptresses. You head to house of Chidi now. Got address from Vandra, I text. Vandra and Zody will meet your team and take them all to Chidi … we join as quickly as possible. Lauren, Annabella and materials all secured in one go."

"Excellent logistics as usual Rosie … I think we're in business again. I'm off, just going to quickly change."

"I just been to loo. Third toilet in ladies is locked. Go there now and you find useful assistance. See you with Lauren later, then when done, we have big party, I look forward to meeting Debbie."

"Yes, I bet."

<><>

Mila immediately departed to the toilets, opened the lock with her penknife and closed the door behind her to see a smart pink holdall on the floor. Flushing the toilet, she emerged, smiled at a couple of Western women washing their hands and went up to her room. Inside was a short and light AR-15 automatic assault rifle, Chinese modified with ammunition, a Glock pistol with a silencer and half a dozen knives. She changed into a pair of jeans, t-shirt and light cotton jacket and put the weapons into a small backpack, then headed for a taxi.

<><>

Lauren and Chidi were pleasantly concluding their final negotiations, the final price having been set at four hundred thousand US dollars. They were waiting for Mwata. Chidi looked at his watch, irritated that the militia leader was already half an hour late. A scratching sound at the rear caught his attention and he called out to his chief guard to investigate but nobody seemed to hear.

"I'm sorry Lauren, would you like another tea. I'll just go and ask my wife to make some more and find a few of her special pastries, a local delicacy you will like."

She nodded. "Yes please but tell me. If we assume Mwata accepts the final offer, how long will it be before Annabella is released?"

"It will be speedy. Once you have the money assembled then the moment he is paid she will be allowed free … we will ensure this is set up so there is no trickery. And my wife's pastries will certainly do no harm to the little one waiting to come out into the world."

"Little ones, Chidi … I'm expecting triplets."

"Good Lord above, congratulations … I wish you and your new family well. Soon, you and your colleague Annabella will be back with your families, I can assure you. Sadly, mediation between factions in this country is something I increasingly do these days. I'll just go and find my bodyguard."

Chidi left the room, sensing everywhere seemed very quiet, when as he turned into the kitchen, a hand with a foul smelling cloth covered his mouth and face. Dizzy and disoriented with the fumes, he was immediately pulled into the next room, blindfolded and tied up, before being carried out to join his wife and five guards, in a similar drugged state, in the back of a battered pickup truck behind the hedge.

The assailant, checking everywhere was quiet, went alone into the house heading towards the large study.

Lauren was waiting, and waited further but could hear nothing. She began to feel initially uneasy and then alarmed, and called out to the half closed door. "Hello? Chidi? Everything okay? Hello, are you there?"

The door opened, and her smile, as she looked up, suddenly turned to immediate horror and disbelief. Standing in front of her … was Olga, makeup immaculate, red hair tied back and dressed menacingly in army fatigues and carrying a large knife.

"Lauren, how nice to meet you again, strange circumstances, I must admit in shithole of Africa but nice. Please, stay seated whilst I explain. My friend Manny, he tell me you are here. So much trouble saved."

Lauren felt trepidation accompanied by a horrible flashback. She was back in Russia, seeing Vaag again and that awful night when he burst into her hotel. She had to stay calm.

333

"What do you want Olga, why are you here? You know Manny Wertheimer?"

"Yes, we go back many years to Chechnya, he commander in my father's anti-terrorist unit. We do nice deal. He gets a quarter of a million dollars and uranium to sell to terrorists and I get you."

"Me?"

"I plan revenge the moment my Philippe jailed for fifteen years hard labour in Russian prison, all because of you. I know you alerted authorities to frame him, you wanted him dead. I love him. I kill you, cut you up into pieces and throw into Congo for crocodiles. But before you die, you suffer much pain, slow and terrifying torture, exactly as I have endured. Philippe loves me and I tell you something you not know. Philippe and I were passionate lovers many years ago, when he had left that silly woman Lyudmila, before you or the West were thoughts in his head. He had vasectomy only for me, as I hate children. So no way are bastards inside you his children ... you also deceive Philippe and for that I make you scream twice as much."

Lauren felt her insides go cold ... she couldn't run, not in her state. Olga was crazy, this was not happening. Philippe how could you do this? Now, of all time ...

"Sorry Olga but your plan has one flaw in its execution ... me."

They both turned to see someone in the other door frame, pistol in hand and pointing it straight at Olga's head.

"Who the fuck are you?" Olga replied coldly.

"Mila ... behind you," Lauren shouted out.

At lightning speed Mila, in a second, whipped her body around and kicked the creeping assailant in the throat, instantly breaking his windpipe and spinal cord. He dropped like a stone, lifeless, falling hard against the wall. She continued, the gun still pointing at Olga. "Down, on your knees, now."

Lauren was standing up and had moved nearer the other door. Still no sign of anyone else.

"Mila? Ah, of course. Your Spetsnaz is good, very good."

"Correction, Mossad and better. Now for the last time, get down on the floor."

Suddenly, without warning, a large roof beam over the door holding up part of the ceiling, fell with a roar, loosened by the impact of the downed assailant against the wall and caught Mila on the head, momentarily dazing her, before she could dive fully out of the way. Olga sprang forward like a tiger as the other men from the truck rushed in behind Mila and jumped on her, forcing her to the ground, the gun levered immediately from her hand.

Lauren watched in horror, her body frozen, staring as they began to tie Mila up, gagging and kicking her. Then her brain unlocked. She took to the door and ran, through the maze of corridors, the effort almost killing her with the dead weight of her body, panting hard trying to find the rear exit. She heard shouting and Olga's voice, realising Lauren had escaped, and was coming after her. Lauren looked around desperately, nowhere to go and not a soul anywhere, only Chidi's old motorcycle standing against the shed. She ran to the ancient Honda, which had the key still in the ignition. It had been a long time since she rode a motorcycle. Her ex-husband had taught her and they used to go scrambling together in the Highlands in the summer when they lived in Scotland. Her brain went into warp-three. She turned the key, seeing Olga running out of the house towards her. The engine fired and she kicked it into gear and sped off, wheels slithering in the dust, when she felt a sudden bang at the back, the rear of the bike dipped and two hairy arms wrapped themselves around her. Certainly it wasn't Olga ... oh my God ... it was Vega the gorilla. She heard Vega screech and her long black arm and hairy hand pointed forward to follow a track, out of the town and into the jungle.

She looked in the mirror to see a cloud of dust following behind. Olga must have grabbed the scooter that was also standing in the yard. She opened the throttle of the old bike and shot away from the scooter, Vega screeching with glee and pointing to a turnoff, which she immediately took, heading out at speed into the bush ...

<><>

Olga realised she would never catch up on her clapped out Vespa and headed back ... she would find Lauren shortly. Tracking her compared to brown bears in Siberia was easy, and no way would she get far. The jungle became thick, dangerous and unwelcoming very quickly. First, she had to deal with this operative Mila, and find out if she was on her own or what else was going on, if anything.

Mila came around with a groan, disoriented. That damned piece of timber, she was not as sharp as she used to be and someone or something had hit her hard, but nothing felt broken, only probably bruised. She coughed, her eyes wouldn't open and she felt a horrible taste and smell in her mouth and nose, not chloroform, probably some sort of mild nerve agent for disabling people, an old Soviet technique of Spetsnaz. She heard male voices shouting, then the unmistakable deep voice of Olga, barking orders in Russian, which of course she knew.

She immediately realised all her clothes had been removed, she was completely naked. Her hands were tied together and her arms were being raised with a rope as she was lifted about a metre and a half or so off the ground to hang from some bar across two beams holding the ceiling. She opened her eyes and adjusted her body to ease the pain having been trained in this form of torture and was strong and could lift herself up if she tried, although her ankles had also been bound.

"Mila, whoever you are, first we have some fun and you will be punished of course for giving Lauren the opportunity to escape. But I track her soon, like bear in Siberian wilderness."

Mila looked down to see Olga, grinning below, holding some kind of leather flail. Olga began rubbing her bare bottom as the men laughed, ogling her naked body.

"Mmm ... nice smooth butt Mila, in fact you have great body, very toned, I admire much. First I whip you hard, and you tell me who you are and why you are here. Then my men fuck you, I fuck you, and if you still tell me nothing I start to dismember your lovely body, piece by piece. The more you tell me the quicker we stop." Olga raised the whip and drew her arm back to strike the first blow.

"Looks like I just arrive in time for orgy. Olga I presume? Well, go on, what are you waiting for? Oh, sorry, forgot to add, you'd better be quick as soon you all die."

Olga and her five compatriots all turned sharply to see a lone female figure, in militia fatigues, standing in the doorway. The burly Russian operatives, also Spetsnaz, laughed loudly. The sight of a slim Chinese woman, unarmed, playing at soldiers was simply too much.

Olga joined in the fun. Mila looked down and grinned surreptitiously at Rosie ... good opportunity to see whether Rosie's speciality of unarmed combat was as good as it used to be, given the amount of training Rosie had done in Alaska to become top-notch fit again.

"Well, well, a Chinese now. Interesting visitors I think this place see." She turned to her men. "Lucky day today, we can now string this Chinese up alongside our new friend Mila. She has a very nice body too, I fuck her first. Bring her over."

The nearest soldier went to draw his gun but in a lightning flash and a blur of movement, he fell back, a knife blade between the eyes, as a large fountain of warm blood spurted over Mila's bare leg.

"I did warn you Olga."

The other four rushed her but it was over in a matter of seconds, necks broken with kicks and hand chops as vicious, quick and deadly as one of the resident gorillas could execute. Mila knew that Rosie was one of the world's top Kung Fu exponents, but was surprised she had become even faster, despite her injury. That was impressive. Olga stared, her mouth dropped as each of her handpicked soldiers fell like dominos to the ground lifeless. She calculated and took the only sensible option … and ran hard out of the other door to the scooter at the back, firing it up and heading off speedily in the earlier direction. At least she would now track down Lauren and finish that job, and then head back over the border to Russia.

Rosie looked up at Mila dangling ignominiously and laughed heartily. "Olga not get far. All our girls, your team combined with mine, ambush hard-man Mwata and his group before they come here. Stupidly they resisted. I was wrong, they refused to run away. Pity really, all dead except Mwata. He is hard and proud man, very hurt his elite militia should be overcome by bunch of stunning women in smart gear and AK47s, so he wasn't inclined to tell us where Annabella and all spent nuclear rods were located. Zody however, remembering, when as child, her family butchered by his clan ten years ago, become very adept with machete. Two toes weren't enough, but right hand finally did the trick. I have alerted Chinese nuclear team who are on their way to make arsenal secure, and

Annabella should now be freed and safely with them. I'm impressed with your team Mila. Destiny could throw silver stars as good as Nadine; you trained them up well in swamp."

"Thanks Rosie, now are you going to stop yackering and get me down?"

"You saved my life once, so I suppose it's the least I can do," Rosie replied grinning. "No, I change mind. I don't get this opportunity often. Olga correct, you have lovely body, so I put knife between teeth and watch you free yourself. I'll just uncut binding on ankles, then you can coil up legs and kick in air ... mmm ... I watch."

"Rosie ... you are just too much sometimes ..." Mila replied, whipping her legs up and around the bar and hauling herself to a position where she could cut the rope through binding her wrists, with her mouth-knife. Hanging upside down from the bar, Mila finally pushed up and out and dropped smoothly like a lithe gymnast onto her feet. Rosie grabbed an old blanket and wrapped it around her, planting a kiss on Mila's cheek.

"Only a small bruise, you lucky this time, Slavic looks as beautiful as ever. You must tell me hairdresser, I love short spiky style. You good as Congo monkeys on bar. Why you end up in air like this? I think you must be getting slower in old age. You need to do weights again like me. Oh ... clothes are in other room, nice underwear, I like Gucci."

"You may be right Rosie. I need to both restart weights and I've decided, acquire a good looking man. Now we must find Lauren. I know she escaped but how or where? We still have a problem? And where is the owner?"

"A man? Really? Now I know you getting old. Chidi, wife and guards tied up in back of pickup. All frightened but okay. Cook, he ran out into fields, and say that Lauren took off on Chidi's motorcycle into deep jungle, with gorilla on pillion."

Mila could only laugh. "I know it's serious and we must find her quickly, but I wish I had a camera when that happened."

"All in hand. Aren't you pleased I have assignment fully managed like old times? Jetta and Vanda have already taken a group of best P30 female militia off to find her. They know jungle intimately and they will track down Olga too. Both should be easy. Neither of them can get far. Congo river restrict escape routes as well as thick jungle."

"Actually Rosie I am very pleased, you've done a fantastic job. Really marvellous to see you back in such good form again. Oh shit, I forgot, Wertheimer, we still need to take him out."

"Now that was interesting part of assignment."

"Was?"

"Of course. Jetta, Evette and I checked out health clinic. No sign of him anywhere, but local women say he visit prostitute house in afternoons. We not need too many female wiles after all. Manny Wertheimer had developed, how you say, predilections whilst in Chechnya which brothel owner confirmed. Jetta decided she like to be his new prostitute for afternoon for laugh, as she has predilection too. Sadly, Wertheimer will be found hanging up in rubber suit and mask asphyxiated ... Jetta was too good, but he die happy exactly as he would have wanted. You can confirm immediately with Mossad, when we find your phone. Now we can have big party later."

Mila looked in the mirror, happy that the bruises on her forehead and left cheek should heal in a week, and laughed loudly. "Phone should be in my bag in the kitchen with your weapons, hanging inside the dustbin. Rosie, when I'm working with you, I just can't believe what you get up to, but I love it. Now, let's see how Debbie and Jetta are getting on finding our two runaways."

Lauren continued hurtling along the track, the thick jungle gradually closing in, long leafy creepers dangling down from branches, with Vega jabbering and pointing towards a clearing. Various brightly coloured birds were zipping from branch to branch, chattering madly and small animals scattered as they roared by. The track was beginning to peter out. Vega directed her to the edge of the clearing, the surrounding thick bushes and grasses providing a lot of camouflage and protection. She stopped the bike next to an enormous black-barked tree.

Vega gracefully jumped off, and brushed her long, hairy limbs, jabbering again to herself as Lauren dismounted with difficulty, leaning the bike against the tree. Vega lolloped off into the bushes, returning, to Lauren's astonishment, with branches and long grass and began to cover the bike over, until it was quickly hidden. Lauren sat on a log and pondered. She could hear insect and bird noises and a faint animal roaring in the distance. This wasn't an environment to be hanging around, although with Vega she felt ridiculously safe, wondering whether Vega had had babies at some stage in her past. Knowing absolutely nothing about gorillas she had no idea how old Vega was, although she wasn't huge but looked enormously strong. Lauren rummaged in her bag for her phone … before realising that there wouldn't be a signal out there, but then saw a faint bar from a Belgian mobile carrier … they obviously weren't too far from town, there must be a mast somewhere. But before she had a chance to dial anyone, another sharp pain in her lower back seared through her body, making her shake. She had felt a strange tingling in Chidi's house, but put it down to nerves, then further uncomfortable feelings when she ran, but that wasn't surprising given the exertion and adrenaline rushing. But the pain was returning, more regular, thirty seconds, then twenty seconds when she felt fluid trickling down her leg. She lifted up her summer dress, and knew for sure. Oh my God, not here and not now! What on earth should she do? She pulled out her phone, but the signal wasn't good enough to connect … her brain went into overdrive, the pains were getting worse. She immediately recalled having Charlotte so long ago. The pains were similar and her labour was relatively quick once her waters broke. Oh no, all those preparations and care she had taken with Edward, a lovely bed booked in a Nice clinic … why the fuck was she now in a jungle in the middle of nowhere. She threw her phone into the bush in despair and cried out loudly. "Oh Vega, Vega what can I do?" She lay on the ground supping the bottle of water in her bag and pulled off her underwear, as more discharge emerged, the pain increasing badly.

Vega was running around grunting and squealing, her long enormous arms gathering up vast quantities of soft grass and thick leaves as she quickly began to construct a kind of bed on the ground. Lauren watched in disbelief, distracted momentarily from the intense pain. She couldn't move and was locked in absolute muscular agony right across her taut stomach. Vega had made what looked like a large and very comfortable looking huge nest, under the canopy of the next tree in the shade. Did gorillas make nests? Then she bounded toward Lauren, and gently with no effort, lifted her up, Vega's hairy arms were tickly and soft under her legs, and carried her slowly onto the soft leaves, feeling just like a mattress. Lauren was astounded, Vega somehow understood, she was the most amazing animal. She drank some more water and lay back, her legs up, recalling what she did when Charlotte was born, as the contractions had increased further. She realised shortly she would have to push. Thank goodness she had done those classes at Edward's clinic … but how can this be happening … everything was so unreal as not to be true but nature was taking hold. She shut her mind off from everything else and began to concentrate hard, as Vega sat quietly next to her, rubbing her own stomach and looking around to ensure Lauren was well protected …

<><>

Olga swore vehemently. She had run out of road and the old scooter sounded like it was about to give up the ghost. Tracking Lauren had been quite easy, fortunately there had been no rain and the motorcycle tracks along the route were visible in the dust to her trained eye. But at a fork, she was confused as the tracks went off in two directions, at a point where the jungle suddenly started to thicken up. She looked around, took off her rucksack, swigged some water, and made a decision to follow the right fork as the tracks had more continuity. Ahead she could see the track was petering out so Lauren couldn't be far … and she would finish the job now on foot and then head back to Russia, via the Central African Republic border. Back home she would use her influences to get Philippe released more quickly … she still had contacts and enough money saved for some bribes.

Suddenly her sharp ears heard a twig snap. Alert, she looked back and five tall black women, AK47's cocked, were advancing towards her in a large semicircle through the bushes. She eyed them up, her Spetsnaz training kicking in, and selected the one looking most apprehensive and lunged towards her, betting that she wouldn't fire. The woman cocked her gun to fire at Olga's legs but Olga was too fast and kicked the gun out of her hand landing a blow to the head, sending Chloe flying. The others turned and ran towards her. They had just been given orders from Mila to take Olga alive, following an interception through Rosie's Russian contacts, but Olga, already adjusted from the different Siberian forest wilderness which she knew instinctively how to navigate like a snow fox, ran through a clearing and disappeared into the dense jungle.

Zody shouted over to Debbie to follow, gesticulating to the others to fan out around and drive Olga onwards … she was familiar with this part of the jungle and knew Olga would soon come to a stop … at the river Congo itself.

Olga continued moving fast, she knew how to navigate thick woody terrains and put attackers off the scent. If she could do it with wolves, her followers would be a piece of cake, despite the abilities and experience of the hardened militia women. Using tricks, she doubled back and took a different direction, listening carefully for the sounds of the militia group receding in the other direction. She smiled. Idiots, she would train them better if she had the chance. She entered another clearing … then what she saw with her own eyes made her stop and stare with disbelief …

Their eyes met, no words were spoken. But Olga now knew and felt something inside unexpectedly take over, compelling and certain for sure. She smiled, she had to intervene. She could hear the river in the distance and knew the militia tracking her would soon realise they had been wrong footed, it was necessary to move quickly.

<><>

Zody looked around for further clues then realised they had been cleverly diverted by false tracks.

"Debbie, you take Alyssa, Destiny and Diamond and follow Vanda in that direction, past the clearing and burned out tree stump to the left. I'll take Michayla and Chloe and we'll detour further right. There is the remnant of an old track which will bring us back to that fork where we were misled in the wrong direction. This Russian operative is certainly highly trained and professional in forest warfare and is good, very good. But the river fans out ahead and that will stop her, whatever she thinks. Either way, we should catch her in a pincer on the bank and then we move together. Let's all keep constant radio contact, and report anything unusual. She may even try and set traps although there probably isn't time."

The two groups set off slowly, annoyed they had lost a good half hour but confident they would soon close in.

Olga continued at a fast pace through the undergrowth towards the sound and smell of the river and quickly reached the bank. She hid behind some reeds and long grass contemplating the width of the river carefully with her high powered binoculars ... at least five kilometres wide but there were some sandbanks in the middle and the flow was not too fast. Her phone began to vibrate and she yanked it out of her pocket and began speaking rapidly in Russian.

"Igor, where are you? I am on my way back to Moscow, once I get over the border."

"Forget that Olga, it's all over. They've rumbled the double cross ... he's out already."

"What? Philippe is released?"

"Yes, the authorities released him immediately under orders from the President. I just managed to siphon the money from Kharkov's account in time, now nicely wired to Belize. Fifty million US dollars. You can't go back to Moscow; in fact you can't go back to Russia full stop. They all want you Olga and now me. The FSB are crawling about everywhere, they have a watch on all the main airports and border crossings. I know how much you still feel about him, but Philippe would be a serious liability if you keep on pursuing him."

"I understand and must recalibrate … Philippe will be lost cause anyway soon, back in love with wife, I now respect realities?"

"Sudden change of heart? How do you know all that?"

"Let's just say … Russian woman instinct but I will always love him … and leave it at that. Where are you?"

"In Luanda. I have two plane tickets, passports and cash for Brazil as well as new identities, I'm already in disguise, beard shaved and you too will need to get a makeover, but I have it all in hand, you must get here quickly."

"Luanda? On coast of Angola? That is even better than original destination." Olga gazed hard at the river again and looked around and smiled. "On my way to Congo coast now, and get boat to Luanda. Will be there nightfall, then I phone. I'm being pursued by black, female militia but fools would be better sticking to fashion, they have no idea of tracking … and that I am strong and swim regularly across mighty River Lena in spring … this Congo big stream is doddle. Bye brother."

She ran back to the water's edge, grabbed some reeds, large leaves and a branch and quickly tied together a makeshift paddle, and then pushed a fallen log into the water. Zipping up her waterproof rucksack, she noted the flow and shoved the log out slowly, swimming hard in the warm water, as it gathered momentum in the current, before swinging skilfully on top, guiding the log away quickly with her paddle using the differing water flow and turbulent eddies; a technique she had practiced and perfected often on more difficult Siberian rivers.

Back on land, the two groups began to converge together following a full sweep down the back, but still no sign of Olga. They met exasperated. Zody, acting as commander, swore hard in her local Lingala dialect.

Debbie smiled back in agreement. "Where the fuck has that Russian bitch disappeared to? There is no way she could swim to freedom in that crocodile infested river of hell, look at the flow."

But Zody was grimacing, peering hard through her binoculars downstream at a tiny figure, paddling furiously into the distance. "Shit … you'll never believe it but she has escaped down the river … on a fucking log! Well I have to say, I'm impressed by Olga the Siberian Houdini — she really is fucking good. I'll alert the authorities, see if they can pick her up enroute, but if she got away from us, I don't think those dicks down there are in with much of a chance either."

Debbie was already on the phone to Mila.

"Forget Olga, she's no longer an immediate threat. The Russians are suddenly now looking for her everywhere; don't know why yet, so when she heads back to Novosibirsk, they'll have a welcome party waiting. I've finally got a fixed tracking location for Lauren. She's stopped in the jungle, probably hiding. Her phone is on fortunately. Rosie and I are on our way with the others to find her. She has a big surprise. Not sure where you are, but I've just texted you the coordinates, you can't be far."

"Okay on it, see you soon. Hope Lauren is okay?"

"Me too … over and out."

<><>

The first armed pickup drew up at the end of the track and the occupants jumped out. DG, feeling like he was back in Vietnam, peered down into the morass of grass, tree branches and creepers with his binoculars, spotted the telltale signs of trampled greenery and headed off in great strides, with Edward Jones struggling at the rear carrying a large medicine bag. And following more slowly behind, much thinner and feeling a little weak ... was Philippe.

They entered the small clearing, pushed through a pile of tall grass towards the clump of trees ... and then they all stopped dead, silent, and incredulous, mouths open so wide their three chins could have hit the ground.

Lauren was lying, quiet and serene, on a bed of grass inside a strange looking nest, her head propped up on a makeshift pillow of leaves. Suckling happily on each breast, through her unbuttoned cotton dress, was a tiny baby with tufts of very blonde hair streaked across each head. She was holding each one inside a large soft green leaf, gazing in wonder from one to the other. Next to her, quietly gibbering, Vega was sat cross-legged, watching over Lauren protectively and patiently holding a third baby carefully with her strong arms, eyes closed and the same sprinkle of blonde hair poking through, and also wrapped in a similar giant leaf, until it was her turn next for mother's milk.

Lauren raised her head and smiled. She was exhausted, her dress was torn and dirty and her hair matted with sweat and obvious exertion. But she had done it. She was miraculously not only alive and survived the most incredibly painful experience she could have imagined, but they came out, in quick succession, and she was so glad she had read up and meticulously digested all the scientific and medical literature on multiple births and what to expect and do. And she'd done it. Given birth naturally to three identical triplets. She knew the odds ... and was pleased ... they were special and so was she.

Philippe walked forward as Vega looked up menacingly.

"Hi Philippe," Lauren croaked, almost hoarse with screaming. "Say hello to your new daughters, Geraldine,

Magdaline and Eveline. Vega, give Geraldine to her father please."

Vega looked warily, first at Philippe, then back at Geraldine, then grinned a wide array of huge yellow teeth and held her out for Philippe to gently pick up and hold carefully. He noticed the stump of an umbilical cord was still there, tied and clamped with some sort of plant thread.

"Another five minutes then it's her turn," Lauren said.

He bent down and kissed her, touching each head in turn.

"I love you Lauren, you are so amazing, I can't believe I'm here and experiencing all of this."

"I love you, but first thing we do girls is to get daddy fed, he's looking a bit thin isn't he. I don't know how you got out of jail but it feels like a miracle," Lauren said with a wide smile.

Edward opened his medicine bag and stepped forward, also noting each umbilical cord had been done the same way. He shook his head in amazement looking around to see the one placenta, carefully laid out next to Vega, with three remnants of cord attached. The baby girls were definitely identical.

He whispered to Lauren. "We need to get you and the babies checked out now. Looks like my classes came in useful. I was indeed redundant, just like you said you wanted in the end! Do you know the mathematical odds of this happening Lauren? Giving birth naturally to identical triplets in a jungle? ... You are a miracle woman, I am absolutely astounded."

"About one in two million, Edward, I like to be special. But I'm so glad you're here now."

With a screech, the second pickup pulled up and Mila and Rosie tumbled out with their teams who they had picked up further down. Annabella jumped out of the front with Chidi, Vega running to him happily, and they all joined the crowd and stared with equal disbelief.

"Doggone it Lauren, you are one heck of a mother-in-law, and I can't even think how those little ones are related to me. I wish I had a camera …" when Mila thrust her smartphone into his hand and directed everyone to circle around Lauren whilst DG took an amazing picture, including Vega … for posterity.

Annabella stroked Lauren's hair. "Thank you, for risking so much to get me freed. I'll never forget this day and look what you've now got back in return. They are so beautiful, and don't they have Philippe's nose and your eyes?"

Lauren smiled, and held Annabella's hand, as Rosie gave her a gentle hug. She was so weak she couldn't talk. And she knew, immediately they emerged, that Vaag could not have been the father.

"Okay, now everyone, let's get organised." Mila shouted. "First thing is to get Lauren, triplets, Philippe and Edward back to the private Oasis Clinic in town, courtesy of Chidi and his wife, which I have booked for checking Lauren and her babies over fully. Then the rest of us have a large room reserved at the hotel, with a bar, for a small celebration."

Jetta and Evette had already brought back a stretcher for Lauren, now with Geraldine to her breast, alongside Magdaline, who was still hungry, and soon they were all on their way back to Kinshasa.

Back at the clinic, Edward took full charge with the consultant obstetrician and senior midwife and a full clean up, examination and series of tests of Lauren and her babies were fast underway, including examination of the placenta.

DG took Philippe to one side, equally exhausted from the ordeal and the travel from Siberia; he hadn't slept for almost twenty-four hours. "Let's leave Lauren and the ladies to get on with the medicals and come back later. You'll have plenty of time with that-there new family shortly." He pulled a small flask of whisky out of his jacket pocket. "I say we have a few celebratory swigs over in that cafe, then you get some shut-eye in that Magnum Hotel Lauren is staying in. You look like shit … I got you a room booked and paid for."

Philippe looked back weakly; his brain was functioning but only just. "Sounds a good idea DG, thanks for everything, you've done. At a stroke my life has changed completely."

"You betcha little ol' Philippe, and hugely for the better I reckon."

They toasted and swigged Jack Daniels whilst DG ordered two large burgers and fries … they were both starving. Philippe didn't ever want to see cabbage or black bread again. "Get some energy back into us both and some weight on you, although I must say overall you don't look too bad considering."

"I tried hard to stay fit, the food was so crap but ended up with respect from the hard guys when I knocked a few teeth out … retired special forces they like."

"Yeh, know all about that, when the gooks took me prisoner."

"You were in a North Vietnam prison?"

"Yep, twelve months. They wanted us to bargain with 'till the Fifth Brigade napalmed the base and Special Forces got us out. That was some period of hell, like in those Japanese war films, but same as you I survived — had to be treated for beriberi though, fucking old rice and nothing else to eat. So I pulled the stops out real good to get you out, however the final hurdle was all down to Olga."

"Olga? Shit DG, I just don't know how to deal with her, I've been such a fool, never again."

"Listen friend, Olga and Igor double crossed both of us, milked the assets and have run off with a load of money. But I was a bit quicker off the mark. I knew something was wrong, the minute they took you away and Igor disappeared. His mild academic manner was a front … he was a clever and corrupt fraudster."

"Olga's run off?"

"We'll leave the full story till later. I've just been onto my friend the Vice President, who pulled all the strings with the Russians. Appears that darned woman and her brother have legged it with a bucket of cash, however all of it is Kharkov's … over fifty million bucks!" DG roared his usual deep belly laugh, causing everyone to look around. "Much of that dough was heading for, let's say, some high-up politicians. They're not happy, FSB is crawling around everywhere … Olga's a darned fugitive my friend. She won't be bothering you no more. And I got most of the drilling gear out in time; it's now all in southern Poland, via Ukraine. We only lost six million dollars, pinprick as far as I'm concerned, and we gained a lot of fracking exploration experience and knowledge … that bit Olga did do right. Shame really about her but there you go. Next stop for you, me and Rubidium is Poland, enormous shale potential and a safer EU backed bet. Hey, there's even Nato there to look after us next time."

Philippe smiled. Would there be a next time? He doubted it. Perhaps his life could turn around, if Lauren was prepared to have him back. But no more gadding about, he wanted to be with his new family, one step at a time.

Lauren had insisted on Annabella and Mila coming with her. Rosie, after uncharacteristically cooing with and holding the babies, had volunteered to help Debbie get the rest of Mila's swat team and the weaponry back to Kinshasa airport, with Iris and the jet on standby, ready to return the team back to the US. Then she would head back to the hotel to arrange the big party with Zody and friends. Meanwhile, Jetta and Evette, knowing the best local places to shop and bargain with, had gone off happily to acquire baby clothes and a couple of nice dresses for Lauren. Edward had some infection concerns about Geraldine and they first carefully restructured and cleaned up the cut umbilical cord area, following on with Magdalena and Eveline. They were so identical, little tags with different colours and their names had to be placed around their tiny wrists.

As Lauren rested in a clean light-blue gown, and Edward carefully examined all the babies in the next room with the other doctors, she chatted and relaxed with Mila and Annabella. Inside her brain, a maelstrom of thoughts were flowing around, particularly how to manage one last try with Philippe, who seemed overjoyed at being a father again. She had to phone Svet as soon as possible too. But she had one secret she was happily keeping. Olga had suddenly reappeared, just at the point when she was struggling, totally exhausted, with the three babies all tied to the placenta. It was Olga, under the careful watch of Vega who didn't allow her out of her sight for a second, who carefully pulled and helped Lauren to release Eveline the last one out. Olga then grabbed a tough thin creeper and showed Lauren, using Geraldine the first baby to emerge, how to cut the umbilical cords from the placenta with a pair of nail scissors and then tie them, claiming she had done it successfully in Siberia with baby bears. Last thing Olga said before running off towards the river was: "Philippe is definitely the father, I know now, he always love you not me … they are beautiful babies, and I go and start new life. Good luck Lauren."

Chapter Twenty-Five

Luigi had become frantically manic during Annabella's kidnapping, and assembled a small army of ex-mafia heavies and weaponry to head off to the Congo and extricate her himself. Lauren had usefully dissuaded Luigi from triggering a diplomatic crisis, after long phone reassurances from Kinshasa that Mila was on board and taking full control of the search and rescue ... Giving Mila a chance had thankfully dissuaded him for a few more days grace.

In fact her first phone call, the moment Edward Jones had confirmed she and her three babies were all amazingly well and that Geraldine's infection was clearing up, was to Luigi. But Annabella of course had beaten her to it and the balmy army was already stood down. Lauren and Annabella both knew how lucky she had been in captivity. She had been treated well, on the insistence of leader Mwata, fed properly and not molested despite the continual inclinations and protestations of some of his wilder militia members, used to daily raping. Luigi was immensely grateful to everyone, especially Lauren, for risking their own lives to get Annabella free ... Lauren insisted that Annabella get the first flight back to Palermo to be with him and her children, especially now that she would be accompanied back to Nice by Philippe, which pleased Annabella greatly. Catching up would come later.

Lauren's first night was one continuous round of feeding, sleeping, feeding again and exhaustion. In between she was already pondering when she could return to work and how she could organise her life. Edward insisted that she remain at the clinic for the next three days, for further monitoring and tests and then she could fly back. She agreed and arrangements were immediately put in place for a private suite where Philippe could stay with her. She smiled, looking at the triplets. They could all begin some bonding respectively with their new father and her new husband. Approval was given for Edward to contact Helena and relay the news, so that Johann could release the prepared press release. Eva and Nimi of course had immediately ensured the internal Cassini jungle drums were beating loudly and an array of congratulatory emails were already flooding into her smartphone by the early morning. She gazed down at Geraldine and Eveline feeding, whilst Magdaline lay in her cot sleeping softly. Her scientific need for rational order and routine began filtering through her mind, mapping organisational pathways and possibilities, depending, of course, on how Philippe was also going to behave ... when she realised the tacit assumption already confirmed in her head ... Yes, she was having him back ... unequivocally. Her instinct was she would not have to dictate terms. A spell in a harsh Russian prison had clearly been sufficient. He needed to get well, and the moment Vega handed him Geraldine was the biggest game-changer of all ...

Suddenly there was a quiet knock on the door and Philippe walked in on tiptoe, with a huge grin of old across his face.

"You look a million times better, Philippe. A good night's sleep in a five star hotel was obviously urgently needed. Now pick up Magdaline, she's just waking and wants a cuddle from her father."

"Shit, darling I can't tell one from the other, they are fantastically alike."

"And they will definitely grow up to be three gorgeous and expensive beauties so you'll have to start saving hard. I'm already beginning to tell, they have different characters linking to their feeding and sleeping which is scientifically fascinating. Geraldine is definitely the most extrovert. Now, no swearing Philippe in front of the children, they don't want your bad habits yet!"

"Sorry," Philippe replied, trying hard to be mournfully contrite before bursting out laughing. "I'm sure Magdaline just gave me a gummy grin, isn't it a bit early? Gosh there's a bit of a whiff, I think she's just pooed."

"She's due for a change anyway, in fact they all are. So, Mr Engineer, are you going to show your daughters how skilled you are at changing their nappies? Spares are in the cupboard over there; these nappies are disposable, bin to your right. Mmm … I can see by your face that Svet never had the benefit of her father's dexterity."

"Actually, Lyudmila took care of everything and when she went back to work after a month her mother looked after Svet every day."

"Presumably whilst you were wheeling and dealing and gadding about … yes? Well we French women are into equality these days … no more Lena River darling, so you'd better watch me first with Geraldine and Eveline and then you copy. Deal?"

"Yes, definitely a deal."

She kissed him on the cheek, his first kiss from Lauren since he left for Russia. He blushed, and decided, now was the moment to say something that had been on his mind since being in prison. He watched Lauren skilfully change the first two babies and put them back in their cots and then attempted Magdaline, with mixed results as she began to cry.

"Mmm … not grinning at Papa now are we Magdaline, which isn't surprising as your nappy is inside out, she has a soft tender bottom … haven't we baby. Papa is going to try again, now that's better isn't it … yes, that was definitely a grin back again. Put her in her cot too, then with some luck we can have two hours of peace. This suite has a little sitting room through that door. Shall we go in there and have a snack?"

They went into the room and sat together on the couch. He put his arm around her and held her closer as she rested her head on his thin chest, like old times … could it be old times back again? No words were spoken for a while.

Philippe began. "Whilst I was in prison, it was only thinking about you every day that kept me sane."

"Only me?"

"Olga was a stupid infatuation, a weakness, she was very … compelling … and I was confused and disoriented with everything that had gone on in Murmansk … such a thing will never happen again, I promise. Olga in cahoots with Igor, her brother, double crossed me and DG, I know now and …"

She looked at him hard. "I believe you. Yes … she told me."

"Told you?"

"She also told me that you had a vasectomy when you had an affair with her the first time, years ago, so you couldn't possibly be the father."

Philippe reddened and sweated. "I had it quietly reversed, the week after we came back from America, but they didn't hold out any hope."

"Well obviously they were wrong. I also learned from Sergei that Vaag also had a vasectomy and was going to have it reversed too, if I had run off to his Mongolian yurt with him, which I didn't, so even if something had happened whilst I was comatose in the bath, which I now think was highly unlikely, he never could have been the father."

"I know, but when he beat the shit out of me whilst I was tied up, he continually boasted of all the things he had done with you … and it set me off … I couldn't get it out of my head and deal with it … my thoughts just festered, then Olga came along again … it was all too much."

"I thought you might have learned not to believe the bad boastful guys after the first time."

Philippe thought … and remembered of course … when they first met … Adrian the other boaster, and Luis too. What was the matter with him?

Lauren continued. "Anyway, Olga won't be back, she's now a fugitive on the FSB's wanted list."

"How do you know that, darling?"

She smiled. "I just know … women's secrets, but it's true isn't it?"

"Yes."

Suddenly his phone rang softly. He looked immediately at the number, still nervous and not always quite believing that he was out of that hell hole labour camp. "It's DG. I'll just shut the door to the girls for a second."

"DG, how you doing buddy? Are you coming over to see Lauren and the babies?"

"Not likely little feller, I'm at the airport, just about to board a flight back to France. Charlotte went into labour last night. I'm now the father of Alex George, all of eight and a half pounds, both are doing fine. Well, I missed the birth of all of my other children, so Alex ain't no exception, but I gotta hurry back. We can have a big celebration when you return. I assume you are coming back? Gotta go, boarding now."

"You betcha, DG. That is amazing news, congratulations. I'll tell Lauren immediately. Cheers."

Lauren, looking puzzled, checked the girls were still asleep and whispered back. "What was that all about?"

"It's Charlotte … you're a grandma again, last night, a baby boy, which they're calling Alex George McCluskey. DG is ecstatic. Mother and son are fine."

Lauren sat down quickly, feeling lightheaded but elated. "That is such wonderful news. I'll call her later, she's probably exhausted and the twins will be hugely excited. Charlotte refused to tell anyone of the sex of the baby beforehand except me, she wanted a surprise, but the twins were looking forward to a new brother. Oh gosh Philippe, our three daughters have now become aunties and they're only two days old! What a weird family we all are."

He kissed her on the cheek … but then she grabbed him and their lips met with a passion and longing as they kissed fully for the first time in almost nine months … before they were disturbed by a couple of small cries. Lauren went into the bedroom and repositioned Geraldine and Eveline on their backs carefully and they went back to sleep, with Magdaline sleeping on through. She rejoined Philippe in the sitting room.

"There's something important I want to tell you," he said, walking back from the kitchen with a teapot and two cups. He began pouring out the teas. "Once I was out of that prison, I decided I would never go back to Russia again. I'm going to apply for French citizenship … I think, given my ancestral background and circumstances, and being married to you, I would be in with a chance; I'm a resident anyway of course so it would be a logical step."

"You'd better polish up your language skills darling."

"Yes, but I'm not that bad, the accent isn't so good though."

"Can't be any worse than your English accent, so I take it then you're definitely returning to our new home in Nice?"

"Definitely … I'll keep on with chairing Rubidium but the first three months at least I'm taking paternity leave … I want to be a full time father and husband."

She kissed him. "Good, that's what I like to hear." She suddenly became thoughtful herself … this had to be the moment for her own big truth-time now; they couldn't restart their lives with any more secrets and misconceptions. She drew a long deep breath.

"There's something I want to tell you as well, Philippe … there's no easy way to say this … and I wish I had said it a long time back but couldn't find a way … I'm bisexual … and whilst you were fucking Olga, I also … became diverted. Sometimes I just need to be close to another woman."

He said nothing. He just sat there, unmoved, no eruption, no distraught face, no moves to run out and disappear forever. Zilch.

"You don't look very angry Philippe," she said, not sure what she should now be saying or doing, but recognising that finally this real and important part of herself had to be said.

"I knew already, and I love and accept all of you for who you are Lauren. I guessed back when we were in Palermo. It was pretty obvious that you and Mila were more than friends, but I realised for sure when we met up with Mila again at Svet's apartment in Boston."

"But you said nothing?"

"I agree, maybe I should have done but there didn't seem to be a reason or an appropriate time, and besides, when I was younger I had made ill-advised and wrong judgemental mistakes, reading into such things inferences which were neither evident nor true."

"You mean you've been in a similar relationship before?"

"Apart from Olga … yes … Lyudmila … In the end, after pressure from me to choose, she did, and became exclusively lesbian, although she and her partner never lived together. I was wrong, I shouldn't have forced her one way or the other, I should have understood but I didn't know how. Compromise and flexibility were out of the question … I never wanted that to happen to you and me."

"Lyudmila … was also bisexual?"

"Yes, as you know we always remained very close … Svet never knew. Which reminds me … will you phone Svet? Since the Olga affair, she has refused totally to speak or communicate. She probably doesn't even know I'm out of prison, let alone about the triplets. Please can you try and somehow make amends for me."

"Yes … on condition that we ring her together and then you speak to her immediately … and apologise."

"Of course, I must do that … You and Mila, I know, have deep feelings for one another. It doesn't bother me Lauren, I accept that's the way it is and I understand why … both of you are incredible women."

Lauren smiled. "Yes, we do and always will … we've never rekindled our affair since you and I became an item … but I need her and she needs me, something special she and I share, which is why it was so hard asking her to go away on a sabbatical. Everything was emotionally just becoming too much."

"Yes I know, especially because of me … today will be a turning point in our lives and I think for the better."

Lauren got up and sidled across to him, planting another warm kiss on his eager lips and holding him tight. "I agree. Now, any more skeletons in the cupboard? I'm done, so let's phone Svet now … then it will be feeding time again and you can practise a re-run of nappy-two when you've finished your call. And when we arrive home, you will meet up with the incredible Marie … so I'd better explain all about her."

"Marie? Who's Marie?"

Lauren began searching through her mobile phone numbers. "My live-in housekeeper and future nanny combined … oh and a dab hand with firearms and security."

"What? All in one? … In a single woman? I'm looking forward to meeting her."

"Good … Svet? Hi … yes, it's me. I know it's been a little while but I have some interesting news … you've just acquired three gorgeous sisters … okay, you can stop shrieking and I'll talk to Nadine and Sergei shortly. We're fine. Your father's here, he's been released from prison and we are all going back home tomorrow for good … to my new villa in Villefrance-sur-mer. Where's here? Err … Kinshasa in the Democratic Republic of the Congo, a very long story … Your father wants to speak to you badly Svet … yes please … I have to go and feed the starving, I can hear the three of them crying. Hopefully, see you and Sergei soon at your next holiday break … we have tons of room, bring Nadine too. Bye, love you." She thrust the phone into his hand. "Now speak to your big daughter please."

He laughed … and thrust her iPad into her hand, opened at the next online Bloomberg magazine. Front cover … was a picture of … Vega handing him Geraldine, with Lauren looking on smiling, suckling Magdaline and Eveline, complete with caption.

Incredible Exclusive: One in Two Million Nuclear Businessmum Solves Midwife Crisis.

"Edward took the picture and sent it to Johann … now broadcast all around the world. Good marketing!" he whispered back, before rekindling the first conversation with Svet for over six months.

<><>

Lauren was waiting patiently at the front desk of the airport departure lounge, the call for boarding imminent, but Philippe had decided last minute to get some bottles of water and a computer magazine. Babies were fast asleep in individual lightweight travel carriers, resting on seats and creating lots of attention from a myriad of admirers and well-wishers. On her insistence, they had booked a row of three seats in the executive business class, giving themselves room to manoeuvre. Her personal phone suddenly rang and Amélie's name popped onto the screen. She connected eagerly. "Amélie, how are you doing?"

"I see we're now into World War Four. Congratulations, but what the fuck you've been doing giving birth in a jungle in the middle of the Congo I shall never in a million years understand! Charlotte just phoned me, I see between you both there's now a nursery full already – seriously, fabulous news. I am just so glad you and the girls are all fine and well."

"Yes, just heading back to Nice with Philippe, now transformed into loving father."

"Philippe? I thought he was breaking rocks until the first manned mission to Mars?"

Lauren giggled stupidly, she was feeling hysterically elated, not caring whether it lasted or not. "A few deals done and then he was out ... we owe it all to DG who orchestrated everything. But what about you?"

"I'm just waiting for Giles and Rufus to transport me to a posh clinic in Preston and be scientifically observed and looked after. I'm late and they're petrified, so if the blighters don't get a move on within the next week, I'll have to be induced. I'm the

363

size of a large mansion, and I have a varicose vein in my right leg showing which doesn't delight me either. However, money and medicine will cure as they say ... the moment they're born I will text you and confirm father, but odds on, as they're already prevaricating and obfuscating, the probability of their father's initial being R is around ninety-nine percent I reckon."

Lauren laughed. "You sound cheerful though, R does look after you well, you must admit. Good luck Amélie, I'll be thinking of you and speak soon. Nursery and live-in nanny will be waiting when you visit and we can dump the tribes there and have some fun."

"That sounds more like it, I'll hold you to that ... and I'm very pleased Philippe is home, about time. Gosh, two worried men are coming through the door, see you soon."

"Bye Amélie."

She looked at her watch, seeing the flight attendants busying themselves to open the gate, when Philippe came flying around the corner, in animated conversation with a tall and fabulously dressed blonde woman, who on immediately seeing Lauren rushed forward to give her a hug.

"Mila, what are you doing here?" Lauren cried out happily. "It's fabulous to see you; gosh what on earth are you wearing? Your dress is gorgeous? Now I've just lost a stone in weight, I reckon I could get into that, once the mummy-tummy goes down a bit."

"I knew you'd be jealous, I felt like a proper treat after that bash on the head. Called in on the best fashion store in Kinshasa, with Rosie and Debbie of course ... a rack just came in, Chanel new season. I felt like a change from Dior. Mmm ... those babies are simply gorgeous."

Philippe interjected. "I found Mila lurking at the ticket desk so I insisted she comes back with us ... and we've got a whole row of five seats. Two were on the house … gift from the government."

"Back to Nice?"

"Yes," Mila replied. "Debbie and the new swat team have truly proved their worth and effectiveness over here … my training programme in Louisiana is complete and Debbie will take charge of all that side of my business. I've decided, now that my luxury pad is suddenly vacated, to return to France for good. This experience has been a game changer, I want a new life. I realise looking at you both that there is much to be said for creating a loving family life again. It's not even too late for me to have a child."

Lauren looked stunned. "You mean … like the normal way … with a man?"

Philippe laughed heartily. "I think she does."

Mila continued. "With permission of the boss, I would like my sabbatical terminated with immediate effect … please. There's some security work to be done down at Cyclops, and I know Seb is a bit out of his depth with the Israelis … because he's already told me."

Lauren hugged Mila hard. "Permission granted. Hey you two, the desk attendant is waving at us. Mila, you take Geraldine, Philippe can take Magdaline and I'll take Eveline. They're freshly changed so no pongs. All sorted. Let's go, I can't wait to get back and see Charlotte."

Mila cuddled Geraldine lovingly. "Isn't she just gorgeous? You're the extrovert one aren't you like your Auntie Mila." "Yes, fabulous news. DG just sent me a text. They're keeping her in for a while to recover. Charlotte has had to have an emergency caesarean section; Alex George McCluskey was a big boy like his dad and ended up breech. But they're both doing fine."

"I didn't realise that," Lauren replied feeling somewhat anxious for her big daughter. "There's a lot to catch up on all round once we get back ..."

<>< >

Charlotte remained in the prestigious Nice clinic for a further time whilst the doctors controlled a potential infection and her stitches healed up. She was fussed over daily by DG, and of course Lauren, who wasted no time with an immediate visit, so all the babies could get to know one another. DG and Philippe had a quiet celebratory ceremony outside in the garden with a bottle of vodka and a Cuban Havana cigar each.

Once they were back in her new villa, Philippe could hardly believe his eyes, not only with how beautiful the new home was, but also how amazingly organised and efficient Marie had become as housekeeper and nanny elect. The triplet's bedroom next to theirs, with warning intercoms and three lovely new cots, had been redecorated with cute animals and jungle scenes, including of course a big gorilla watching carefully over Geraldine's cot. Philippe already was planning to buy a black stallion to ride along the beach in the early morning.

Lauren was insistent that the three babies had their own cots from the beginning so they could get used to their personal space quickly whilst remaining close to each other in the same room, until they needed their own privacy when older. Already their differing characters were becoming evident, with Geraldine quite outgoing and noisy, whereas Eveline was quieter and liked to be by herself more. Magdaline was somewhere in between.

By day five Charlotte, whilst still sore, was feeling much better and had been given the all-clear to be taken home. DG, who had some business to take care of on his yacht, would be down in the evening to collect her and AG, as he was already calling Alex George. However she was mulling over what to do with her secret dilemma, and was expecting an imminent visitor who had phoned the day before and insisted on coming that afternoon. Henri-Gaston was insistent, not only that he come to see his daughter but also his first grandson. Charlotte had been so preoccupied with the imminent arrival of Alex that she hadn't really thought through how to handle the situation … and he was still constantly asking about Lauren … which she had evasively batted away once more as not being quite the right time yet.

Fortunately, Lauren had also just phoned and apologised for being late for her intended afternoon visit as she had to lead an urgent Executive team meeting in Brussels by video-conferencing, which Marie had just got set up in the study, after conferring with Mila over the best software for speed and security. Baby births and the Congo adventure were already well over. Lauren was also anxious about Sonja who was on maternity leave and due in the next four weeks, but Seb had installed the same system in her old apartment, which Sonja and Johann were now renting, so Sonja could also join in the meeting. First agenda item would be showing off the triplets to everyone … and introducing them of course to computers and screens … as Lauren chuckled to herself, looking forward to bringing up her daughters in the world that she lived in of advanced technology. Would they inherit her natural love of mathematics and science or be artistic and creative like their grandmother, following in the footsteps of Kat and Lexi? Or maybe they would be wayward fickle wanderers like their father? Mmm … not if she could help it.

But she had also been working through a suitable plan for managing the next three months … deciding she would take that whole period off from Cassini and then return full time …

Her triplets were not only going to be a special family challenge but she wanted an opportunity to really bond with them, and to be with Philippe properly for the first time since they were married. But there were serious leadership issues to resolve, not least the lack of Executive boots on the ground shortly once Sonja and Johann took family leave … she needed to enact a radical solution, credible and acceptable to both inside staff and outside customers, and began to think hard, realising that she may have lost a stone but her brain felt back in full business gear again … which pleased her enormously.

<> <>

Despite having five sons, Henri-Gaston hadn't been very good with babies. His deceased wife had deftly got on with it each time and had been happy to see him slink off to his art studio and paint when matters of nappies and feeding arose. But he did at least learn how to hold and cuddle one, and like riding a bicycle, it all came instantly back as he gurgled and gushed happily to Alex George, his first grandson, whilst Charlotte looked on equally happily, quietly working out the next steps to introducing Henri-Gaston to DG, and then ultimately to Lauren herself. None of that was going to be easy.

"Henri … will you be free next Sunday? I would love you to come to my home and meet DG … time my husband found out he has a real father-in-law and … that may be a bit of a shock but I'll prepare the ground. Anyway, DG always does as he's told. Equally, Kat and Lexi will be fascinated to meet their new grandfather."

Henri-Gaston reflected hard. He hadn't bothered bringing his pocket diary, wishing that he had started using his smartphone as his son Charles insisted he should and get into the high-tech age of appointment management and social media. He suddenly remembered. He had a cool date with

Claire, the new thirty year old blonde curator of his latest gallery, but that could wait. This opportunity was more important than anything.

"Of course Charlotte, that would be tremendous … do you think it might be possible to also arrange …?"

"No, I can't guarantee that but I will find out if Lauren could be there too."

His face brightened up. "Great! I'm sorry, I'll have to get back to Marseille, there's an important event at the gallery I need to be at, launch of one of my new Chinese urban scene collections."

Charlotte realised her father hadn't been keeping up with the latest celebrity gossip and news, probably too busy with his latest womanising and commissions, so he still had no idea of Lauren being pregnant or having given birth to triplets. She would keep it that way for the moment. There was going to be a lot of explaining to do first once she got back home, and in a very short period of time.

After a quick hug and kisses to daughter and grandson, Henri-Gaston departed out of the maternity room intending to head past the nurses for the exit door to the main corridor. As he closed Charlotte's door, his gaze was suddenly diverted. Sat next to the nursing station was a striking blonde, early forties, with her back half-turned to him and talking avidly into one of their phones. His sharp artist's eye instantly noted her expensive blue aquamarine business suit, recognising a bold creation of Corsican couturier Jacques Saint Jack, who he knew well amongst his cultural circles in Paris. Her short skirt had ridden high up her lengthy thighs as she sat cross-legged, her sheer tights glistening provocatively in the ceiling spotlights, and a black Ferragamo spike, dangling sensuously from her raised moving foot. He appreciated women better than most men, and the way she was talking, confident, poised, in control and obviously seizing the moment of the topic of conversation and turning it to her advantage, was both sensuous and compelling. There was only one woman, obviously on her way to see Charlotte, who would fit that description.

She put the phone down and smiled to herself as he called out. "Lauren?"

She turned round slowly, not recognising the voice and looked hard at the grey haired stranger, just emerged from Charlotte's room. His face was unknown but he was surprisingly handsome, with a strong jaw line and expressive eyes perhaps mid fifties, tanned and an air of intelligence and charm, especially the smile. From the way he was dressed, he was rich and he had style. She immediately recognised the Dolce and Gabbana expensive and sultry Italian look, from his smart casual tan jacket and slim matching chinos right down to his brown leather shoes. He certainly wasn't a medic. Her razor sharp brain began immediately calculating in a micro-second. Who was this guy? He had obviously just emerged from Charlotte's room so had been a visitor. He must be someone important to her and close, given the intimate nature of her present stay and situation with Alex George beside her too. Then she realised. She got up and held out her hand as he walked forward to greet her.

"Hi … you must be Henri-Gaston. My name is Mila. I'm Lauren's new Acting Chief Executive of Cassini. I was just on my way past and thought of calling in to see how Charlotte is doing."

He gazed at her up and down, almost as tall as him and so elegant, stunning and mesmerising, those luscious green eyes boring into his head. He felt strangely bowled over. "Err … yes; I am indeed Henri-Gaston. You obviously know about me.

Charlotte and my new grandson are in fine form, she's being allowed out this evening."

"Excellent … in that case, I'll see Charlotte tomorrow when she gets back home. I'm going to the Hotel Negresco for an afternoon drink. Are you going anywhere?"

"Nowhere important, I'll come with you."

She smiled, he grinned … and they left.

End

About the Author

Roy Baldwin was born in South Lancashire and has lived and worked around the UK in various mathematical and scientific guises as an educationalist, night club owner, civil servant, musician, house conservator and management consultant. His last novel, Mauveine, a contemporary ghost story, was conceived, written, edited and published in thirty days, during the NaNoWriMo 2013 competition.

Rhapsody of Succession is the fourth book in the Rhapsody series, which follows the exploits and challenges of nuclear scientist, Professor Lauren Hind. He is a full time writer and women's fiction publisher, and regularly commentates on books and indie publishing through twitter. Other books in the Rhapsody series are Rhapsody of Restraint, his fictional debut and the first Rhapsody novel, followed by book two, Rhapsody of Power and book three, Rhapsody of Fate.

In between writing and digital publishing, Roy tries to enjoy the fabulous beauty of the Norfolk countryside and seashore where he now lives.

All Rhapsody novels can be bought in both eBook and print versions from online and traditional bookstores worldwide.

Further information can be obtained from the author's writer site: www.creativepubtalk.com

The author hopes you have enjoyed this book and welcomes any feedback or questions on any aspects of the story, characters or settings. Please support the author by providing a personal review on Amazon, Goodreads, Twitter or any other favourite online book site or social media.

Author Twitter Feed: www.twitter.com/creativepubtalk
LinkedIn: Roy Baldwin - Women's Fiction Author

The next book in the Rhapsody Series, titled Rhapsody of Moon and now being written is planned for release early 2015.

Have you read the others?

RHAPSODY OF RESTRAINT

Professor Lauren Hind is a scientist who appears to have it all. Global recognition for her nuclear energy work, a doting designer husband who she loves and a mega salary in a large corporate so she can indulge in her joint passions of haute couture and mathematics. After leading a prestigious research conference, she unexpectedly meets up with the mysterious and beguiling Luis who lures her into a culture she had not experienced. Fuelled by drink and intrigue, a train of events takes off and Lauren finds herself desperately buffeted by a seemingly irresolvable kaleidoscope of emotional and confused outcomes, which threaten to violently overturn her well-structured lifestyle and relationship bearings. Trying hard to salvage her way out of the mess she has created and save her marriage, new and interrelated twists and turns throw her into further turmoil, entanglements and more betrayal as she is forced to question everything she has stood for and make fundamental choices. But someone else turns up who has the capability, passion and desire to take from Lauren whatever she wants. Lauren needs to find the will and strength to confront this additional adversity and resolve her own complicated needs - but can she overcome the temptations...?

RHAPSODY OF RESTRAINT is the first book of the Rhapsody series which tells the story of the intriguing scientific and emotional destiny of Lauren Hind. "Where romance and adventure meets nuclear fusion!"

An excerpt from Rhapsody of Restraint …she sauntered to the table already occupied by around a dozen other Sicilian men, some similar in age to Luis but many others younger. As they surrounded her, she sat down deciding not to take off her jacket immediately but flaunt her new outfit a little longer. They were dressed smartly, like they were all part of a group and were engaged in what appeared to be quite intense discussion on some hot topic or other in Italian.

"May I please ask your name?" He grinned warmly towards her. "We think you are the most interesting and desirable person to have crossed past our table tonight … well so far anyway! It is nice to meet again in much more pleasant circumstances."

"I'm sorry?" Then she looked again and that minute before of déjà vu was confirmed with a jolt, the colour draining from her cheeks as her mouth dropped. He laughed vigorously at her seeming discomfort.

"Let's say my near decapitated legs in the airport are now fully recovered. Don't worry. I could see you were somewhat preoccupied then. Now tell us about yourself. I hope you're happy that we speak in English. I sense somehow that your Italian is less well developed."

"Gosh … Yes thank you, please continue in English that's fine. I don't know what to say except to apologise profusely. It was rude and unacceptable of me to react that way when I had just arrived and …"

He interrupted her gently. "My response back to you was not exactly civil either, so let's call it quits. No harm done and anyway I admire assertiveness in a woman and you certainly appear to have that in spades, as they say!"

Lauren, although embarrassed and somewhat taken aback with his immediate forwardness, nevertheless returned the smile and replied warmly, her composure returning quickly as she surveyed all the inquisitive faces.

"Hello everyone, I'm Lauren. I've been staying in the hotel over the last couple of days with the conference which has now ended. We've been doing some international exchange work in sustainable nuclear energy, networking, new developments all that sort of thing," she said clearly and deliberately.

She could hear herself sounding unnecessarily formal and not really knowing why she was speaking so wooden, when everyone around was being quite casual and laid back. She felt displaced with her thoughts, and especially with Luis who was deceptively and deliberately disarming her normal flow of reaction when meeting new people ...

RHAPSODY OF POWER

Nuclear scientist Lauren Hind returns to Brussels to find her company, Cassini Power, riven by upheaval and turmoil and her Director role threatened. Confident in her adaptability and desperately needing a change of direction, she decides to face down her antagonistic Chairman, whilst seeking solace in a splurge of fashionable indulgence in advance of her expected big payoff. Appearances however can be deceptive and out of the blue an unexpected turn of events shakes up her perception and sets her off on a new path towards career possibilities and a world stage she could only previously have dreamed about. But threats and a puzzling technical dilemma shake her out of any cosy feelings of finally being in control of her life because she has to decide where her loyalties lie, and confront once again who she really is and her true feelings. Aspects of her recent past have not quite gone away as she had hoped and expected. A looming catastrophe, with enormous consequences for Europe and the rest of the world reveals the true extent of her capability to deal with serious dangers. To add to her confused feelings and foreboding, her Chairman is at the centre of the murky wheeling and dealing and she is summoned to engage in an adventure which could lead to her death and destruction. She badly needs help and there is only one person to turn to again - who could annihilate her in a moment. Can she let this happen or are the consequences and payback already drawn in the sand? And there is still her Chairman...

RHAPSODY OF POWER is the second book of the Rhapsody series continuing the science adventures and romantic escapades of Professor Lauren Hind

An excerpt from Rhapsody of Power ... Lauren saw immediately that Amélie was massively irritated and annoyed by what had been said in the first five minutes. "Honestly Amélie, I have not got a clue what all this attention is about. Listen, you can bank on me, once we get into the meeting, to step swiftly into the background, I'll back you up at every turn and when the time is correct follow your lead into what Cassini can do on fast plutonium reactors. And then let's sew up whatever deal we can muster; first and foremost to benefit you, remember just like we did in the old days? Anyway you look stunningly immaculate as ever, whilst I look like I've been dragged through a hedge backwards after that damned gust of wind outside. Have you got a decent hair brush?"

The tension in Amélie's face dissipated as she dug into her handbag. "I'm sorry Lauren for snapping. This deal is actually potentially more important to me than maybe I let on. Things have become a bit tricky back at the ranch, you know what I mean?"

Lauren patted her arm affectionately. "Of course, fully understood, you can tell me later. Hey, what are friends for. Now, let's get in there and give them the old one-two sales patter. I just hope my Chairman isn't there, I really do."

They strode out and over to reception where a smiling Valerie whisked them off to the lift and up to the fourth floor. As they stepped out into the executive corridor, an amazing view of the sea and the coast hit their senses, an immediate impact from the unusual design of the building, built like a glass atrium with a steep vertical wall immediately beneath going directly into the sea.

In a few seconds they entered the Board room to be greeted by a sea of male faces stood around the large buffet table, beautifully set out with an array of hot and cold food, salads, vegetables and sandwiches. Amélie immediately took a glass of white wine off the waiter near the entrance, with Lauren in close pursuit of the red, when a deep, clearly very English accented voice, familiar but unfamiliar, spoke out softly from behind.

"Ah … so you must be Professor Lauren Hind. I have waited quite a long time to meet you." Lauren turned around and her face dropped as she found herself shaking hands — with the UK Prime Minister!

RHAPSODY OF FATE

A fun holiday in Rome beckons for scientist and Cassini CEO Lauren Hind to forget the recent nuclear debacle in Sicily. Looking forward to a new relationship with Philippe, her Chairman, her business and personal life should at last become rosy and settled. One revelation changes everything, discovering her lost adopted daughter, Charlotte and new family. But will this upheaval be a force for good or an uncontrollable disruption in her life?

She needs to find out, confront the demons and reconcile her feelings and admit who she really loves. But unexpectedly, in China, the marital happiness she had sought and won is violently disrupted leading to unwanted challenges and distractions. She is forced to question Amélie, her best friend, who she had always understood and trusted.

Something oddly sinister unfolds leading to a set of destabilising coincidences and finally a kidnapping which even her worst nightmares couldn't have predicted. Never before have her technical skills and bravery been tested so much. Could there be a man even more evil than Luis, capable of lacerating her emotions and loyalties at a stroke? And why does she have to travel to the Arctic to find out?

Many may die, the dice is thrown and she must finally make the ultimate decision, one way or the other.

But which way does she turn? And who really loves her enough to pull her away from the deadly consequences?

RHAPSODY OF FATE is the third book of the Rhapsody series, continuing the science adventures and romantic escapades of Professor Lauren Hind

An excerpt from Rhapsody of Fate: They were soon heading out of town and into the surrounding countryside. The wide city beltway had dropped from a major highway down to a series of small rural lanes. Lauren gazed with interest at the great expanse of landscape, a mixture of parched and green rough grass, undulating hills and some meadows, but also randomly interspersed were a number of flat desert-like areas, on which stood interesting large contraptions with long beams, bobbing slowly with a counterweight and some kind of motor. Lauren immediately began working through the physics of turning the fast rotary motion of the motor, through a crank to upwards and downwards slow reciprocated pumping. But what was being pumped? Presumably, she thought, oil, but there were a lot of them and she was under the impression that inland oil reserves in Texas were long depleted.

"I can see you are intrigued Lauren. They're called pump jacks or nodding donkeys. Most of what is coming up is water with a bit of oil, but it remains extractable as does the gas often associated which can power the motor."

"Fascinating," replied Lauren, quietly.

"Okay, I'd better warn you in advance. Lyell's father Doug, who you are going to meet, although everyone, including us, calls him DG, is not only a Senator but the family have been big in the oil business for four generations and made a lot of money. I was just getting going with my engineering company when I met Lyell, but all the family connections and expertise were so useful, which is why I supply specialist parts to the industry. DG was a big help, and when we got married he insisted on buying us the ranch as a wedding present, as all my money had gone into the business. I lived in a small apartment in downtown Dallas. The ranch is a fabulous place.

"Really big Grandma," added Lexi. "And we keep our own cattle as the ranch used to belong to a cowboy. And we have our own nodding donkeys as well."

"Yes, DG insisted we exploit the mineral assets which had never been done, and he got it sorted out. In the US, mineral rights belong to the landowner not the government, like many other countries. Now it provides a useful addition to our overall income."

"But Lyell never wanted to be part of the oil business then like his father?"

"No, he never took to it. He loves the outdoors, and is very physical. He was a bit of a rebel in his youth, which is why he ended up in the army when he left school, but did very well and yes; he was in Special Forces when we met. He is very talented too with computers and software when he can be bothered, and has written some software for me, which has got me a load of new business, but I just wish he stuck at it. But when you see his wood carvings you will see why he doesn't need to."

Lauren nodded, taking in the information, her mind ticking its inexorable way through detailed analysis then synthesis of the data. Charlotte didn't seem to have anything in common with Lyell, but then again, who was she to judge or comment, three time married and soon Philippe the fourth to be added, especially on her own daughter? Everyone has to find their own way in life, even Lexi and Kat. She thought of Svet and wished she was here to enjoy this outing and vowed to bring Svet the next time she and Philippe visited Charlotte, although everything was getting so busy and the original planned arrangements with Svet had gone astray. When indeed would she have the time? Many mothers with a daughter of Charlotte's age would be more carefree in their later middle-age — shit, she was just forty-three and Charlotte was twenty-seven, they were like sisters. Then she reflected on the twins, nine years old. Something wasn't mathematically quite stacking up.

Without warning, Charlotte suddenly swung the steering wheel to the right and she put on the four-wheel drive as they headed down a dusty and very bumpy track through glades of trees, more meadows and quite sandy soil. Lauren noticed a large blue lake in the distance, when they rounded another corner and came to a wide, but ungated entrance, flanked by two light grey stone pillars. An iron cattle grid was placed over the entrance which they slowly rattled over.

Edging around a final bend, the full extent of the lake fringed with beautiful willows and occupied by a small rowing boat and lots of ducks of all shapes and colours, came into view along with the Half Moon Corral. Lauren simply drew breath at the view and the size of the ranch, if you could call it a ranch at all. She had a picture in her mind of a typical Southern State cowboy ranch, with lots of brush blowing outside, rather derelict, and all wooden, with verandas and rocking chairs. Obviously, she realised, she had watched too many Westerns. A massive white walled, sprawling building, like a snake with a two storey extension on its head, wound itself into a rectangular shape, all gorgeous windows and fronted by a huge stone laid veranda going on forever, with the tiled roof covering held up by endless archways, like a railway viaduct. Fronting all this were a series of beautifully laid out gardens, blooming with masses of colourful flowers and various small shrubs. The driveway cut in through a well tendered lawn interspersed with majestic oaks.

As they stopped, Lauren could see, though the archways and entrances, the inside of a square courtyard, centre-pieced with a large swimming pool and all kinds of levels, stairways and tubs of flowers, leading to different inner building areas, including a spiral staircase up to the second storey building. She sat mesmerised before being distracted by Philippe, waving from a table on the veranda, perfectly placed out of the sun but catching the full view of the lake and trees from the house. Lyell was sat next to him, grinning, bottles of beer and plates of nibbles being consumed avidly by the pair of them. A third man in a large black Stetson almost hiding his face, sat next to them who she didn't recognise.

The main door opened and a tall, well built African-American man, possibly late forties or early fifties, in green overalls and a floppy straw sun hat walked briskly to the car as they all got out.

"Charlotte, great to see you back. I'm just cleaning up the pool, reckon you might be needing it tonight; it's been as hot as Hades here."

Charlotte beckoned the man over to meet Lauren. "Lauren this is Orlando, our gardener and handyman, who keeps this place as spick and span and as amazing as you can see."

Orlando shook hands with Lauren. "Glad to meet you Ms Lauren, something tells me this is the first time you've been to Texas. I hope you like big steaks; my wife Marcie is cooking the most delicious T-bone's you will have ever tasted in your life, all to a secret family recipe we had in my family since them old slave days. Charlotte here, she keeps wanting to buy it off me, but I won't sell that recipe for any amount of dollars!"

Lauren laughed and felt instant warmth for Orlando as she looked into his eyes and could see a man with a lot of hidden depths, especially his do-it-yourself and gardening skills, which she might be able to learn a bit about.

"That's true Lauren. One day Orlando and Marcie want to open another simple family restaurant downtown. It will be a big hit with her steaks and special pumpkin pie. Orlando, Lauren is a special guest — she is my mother."

Lauren felt startled inside at that admission, said so informally and off the cuff. It was oddly peculiar being called a mother. She looked at Orlando, who looked her up and down back, but never blinked an eyelid or appeared in the slightest bit surprised.

"Well now, isn't that just something Ms Charlotte, and can I see the resemblance. I thought at first you and Ms Lauren might be sisters or cousins. Hope you enjoy your stay here Lauren. We've put you and Philippe in the guest building, best view of the lake too." He pointed to the beautiful two storey end building with the spiral stone staircase winding up and wisteria splattered all over the while walls. "Your things are already up there." He began to head back inside. "Charlotte, I'll just get off and help Serena get everything ready for dinner."

Lauren looked casually around. The twins had already gone inside too, probably off to their rooms. Charlotte touched her arm and pointed to a Gazebo at the other end of the ranch. "Philippe looks fine in the company of Lyell and his father. I want to tell you something, let's walk over there."

"That's DG in the Stetson?"

"Of course. He thinks he's like JR Ewing sometimes and makes us all laugh, although Lyell doesn't see the humour so much. DG is always wheeling and dealing at any opportunity to make even more money…!"

www.ingramcontent.com/pod-product-compliance
Lightning Source LLC
Chambersburg PA
CBHW030546180626
46816CB00005B/1422